DARKSHIP

1/10

BAEN BOOKS by SARAH A. HOYT

Draw One in the Dark
Gentleman Takes a Chance

Darkship Thieves

DARKSHIP THIEVES

SARAH A. HOYT

BAEN

DARKSHIP THIEVES

This is a work of fiction. All the characters and events portrayed in this book are fictional, and any resemblance to real people or incidents is purely coincidental.

A Baen Books Original

Baen Publishing Enterprises
P.O. Box 1403
Riverdale, NY 10471
www.baen.com

ISBN 13: 978-1-4391-3317-0

Cover art by Allan Pollack

First printing, January 2010

Distributed by Simon & Schuster
1230 Avenue of the Americas
New York, NY 10020

Library of Congress Cataloging-in-Publication Data

Hoyt, Sarah A.
   Darkship thieves / Sarah A. Hoyt.
      p. cm.
   ISBN 978-1-4391-3317-0 (trade pbk.)
   I. Title.
   PS3608.O96D37 2010
   813'.6—dc22

                                        2009039743

10 9 8 7 6 5 4 3 2 1

Pages by Joy Freeman (www.pagesbyjoy.com)
Printed in the United States of America

To Robert A. Heinlein, the man who pointed the way
to the stars, and who taught me that the future is
always better than the past. My work is unworthy
of the master, but it is the best I have to offer.

Acknowledgments:

Thank you to my wonderful publisher, Toni Weisskopf, for letting me play in space. Thank you to Eric S. Raymond for catching some of the technological miscues in the early manuscript. Thank you to the usual gang (pressed) first readers: Pam Uphoff, Amanda Green, Kate Paulk, Rob Hampson, and others, who helped me make this a better story. And as always, thank you to my husband Dan and my sons, Robert Anson and Eric Marshall, for putting up with the insanity as I wrote this.

I

Father's Daughter

⮐ ONE ⮑

I NEVER WANTED TO GO TO SPACE. NEVER WANTED TO SEE THE eerie glow of the powerpods. Never wanted to visit Circum Terra. Never had any interest in discovering the truth about the darkships. You always get what you don't ask for.

Which was why I woke up in the dark of shipnight, within the greater night of space in my father's space cruiser.

Before full consciousness, I knew there was an intruder in my cabin. Once awake, I couldn't figure out how I knew it. The air smelled as it always did on shipboard, as it had for the week I'd spent here—stale, with the odd tang given by the recycling.

The engines, below me, hummed steadily. We had just detached from Circum Terra—a maneuver that involved some effort, to avoid accidentally ramming the station or the ship. Shortly we'd be Earth-bound, though slowing down and reentry, let alone landing, for a ship this size, would take close to a week.

My head felt a little light, my stomach a little queasy, from the artificial grav. Yes, I know. Scientists say that's impossible. They say artificial gravity is just like true gravity to the senses. You don't feel a thing. They are wrong. Artificial grav always made me feel a little out of balance, like a couple of shots of whiskey on an empty stomach.

Even before waking fully, I'd tallied all this. There was nothing out of the ordinary. And yet there was a stranger in my cabin.

Years in reformatories, boarding schools and mental hospitals

4

had taught me that the feeling I woke up with was often the right one. Something had awakened me—a door closing, a step on the polished floor.

Now, why? Knowing the why determined how I dealt with it.

Three reasons came to mind immediately. Theft, rape, murder. But all of them were impossible. The space cruiser belonged to Daddy Dearest and there was no one aboard save Daddy Dearest, my charming self—his only daughter—and his handpicked crew of about twenty-five, half of whom were his bodyguard goons and half maintenance crew of one description or another. Far more than I thought it would take to run a ship this size, but then what did I know about ships?

Now, whatever I thought of my father, the Honorable Patrician Milton Alexander Sinistra of the ruling council of Earth, I neither thought him stupid nor stupidly inclined to trust people. His goons were the scum of the Earth—only because there were no real populations on any other planet—but they were picked, trained, conditioned and, for all I knew, mind-controlled for loyalty. Hulking giants all, they would, each one of them, have laid down their lives for my father. Not the least because without Father they'd only be wanted men with no place to hide.

As for his other servants and employees, they were the best Father could command, in any specialty he needed.

None of them, nor anyone who had ever seen Father in a white hot rage, would ever do anything against Father or his family. Well...except me. I defied Father all the time. But I was the sole exception.

There were no crimes at our home in Syracuse Seacity. There weren't even any misdemeanors. No servant had ever been caught stealing so much as a rag from the house stores. Hell, no servant broke a plate without apologizing immediately and profusely.

So the three reasons I could think of for an intruder to be here didn't apply. No one would dare steal from me, rape me or murder me under Father's roof. And no one—no one—who had even heard rumors about me would do so absent a fear of Father.

Without opening my eyes, I looked through my eyelashes—an art I'd learned through several sojourns at various institutions—and turned in bed. No more than the aimless flailing of a sleeper seeking a better position. The cabin was dark. For a moment I could see nothing. I could turn the lights on by calling out, or by reaching. But either of those would let the intruder know that I wasn't asleep.

And then, my eyes adjusting, I saw him standing out of the deeper darkness. It was a him. It had to be a him. Broad shoulders and tall. He stood by my bed, utterly still.

My heart sped up. I tensed. I didn't know who he was, nor what he was about to do, but it couldn't be good. No one with good intentions would come in like that, while I was asleep, and then stand there, quietly waiting. As if to make sure I really was asleep.

Then I thought it might not be one of Father's people at all. Our security was good. Really good. But we'd just been on a four-day-long state visit to Circum Terra, where the population were the top scientists in their field. Smart people. Smart people who had been isolated for a couple of years. Smart people who had stared and sighed when I walked around and attended parties and was my most flirty self in the clothes that were one of the few perks of being Father's daughter.

If one of those people had sneaked aboard...

Moving slowly, in the same seemingly aimless movements, I clenched my hands on the blanket about an arm's length apart, and made fists, grabbing handfuls of the stuff. I'd have preferred to twist it around my wrists, so it wouldn't come loose, but that would be way too obvious.

The man in the dark took a step towards me. He was good. If he was a scientist, he must have been a cat burglar in a previous life. If I hadn't been awake, he surely wouldn't have awakened me now.

I sprang. I hopped up to the edge of the bed. The ceramite bed rail gave a better surface for bouncing. I bounced on my tiptoes and flew up, blanket stretched between my hands.

There is this state I go into when in fear or anger. It seems as though I can move faster—and be stronger—than normal people. At least enough to take everyone by surprise. It had seen me through countless battles in boarding schools, hospitals, detention centers. I never understood why people didn't match it. They didn't seem able to.

As time seemed to slow for me, I wrapped the blanket over the head of the intruder and pulled, with the blanket still held in both hands. A blanket is the worst garrotte possible. I much prefer a scarf or a rope. But even I couldn't have everything. Where would I put it? Who would polish it?

As my prey started to flail, I knew that however much slower than I he was, he was stronger. And bigger. I pulled the ends of the blanket I had grabbed, as tight as I could around his neck. It wasn't pliable enough. I needed something big and heavy to crash over his head. But—damn the space cabin!—everything was locked behind drawers and doors. And he was thrashing, struggling, grabbing my arm.

I did what comes naturally in these circumstances. I lifted my foot, aiming with my heel because bare toes aren't very effective, and kicked. Hard. Right at the center of his manhood. He screamed and let go of my arm.

Just long enough for me to find, on the floor, the boots that, according to my bad habit, I had taken off and left by the side of the bed. I mustn't have been asleep very long, since my maid hadn't picked them up yet. This meant that most of the people on board should be awake still.

As I thought this, I grabbed the boot. It was more fashionable than practical, a boot designed for walking indoors and looking good. Fortunately at that time looking good—in the short silk dresses I normally favored—demanded a fairly high heel, plated all around with a thick layer of silver. And chunky, according to current fashion.

I had just time to weigh it in my hand. My uninvited guest was trying to pull the blanket off and calling out some nasty words that good scientists shouldn't pronounce.

When hitting someone on the head it's all a matter of knowing the point where it will do the most good. Or harm. Long experimentation had told me the point above the ear would work, only of course, he was moving around too much to make it exact. I did try.

I visualized my hand going through his head—because otherwise the blow would lack the needed force—pulled back, to gain momentum, and brought the heel of the boot hard on his head. As hard as I could from the disadvantage of a lower height. If he hadn't been half-bent, trying to unwrap the blanket, I'd never have managed it at all.

As it was, the first hit made him pause. Just pause. He didn't fall and I thought I hadn't hit hard enough, so I hit again, harder.

He made a sound like choking and went down. The blanket, which he'd managed to loosen most of the way by the time he fell, came off his face.

"Lights on," I said, and jumped back, holding my boot, because if he came back at me I was going to hit him again, and this time I wanted to be able to see where.

But as the soft glow shone on his pale face, I recognized Andrija Baldo, the head of my father's goons. And he was very still.

His square face was pasty grey. The brutal lips another shade of grey. There was a drop of blood running from beneath his hair. I wondered for a moment if I had killed him, and exactly how mad Father would be if I had.

Then I realized his chest was rising and falling minimally. So, still alive.

And in his right hand, firmly clutched, was the oval shape of an injector. I knew the color too. There was only one medicine they packaged in those piss-yellow injectors.

Morpheus. The strongest knock-out juice in the universe.

⟨⟨ TWO ⟩⟩

A FULL INJECTOR OF MORPHEUS AND I'D HAVE BEEN DEAD TO the world for the rest of the night. Was it really rape after all? Or murder?

I frowned down at the passed out goon on my floor. Right. Andrija Baldo, who—as far as I knew—had been with Father since Father had rescued him from some correction camp or other, had been about to drug me and . . .

My mind stopped there.

Oh, he could have raped me. And maybe I wouldn't even have known, come morning. Or he could have killed me.

But none of us, and Father's goons certainly least of all, could imagine that we had any real privacy aboard this cruiser. Father had it built to specifications. If there were no cameras and microphones covering every possible inch of every possible compartment, then Father was not the paranoid bastard we all knew him to be.

So . . . Why would Andrija do this?

Truth was this whole trip to Circum Terra stank to high heavens. Yes, Father was a member of the Earth's ruling council. But he was not one of those who interacted with the public or who gave the benighted multitudes the idea that they had any say in their governance. Father stayed behind the scenes. He planned things. He hired people. He saw that plans came to fruition. So, why go to Circum Terra? Why meet with scientists whose influence on the public opinion was slim to none? And why bring me along?

Oh, I was decorative. I'll admit that. I could be decked out and made up and—at all of five-five, with long wavy black hair and breasts the size that make other women call you fat—I could look like the perfect young lady of Patrician class. For a time at least. Before the next clash with Daddy Dearest made me tear a broad swath of rebellion and rage out of his proximity. And four days in Circum were a short enough period to allow me to pass.

But why would Father want me with him? And why the trip to Circum at all? And if he had to go there, why not use an air-to-space, which traveled much faster and could get us to Circum in a day? Why the huge, slow space cruiser with its full complement of personnel? I shoved the thoughts out of my mind. Nothing I could do about them now, and I *must* do something about Baldo.

Alive or dead, an inert goon made for a terrible room decoration.

I stood by Andrija's unconscious body, holding my boot in one hand. I could shove him into one of the closets around the room, under all the gowns, and then lock my door and go back to bed. And hope he didn't wake up in the night, and come after me. Or I could hope that someone had seen all this on a camera and came to my rescue.

No. I'd never before waited for someone else to rescue me. I didn't think it would work if I did so now. For one, I couldn't really believe Andrija was working on his own. Not in Father's ship. Not when Father would surely find out.

Someone knocked at the door. It was a tentative knock—the type people give when they don't want to rouse anyone else. My hair prickled at the back of my neck. If someone had spotted the attack on the security tape and had come to rescue me, the knock would be loud. They would be calling my name.

But there was only the tentative knock. Repeated. And then the doorknob shook.

I slid around to the right side of the door. The door was set on a wall with a slight angle, so that the right side formed a shallow angle with the closet. I squeezed myself against the wall there, as the knob turned completely and the door opened.

A dark head poked in, there was a muffled sound of surprise at seeing Andrija on the floor. I acted on instinct. Before the newcomer could open his mouth to call out, I reached over, and hit him hard with the heel of the boot. He went down.

As he fell, I recognized Friso Sikke, the second-in-command

among Father's goons. What was going on? Had Father's goons all turned on me? Would all of them be coming after me?

I had to get out of this room. When under attack, a place with only one exit—through which enemies arrived—was the worst possible refuge in which to make a stand.

I could not wait here to hit them one by one as they came in. I took a quick look down at myself. I was wearing only the thigh-long silk slip in which I slept. I cast a longing look at my closet, full of all sorts of work suits which would be much better for fighting or fleeing in.

Steps approached. I couldn't take the time. I didn't have a moment. I had to get out before they blocked the door.

Boot still in hand, I ran out of the cabin. Outside, a broad hallway opened. In the middle of the hallway stood two men. They weren't familiar. Servants. Or at least I assumed they were servants, hired for the trip.

Blurrily, I noticed they were pushing a grey antigrav platform between them. A stretcher, of the type used for hospitals. I ducked under it. They yelled something as I passed, but I had more important things on my mind.

My father's cabin was at the other end of the hallway from mine—presumably so that should I decide to hold a party by myself in the dark of night I wouldn't disturb him. Across from Father's cabin was the antigrav well that led to the next level. I ran towards it.

If Father wasn't in on this, then the safest thing would be to run towards him. I couldn't imagine why Father would be in on this, but all my instincts warned me off running to his room. At the very least, if Father weren't there, or if he weren't capable of stopping their coming after me, I would be stuck at another dead end. The antigrav well, and the working levels of the ship below it, were the only way open.

I heard screams and running feet behind me, but I'd already jumped into the cushioning currents of the antigrav well. The landing at the other end was soft enough, and I started running immediately, faltering only slightly as I pulled free of the antigrav. I felt more than heard the two men hit the well behind me.

This corridor was the working level used by Father, not his personnel. During our time docked at Circum it had served a mobile embassy for Syracuse Seacity. Three of the doors on either side led to ballrooms and one to an office/workroom. I had no idea what the other three were for. We had never opened them. At the other end of the hallway another antigrav well led to the servants' quarters and, at the end, to the lifepod bay.

In between was a hallway twice as broad as the one upstairs, with the walls covered in holo-windows that displayed sunny Mediterranean landscapes—beaches and olive groves and pastoral-looking mountains.

The ballrooms sprawled spacious, and the office had more places to hide than my cabin, but in the end they remained enclosed areas. Not a good place to get trapped in. Running full tilt on my bare feet, boot in hand, I wondered if one of the other rooms might hide an armory. Unlikely. Our home had an armory, but Father—being almost eighty years old—never used it.

Still, one of the other rooms might hold something...Or it might lock securely till I could figure out my next step.

In despair, I slowed enough to test the door of the first room I'd never opened. And found myself staring at a state-of-the-art operating room. Father lay on an antigrav stretcher.

I had time to register that he was clearly unconscious before a hand touched my arm. I felt more than heard movement behind me and spun around, in combat mode, that mode in which I felt as if I were going twice as fast as everyone around me.

The boot, clutched in my hand, caught the medtech full force on the forehead. He grunted and stepped back. This surprised him just long enough to allow me to pull my arm free and run again.

No escape there. No escape in the medical rooms. Medical rooms!

Why were there medical rooms in a space cruiser? There was no way we could take a trip longer than a week. There was nowhere to go! The moon bases didn't take visitors—not even Good Men—and even so, it only took two weeks to get there. What could happen to Father in two weeks? Father was old but not that old. And he was in good health. Father. Why was Father unconscious in a medical room? There had been...trays of instruments. Medtechs. And medical machinery. Why?

I legged it as fast as I could towards the antigrav well. A sudden shrieking alarm broke the silence, and then a strobe light effect kicked in, making the Mediterranean landscapes on the walls look like they would if the Earth was hit by a meteorite cluster.

The voices that went with the shipboard alarms came in over speakers, seemingly from everywhere at once. One of them was the fire alarm saying, "Fire, fire. Please rush to the lifepod bay." The other one was the one for piracy and it said, "There are intruders aboard. Please secure your area and do not leave." And yet another talked about a mechanical malfunction and my absolute need to rush to assist.

It seemed to me that someone had clapped his hand across all the alarm buttons. In my particular emergency—unable to understand what was going on—finding an area I could secure seemed like a really good idea. Perhaps the kitchens downstairs. Kitchens would have knives and cookers and poking implements that could cut and stab and burn. They also contained provisions.

Once, at twelve, I'd held an entire finishing school at bay and barricaded myself in the kitchen for a week, until Father had come to get me.

I threw myself down the grav well. Landed ready to run. For my money, of all the self-defense, street fighting and other offensive arts I'd taught myself, the best training of all as far as running and staying on my feet and even fighting back had been my time spent at the ballet school in Paris when I was fourteen. It helped me keep my balance now, as I landed on tiptoes and leapt out of the antigrav field.

I loped two large steps down the hallway. And became aware of steps behind me. Coordinated steps. Large, heavy bodies on large heavy boots, hit the floor in the grav well, and fell into a run as easily as I had.

A look over my shoulder showed me what remained of my Daddy Dearest's goons. They were dressed in full dimatough armor from head to toe. At a casual glance they looked like men in black masks wearing suits made entirely of black scales. Which they were. They were also men protected by material that nothing—not even diamond—could cut.

Nothing I might find in a kitchen could hold them at bay. It would have to be the lifepod bay.

The *clump-clump-clump* of their boots behind me cut through the mishmash of warnings, sirens and alarm bells. I wondered why no one came out of the kitchen or other dependencies. Where were they? Had some word of warning gone out? Or were most of them in their dormitories and confused by the cacophony of alarms? Of course, Father's long-time servants knew me. Not one of them would volunteer to grapple with me.

At the end of the hallway, the huge double doors led to the lifepod bay. Next to them was a panel for the palm print that would allow one to open the doors. I lay my sweaty palm against it. I was afraid it wouldn't open. The law said it had to be coded for everyone aboard. But this was Father's cruiser, and where Daddy was concerned, laws happened to other people.

Slowly, ponderously, the door started sliding open. One handspan. Two. I slid through into the opening and squeezed into the bay.

Inside, the lifepod bay was cavernous, and lifepods were set in a circle around the bay, each of them in front of its own eject lock. There were thirty-five. Enough for everyone aboard. I dove towards the nearest one.

And saw one of the goons—from the bulk, Narran, another of Father's favorite bodyguards—near the control panel inside the lifepod bay. He was about to press the button that would lock the lifepods. Not that I knew there was such a button, but it stood to reason. He could prevent my leaving.

Instinct is a wondrous thing. I turned around, grabbed my slip and tore it, top to bottom, exposing my naked body.

It was only a second but, if I knew the male brain—and I did—long enough to short-circuit his reactions for a couple of seconds.

Enough for me to jump into the lifepod and push the red eject button. I suspected once that was done nothing could stop it. But still, relief flooded me as the pod shot out into the membrane that divided it from the airlock. The membrane opened to let it through. Then the other membrane opened.

I shot out into space in the lifepod—which was a triangular vessel made of transparent dimatough and barely large enough to hold me—in an awkward position, effectively straddling the central axis of the vehicle, with my knees and legs on the floor of it, and bent forward over controls that consisted only of a joystick and a com button.

Trembling, I took a deep breath. Whatever was going on, I was sure my father's goons would follow me as soon as they could strip off their dimatough armors and squeeze into the lifepods.

I had to get away from here. I had to get help.

Grabbing hold of the joystick, I pointed myself towards Circum

Terra, which hung like a glowing doughnut in the eastern quadrant of the sky. With my free hand I pushed down the com button.

"Help," I shouted into whatever frequency might be picking up. The cruiser for sure, but perhaps Circum Terra too. "My name is Athena Hera Sinistra. My father's space cruiser has been highjacked."

⦆THREE⦅

I WOKE UPSIDE DOWN. OPENING MY EYES, I REALIZED I WAS IN a lifepod, surrounded on all sides by space. So it wasn't strictly true that I was upside down. Lessons from childhood bobbed up in my mind. *In space there's no up nor down.*

Which was another of those things like antigrav not making you sick to your stomach. It's fine to say that, but clearly the scientists who thought so didn't live in my body. In space, with null-grav, with a minimal vehicle between me and the void, everything was upside down. Always.

I tweaked the joystick to bring me "up" the other direction, but I still felt upside down. It must be two hours at least since I'd fallen asleep. The reasons for falling asleep of course were that I was exhausted, Circum Terra wasn't answering, and the pod moved straight ahead at a constant speed no matter what I did.

But now things looked more interesting. In front of me, Circum Terra loomed—doughnut shaped, shining with the lights of myriad docking stations and beacons. And behind me...

Looking over my shoulder, squinting, I could see a straggle of other lifepods, in hot pursuit. Er... in pursuit as hot as they could manage. Which wasn't much. These lifepods had no speed controls. They had a fixed speed and—I thought—twelve-hour air supply. I wished I'd paid more attention to Father's lectures about the lifepods. But I knew they all had fixed speeds. And so Father's goons were as far behind as they'd been when they'd left the space cruiser.

17

I had to get to Circum, dock and make my case quickly. To be honest, I doubted anyone would take the opinion of the goons over mine, but one never knew.

I looked down at the front of my torn slip. Not much chance of making myself look respectable before I reached Circum. As for my hair, with the best hairdressing in the world, and lots of work, I could tame the wild black curls. With my fingers, in a small space vessel, I'd have to hope I didn't look too savage to ask for refuge.

My eye on the goons behind me—just in case they magically gained on me—I reached for the button of the com, and pressed it. Before I could open my mouth, a voice came from it. Father's voice.

"Athena Hera Sinistra," he said, "has left my space cruiser while hallucinating. She might be in the grip of mind-altering drugs. She must be believed to be armed and dangerous. We're asking Circum Terra to detain her till she can be retrieved by my employees."

Several shocks hit me in succession.

First—the com was two-way? My mind accommodated to this quickly, though. Of course it was two-way. How else could a base talk a stranded castaway through landing?

Second—my father was talking? My father? Last time I'd seen Daddy Dearest, he looked about as likely to talk as to sing opera. So what had happened? Had he been behind this all the time?

No. I couldn't imagine Father being part of any plot that involved his lying there, in a medical room, cold and dead-looking like landed mackerel. I knew for a fact that most procedures he'd had done on him, from minor regen to surgery he had insisted on local anesthesia only, because he didn't trust anyone to operate on him while he was out cold.

So...no. Father wasn't behind this. He couldn't be. But whoever was either had awakened him and forced him to issue this warning, or found a way of faking his voice—not hard with computer generation—so that it even fooled me—a little harder, but possible.

That it was recognizable as Father's voice was all that mattered. No one at Circum would doubt it. Not for a minute.

And though I'd been on my best behavior while in Circum— the charming socialite Athena Sinistra—I was sure even they got casts. And the casts had been full off and on of my misdeeds.

The running with wild broomers. The time I'd flown my broom right up against a wall and everyone had thought I'd die. Drugs? They'd believe that. Psychotic behavior under drugs? They'd believe that too.

This was the last shock, and the worst of all. Because it dawned on me slowly: I couldn't go to Circum.

And this was a problem indeed. Because space lifepods depended on the fact that the ship in trouble would have sent a rescue signal. And faster ships would have come to rescue any survivors within hours.

This meant . . . I had oxygen for a few hours more—I wasn't sure how many as I didn't know the speed of the lifepod nor how long I'd slept. Not nearly enough to make it to Earth.

I looked behind me, at the lifepods pursuing me. The formation they were in. I could only go to Circum or into the dangerous powertrees. They'd never catch me before I made it to Circum, but what was the point, if they could capture me without getting there before me?

I thought of my time in Circum Terra. I'd flirted with scientists and befriended techs, but the ones I'd felt most comfortable with were the powerpod harvesters. These men, who risked their lives daily navigating through the thorny, dark labyrinth of the power-trees and harvesting the unstable powerpods, were somehow the same kind of person I was. We were kin. We understood each other.

Now, with Circum up and to my left—well, to my insides everything felt like down and left, but it was relatively above the lifepod and I knew it—I had the forest of powertrees, the powerpods glowing upon them like captive fireflies to my right. Earth cast its shadow on us and put us in night.

If I couldn't go to Circum, why not the powertrees?

Fine, fine, any rational person would refuse to consider the powertrees. Ever. But I was never a rational person. And what choice did I have? They wouldn't pursue me in there.

And if I could find a harvester there, in the forest of coiling branches, if I could get the harvester to take me on, I'd have a chance, wouldn't I? I could talk to the harvester operator and convince him of my story, and get him on my side before I landed in Circum. I might have a chance. Just a slim chance, but better than none.

I veered off towards the powertrees. Calling them trees is, of course, a misnomer. They have no trunks and no roots. They are rather a conglomeration of twisting branches with what appear to be gigantic thorns growing out of them. And here and there, amid them, the powerpods in various stages of ripeness, radiation glowing through their skins.

What did I know about them? Absolutely nothing. Or nothing more than you learned in your primary programs. That the trees are a biological solar collector, planted and grown in the late twenty-first century during the reign of Earth's bio-lords. That they were fed organic matter from Earth via the ancient beanstalk that predated Circum Terra and which was no longer safe for people, but which still worked perfectly for cargo. That they collected the sun's radiation into the powerpods which, in turn, brought to Earth, powered our civilization.

How the trees grew in space, in vacuum? No idea. Clearly they were a closed system, their skin immune to the vacuum of space. How? No idea. But then again, neither had our leading scientists any ideas. The bio-lords, fortunately deposed in turmoils long before my birth, had been bioengineered to be well beyond our intellectual capacity. None of us could match it. But we still used the power system. All of our technology was keyed to it. And it was so abundant and inexhaustible.

Even the harvesters had no idea how the trees grew in vacuum. All they knew was how to pick the pods at the sweet spot between ripeness and instability. Too little ripe, and they would have too little power, barely worthy transporting to Circum. Too much and they would blow up and take the harvester with them before ever getting to Circum's extruding chamber.

Oh, another thing they knew—or said they knew—and that was that darkship thieves, the descendants of a few escaped bio-lords, lived somewhere beyond the stars and stole ripe pods. Or so they'd told me. I wasn't sure it was a true legend, or the equivalent of stories to frighten a child.

I'd given them no thought at all—not until I found myself flying into the tangle of powertrees.

The joystick was sweaty in my hand, and it was hard to maneuver—even this small a ship—between trunk and powerpod, carefully, carefully. Harvesters had precision controls and computer-aided steering. I had a joystick and an unwieldy lifepod that reacted just a little too slowly.

Down over a branch, I dodged above the next just in time to avoid smashing into it, and then there was a huge powerpod in front of me, the fissures in the skin indicating it was overripe and about to blow. I twisted sideways and barely skidded away from it. And found myself threading a needle hole, barely large enough for the pod to dive through. I hoped.

I swallowed hard, as I went into it. I'd have prayed if I believed in gods.

And then, out of nowhere I hit something. Not hard. And whatever I hit was not as deadly solid as the diamond-hard trunks and certainly no powerpod. For one, it didn't blow up.

Even after hitting it, I couldn't see what it was. It was ... dark. Straining, I could make out a rounded outline, but barely distinguishable from the surrounding gloom.

My throat closed. It was a darkship. It was a darkship piloted by the descendant of the biorulers. The biorulers had been inhumanely intelligent, modified to be that way. They'd also been unable to reproduce—leading to their being called Mules—to ensure that the human race survived. But if this was a descendant, they must have been able to reproduce. Or was this one of the original biorulers? How long did they live? And what did they want with us? Their rule of Earth had been utterly ruthless. They'd moved and eliminated populations without regard. What would they do with me?

In a panic, I looked behind, looked around for a harvester. But there was no one in sight. I tried to move away from the ship, but I seemed to have caught somehow. All I managed was a long, painful scrape.

And all of a sudden my com button pushed itself down and a voice came over it. A deep, male voice, with an odd accent. "Blazing Light," it said. "Why are you scraping my sensors?"

I froze. This thing wasn't a ship. It was a creature. A dark, huge and powerful creature. And I'd injured it.

◦◦ FOUR ◦◦

"SENSORS?" I SAID, IN THE GENERAL DIRECTION OF THE COM, sounding far less assured than normal.

There was a pause. Then the voice said, "Light," as though that ought to mean something. "Ship sensors," the voice said at last.

I blinked at the dark sphere. So it was a ship? Not a being? I felt fearful, which was odd.

It's not that I didn't understand the meaning of fear. I understood it perfectly. Fear was what little old ladies who ran expensive boarding schools felt when they took a look at me. That was why they refused to admit me, unless Dad brought force or money to bear. Fear was what larger young men who ran military academies felt after I got the first one over on them. And that was why they called Daddy Dearest in hysterics and demanded I be taken home again.

What I didn't understand was *feeling* fear. But neither could I deny I was afraid of this dark, secret ship—this legend come to life. Could it just be another type of harvester? What, all black? To...what? Allow its fellows to ram into it? Or to play a prank on tourists? Except that Circum Terra and the powertrees were not open to tourists. Only to butting-in juvenile Patricians. And those were few and far between.

Trying to understand who this might be, trying to figure out how to react, I stayed quiet long enough that the voice said, in the tone of one who has reached an unpleasant decision, "Right. I'm bringing you in."

Bringing me in? "Bringing me in to where?"

"The *Cathouse*," the voice said, with an absolutely matter-of-fact tone.

I blinked, and my panic receded. The whole sequence of events from waking up with Andrija Baldo in my room to some space-borne bordello's kidnaping me only made sense—and perfect sense at that—if one assumed that I was dreaming.

The certainty that I remained safely tucked away in my bed, in the space cruiser, kept me still and only *mildly* curious as something grabbed the lifepod. I didn't know what it was, not to draw a diagram, but it looked like a mechanical claw that enveloped the transparent ship from all directions and... pulled and shoved. My stomach, already tempted by lack of gravity, now did its best to catapult towards my mouth.

I had a moment of doubt, because one doesn't normally feel queasy in dreams, and then stopped thinking about it because the claw shoved me neatly through a membrane, then another—an airlock?—and into a vast, dark space.

How vast it was, I couldn't tell, because it was dark. Though not dark as outside. More a twilight type of darkness, a veiled light—like a late summer sunset over the Mediterranean.

My lifepod was set down, with a resounding metallic thud, and then the claw withdrew. I counted to five. Then to five again. Everything in me wanted to move. I wanted to open the door. I wanted to take off running. I did not want to sit here, waiting, confined—my legs bent backward and fast growing numb.

But what if there was no air out there? Nonsense. Nonsense. Why would there be an airlock if no air? But what if it was ammonia? Or something like that?

No. If he—whoever he was, Mule or darkship thief, or whatever—was anything human derived, he breathed air.

I'd just made up my mind, and set my hand on the release bar for the lock that would allow the upper part of the lifepod to open, when there was a thud from somewhere near the nose of the lifepod. A thud like... like a giant door sliding open. Someone was coming. *Something* was coming. For *me*.

I'd be damned if I was going to meet it while cramped and bent in here. I pushed down the door-opening release very fast, then pushed the lifepod open, in one move, while holding my slip—what remained of it—closed with my other hand.

And found myself facing someone who looked utterly alien. Oh, not alien like with tentacles and stuff like the bad mid-twenty-first-century sensies. I mean, those were not really scary. What's so scary about a squid or an octopus? Even if it's walking on land?

No. This...creature was scary because he was human, undeniably and certainly of the same human stock I was—bipedal, general body shape of human male. Truth be told, wonderful body shape of human male. He was tall, with broad, straight shoulders, a narrow waist, the muscular legs of a dancer or runner. All of which were clearly visible because he was wearing what could have been a dancer's costume—bright red and made of some material that molded to every inch and possibly every pore.

I noticed that first, but then I looked up. And above the neck... Oh, don't misunderstand me. He didn't look deformed. Just familiar and different in an unbearable combination. His face was that of a human male, in bone and skin—a broad face, with a hint of the Nordic and a square chin, that would not have looked out of place on a redhead.

Only the hair above the face was not red. It was...calico, like a cat's. A mixture of blond and brown and red, bright enough to be visible in this dim light. And his eyes, broad and bright, had no sclera at all. They were green like a cat's and, like a cat's, slanted and shining in the dark.

"Cat got your tongue?" he asked, and seemed to see this as the epitome of humor.

I must have made an inarticulate sound, not so much of fear as of shock. And I let the front of my gown drop open. His eyes widened, just a little, and he did the quick once-over, up-and-down checking movement. So, strange he might be. But human he was. And male.

"Where am I?" I asked. "Who are you?"

"What? Are you mentally defective as well as an Earthworm?" he asked. "You set out to catch a darkship thief, and you're surprised you caught him?"

"I'm not..." I said. "I didn't..." Never had I found it so difficult to express myself in the right words. And then I realized what I'd first missed in the low light. In his hand, he had a weapon which he pointed at me.

It wasn't like any weapon I'd ever seen—narrow and bright yellow and thin at the tip, it looked like...a pointer of some sort. But I had no doubt from the way he was holding it that he was armed and from the way he was looking at me that he was dangerous.

I grabbed my ruined slip and held it one-handed, calculating how fast I could move to kick that weapon out of his hands, before he could—

"Don't *think* about it, Earthworm," he said and smiled. Even teeth, but not a pleasant smile. "I don't have the time to play with you. I'm mid harvest, and I can only leave the ship on autopilot so long. So, I'm going to put you somewhere where you can't trouble me." He stepped out of the way and let me see, past him, an open door leading into what looked like some sort of corridor. "Go. Forward. Past me."

There are only two things anyone can do in that situation: Obey or not obey. I chose the third. As I was walking past him, I turned and attacked him aiming a high kick at the gun and getting ready to fall again, entrechat, and kick his groin on the way down.

It should have worked. It always worked. But his hand met my foot, held it. Sending me spilling backward, my head hitting the floor, hard. Dazed I looked up, to catch again that brief look of appreciation at what my split-up slip revealed.

Oh, yes, he was male. And human. Very. But the expression of interest passed as soon as he'd shown it, his—warm, viselike—hand let go of my foot, and he seemed to jump back. Or rather, he seemed to fade out and appear further back. Quickly. "Up," he said. "Up. Don't try that again. Next time I'll fire. I swear I will. Up."

He looked discomposed, which was odd, because he'd stopped my kick just in time. Why did he look like he'd suffered an unexpected blow? What was he afraid of?

Whatever it was, it wasn't my fast moves. And I wasn't stupid. If at first you fail, you don't try and try again in the same manner. You fall back and think of a better way to succeed. So I walked past him—as dignified and composed as I could be—into a narrow corridor, where the walls appeared to be made of some hard, poured material, ceramite or perhaps dimatough, in an iridescent, pearly grey. At least that's what I thought the color was; it was hard to tell in the almost-darkness.

As I walked on, ahead of him, I smelled the vague, rancid smell of long-distance ships. Not as bad as in the Circum harvesters, but worse than in Father's cruiser. Not too bad, though. Not nearly as bad as that lifepod, with my sweaty self in a far-too-small space.

The floor under my feet felt carpeted. Plush carpets. Living quarters? He walked me round and round. Ramp. We were taking our way up somewhere. Didn't he have stairs or antigrav wells? Of course he must. Somewhere. But only an idiot would take a prisoner up stairs or antigrav wells and give the prisoner the advantage of high ground. Instead, we were following a spiral corridor along the outside of the ship, climbing up and up. Till he said, from behind me. "Left, sharp. Don't try anything funny."

I didn't feel even vaguely humorous. I remembered that move downstairs. He was faster than I. I'd never met anyone faster than I. And I didn't want to die. I'd gotten lucky he had grabbed me with his free hand, instead of blasting me with his burner.

"Is that gun a burner?" I asked.

"No," he said. "It's just a flashlight. What do you think?"

I swallowed. "I rarely think about—" I said.

"Noted," he said. "Only an idiot would take a ship like that thing back there through the powertrees. I've half a mind to space you and save you the trouble of committing suicide going back in that."

"Going back—" I said blankly.

"When I'm done collecting and not a minute sooner," he said.

We were following another corridor, and it opened onto a large, circular space. I had to blink to realize it was a bedroom. It wasn't just the darkness, but it seemed so odd to find an utterly human bedroom—bed, chair, closet doors on the wall, a sensi cabinet, a gem storage unit—in this creature's lair.

He grabbed me. For the space of exhaling, I saw images of women captured by space monsters of . . . But he threw me down on the chair. The hard, straight-backed chair. Then he moved again with unreal speed. Tying me to the chair.

There are very few things I truly can't stand to have done to me. Being tied up is one of them. As he tied me with something elastic and fabriclike at middle, legs and chest, I panicked and tried to struggle. But he was fast, and I hadn't a chance.

When he finished tying me, he pocketed his gun and grinned at me in the dark. "I'll let you go once I'm done harvesting," he said. "I really can't afford to be on autopilot anymore. We could blow at any second." He got a strip of fabric from his closet. "Just an extra precaution."

"No," I said. "Do not blindfold me."

"Why?" he said. "Because it will make it harder for you to get free? Good."

And then he seemed to speed up again. Before I could do anything, I was blindfolded. And tied. To a chair.

Right. He was going to die. He was going to die a slow and excruciatingly painful death.

꜀⊙ FIVE ⊙꜄

MY CAPTOR DIDN'T KNOW HOW TO TIE UP WOMEN. I WASN'T SURE what that meant precisely, but right then I was grateful for his ineptitude.

His first mistake was in tying my hands in front of me. I suspect he thought he was perfectly safe, because he had tied my hands together and then tied me to the chair with my hands bound, so that two strips of what felt like fabric ran over my secured-together arms, one at chest height and one at waist level. Another strip of fabric tied my ankles together.

The second mistake, of course, was that chest-height thing. Either the man hadn't been around many females, or he simply didn't think. Then again, didn't they say the Mules had no females? All male, all sterile with human females. Yes. That had to be it. He had no idea of the...ah...springiness of the female breast.

I'd held my breath as he tied that bind across my chest, so it was already loose. Deep breathing and cautious wiggling made it fall past the fullest part of my breast to hang loosely around my waist. This left me free to shrug, and pull, and shrug again, till I freed my hands from the tie, now looser, around my waist. And this allowed me to bring my hands up to my mouth and gnaw through the fabric—whatever it was, it felt like fine silk against my teeth and lips—that held them.

Silk tears easily, once it's started to tear, and once I had the first hole in, I pulled my hands apart, till at last it tore across,

29

with a ripping sound. The fabric fell loose, and I massaged my wrists, then removed my blindfold and untied the two binds at my waist and chest, and bent to untie the one at my ankles.

That last one felt elastic and beaded. Having untied it completely, I brought it up near my face to see it in the dim light. It was red fabric embroidered in every possible color of the rainbow. It was either a belt or a headband, and in either case it meant the cat-critter had atrocious taste. However . . . I tested the tensile strength of the thing and it would make an ideal garotte. I tied it around my slip, to hold the halves together, as I got up to investigate my surroundings.

I really didn't want to waste more time than I needed to, but I had learned through going off on half setting more than once that it paid to reconnoiter and to know what I was up against. Particularly—I thought as I stretched—since I had no idea at all if the creature was human. Or quasi human. Or . . . a Mule. It was said, and it fell in the realm of legend more than anything else, that when the Mules escaped Earth in the spaceship they'd secretly built, they'd taken with them the most grossly bioengineered of their servants.

Perhaps it was true, though enough had stayed behind to be chased down all over the Earth, hanged and burned and—for those that fell to exceptionally creative mobs—crucified publicly all over the globe. The vids of the time were not supposed to be accessible unless there was need to know, but I'd defeated the security in my education computer and seen them all. And hadn't been able to forget them since. And there had been people left behind to be killed who could only vaguely be called human, such were their bio-modifications. So if the Mules had taken their more bioed servants with them, exactly what were we talking about?

If I didn't know what this . . . person/male/creature was, then I'd worry about things that might not be within his capabilities. So far, I knew he was human-shaped, save for eyes. His hair could be some odd fashion. Humans had been dyeing hair presumably since they'd had hair, and I'd seen weirder affectations in the stranger parts of Syracuse Seacity. But those eyes seemed real, and he could see very well in the dark, which probably meant they weren't contact lenses or some other purely cosmetic artifice. I also knew he could move fast. Faster than I in my speed-demon mode. Oh, and I knew he liked the sight of naked female. Which was just as well. But if I was going up against him, and if I was going to convince him to take me to Earth, I needed more.

I walked slowly around the room, in the half light. It was roughly hexagonal and sparsely furnished. Near the closet, I found a slide that looked like the old light-adjustment slides, not in use in modern houses on Earth for two centuries, but still present in historical buildings. I slid it upward slowly, and light came flooding into the room, revealing it just as I described, save for the colors. The colors made me question the sanity, or at least the balance of the creature who had chosen them.

Walls the deep red of arterial blood fought for notice with a bedspread the purple of a bruise. No piece of furniture was safe. The sensi cabinet, which, on Earth, came only in black and white, here rejoiced in a deep, dark, shining gold. The bedside cabinet, following the rule of no two things sharing a color, was bright, almost fluorescent green.

I was tempted to turn the light down again, but I didn't. Instead, I walked up to that closet on the wall and opened the door. The clothes inside . . . Well, they would make an aesthete weep. Or perhaps curl in fetal position in a dark corner, whimpering in horror. There was purple and gold, silver and bright sky blue, sick green and piss yellow—sometimes all in one garment.

Repressing a desire to vomit, I looked closer. Tunic and pants and pants and tunic. Fairly boring clothing, except for the colors. Either wherever this person came from was far more regimented than Earth, or he was the type of male who favored simplicity over fashion. Although if that was the case, someone should clue him in on colors.

One suit stood apart from the others, having more elaborate tailoring. Instead of a tunic, it had a jacket, and the pants were tailored, rather than elastic to mold on the body. Dark red, with white piping at sleeves and pant legs, it had the feel of a uniform. Adding to this, the chest showed an insignia. I looked more closely at it and it was like nothing I'd ever seen. The insignia was shield-shaped, about the size of my palm. On it, embroidered, was a dark red apple, with a serpent coiled around it. Either the serpent had human dentition, or a human had taken a bite out of the apple before the serpent got there. Above the figure, a single word: "Eden." Beneath the figure, in ancient French—which Father had forced me to learn—the words *Je Reviens* which meant "I return."

None of it made any sense. I knew Eden was the place human-ity had started in one of the creation myths. But Father—and most other rulers of Earth—was not in the least religious. I'd learned all of it as myth and history, but I had a very foggy idea of what it meant. I knew it involved a serpent and an apple and the feeling started to grow on me that the whole thing was a joke I just couldn't get.

I closed the closet doors and looked over the rest of the room. The bed was neatly made. So whatever the bioengineered freak was, he was neat. Good for him. Next, the bedside cabinet, which had a series of drawers. I walked around the bed to get there, and then I saw it...

It was one of those holos which is only visible from a certain angle, and it must proceed from a chip mounted on the top of the cabinet itself. It showed a family group. A very odd fam-ily group. There was an older male—probably the father—with normal-issue human body and features. On his arm, and leaning slightly against him, was a female with the same eyes as my feline friend, only in dark blue. Both parents were dark-haired and solidly built. On the left stood a young woman who could have graced the halls of a Roman palace. Except her eyes, dark blue, were also catlike. A normal Earthlike male with blond hair had his arm over her shoulders. Right from the female, presumably the mother, stood another young lady, this one looking much like her dad and perfectly Earth-normal. Behind her and to the side, his face visible, but his body only partly so, stood a dark-haired gentleman with golden cat eyes. Right of this couple stood my acquaintance, in all his calico-haired splendor. And from his arm hung a perfectly normal Earth female, blonde and petite, one of those self-contained, perfectly groomed women who always made me feel like breaking something. Preferably something attached to them.

Um...So, the critter didn't reproduce by fission. And he had a family somewhere. Were any of them here?

Points against—he had said that he was alone and had the ship on autopilot. No, correction. He'd said he had the ship on autopilot. Didn't mean he was alone, only that Little Miss Blonde couldn't pilot. And—points for someone else being aboard—that light slide went all the way up to normal lighting, which Cat-Eyes didn't seem to enjoy or need.

Fine, I'd go on with caution. If there were two of them onboard, it would make things harder. Not impossible, mind, not by a long shot, but harder.

I left the room and met with a choice of going to the right, which angled down into the ramp I'd taken coming in. Or to the left, which led around in a lazy, level circle. I went left. These were definitely the living quarters. Not particularly impressive, but far bigger than in the harvesters from Circum and denoting a long-distance ship. There was a small room, with an exercise machine so complex that I couldn't imagine how to use it, followed by a slightly larger fresher with the usual appliances and a cleaner with the options for water or vibro. Down the hall from that was a kitchen with a large automated cooker, a small table—affixed solidly to the floor—and two chairs, ditto. The cabinet revealed two plates, two cups and two sets of cutlery. Perhaps Blondie was around after all.

Further down the hall, a vibro closet for clothes, filled to almost capacity with dirty suits that no one had bothered to put in the small, efficient-looking vibro unit. The clothes smelled musty and contributed in no small measure to the smell of the ship. So... either the unit was broken—I lacked the time or interest to try it—or there was at least one very bad housekeeper aboard. A poke with my toe—as close as I wanted to get—seemed to indicate all the clothes were of the type and size of the clothing upstairs, and, truth be told, there seemed to be clothing only for one in the bedroom. So, then again, maybe kitten was alone.

I went down the other way, till I came to the set of stairs I'd guessed existed somewhere. The stairs led to another floor. Most of the doors here were marked with the timeless radiation-hazard sign. I knew that signs often lied, but I didn't feel foolhardy enough to try just yet. And besides, this seemed to be a small, intimate spaceship, so to whom would the signs lie?

While the level upstairs had been carpeted in bright red, plushy stuff, this level was all dimatough, polished and cold.

I came upon another staircase—with a ramp to the other side, which was odd. Was this spaceship set for disabled access? Who was disabled? Blondie? And why? If bio-improvement were allowed and not forbidden as on Earth, why have disabilities?—and took the ramp down, as silently as I could. It wasn't difficult to be silent, as the steps were made of dimatough, solid as stone and immovable, and I was barefoot.

This level was carpeted again, and as I moved slowly clockwise, I could tell it was inhabited. It had that feel. I passed a broad, empty room full of monitors and what looked like blank gemboards. And then I came to the door of another broad room.

My calico-haired friend was there, sitting, with his back to me—such his confidence—fully absorbed in something taking place on the screen in front of him.

The screen was too dark for me to see exactly what he was looking at, but whatever it was, it had his attention, as he worked a joystick with his right hand and ran his hand frantically over a sensepad to his right.

I removed my belt as soundlessly as I could. I wasn't going to kill him. Yet. But it was essential that he thought I was. Winding the belt around both of my wrists, with a generous strip left free in between, I waited till he looked down for a moment, so he wouldn't see my reflection on the screen.

He looked up, just as I surged into the room, and I saw his eyes—reflected on the screen—widen, just as I wrapped the belt around his neck and twisted.

⋙ SIX ⋘

IN REFLECTION, ON HIS ALMOST DARK SCREEN, HIS EYES WIDENED further, while his hands came up, to claw at his own neck, trying to dislodge the belt. Not a chance. What there was a chance of, was my killing him. Which would be a problem.

I've had an easy time with machinery and electronics since I could remember, but these controls looked a little complex to learn before I blew myself up on the next ripe powerpod. So I had to be careful, and bring my prey within sight of his own death without pushing him over.

This required my knee at his back, in between his shoulder blades; my hands pulling just enough to keep him struggling without making him lose consciousness. I watched his eyes. As soon as he looked dazed enough, I would let go and I . . .

His foot kicked at a lever on the floor. I had a millisecond to wonder if it was reflexive action. In the next moment his hand let go of his neck and he unbuckled himself from the seat. And we floated.

No gravity. No gravity. I whimpered, as my feet lost all contact with the distant floor, and there was no floor, no ceiling. My stomach twisted.

The creature freed himself from the belt, and growled something that sounded like another language under his breath. He turned around, mouth in a snarl. His hand, massive and square, positioned just below my breasts, pushed. I went back and spun.

35

I tried to fight. I've fought many men, many who should fight better than I or who were stronger. This was like fighting a shadow. He moved... He was everywhere. He slid past me, fast. Fast like being in a dream where people change positions before you can track them.

I tried to kick but never made contact. I tried to claw and scratch, but it seemed to have no effect. His features were frozen in stony anger, his teeth clamped together and showing between his drawn lips which had, in turn, gone pale. And he was muttering something that was little more than a growl, as he pushed me back and back and back, and pinned me against one of the walls.

I bit him, hard, on the arm that held me pinned. He grabbed the back of my hair and pulled till my mouth opened and I let go. He didn't give his bleeding arm more than a glance.

Glaring at me, his lips drawn into a rictus of fury, he muttered things, of which only a few words were understandable. "Earthworm... vicious... uncontrolled... I was going to let you live. I was going to... Tell me why in Blazing Light I shouldn't space you?"

I opened my mouth, but no sound came. My throat felt dry and abraded, as if I'd been screaming for a long time. Whatever he was, he wasn't human. He certainly wasn't normal human. He wasn't... No one could move like that. I swallowed, but there was no saliva to soothe my throat. Instead of words, a pitiful whimper came out of my mouth.

I didn't think being cute was going to save me this time. He wasn't even touching anywhere near my breasts. Though my slip was split open, the halves floating, his hand pushed solidly between my breasts and my stomach. And in his odd eyes there was no sign at all of masculine appreciation for curves.

"Tell me," he said, his voice more understandable, but not that much calmer. "Now."

Something exploded. At first I thought it was my head—such the sense of pressure and danger, such the need to answer, somehow. And then I realized it came from outside the ship. And then we started rolling, rolling, end over end, accompanied by thuds and pops of hitting something—several somethings outside.

I had time to think of the dimatough trunks, the explosive powerpods. My companion clearly thought the same, as he let go of me, and said, "Oh, hell."

And then the lights went very bright, then dark, then normal. Gravity reasserted itself and I fell. I saw my playfellow on the floor, pulling at the lever with both hands.

So the lever was gravity, was it? I'd never seen a ship that could turn gravity off and on that easily and I wondered why. But he wasn't paying any attention to me. Which might be a good time to attack him, only, of course, I wasn't sure I could win. I also didn't know anything else to do. It wasn't like he was just going to forget I'd tried to strangle him. Was he?

He sat down in his seat, and buckled himself with what seemed to be a reflex motion. He ran his hands along the keyboard, and along a panel next to it, where a series of raised dots shifted places quickly—whether in response to his touch, I didn't know.

Words still came from him, under his breath, but now they seemed to be more the muttering of someone who is cursing fate. "Can you see the screen?" he asked me. "Can you see anything on the screen?"

I'd thought we were not on speaking terms, but I squinted at the screen, and could make out, amid the prevailing darkness, some twisting darker lines and some brighter spots. "Pods and trunks?" I asked.

"So you're not completely stupid," he said. "Can you tell me how to get out of here?"

"Why . . . why . . ."

He made a sound at the back of his throat. "Because I'm blind. The flash of light blinded me. Temporarily. My eyes are light sensitive. It's part of my ELFing."

His . . . ELFing. Oh, no. I wasn't going to ask. He could be any mythical critter he wanted. I was not going to ask at all.

He mistook my silence for something else. "Don't even think about it. I can beat you, even blind. Besides, if you don't help me, we're going to run into something and die. As far as I can tell, from my memory of where we were and how we rolled, we're in a cul de sac, surrounded by pods and trunks. How do we get out?"

I wasn't thinking of anything. I knew he could beat me with his eyes closed. And probably without hands. It was a novel experience, meeting someone who could do this. Aloud I said, "Forward . . . um . . . the way you're facing. At least if the screen is the same orientation we are. Slowly."

He obeyed, his hands dancing on the keyboard with eerie

precision when one realized he couldn't see. We slowly advanced amid the cul the sac of branches. I could now see—well, sort of see, a lot of the screen took guessing—that we were surrounded above and below as well.

"There's a branch at the end too," I said. "We're going to have to squeeze out."

He only grunted.

"Slightly down," I said. "Down, down, down. A little more. Faster than that, damn it."

And we were in the gullet, we were squeezing out. Squeezing. A scraping sound from outside, a faltering in the sound of motors I hadn't even noticed before, and then the sound picked up again, on a higher note, and a muscle jumped in my... captor's jaw.

But we were out and I directed him: "Up now. Now forward. Now down."

We wound like a bit of string through the knotted trunks of the powertree ring. The thing is, though it's called a ring, it is no such thing. It is more like a ball of yarn, thick and huge, an artificial satellite the twin of the moon. It might have been a ring in the time of the Mules but for the last two hundred and fifty years it had been fed overtime to satisfy the ever-larger craving for energy from Earth populations. Add to that the random blowing up and reseeding of ripe, unharvested pods, and you had... a cat's cradle for a particularly large and radioactive cat.

We wound through it and spit out the other side, into what the screen showed as a space free of pods and trunks.

My captor turned his sightless eyes—huge and more bewilderingly catlike than ever—towards me. "How good are you with machines?" he asked.

"Why? Why...?" I asked.

"Because if you can't go outside and fix the node we scraped off in that tight place, we're going to die."

ꞁꞁꞁ SEVEN ꞁꞁꞁ

"WHY ARE WE GOING TO DIE?" I ASKED. "WE'RE OUT OF THE powertrees." I told myself he was trying to scare me. That was all he was doing. But why did he need to scare me? He'd already fought me into a corner. And I knew he could still do it, even blind.

"Because we're on auxiliary power. If you don't fix the node, the power will fail."

"We won't have lights?"

"Or water," he said. "Or air."

"Oh.

"So, how good are you with machines?"

"Very," I said. And it occurred to me it sounded like I was boasting, but it was the plain truth. "I keep the brooms in the lair flying."

"Brooms? Never mind. This is quite beyond household machinery, but you're all I have."

I bit my lip. The brooms were not household machinery. They were antigrav wands that could be ridden. Though highly illegal everywhere on Earth, except as means of lifesaving in an accident, they were, of course, used. I'd been riding them since I was twelve and most of my time on Earth was spent at my broomer lair. But if darkship thieves didn't know about brooms, I wasn't going to enlighten them.

He got up, tentatively, hands flitting around him, to orient himself. "I have a spacesuit," he said. "Should fit you."

If it belonged to him, it would fit me like a pair of galoshes fit a snake. My head still hurt from where he had slammed it into the wall.

He passed me—flit of the hand in my direction, barely brushing my shoulder—and said, "Follow me," as he rushed ahead. And I mean rushed. I could tell, from the way he put his foot down hesitantly, at first, then firmed the step, and from the way his hands fluttered to the walls now and then that he was indeed blind and trying to orient himself. But he walked faster than I'd ever seen anyone walk while they lacked use of their eyes.

He led me up to the curving corridor, to the floor without any living quarters or steering arrangements. There he stopped, in front of what seemed to be a solid wall. He felt at the wall, then punched it in three points. His face had set in something between rage and pain. I didn't want to disturb him. I was half afraid he was punching the wall because he was crazy, and even more afraid he would turn around and punch me if I made a sound.

But to my surprise, the wall slid open, a panel disappearing into another panel. Revealed was a small compartment in which a bright blue suit hung. It didn't look like a spacesuit. It looked like a bright blue, knit stretch one-piece. As he picked it up, it hung limply from one hand.

"That's not a spacesuit," I said. Could he be confused? He was blinded.

"Of course it is," he said.

"The pressures..."

"It's bioed fabric. Do you mean Earthworms' suits are different?"

I didn't say anything, just reached for the thing. It felt cold and scaly to the touch, though it looked absolutely smooth. I couldn't see any way of opening it. It seemed to be a single knit piece, but when I pulled at the front, it opened, from top to bottom, like stickfast or a zipper. I slipped it on, then closed it down the front. It felt oddly warm once I was in it, though nowhere like my spacesuit back in Father's ship. And the gloves that were part of it felt like a second skin, even more sensitive than surgical gloves.

"It will stay closed until you pull it forcefully apart," he said. I jumped. Was he reading my mind? But he grinned—a fast and unfriendly flash of teeth. "It would be like Earthworm brains to worry." He was holding something that looked like a ski mask. "Helmet," he said.

I was past arguing and slipped the thing on, to find that it was completely enclosed, something as transparent as glass, as malleable as fabric, covering my face. I had a moment of panic and suffocation, and then he straightened, from near the compartment, holding two large, reflective cylinders that he slapped on my back. They stuck there, and he did something, and suddenly fresh oxygen filled the suit. So, it was airtight. But I had no time to dwell on it, because he was putting boots in front of me. They looked like stylish metallic ankle boots and they fit me perfectly. The whole suit fit me perfectly. I looked at mine host and knew there was no way, there simply was no way this was his. Well, his chest was broader than mine, which might make accommodation for my breasts, but there was no way his height or bulk converted to mine. And in no way could his boots ever fit me.

He walked ahead of me again, to a door marked—surprisingly in Glaish—with DANGER. DOOR LEADS TO VACUUM. It had a genlock, on a grey membrane, upon which he lay his palm flat. The door retracted open—it was the only way to describe it. Each half contracted soundlessly, like a membrane, though it looked mechanical, and he stepped through. We were, clearly, in an airlock. He took a box that was attached to the wall near the outer door. "This is a tool box," he said. "It will open the node. It should be the one closest to this door. Inside the node, the blue...it's not a wire, but it will look like one to you, if history vids are right, should be feeding into the gold one. If it's not, change that. There's diagrams on the lid of what the circuit inside the node should look like."

I looked at him. "What...how will I hold onto the ship? Are the boots magnetic?"

"No," he said. "But that's fine, because the ship really isn't metal either. It's...localized gravity. The boots are attracted to the ship. The suit too. You won't drift away." He gave me a tight smile. "And the tool box is attracted to the ship too, so you can set it beside you. The tools are locked in it, just don't put a tool down out of place. It will float away." He approached the grey membrane on this door, and placed his hand on it, but it didn't open. "I'm going to leave. That door has a minute delay to make sure you're ready."

"But—" I said.

He stopped and turned around. "I'll let you in when you're done," he said.

Frankly, that was the least of my worries. And there were

many worries. Like, what exactly a node was and how I'd find the one that was broken. It *should* be the one closest to this door didn't exactly reassure me. It *might* not be that one. And I wasn't absolutely convinced this spacesuit would work, either. It was like nothing I'd ever even heard of on Earth. Were the darkship thieves truly that advanced? Could they be?

But my captor had left. The outer door was spinning open. And I couldn't go back in the ship. I was sure the genlock in the middle of the inner door wouldn't open for me. And if it did, what would it mean? Other than that I would be able to die inside, without air when systems failed?

I stepped out of the door, to find there was a narrow little walkway around the ship. Kind of like the representations of the rings of Saturn. I stepped onto it, and began walking around it, looking for anything that might be a node.

Ahead, there was a rounded swelling in the skin of the ship. I grabbed onto it, and it pulled open as though on hinges, though no hinge was visible. Inside . . .

Inside was a jumble I couldn't begin to understand. The creature had said I'd see wires, but there was nothing like wires. There were . . . capillaries, maybe, plus a confusion of painted circuits linked by those pulsing capillaries. The color of the capillaries was dark grey. All of them were dark grey, except if you squinted, you could sort of see, against the dark grey color, as though flickers of another color.

Instantly, despite the coolness of fresh oxygen, sweat sprang up inside the suit and beaded on my forehead. I looked over my shoulder at space, immense and looming out there. To my right the powertrees glowed eerily. To my left, blackness punctuated with pinpoints of light, immense and dark and presumably devoid of life, save the Mules beyond.

Then I looked at the circuit again. And still could not make heads or tails of it. Sweat was pooling above my eyebrows, a little trickling down and making my eyes sting. I would never get done here. And if I didn't get done, I wouldn't be able to get back in. Not the least because my captor would be dead of suffocation.

My hands felt slippery inside the gloves. A single thought formed in my mind, overpowering all. *I don't want to die.*

Who are *you?* The creature's voice sounded in my mind, unmistakable. *Can you hear me?*

⟪ EIGHT ⟫

OF COURSE I CAN HEAR YOU, I THOUGHT, ANNOYED THAT HE doubtless could hear me too.

The thoughts forming in my head were not a pleasant form of communication, even if they came with so much of my friend the ELF's intonation and feel that there was no imagining they could be mine. I assumed something built into the suit made thought transmission possible. Or some form of subperceptible sound that sounded like thought. Looking at their circuits, I thought they'd developed centuries ahead while we stayed, more or less, still. *And what do you mean, who am I?*

I got the impression of his glare, catlike eyes widening, mouth frowning. *You're right. What are you, more appropriate perhaps.*

What I am, I answered, testily, *is out here, with a job I don't understand.*

Let me see it.

I hesitated, confused by what exactly he might mean by that.

Look at the node, please, so I can see what's confusing you.

He could see through my eyes? That was about as comfortable as being lost in someone's underwear. But I still didn't want to die, so I looked down at the open node, at the mass of pulsing capillaries, that made it look like a nest of very thin worms.

The gold one, he gave me a mental image of the writhing caterpillar with the little gold sheen to it. *Make it feed into the blue one. Use this tool to disconnect it*, mental picture of a pincerlike thing. *And this one to connect it,* mental picture of a little spatu-lalike implement.

I followed his instructions. With the mental pictures, it wasn't really hard. The idea that he was in my mind, giving me images directly to my mind, still gave me the shivers though. If he was knocking about in there, what else would he find? See? Think?

Even Daddy Dearest had never invaded my privacy this far. I closed the node, and the tool box. The question was if the creature was this likely to become temporarily blind, and the nodes out here could go hairy, why was he traveling alone?

There was a sense of displeasure from the other end, and then a curt, *I don't work well with others.*

No, really? Would wonders never cease? I tried to keep that thought to myself, but from a certain hint of offended dignity coming from the other end, I suspected I'd failed.

Is the node working now?

No, sullen, with a hint of resentment. *Kick it.*

Beg your pardon?

Give it a good kick. Kind of stomp on it.

I stared at the blister on the ship's skin. Was he joking? The node was out here, where it might rub a stray trunk in going through the powertrees, or where a microasteroid, even, might hit it. And a kick could fix it or, presumably, break it? He had to be joking.

It's an old ship, came the tired answer. *A very old ship. Used to be a teaching ship.*

Aiming the kick so it wouldn't open the cover, I slammed my foot against it. *And now?*

For a minor eternity, no one answered. I was here alone, on the outside of the ship, with the eerie glow of the powertree globe to one side, and the eternal night of space to the other. The stars shining in that night seemed very distant, very small. For no reason at all, a memory of one of the last happy times before my Mom left came to mind.

I was very young and we'd taken a family vacation to Pamplona, in the Southern European territories. And there, I'd seen some old ritual that involved countless people strolling around in the dark of night, holding candles. The windows had been ornamented with tapestries, and there had been flowers everywhere, making the night air redolent of wax and roses. I remembered leaning out a window, over the soft, silken tapestry, while my mom held me around the middle of my body. "Thena, look how lovely," she'd said, whispering in my ear.

Thena. Is that your name?

The creature's voice, directly into my mind, made me jump. I answered in offended dignity and horror that he'd been in my mind and seen that memory of all memories—and fear he'd think me soft and easy to subdue because of it—*Athena Hera Sinistra, Patrician of Earth.*

Oh. Earthworm and *inbred. Yes, yes, something to be proud of,* he said, his tone just as haughty as I suspected mine had been. *My name is Kit to my friends, but you may call me Christopher Bartolomeu Klaavil.*

Are you going to let me in? I asked.

Your wish is my command, he said, in a voice that didn't sound the least like it. *Look to your right.*

I did, in time to see the door open on the ship skin. I scrambled over with unseemly haste. Being on the outside and subjected to the creature's whim on whether or not to let me back in was not my idea of a rousing good time.

He was inside the airlock, attired in a bright blue spacesuit, similar to mine, but clearly his size. Of course, that made one wonder, exactly, who had worn the suit I was wearing. I thought of the blonde woman in the picture. What had happened to her?

His words, *I don't work well with others,* came to my mind and made me shiver.

I never . . . His voice said in my mind. *I wouldn't*—I had the impression of a door, forcefully slammed down on his thoughts. *Oh, hell, what does it matter, anyway. Please get in, so I can close the airlock.*

I obeyed, and he closed the outer door, then did something with a valve and a control on the wall. I could hear air hissing into this tight compartment. "What do you wish me to do?" he asked.

I looked at him puzzled. His face was just visible through the helmet, half in shadows, making his catlike eyes even more alien and stranger.

"You saved my life," he said. The voice had the tone of something spoken through clenched teeth. "I owe you a debt of gratitude. I don't think you can go much farther on the ship you used to come here. Your power reserve is almost empty and I don't know how to recharge it. Our tech *is* different. But I owe you my life, and so I must repay it any way you wish. Where do you wish to go?"

"To Earth," I said immediately, without thinking.

He cackled.

"You said—"

"I'll help you as I can, but that doesn't include an offer to have myself stuffed, mounted and hung in a museum as a specimen of forbidden bioengineering modifications." The air had stopped hissing in, and he now opened the interior door and motioned for me to go through ahead of him, which I did.

He followed.

"You're a Mule," I said, shivering. It was a leap of reasoning.

He gasped. "No," he said. "Merely an ELF." And then, as though perhaps catching some trace of surprise from my thoughts. "An enhanced life form. I was bioengineered in a womb, via a designed virus."

"With cat genes?"

He shook his head, his face in shadows. "Of course not. The hair is an accidental, rare, side effect. And the eyes only look feline, because the function dictates form. They're best for seeing in the dark, tracking motion. With improvements to reflexes and speed of motion, they make people like me ideal for piloting harvester ships."

"The darkships?"

"Well, of course they're dark," he said. "We really don't want Earthworms...er...Earthers to catch us, do we? We work in the dark, and use ships without lights. Hence the modifications to my eyes. I work well in the dark."

"But not in light," I said.

"Don't get—"

"Ideas," I said. "I'm not." We'd got to the compartment in the hallway, and I removed each piece of the suit, while he sometimes helped.

"Your eyes have recovered," I said.

He snorted. "No. But I'm using yours. Grossly inadequate."

I tried not to think he was still in my mind, somehow, and also not to react to the insult, but my voice came out tight as I said, "What tech in the suit allows you to do that?"

"The suit?" he said.

"Isn't that what allows you to hear my thoughts? Use my eyes?"

"No. You...It's...I don't know. It's one of the traits bioengi-neered into me. It is also bioengineered into navigators, who are normally the other half of a traveling power-collecting team. So a team can communicate without using any frequencies Earth... Circum harvesters could possibly intercept."

I'm not telepathic, I thought in a panic. *I've never—*

Yeah, he answered back in my mind. *Neither have I with anyone but a nav, and my nav at that. It's a bonding thing. You have to be trained to do it. That's why I asked you to explain. No human I ever heard of has developed natural telepathy.*

Bio improvements are illegal on Earth, I said. *It has to be natural.*

"It can't be," he said.

I shook my head. I was still holding on to the last of the suit. It was the suit. It had to be the suit. I dropped the suit to the floor and then, very quickly, aimed a kick at my captor. There was air and energy now, I could make him—

He grabbed at my foot before it made contact and down I went, cracking my head against the floor of the hallway.

"Do you like hitting your head, or is it just something you do to pass the time?"

"Bastard," I said.

He straightened his spine. "Quite possibly," he said. "By several definitions. Now, if you let me remove my spacesuit, I'll be glad to take you near Circum. Your ship should have enough fuel to make it a very short drop from my ship to Circum and my ship is dark enough, if we go to an unused bay area, we might not even be noticed. Your...harvesters must fly back regularly—what, once a week? To take back pods. You must go with them."

I shook my head. Harvester ships never went to Earth. This I knew. It was why I'd been such a hit with harvester pilots. They might be stuck at Circum for years at a time. "No, they sent the energy some other way," I said.

"How?" he sounded suddenly curious.

"Don't know. Something invented by an ancient Greek, I think. Or a Frenchman. Or maybe Usaian. Something from one of his writings." Now he looked doubtful, so I exerted my mind. "Tekla, no, Telec...um...no, wait. Tesla."

"Nikola Tesla?"

"That," I said, triumphantly.

He hid his face in his hands. When he looked up again, he

was composed. "I'll take you into drop distance of Circum. I'm sure you still can find your way to Earth, anyway?"

"Oh, I'm sure."

"Right. At least," he added, his voice pensive. "It's not quite as certain a death as going near Earth, and the risk is worth it to be rid of you."

◖ NINE ◗

BUT AN HOUR LATER, AS HE ESCORTED ME INTO THE BAY WHERE the lifepod waited, he looked strangely hesitant.

He opened the door to the lifepod for me, and waited till I got in. He looked concerned. Though his expression was not easy to read—not with those very odd eyes—there was a crease above his nose, and his eyebrows were drawn together beneath the mop of calico hair.

"Anything wrong?" I asked, as I bent forward over the controls.

He frowned more, glaring thunderously at me, as if I'd said something wrong. "No," he said. "I'm going to take you as close as I dare to one of the dark bays. It might not be very close to it, but I looked at your gauges and you have oxygen for at least an hour. And a ship that size should be easy enough to maneuver back."

I nodded. He was probably just afraid of being captured. And I had other things to deal with.

As he closed the top of my lifepod, tapped the front in what appeared to be a nervous gesture, and turned to walk away, I thought of what I was going to do when I got to Circum.

I'd best find one of the harvesters first. Someone I could convince I was neither hallucinating nor drugged. It wasn't much fun going to Circum this time. I mean, my lifepod was completely encased in what must be the cargo bay of the ship. I could feel the maneuvering and turning, in a way, but more because the lifepod slid just a little bit this way and that.

49

And I had a lot of time to think. A lot of time. Getting into quiet rooms, in the dark, to think was one of those things that several counselors, psychiatrists and terrified people had told me to do. I'd never taken their advice till now, when I had no choice. I failed to see what was so special about it. So here I was, sitting in the dark. And slowly smiling at the idea that I had not been very nice to the poor ELF in his darkship. I'd attacked him... Four? Five times? And by his view of it, had tried to kill him at least once.

So why was he being so nice and taking me to Circum?

I sat up suddenly, alarmed. What if he wasn't? What if this was some elaborate scheme to—I stopped, the mind boggling. To have me completely at his mercy? But he did. My attacks on him had been countered. I'd never managed to do more than, as he put it, making a hobby of cracking my head on the floor. Repeatedly.

And besides, how could he have me more at his mercy now than he did when I was out there, on the ship, with nothing but a door he controlled between me and space?

The truth was, he could have killed me any of a dozen times, in there. Oh, forget counted times, he could have killed me at any moment. I'd have been completely in his power. So...why hadn't he, exactly?

Frowning at the memory of what I'd done to him, I couldn't figure it out. Anyone else—even those nice people who ran reformatories for young girls, and who had reason to be scared of Father and Father's money—would have killed me if they had a chance. At least they would have after I had tried to kill them. They'd just have told Daddy Dearest that there had been an unfortunate accident.

But the ELF should have no more reason to be scared of Father than of anyone else from Earth. He had a far greater reason to be scared of me. He could have killed me at any time, and he hadn't. And now he was repaying my saving him—while saving myself—by serving as taxi service to a location that was dangerous to him.

And he'd vibroed my slip on the repair setting, so that it was closed down the front, the silk shining slightly unevenly—clearly the man had no idea how to set a vibro, really—and lent me a brush to tame my hair, so that I didn't look like a refugee from a reeducation institute.

Which meant...

It wasn't possible he was stupid. No, really. He couldn't be. Not and keep anticipating me the way he did, let alone answering my jibes faster and more incisively than even Father—who just tended to yell. And it wasn't like he could expect kindness to me to pay him back. Father didn't know he existed and if he did, as a member of the ruling council of Earth, Father would be more interested in catching the darkship thief and imprisoning him and stopping the raids on the powerpods than in thanking him for saving me.

The ELF couldn't even expect me to put out in recompense. Well...he could have, but he hadn't tried it and now he was taking me to Circum and unless the telepathy came with some sort of mind-sex setting he was screwed. Or rather, not.

So...so it had to come down to he was mad. Mad, loony, crazy, touched in the upper works, driving with a defective power pack, flying without a stabilizer, brooming in the dark...

Fortunately, his madness seemed to be of the kind that wanted to do me a favor, not the kind that would kill me on sight. So much the better.

Having reached this point in my reasoning, I jumped at his voice in my head, icily polite and strangely calm for an obviously mad man. *We're as close as I dare go now. The door is open. Please maneuver your pod out.*

As he stopped speaking, light came on—low-level light, granted—but enough for me to see the less reflective black of the membrane to outer space. Of course, I couldn't be sure that the door was open beyond that. But again, why would he kill me that way? Wouldn't it be a very strange way to kill someone? And one that might damage his ship, as he couldn't know if my pod would go out in an explosion?

Right. Just a touch of paranoia, Thena. The result of growing up with Daddy Dearest.

I started the pod to liftoff, aimed for the membrane and sped forward. By the time I crossed the membrane, I was going fast enough that the airlock went by in a blur. And then I was... Up-side-down. Up-side-down whichever way I turned.

In space. Looking straight at the dark bays of Circum, the ones out of rotation for the harvesters.

In my mind something echoed, that might have come from

my friend the ELF, or else, might be completely imagined—it was that faint. *Good luck.*

Probably imagined because, first of all, why would he wish me well, after all I'd done to him? He might balk at actually killing me, and it was only sane for him not to want me in the ship with him, headed back wherever he was going. But why would he wish me well, after everything I'd done?

I had a memory of his eyes, wide and terrified as I tightened the garrotte around his neck. Right. The chances of his saying something more than "good riddance" were very low indeed. And second, there had been an almost wishful sound to his mind-voice, a sound I'd never heard from him. Right. So now I was imagining ELFs in my mind. Just great. Let's add madness to your many accomplishments, Thena.

Clenching my teeth tight, not looking behind at the darkship, I headed straight for the deserted bay in the middle, and crossed the outer membrane at speed. At which point the sort of inner voice that has kept me from killing myself a dozen times—at least—whispered to slow down. So I crossed the second membrane slower. Which was good, because it meant that I managed to stop the pod just behind the huge, blue metal harvester parked there.

Earth harvesters were massive compared to the darkships. Still slim, mind you. Slim enough to maneuver between the powertree trunks and collect the powerpods. But they were more cigar-shaped, bright metallic, and looked like some decadent artist's depiction of a glorified sewing needle.

Fortunately my inadequate pod was so small that I had plenty of room to park behind the harvester.

As I opened the canopy, I wondered what I should do. That bulletin claiming I was in the midst of a psychotic episode probably made it unadvisable to just use the two-way com and tell everyone I was here and to come get me pronto, with the red carpet, the fawning and the—please, for the love of heaven—ready bathwater.

If I commed my arrival, I'd just get medtechs stacked three deep and dying to put me to sleep and deliver me to . . . who knew whom? I wasn't sure that Daddy Dearest was even alive.

On the other hand, I had to talk to someone eventually unless I planned to be one of those space legends, living in hiding in the space station and seen only by the unlucky few.

I'd go in. Go in and find some of my harvester friends. They'd listen to me. They wouldn't believe that I was psycho.

Still, the idea of marching in there unprotected set off alarms, and put cold shivers down my spine. Unfortunately, and contrary to normal procedure, I'd failed to beg, borrow or steal a burner from the ELF. Well, it would have been stealing for sure. Even he wouldn't be crazy enough to give me a weapon.

But I hadn't stolen it—frankly because he was so much faster than I, he would have taken the weapon back and possibly shoved it somewhere unpleasant. I smiled faintly despite myself. I'd found someone who could match my speed and I was starting to understand why those who tangled with me usually got scared. Looking down at my feet, I realized I had only the weapon I'd first taken with me—the thick silver heel of my boot.

Grabbing the boot, I jumped off the lifepod and crept into the deeper shadows starting to round the harvester.

There was a movement in the shadows. Or so I thought. But it might have been just a reflection on the carapace of the harvester. I waited. Nothing moved. So I started forward again.

And then, suddenly—I struck out, before I realized what I was striking out at. Crashing into something hard shocked me so much I almost dropped the boot. Lightning fast, between the first strike and pulling back to hit again, I recognized the square chin and brutal straight lips of Lars Einar, yet another of Father's goons. The second time, I hit out with a sense of relief, because when I'd first reacted, I wasn't absolutely sure I wasn't merely attacking some poor harvester doing a last inspection of his ship.

I heard a rustle behind me, and pirouetted, foot raised, to kick another of the goons square on the balls, and take him out with a smack of silver heel to the temple.

I wondered why they weren't wearing dimatough—but of course, that would look weird on Circum when supposedly all they were doing was recapturing a Patrician's daughter. Without thinking, I hit with the heel again, to my left. I wasn't aware of having heard anything. Or seen anything. But I was aware of having hit human flesh and bone. And a soft sigh indicated someone who had gone off to a happy goodnight.

I had entered my speeded-up state. I spoke to the shadows, "You can't get me. I don't care how many of you there are, you can't get me. Just let me go in and leave me alone."

There was no answer, though my heightened senses could feel a dozen expectant presences, composed of little more than a stray breath, an odd rustle within the shadows. "Come on, come out of hiding. I'll take you all together or one by one. Come on, you piss bastards!"

"Athena."

It was the voice I last expected to hear. I turned, startled. In the shadows there was—

"Father," I said, at the same time I identified him. He looked like hell, pale and trembling, holding on with both hands to a cane—something he hadn't used in a very long time and only when he was feeling ill. His face looked more wrinkled, too, like crinkled parchment.

Above it, his merciless dark blue eyes, the exact color of mine, shone at me. "There is no need for all this, Athena."

Was he really here? Was it a hologram?

I took a step towards him, trying to see more clearly.

It caused me to miss the rustle to my right side. I struck out with the heel, but not in time. Something cold was already touching my neck.

As the whole world seemed to recede from my sight, I saw something fall and roll at my feet. A piss-yellow injector. Morpheus. *Oh, shit.*

The world went black.

⨾TEN⨾

ARTIFICIAL GRAV, I'M GOING TO THROW UP. THE THOUGHT
assembled in my mind, bit by bit, as if I were thinking with
instruments totally unsuited for the task. My toes. Or perhaps
my stomach. Which was clenching and...

Easy, a thought formed in my mind, and it was easy, as if
it had come from outside my head. *Easy there. It's Morpheus
reaction.*

Hands, firm but gentle, helped me turn and something must
have been proffered to catch the contents of my stomach, because
there was no hint of dismay as burning bile came shooting out
of my mouth. Just, *Easy, you'll be all right.*

Don't be foolish, I told myself. *There was no Morpheus. I took
Andrija Baldo down. I escaped in the lifepod. No Morpheus.*

As you say, Madame Patrician, This time the voice had a tinge
of almost sad amusement. Like the emotion evoked watching the
vain efforts of a child to do something she's not capable of. And in
my mind, slowly, another scene involving Morpheus assembled—a
landing bay and—*Father!*

There were no words in answer, this time. Something clanked
nearby, sounding like a space cruiser's disposal chute leading to
recycling facilities. Something soft wiped at my mouth. A hand
touched my hair, pulling the curls back. For a moment, in total
confusion, I thought it was my mother. My mother was the only
person who did that as I lay down. *Mother.*

My answer was a soft chuckle that sounded not at all feminine. I went into the darkness again.

I woke up in space. My first thought was that I was in Circum, that I'd somehow hallucinated the ambush and Father and the Morpheus and all that. But the artificial gravity of Circum Terra was almost like real gravity and didn't bother me. But then again, this didn't feel like the artificial gravity in Father's cruiser. This was a completely different quality of feeling, something that made me feel lightheaded, but not exactly nauseous.

Also, the bed beneath me did not feel like my bed in Daddy Dearest's cruiser. It was firmer, and somehow cooler. A hand flung sideways felt a handful of silk, not the dimatough bed frame.

My head hurt like all the blazes, a rhythmic headache, concentrated on the top of my eyes, flashing, flaring, making me wish to whine with pain—only I had learned long ago not to whine. If you cry, if you give a sign of frailty, they pounce. It doesn't matter who they are. They are always there waiting to pounce. At the last instance, there was always Father, waiting for a weakness, ready to subdue me. I'd learned early and I'd learned well not to whimper, not to simper and not to cry. Unless of course it was to make someone think I was weak, just before I pounded them.

I forced my eyelids open against all my preservation instincts, making my eyes open, making...

There was no light. Or at least not the light I was fearing, the light I was sure would make my headache pound and make me throw up again. Instead, there was a soothing twilight, full of shadows. *Shadows.*

I started to sit up, and the round bed—like something from Decadent Earth—the cabinets, the straight-backed chair, all found a home in my memory. *The darkship.*

How and when had I come back here? Had he kidnapped me? Did he...?

A memory of being ambushed, of Father or perhaps a hologram of Father being used to surprise me, to stop me long enough, made me flinch. If it wasn't Father, then his bodyguards had been set to capture me. And if it was Father...I didn't want to think about it. I couldn't think.

The door opened and closed softly, and there by it stood the strange ELF, staring at me. "Would you like light?" he asked politely, like someone asking you if you wanted water, or perhaps food.

"A . . . little," I said. "But not if . . . not if it's going to blind you."

He slid his hand up the light switch. By the faint glow suffusing the room, I could see him smile, a tight smile, like he needed all his self-control to deal with me. The catlike eyes were attentive. "It won't blind me," he said. "I have my lenses in." And then, to what must have been a look of incomprehension on my face, "I wear them when I'm not alone, and when I'm not harvesting. Most cats do. We can't ask our families to live in the dark, after all." The tight smile flashed again. "I am told it makes our vision almost normal, but that we don't see colors quite the way the rest of you do."

"Oh." And I supposed that was an explanation to the glaring colors everywhere, but I wasn't about to ask. "Where . . . We're not in the powertree ring."

"No."

"Earth orbit?" I asked hopefully.

He actually cackled. A short, dry cackle. "No."

"I . . . what are you . . . Where are you taking me?"

There was a hesitation. The generous lips tightened, and a wrinkle formed on his forehead. It made him, somehow, look more human. Also upset. "I only have one place to take you. Home with me."

The unsaid words *but I don't have to like it* hung in the air between us. I didn't ask for it to be made explicit. He didn't try to tell me, either. Just looked at me with the expression of someone who is not quite sure how to avoid the wall his broom is heading towards.

"How long will it take us to get there?" I said. I felt oddly vulnerable. I was locked in this ship with a person who had no reason to like me. I assumed it was better than being in Circum Terra, or perhaps back in Daddy's ship, with whatever the goons wanted to do to me. I had a strong feeling if they'd gotten their way, I'd no longer be consuming oxygen.

He shook his head and didn't say anything, and I realized he thought I was trying to get information about the darkship's base. Which I was. Of course I was, but not as a spy. If I was going to this place, it seemed logical that I ask where it was, what it was and . . .

"It's not that I don't want to answer," he said. "Though I would like to say, even if the setup I rescued you from was elaborate, it wasn't impossible. It's quite likely that the people of Earth, wanting at long last to trace us, would have set up just this elaborate trap with tasty bait for the one cat without a nav, the one cat who travels alone, the outcast one. It would make me think more highly of Earthwo—of your people's policing efforts, but it would not be impossible."

He raised his eyebrows at me, as if thinking through the implications of such an unlikely trap. "But in that case, I suspect they would have put a tracer on you, rather than get you to ask me where my home was.

"My equipment could not detect a bug, but that doesn't mean there isn't one. Just that the bug is well hidden, or perhaps of a type I can't detect. Of course, if that's the case, whether I tell you or not is largely inconsequential. But the thing is that I truly don't know. Our . . . home is on a variable orbit. I have alarms and detectors and an idea of in which direction to head. We'll reach it when we reach it."

His reasoning was almost as paranoid as mine when faced with Father's plans, or Father's when faced with the universe at large. And the variable orbit made sense. I had a vague idea that when the Mules had first left, while the space travel capacity they had endowed Earth with still endured, and before the last spasms of the riots had destroyed it, they had swept the Solar System for a trace of the Mules.

Of course, these couldn't be the Mules. Not as such. The Mules had no women, and my captor had Blondie and the family group which either had women or some spectacularly odd-looking males. Not that this would be unlikely. One heard stories even from Circum Terra, where females were scarce. Year after year, much less century after century, with few or no women led to creative arrangements and given bioengineering . . . "How old are you?"

His eyes widened. Whatever he'd been expecting, that question wasn't it. "Twenty-two," he said, in the bewildered tone of someone who can't be bothered making up a lie.

Oh. So no Mules, because unless they reckoned years differently— "Years?"

He grinned this time. A genuinely amused grin. "Millennia. What do you think?"

"I don't know," I said, slowly. It hadn't mattered. Not so much. Not while I thought we were going to part ways and never see each other again. But thoughts of the things the Mules were alleged to have done, the people they were said to have killed— hundreds of people, thousands, millions, for reasons that only the Mules could understand. And the things that had been done to the Earth under their watch. All of it made my hair stand on end at the thought of being in this ship with one of them for who knew how long. What would he think of me? What would he care for a mere human? "Are you a Mule?"

The smile vanished, the mouth tightened. The odd-looking eyes—which were becoming readable the more I looked at him— turned guarded. "What do you care? Does prejudice against bioing still hold on Earth?"

"No," I said, because prejudice is a charged word. At any rate, I was truthful. There was no prejudice as such. Bioing was a death-bringing crime. For those perpetrating it and the results. "But I want to know."

He shrugged. "I'm twenty-two Earth years old. Does that answer your question, or do you need my universal birth date, too?"

No reason to get rude, but I wasn't going to argue. I just nodded. It answered my question well enough. If he was twenty-two, he could not have been alive when the Mules left the Earth and therefore he could not possibly be one of *them*.

"I've set the cooker to prepare some food," he said. "Since you didn't seem to have eaten in quite a while."

Quite a while. Depending on how long I'd been asleep it could be almost twenty-four hours. At any rate, I'd never heard of Morpheus knocking anyone out for less than twelve hours.

I got up, and found myself swaying on my feet, not so much dizzy as unsure of my footing. It was like when Father had taken me on a cruise in the Mediterranean, years ago. The ship had been large enough that the floor felt as if it were stationary. But I hadn't felt it as stationary, rather as bobbing and bouncing.

Now there was the same unsteadiness to the ground under me, that my back brain knew about, even though my feet couldn't quite feel it.

"Easy," my captor said, sounding much like that voice in my head. "We're under way. It's a different drive, and for someone whose brain is sensitive enough to feel artificial gravity, it would be disorienting." He extended a hand towards me, as though to help me.

"You're making fun of me," I said, almost wailing in fury and waving way his hand.

His eyes widened again. "What? No. You're clearly sensitive to artificial gravity. A lot of navigators are. It comes with the built-in sense of direction."

"Oh." I gave him a close look, to make sure it wasn't some joke I just didn't get. But he wasn't laughing. He was extending his hand, still. "Come on. You'll be unsteady until you get your space legs."

I allowed him to grasp my wrist. If this was a seduction ploy, he really wasn't very good at it. Like his inability to tie up women properly, it was oddly reassuring. Actually, he didn't even hold my wrist. just clasped it when it looked like I was about to fall, and the rest of the time let me try to progress on my own. I remembered the way, sort of. I'd come through here, trying to figure out what sort of creature held me captive. Now I looked at him and found him looking at me.

"You wouldn't be feeling the need to garrotte me, would you?" he asked.

The question was half coy and half teasing, and my first reaction was that I would, of course, not tell him if I had any such intention. But the next reaction was to think it through. Could I attack him, turn the ship around, get to Earth?

Perhaps. No. Almost certainly. The ship was not that difficult, I thought. Well, all right. There were all the implements for collections and all the various navigation systems, and I'm sure they took some learning. But I also had no doubt I could learn them. The system had yet to be created that I couldn't back-engineer and figure out. On the other hand, I remembered the gauges in the control room. There was no way—absolutely no way—that I could learn it on the fly, without weeks of practice. And there were other considerations. Such as the fact that, if I took this ship to Earth, Earth defense systems in whatever continent I landed in were likely to think I was an enemy and shoot before asking questions.

But beyond all that, I couldn't be so crass as to hit my captor on the head and then head off.

But why had he come and gotten me? Obviously the mind link had sent him feelings of my surprise. He knew I'd been hit with Morpheus. And doubtless he'd come in the nick of time. I had no idea what Daddy's goons intended to do to me, but I was fairly sure it wasn't pleasant. But why had he come? He hadn't told me.

And, I realized as we entered the kitchen and he gestured for me to sit at the table, he wasn't about to tell me. Instead, he fiddled with the cooker, peering in screens and making half mutters as one absorbed in a task.

After a while, he set a cup of broth in front of me. It tasted odd. Very odd. It was like...chicken broth, with an odd hint of fish. "Fish?" I asked.

He looked surprised. "Most of the protein in Ed—at home is fish. Not much space for cows." He smiled as he got himself a bowl of the broth, then handed me a spoon and took one for himself from some receptacle beside the cooker. "If you don't like it, I can program other flavors."

But the broth, strange flavor and all, calmed my hunger pangs, as did a sort of flat bread filled with what appeared to be a nut paste. He ate also while staring at me. When I was almost done, he said, "I have moved my clothes to one of the storage rooms," he said quietly. "You may have my room."

Well, I thought, that figured. It was probably the most secure place in the ship. I wouldn't put it past him to have put some sort of alarm on the door too. "And where will you sleep?" I asked, wondering if, after all, this was some form of backwards seduction—if he intended to share the bed with me.

He shrugged. "Probably the virtus. It's where I sleep most nights." He sipped his broth. "That or the exercise room. I'll show you where that is, later. I don't know how long the trip will take, but it will take more than a few days, and probably more than a month. I don't want you to feel uncomfortable."

It was, of course, much too late for that.

∾⊙ ELEVEN ⊙∾

"AIM HIGHER," MY CAPTOR SAID MERCILESSLY, AS HE GRABBED my ankle, halfway through my jump, and caused me to fall on my back, with a nerve-jarring thud. "There is more than one vulnerable zone on a male."

Fortunately for my hard head, considering the number of times he did this on any given day, we were in the exercise room and I had a heavily padded mat beneath me.

"Had enough?" he asked, stepping back as I rose, trying to get my bearings.

"I still don't understand how you can move that fast," I said.

"It's part of the ELFing," he said. "To maneuver in tight spaces. More to the point is how *you* can move that fast. Almost as fast as I do."

"Oh," I said. "I always have."

He raised his eyebrows at me. "I wonder," he said. "If one of ours, a nav, went missing on Earth..."

I picked up a small towel from the pile on the complicated exercise machine next to the padded area on which we stood. I didn't need it. Oh, the exercise had been violent, but the ambient temperature was low and I was not sweating, at least not as such. However, making a show of wiping my forehead provided me with time to think. "What do you mean one of yours? A nav?"

"An ELF," he said.

"Bio-improved?" I asked. "The navigators? They're ELFed, too?"

"Oh, of course," he said.

"Of course?"

"Well," he shrugged. "The ELFing is less costly than for a cat, so more likely to happen if a family is strapped for cash, but..."

"But they too are improved?"

He'd explained to me that the designation for his function had started out as *pilot* but had over the centuries changed to *cat* because people couldn't overlook the eyes.

"Oh yes."

"But...no eyes, no..."

"No. For sense of direction. Ability with mechanics, and the..."

"Speed?"

"Not normally." He frowned. "Cats are. But I can see a nav passing on Earth, never a cat. Which is part of what confuses me about your speed. But navigators usually have very good visual memory and even better spacial reasoning. It allows them to remember cul-de-sacs if their pilot gets blinded. In that way they're invaluable backup. One person alone in a ship is dangerous. A pair with the same abilities—they'd both be incapacitated at the same time. So the navigator is a...redundant system to the cat, with some...modifications."

"I see," I said. "But how could I have inherited my abilities from my parents? Even if my parents were...a nav or something?" I couldn't imagine how it could possibly be, since Patrician lines were fairly well guarded and certified. I couldn't imagine how Father, with his line of ancestors that had all been Patricians of Syracuse Seacity stretching back to the twenty-first century, might have been replaced. True, I'd never seen him in a fight, and I'd never seen him fix anything, so there was no telling whether he had mechanical ability or super speed. And Mother...I knew next to nothing about Mother, only that she must have been sane, because she left about when I was six. And no sane woman could have endured any longer with Father. "And what would super speed have to do with it? You said that's not a nav thing. And anyway, didn't you say that the...ELFing costs money and needs to be introduced via a virus in gestation?"

He shrugged and frowned, the expression of a man deep in thought. "Yeah," he said at last. "It doesn't make a lot of sense, but there have been cases—rare—where ELFing passes on a generation. Or some characteristics of ELFing. And particularly your ability to mind-talk with me, since the cat and nav telepathy is of a specific type, and normally has to be trained between a couple, makes me think that—"

I jumped, suddenly, in a perfect leap, which is difficult when you start from a standing position, but which was good enough for me to hit first his left knee, then as I fell, the right.

His eyes widened, then he grimaced and went down on his knees. I smiled. I hadn't hit him hard enough to break his kneecaps—not only was that nearly impossible from a stand, so that if I had truly been in a fight with him, I'd have needed to now hit him, quickly, with something heavy, but also I had no intention of permanently maiming him and then having to spend I didn't know how long in there with him, before we got to his home where, unless I were very wrong, I was going to need his indulgence and good will.

He knelt and folded over, and then fell on his behind, and stretched his legs, rubbing at the knees. "Very funny," he said. His expression was closed and grave, even though his voice came lightly.

"You said there was more than one sensitive zone on a male," I said. "Although I'd like to point out that it's not as effective as hitting you where it mainly hurts. Because that would disable you longer."

He gave me a look, part guarded, part considering. "Somehow, *Princess,* I suspect if you had hit me on the knees as hard as you could, it would have done for me fairly effectively too. I suspect your hitting where you normally do is psychological."

I set my hands on either side of my waist. "Freudianism was a discredited religion that led to—"

"Uh. And that's all you ever heard of psychology, is it?" he said, getting up. He made a show of flexing his leg, that I expected was exactly that—show. "Remind me to give you a couple of data gems later."

And that was par for the course and again confirmation that he was a completely normal human male. In the times when I wasn't causing instructors and trainers at various academies to hide in fear, I was earning their respect, trust, and good will by allowing them to lecture me. It must be something set deep in the human male from the time the first one of them crawled out of the cave. Doubtless the first thing a man did after learning to speak was to explain to the nearest woman that Ooog was not the same as Ooooog.

I'd learned the darkship thief was only very much human in that he delighted in giving me history gems and music gems and literature gems.

The music gems hadn't been a surprise, or not exactly. At my social level, I was expected to have a decent, classical education, no matter how many schools were left torched in my path. I had learned all the classical composers, though I can't say I mastered the passion with which he spoke of Haydn and Liszt. History and literature and even science seemed completely different from what I'd learned. And not in the obvious way. You'd expect them to speak of the time of Mules as a golden age, of course, a time when Earth was well ruled. Strangely it wasn't so. Rarely referred to, and when at all, it had the tone of an embarrassing time. It was called Earth Authority or the Time of Servitude.

Other things too had a different weight in those books. Take the Usaian experiment. All the analyses I read back from primary program on talked of it as a failed experiment and everyone agreed it had been doomed from the very beginning, where it had put the emphasis on private rights and individual decisions about government. Eden's books . . . well, it wasn't that they had never heard about Marx, or Pseudo-Gurion, and they seemed to have a startlingly low level of respect for Moore, though his work was referenced in passing once or twice, mostly as an example of what not to do—it was more that they looked at everything I'd learned from the other side.

In their view the Usaian state had collapsed not because it had reposited too much confidence and too great a power in the individual; not because it had allowed private citizens to own dangerous weapons; not even because it had enforced the right of the individual to associate and trade with whomever he pleased, but because it had, by degrees, slid into the same sort of oligarchy that governed most of the world at the time. It was—the darkship people's treatises said—because the Usaians had surrendered, intellectually, to the older ways of doing things that they had lost their place as the most advanced and powerful state of the early twenty-first century. And it was because of that that it had eventually become just the North American protectorate of Earth's government.

If only the Usaians had restricted their government, if they'd kept it small and powerless, the world might still eventually have united under the bio-lords and led to the debacle and disorder and the current government of the Good Men, but probably not.

I'd learned soon to keep my mouth shut about how strange these ideas were. I'd tried arguing once, after a week in the ship, when I'd read only a few gems. "It's not true, you know," I'd told my captor over lunch.

We rarely ate lunch together. In fact, he seemed to avoid me as much as he could, almost as much as Father did, only with less reason. Or perhaps not. I had never tried to strangle Father. But this one time, I'd come in, with the small gem reader he'd loaned me in one hand, reading my fourth history book of the week—more than I had read in my entire educational career.

He looked up from what he was eating—something that smelled and looked like fish over rice—and gathered his eyebrows over his eyes. "What is not true?" he asked.

"That the government of the Mules collapsed not because of the Mules but because too much power was concentrated in the hands of too few individuals. The Mules were different—they weren't human. They didn't think—"

"Perhaps," he said, and lowered his eyelids a little, whether to think better or to hide his eyes from me, I did not know. "And perhaps because they were different the system survived longer than it would have with normal humans."

"Uh?"

"Well, think about it. What is the rationale for having all the power concentrated in the hands of a few individuals?" he asked.

"That..." I thought about it and fished from my imperfectly remembered lessons the answers I'd learned. "That governing can then be done by experts. It is too much to hope for, too much to believe that regular individuals, concerned with their families and their work and...daily life, will have any interest in the government of the Commonweal beyond the marginal interest in enacting what will benefit them, but which might be disastrous for the country, region or world."

"And why shouldn't they enact what's in their best interest?"

"Because they don't always know what's in their best interest."

Kit Klaavil waved the whole thing away, as if it didn't matter. "I must remember to give you Gilbert's *The Election of the Few*.

What you're reporting is a fallacy caused by whoever interpreted history to write the books you read. They had assumptions a priori and—"

"In the twenty-first people believed the zaniest things. That there are no gender differences in the human brain; that race predetermines culture. That—"

"Granted. That whole period was psychotic. It could be argued that it was a psychosis from which the Earth as a whole has yet to recover. But the thing is, unless the analysis I've read got it grossly wrong—and they investigated electronic documents of the time—mostly the mass psychosis was pushed from the top down. Yes, people came to believe it, but it was taught in colleges, by professors trained in the best universities."

"But how could the common man not notice reality right in front of his eyes?"

"They did. The masses as a whole made jokes about these notions. But they weren't truly given an option not to apply them. By that time, government was already too divorced from the common man."

I was lost. This was such a complete contradiction of everything I'd learned, that he might as well have announced that the sky was normally green, or that this spaceship was made entirely of fish. "I suppose," I said, "if what you say is true..." Part of me was trying to adjust to the idea that anyone could say it was true—that this anarchic vision of individuals ruling themselves could in any way be the work of a sane human being.

The rest of me, meanwhile, wanted me to back away from the dangerous madman, before he reached out and stabbed me with his fork.

He grinned at me, as though reading my mind—which he might very well have—"Patrician Athena Sinistra," he said. "Tell me—who is better equipped to decide what you should be doing with your life? Yourself or your father?"

"Myself," I answered without thinking.

"Then what makes you think that your father is better equipped to decide what's best for total strangers?"

I hesitated. "People would say he's best qualified to say what I should be doing," I said. "They would say he knows how the world at large works and what I will have to do when I inherit."

"Does he?" It was a mild enquiry.

"Like hell he does," I'd tried to constrain my response, but it wasn't going to happen. "All Father cares about is the Sinistra name, not me. Given enough time, he'd have found me a nice Patrician husband, probably the younger son of a ruling Patrician, and he'd have me marry, have the man take our name and then..."

"And then?" He looked half interested, half horrified.

I shrugged. "And then I become a broodmare," I said. "To make sure the Sinistra name never comes to this point again." I looked up and couldn't read his expression. "I know it sounds childish. Yes, I'm aware that forced marriages have occurred in every culture and place, throughout history. And it's not like anyone will force me to choose a man I hate. It's just that I... ah. Never mind."

He didn't say anything for a long while, then put his empty plate in the cleaning area of the cooker. "Let me show you the gym," he said. Which is how we'd started our habit of exercising through mock fights. At least most of them were mock, though sometimes our discussion got more than a little heated and it extended into the exercise room.

Which is how we'd got to the point where he was making a great show of flexing his legs. The pity-mongering worked. "You may have the fresher first," I told him.

He flashed me a half-surprised smile and went past me and down the hallway. The only fresher in the place opened off the bedroom—in keeping with the idea that the ship was supposed to contain a married or otherwise bonded couple.

I walked after him, far enough to see him go into the bedroom. And then I turned and went back to the virtus closet where he slept.

It was normal for a full-size unit—not like the little holo projectors that I used to watch the gems he gave me and the ones I found on my own, but real virtus, the kind where you can live through an experience—a little longer than seven feet, a little wider than five. It contained a single bed and the apparatus, which consisted of helmet and a sort of blanket you could pull over yourself while experiencing the virtus—unlike the ones on Earth which had rigid gloves and leg enclosures as well as a mid-body shield.

Here's the thing. While the virtus closet was the logical place for someone to sleep if your bedroom was taken up by an unexpected guest in an otherwise bedless ship, to be honest, the virtus closet was the most logical place for the guest, herself, particularly when she was half your weight and a little over five feet.

Even conceding he'd given me his room out of courtesy and the kindness of his ELFed heart, I knew for a fact that every time I'd chanced to glance in the closet—as I walked by when he opened the door for example, I saw him removing the helmet or turning off the unit. From that and from the general overneat look of the bedroom, when this man was just as likely to not vibro his clothes or not pick up after himself, I got the impression he'd been sleeping in the virtus.

All right, you'll say it was none of my business. If he wanted to lock himself in and have vivid dreams, instead of sleeping normally, it wouldn't make any difference. Except for two things. First, I, just like everyone else for the last hundred years, had heard the horror stories of people who used virtus instead of sleeping and who went completely insane within weeks. I figured I'd been here for just over a month, and if he were going to go berserk, I'd like to know and be ready. Second, if he was living through vivid experiences of, say, dismembering and eating female guests . . . It would be good to know.

He had the gems preloaded into a chute and fortunately the virtus had a little preview chamber next to it. I flipped through it rapidly. He had maybe twenty gems. The preview chamber didn't show the events happening in motion, of course, nor the sensations and feelings while they were happening. Instead it showed still holograms of various scenes in the virtus gem.

They were all variations on a theme. Birthday parties and celebrations. Family dinners and picnics. Children and butterflies. All right, I'm making up the part about the butterflies, though there might have been some in the scenes that didn't preview. In all of them the young blonde in the family picture showed, in various poses and moods. Sometimes in a uniform that matched his, sometimes in a dress, sometimes in nothing at all. But it wasn't the kind of virtus you'd expect a man to review about his girlfriend or wife. It wasn't intimate moments, or sex. It all seemed to be fairly innocent scenes.

I previewed virtus gem after virtus gem, watching the amber-colored balls sparkle into the chamber and the scenes form. They were all the same.

Behind me, a throat cleared, and I just about jumped out of

my skin. I turned around, ready to defend myself, expecting him to look disapproving or upset or perhaps angry. Perhaps he would lash out.

But when I turned around, he looked perfectly normal, except that the *closed* gaze was back. He stepped back to avoid me, as I emerged from the virtus.

"The fresher is free," he said. And as I nodded and started to walk down the hallway, my face—I'm sure—burning red, he added to my retreating back, "If you wish to use the virtus, you may ask me any time."

I called "thank you" and went into the fresher, my cheeks stinging. I removed the suit I was wearing. All my suits—three, which he had vibroed and programmed in alterations for—were his suits, which he allowed me to wear. He'd even picked—possibly out of consideration—the most sedate of the suits. A solid color blue, which was what I was wearing, a grey one and a black one.

I stripped the suit off in brisk movements, tossed it into the vibro, then stepped into the fresher. It was the normal fresher deal, a little smaller than even those in Father's space cruiser. Just about large enough to hold me—I had no idea how Kit Klaavil stuffed himself in it—it had the normal pressurized water and air jets. It ran for precisely timed periods, and turned off promptly and without my intervention. And I supposed the water was recycled, of course. Some days like right then, I could have killed for the free-flowing water back home in Syracuse Seacity, but I was aware that, as it was, I was probably straining my host's resources. There were times I noticed him reprogramming things and I suspected he went without meals to provide for mine—I couldn't be sure, but on weight alone, the spaceship wouldn't be outfitted for two people, would it, at least supply-wise? So my food must be coming from somewhere. And while I resented him for not having taken me back to Earth, I also knew that, once Circum had proven inhospitable, I could not ask him to commit virtual suicide just to take me back where I belonged.

I'd gotten out of the fresher, dried, and was pulling on the grey suit, when there was a polite knock on the door. I pulled the grey tunic down and said, "Yes?" in the general direction of the door.

He opened the door just a little and said, "The alarm has gone off. We're approaching Eden. I thought you'd like to see the approach."

ⵜTWELVEⵐ

KIT CHANGED INTO HIS UNIFORM WHILE I WAITED OUTSIDE HIS room. Then he led me along the hallway to the cat cabin, which was what he called the place from which he controlled the piloting and harvesting. The same place where I'd tried to strangle him.

He didn't seem to remember it, or perhaps he remembered it all too well, as he had me strap down into an extra chair. "Are there two cats, sometimes?" I asked.

Kit gave me a sideways look, as though surprised I asked. "No. This was a training ship, before being retired," he said. "That is the student's seat. Which means you should be able to see everything."

It wasn't like that, of course. Well, it couldn't be. He was working without his lenses and with his screens at comfortable cat lighting. If I looked carefully I could just discern movement in the dark blue depths.

"You said the alarms went—" I wanted to ask how it worked. But I wasn't sure how much he would tell me.

He looked at me again, that half look, and smiled a little, the sort of smile that in our discussions or mock fights told me that he'd seen through my attempt to ask, and it amused him. "The orbit of Eden is so irregular," he said. "The founders chose an asteroid with a highly irregular orbit because it's easier to keep hidden. No propulsion. They also set a proximity alarm. It will only be activated in the ship when we get close enough to maneuver into the landing area. And it is activated in Eden at the same time, so they can prepare for our arrival." He paused, while his fingers danced on the keyboard.

It was like watching a trained pianist play soulful, intense music, in precise, fast movements, all the while staring in front of him at . . . something.

The something, in this case, was the shadows in the screen. I frowned at them, trying to discern something resembling a planet out there in the dark.

I know I said I didn't want to go to space, and that was true. I'd read enough and taken enough virtus to know that Circum Terra was all regimented, scientific rooms, with the creature comforts thrown in as an afterthought. I knew that the few colonists on the Moon lived in confined, miserable quarters, little better than those in my father's space cruiser. Worse, probably, for comfort even if larger.

Earth had much more room for me to get away from Father. Even in Syracuse Seacity, I could disappear into my broomer lair, and not be found for quite a while.

So why should I want to go to space? Why should I want to trade my life for the arduous one of a scientist?

But now I was here, and whatever that world was in front of me, it was likely I'd have to remain there until I could find a way to make it back to Earth. In fact, most people would say it was impossible for me to make it to Earth ever again, given that I would be in a world that had become legendary through not being discovered for centuries. But that was underestimating me. I'd always found my way back, from boarding school and mountain fastness, and I failed to see why this should be any different.

Still Eden—whatever it was—the place of the bitten apple and the serpent, would be my home for a while, and of course I was curious about it. Yet watching Kit Klaavil click through what seemed to be memorized sequences, while he looked at shifting shadows in the screen, was as puzzling as watching foreign language words flick across the screen of an unknown system.

After a while he seemed to realize my problem. He looked over at me, and must have read the glazed expression in my eyes. "I'm sorry," he said politely. Then, "Here." He flicked a switch and the screens remained deep and dark and blue, but now I could make out a shape in them.

The shape was potato. A large potato, mind you, but still

unmistakably potatoish, floating in darker blue. It was more oblong than wide, and not a sphere or a cylinder, or anything else that could be identified. All that was missing, I thought, were some sprouts growing out of the eyes.

"It looks like a potato, I know," my host said. "We call it the Primeval Potato."

He seemed to think he'd made a joke, so I smiled politely and asked, "How long will it take us to land?" I didn't see anything that we could land on, on that surface. No cities, no lights. Nothing. I started wondering if my ELFed host, addled from reliving too many hours of children's birthday parties and family sing-alongs, had gone completely insane and was in fact going to land us in a bare rock in the middle of nowhere, in space. Would he also require that we saunter out without spacesuits and helmets? Perhaps this was what darkship thieves did when they found themselves discovered? Perhaps it was their elaborate way to commit suicide.

"We don't land," he said. "They pull us in."

"Oh."

"Well, you know, we have defenses, in case . . . Earth comes looking for us."

"Earth thinks you are legends," I said. "Earth thinks you don't exist."

He gave me a considering look. "At least according to you, yes." And before I could react to the implication that I was either lying or had no idea what I was talking about, he continued. "But my people don't know that. My people can't be sure of that. We have holos and virtus of the riots and the disorders. We remember the hunting down of anyone who was biologically modified. I was exposed to the materials as part of my education."

"I was too," I said, irked.

"You were?" he said, looking surprised. "Good for you. And did you get to do virtus hunting down of the dirty bios and ripping them limb from limb?"

"It was only holos," I said, stung by the sudden anger in his voice, which seemed to have come from nowhere, and which I knew I'd done nothing to cause.

I would be damned if I was going to tell him that the holos I'd seen had disgusted me and caused me to wonder if it wouldn't have been better to allow bio-modified people to live, than to indulge in that kind of orgiastic blood-letting. In the messes of the riots people had been killed who were innocent. They just happened to be naturally beautiful or intelligent or something. And I'd started to wonder if the bios weren't innocent too. Oh, sure, the bio-lords, the Mules themselves and their closest associates might have committed horrible atrocities. But was everyone guilty? Or just them? How many of the bioed people had simply been entering data into some system? And could they help the way they looked or the way they had been born? They'd been created by their parents or their state for specific posts. That they should be killed for it seemed horrible.

But I'd rather bite my tongue in two than admit that to the bio-improved man who shot me a glaring, sideways glance. "That must have been very disappointing for you. I must be sure to line up some virtus so you can experience it. I'm afraid you can only do so from the victim's side, but you'll doubtless enjoy it anyway."

I was stung now. I had forgotten, in the time I'd shared his ship—in the time he'd been polite to me, except for that tendency to lecture which might very well be inborn in the Y chromosome; in the time I was sure he'd curtailed his food so that there would be enough for me; in the time when he'd talked to me about music and history—the fury that he'd inspired in me when I first met him.

Okay, so part of it had been the fact that he looked so different, so alien. But the other part had been that anger as if I'd done something to upset him. When all I'd been doing was escaping. He had no reason to meet me with drawn weapon. No reason to force me ahead of him at gunpoint. And absolutely no reason to tie me to a chair.

And he had no reason to talk to me as if I'd shot his favorite dog. Whatever those virtus of being chased as a freakish bio through the streets of a long-vanished Earth had done to him, it was not my fault. I had been born centuries after that. Even if some of my ancestors had been involved in the chasing—and I doubted it, as Father was fond of reminding me, people like us hired others to do that—I had not been. I curled my lip at him, remembering how surprised he'd looked with that belt around his neck. "I don't know what you think—"

"Identify yourself." The voice boomed all over the cabin, seemingly from everywhere at once, the sort of voice that leaves your ears ringing and makes you wonder exactly what kind of a giant can have spoken. It had the same accent as Kit Klaavil's.

Kit said "Light," and something that sounded like a word in an ancient language under his breath, then aloud said, "Cat Christopher Bartolomeu Klaavil, piloting the *Cathouse* for the Energy Board."

There was a silence on the other side, filled with crackling and the sort of rustles one hears on the other side of a com link while the other person gets up or shifts about.

"The responder must be broken," Kit said to me, in a tone of explanation. "Normally it identifies on approach."

"Cat Klaavil?" the voice boomed again.

"Would you mind giving us your ID number?"

Kit rattled off a long string of letters and numbers. Crackling again. He was now frowning at the console, as if something either in the screen or in the keys were deeply offensive.

"Tell us the date on which you left?" the voice asked.

Kit rattled off a universal date three months back, only to be asked another string of questions, including his address. His frown deepened.

At the end of it, as the crackling silence filled the cabin, he cleared his throat. "This is Cat Christopher Bartolomeu Klaavil, piloting the *Cathouse* on behalf of the Energy Board. I have a full load of powerpods. Is there a problem?" No one answered and he repeated louder. "Is there a problem?"

"Our sensors show another living ... being aboard your ship? We believe about fifty kilos?"

I wanted to protest that fifty kilos. At what I'd been eating—or not. I was never fond of fish—aboard the *Cathouse*, I'd probably lost at least two of those.

"About that," Klaavil said, which goes to show the only parts of my anatomy he ever noticed were the rounded ones.

There was a silence from the other side, this time without crackles. I felt as if the silence itself held its breath, trying to determine what Kit Klaavil meant. When the booming voice came back, there was a vibrato of uncertainty behind the booming. "You have another person aboard? Identify him."

"*She*," he said, and followed it with a pregnant pause, "is Patrician Athena Hera Sinistra of the Seacity of Syracuse on Earth."

"Pat—" Well. At least my title made someone choke, though perhaps not in a good way. "Where did you capture the Patrician?"

Capture. I almost snorted.

"Patrician Sinistra was fleeing through the powertree ring. I rendered assistance." A steely kind of casualness had crept into Klaavil's voice. It was a tone that should have been impossible, except that it was exactly how it sounded. He wanted to—and did—sound offhand, but at the same time it was clear he was wielding that casualness as a weapon. He knew that picking me up was, if not a crime, a serious disruption of routine. There was no possible way he could have failed to know it. But he was too stubborn to admit that he'd done anything at all out of the ordinary.

"You rendered..." the voice boomed away into speechlessness, which went very badly with whatever was being used to amplify it. "You can't have rendered assistance to a Patrician of Earth! And what was she fleeing from?"

He looked at me, as if for a cue. I'd told him the whole story in the last month, but he seemed to be deciding exactly what he should tell them. Or perhaps, I thought, taking the measure of the man, or perhaps thinking up the most outrageous response possible.

"Mutineers," he finally said.

"Mutineers?"

"Mutineers took over her father's space cruiser, waylaid the Good Man Milton Sinistra and pursued his daughter, after she escaped in a lifepod, intending to make Circum. I found her in the powertree ring, and I rendered assistance."

This time the silence was absolute. It was an unnatural silence, without even the traces of breathing or of clothing rustling, or of anything at all that might indicate a person on the other side. I wondered if they had turned the sound off completely. Had they gone away and decided to ignore us?

The silence extended, becoming, of itself, an answer. Kit at first sat expectantly, leaning towards the sound receptor on the console. But after a while he sat back, frowning at the screen, and then at the keyboard, and then at the screen again. He looked up at the domed dimatough ceiling, as if he expected the voice to be cowering up there, somewhere, possibly scared of his glare.

Then, in an undertone, sounding like he was putting an end to a long drawn-out conversation, he said, "Right." He paused. His fingers drummed on the console. "Right. "

He leaned forward, once more alert, full of purpose and pressed a red dot on the console. "Eden Base," he said. "Please give me docking coordinates, so you can bring me in."

He let go the red dot, which must have been some sort of emergency communication device, because immediately after his words, there was frantic crackling, and the sound of someone breathing fast, as if he'd run a long distance. "Cat Klaavil," the voice said, sounding monstrously amplified, but far less sure of itself. It was as if the voice were a kid dressed in daddy's shoes and stepping on stilts, trying to appear bigger and utterly failing. "We regret to inform you that we cannot bring you in."

"No?" Kit sound terribly calm. I wondered what he intended to do? Were we to live off space and virtus of family gatherings?

"We don't have a procedure to deal with this issue. I ... in two hundred and fifty years of recorded landings, this has never happened."

"I see," Klaavil said. He still sounded very calm. He took a deep and deliberate breath, which I was sure was as much to be heard on the other side as to steel himself. Something like a light of battle came into his eyes, and he said, "I am Christopher Bartolomeu Klaavil, flying the *Cathouse* on behalf of the Energy Board of Eden." He ignored an attempt at interruption, what sounded suspiciously like a voice about to tell him they knew *that*. "I have collected six ripe powerpods, which are right now in my cargo hold. I am now requesting landing coordinates so I can be brought safely into Eden—"

"We explained we cannot—"

"Should I fail to get landing coordinates, considering I have no other alternative for landing, I will have to fling my ship at Eden, in the hopes of somehow hitting near the entrance of a landing bay. Of course, I have no idea where that might be located. I'll have to do it visually, and you know how deceptive it can be. I could accidentally miss and end up crashing through into ... oh, the half-g gardens? With a full and explosive load."

"Uh. Oh. Uh. Don't ... don't do anything. We ... we will give you coordinates shortly."

"Certainly," Klaavil said magnanimously. "I'm not an unreasonable man. You have a full three minutes. I'm setting my timer."

He looked at me and, rather deliberately, winked. The effect was only mildly disrupted by the fact that inner, nictitating eyelids blinked the other way first. I was speechless. The same haughtiness and high-handedness was not all that bad, I thought, provided he was on your side. Of course, the question with Kit

Klaavil was which side he was on and exactly why. I wondered if he, himself, knew.

It didn't take three minutes. Or two. Or much more than one. A voice crackled over the com, "Please come in at twenty-two A by twenty-four D."

It made no sense at all to me, but not only did it obviously make sense to Kit Klaavil—his hands moved purposely on the keyboard, playing their inaudible symphony of directions—but he raised his eyebrows as he did so. I thought that whatever the move the other side had made surprised him, and I wondered how exactly. He didn't seem upset, more curious.

The ship swayed gently this way and that, and I settled in for what I expected to be interminable hours. After all, to land Daddy's space cruiser in Circum, which was considerably smaller than the Primeval Potato, took the best part of a week. It would take at least hours here, even accounting for coordinates and however improved their steering mechanism might be.

Only the potato exploded. At least it looked to me as if it exploded, though as I blinked, I realized it was shooting something like a sleeve towards us. The sleeve covered the screen, giving the impression that we were being swallowed whole.

We flew down what felt like a tunnel, though I had no other indication than the view screen and Kit was too busy doing whatever he did on his console to answer my questions.

After a long while it felt like we came to rest on something. Kit, carefully, slid his foot along the lever that I now knew turned off artificial gravity. I braced for my body to be only held on the seat by the belts, but nothing happened. Kit nodded. "Eden artificial gravity field," he said. "It encompasses us." As he spoke, he unbuckled himself and stood up, then gave me an uncertain look. "Would you rather...uh...put on the dress you had when you came into the *Cathouse*?"

"I-it was a slip!" I protested.

"I don't think anyone in Eden would know that," he said. Then shrugged. "As long as you don't think you're ill dressed or..."

I shrugged in turn. I might as well be seen in a hand-me down, glimmering grey pants-and-tunic suit which if anything ended up molding my curves rather too well, as in a hastily mended slip. If my captor's handling of the situation was any indication, my arrival here *already* wasn't a rousing success.

"I'm sorry," he told me, as we walked along a corridor which I assumed must lead to an exit, "about the confusion up there." He pointed vaguely upwards, which I assumed to mean the exterior of the asteroid, because, at least as I understood it, we were not on the asteroid but inside it. At least that accounted for the fact that I hadn't seen any cities or constructions on the outside. And it made perfect sense. It was not only a way to hide their presence from any stray Earth telescopes turned this way but also probably the most efficient way of colonizing an asteroid. Provided they contrived a way to bring sunlight within—and I was sure they had one—the interior area could be much larger than the exterior because the world could be colonized in layers. "They truly would sit there and dither forever because there was no precedent..."

I was amused and for once completely in sympathy with him. "I've met the type." In correctional facilities, hospitals, rehabilitation programs. "I call them the mark-the-right-answer-or-die tribe."

He gave me a fleeting smile, "I guess bureaucrats are the same everywhere."

As he said this, we'd come to the end of the hallway and were facing the sort of irised door that blocked airlocks. Kit pressed a button and it swirled slowly open. Then the membrane behind it followed suit.

We crossed ten steps, faced another door. Kit touched another button. The door swirled open, a staircase extruded from the ship.

And we found ourselves facing fifty men with burners pointed at us.

II

The Earthworm Turns

⟨⟨THIRTEEN⟩⟩

I SURGED FORWARD, ABOUT TO ENTER INTO MY FAST MODE. IF I rushed them—and Kit was faster than I—I could get half the guns and he could easily get the other half.

No. His voice in my head admitted of no dispute.

Do you want them to take us prisoner? What do you...

No. Let me handle it. My place. My people.

I didn't answer back, not with coherent words, more with the half-acknowledged hope that he knew what he was doing. What I got back from that was a mental half-laugh. His features showed no expression.

We stood at the door, side by side, looking out at the men holding guns pointed at us. *Men* was sort of a courtesy title, because I'd judge the oldest to be about nineteen, and the others much, much younger. I'd swear the one at the corner, looking at me as though he expected me to grow a second head and holding his gun in trembling hands, couldn't be more than thirteen.

I looked from one end to the other, from blond, closecropped heads to dark, unruly long hair and realized that these boys looked like they'd been sampled from all over the world, though the overwhelming majority were tanned looking Caucasian. There were no truly dark skins and no pale blond hair. Which figured. I didn't know how many people had made it to Eden, but a small population would tend to homogenize. There didn't seem to be a standard hair length or a standard hair color. I saw a young man with wild calico hair, as bright as Kit's and open-wide brown cat eyes. They wore a uniform of sorts, a pale blue jacket and darker blue pants, but each of them seemed to have gone for his very own cut.

The only uniform thing about the way they all looked was their eyes. They all stared out at us with an expression of frightened decision. The expression someone has who is scared to death of having to shoot.

Early on, when I was very little, after a failed attempt on his and his family's life, my father had told me the one thing to watch was not the gun nor the hands of the person holding the gun, but the eyes of the person holding it. The eyes would tell you if the person was bluffing. The eyes would tell you if the person was willing to shoot. And the eyes would tell you if the person was scared. That last was the one to fear, because the scared man would shoot as he flinched.

Kit must have come to the same conclusion because he said, *Don't move unless I ask you to.*

I didn't so much agree—I wasn't about to entrust my ability to fight completely to someone else—as send back wordless assent that I would not move for now. This seemed to be enough for him. He stood very still, both hands in full sight.

From the side, not getting between us and the guns, a man emerged. He was older than all the assembled boys, older than Kit. If these people aged like on Earth, he was probably thirty years old, with a blockish build and a square face topped by receding dark hair. He wore the same colors as the boys and stood at the extreme left edge of my field of vision, closer to Kit, and said, "Cat Christopher Bartolomeu Klaavil?"

The voice seemed to call for a military response, but Kit looked slowly in his direction and said, "Yes?"

"You must be searched and debriefed before we can admit you to the common areas."

"Oh?" Kit said. "And my passenger?"

The man looked in my direction and he, too, looked like he expected me to have three heads and a complementary set of arms. I was sorry to be disappointing everyone. "We will deal with her afterwards," he said. Then towards Kit again, "First you, Cat Klaavil. Easy and slow. Hands in full view. At the first sign of cat-speed, the hushers have my instructions to shoot."

Kit gave a quick, dismissive look at the boys with guns and then, hands in full view, climbed down the two steps from the ship to stand two feet in front of the man who seemed to be running the show.

The man stepped aside, to let Kit pass him, and I realized he was holding a gun pointed at Kit. Right. So the fifty trembling teens could be left to point their guns at me, and to keep me under watch. Too bad.

Kit walked all the way to where the only furniture in the room—a desk—stood against the wall. There he turned and stood, looking at the official with the quizzical expression I knew so well. He gave me that look when he expected me to do something particularly stupid.

The officer frowned up at him. Being a good five inches shorter than Kit clearly put him at a disadvantage he did not enjoy. "Strip," he said.

"Beg your pardon?"

"Strip. We must check you for bugs. You've been to Earth. Who knows what might have happened there. They might have implanted a bug on you, or a controller of some sort."

"I was never to Earth. Never came near it," Kit said.

"Who knows if that is true? Would you tell us? Would you tell us if she"—he pointed back at me—"had put a controller on you that could kill you or hurt you if you said the wrong word? How do we know there's not a bracelet or a clinger on you somewhere, controlling you? Strip."

Kit looked at the officer, then back at the boys with guns, then at me. I swear there was something akin to amusement in his gaze, though the primary look was of bewilderment. He pulled on the front of his jacket, unfastening it. It looked like it was buttoned, but clearly the buttons were decorative, and the two halves held together with stickfast. He tossed the jacket at his feet in what was also all too familiar. Not that I'd seen him undress before, but I'd seen his clothes piled just outside or just within the virtus and around the vibro, with complete disregard for housekeeping or the clothes.

Under the jacket he wore a simple tunic, so thin that it must have been designed as an undergarment. Through it his muscles—which I had only felt but never seen—were visible, delineating a powerful torso and a flat stomach that disappeared into the closure of the pants. He looked at the officer. The officer barked back. "I said strip."

Kit sighed again and pulled off his undertunic showing me first a back where the shoulder muscles stood out in relief, a testimony to the many hours he'd spent in the exercise room before and after I joined the *Cathouse*. I'd seen male backs before, of course—I mean casually, not just those of my bed partners—the members of my broomer lair for one. Male backs were prone to pimples and other such excrescences, but his had clear, even skin. As he turned around, at the officer's command, his front revealed more clear skin, more muscles, a dusting of reddish-gold hair and a nice belly button.

"Strip," the officer said again.

Kit reached for the fastening to his pants, and pulled it, and let those fall, appearing in underwear of the sort I'd found in his drawers when I'd searched—male variety, designed for the sort of male who preferred his under things well girded and held firmly in place. Which, of course, meant it was also rather revealing. I looked away. More the pity, despite the fascinating show, the young men with guns were still looking fixedly at me.

"Strip," the officer repeated.

Kit glared. "Further than this I present you with a fee scale," he said.

It took a moment for the official to absorb what Kit had said. When he did, he looked like he would like to spit, or perhaps slap Kit. He did neither. Instead, he stepped back and said, "Strip, or I order you shot. We must make sure you are not controlled by Earth, that they don't have a bug on you. The fate of Eden—"

"The fate of Eden is horrible, if you are an example of its protectors," Kit said, raising his voice just enough that though he was neither shouting nor sounding angry, he sounded intent and purposeful. It managed to stop the official long enough for Kit to add, "What do you intend to do after I strip? Cavity search? And when that fails? If I had gone to Earth—which I didn't—or if Patrician Sinistra were a spy, which she almost certainly isn't, why would they be so stupid as to implant a bug on my skin or in my clothes? Why not inject it into me or—"

The official jumped back and pointed a trembling gun at Kit. "You're telling me they injected a bug—"

"No," Kit said. His calm was all the more admirable in that the way the official was waving that gun around there was a good chance he'd fire it by accident. Of course the way it was trembling, shaking and moving, the chances of the ray actually hitting Kit were minimal. "I'm saying if they'd implanted anything in me they would probably have done it in a way your strip search would not discover. So unless you are interested in seeing me naked—in which case I should see what the going fee is—there is no reason for me to undress further."

The official looked like he was about to have an apoplexy, and he did what bureaucrats do in such situations. He turned to the pimply boys with guns and waved and said, "Fire."

Which was the most confusing command he could give boys who already looked none too steady. They glanced at him, and Kit, probably realizing that if they turned to burn Kit, they would burn the official too, in the process. Then they looked back at me. I was ready.

I had to be ready because one couldn't discount that they might simply decide to shoot me. So in the time they looked away, I pulled my shirt off. There were fifty wide eyes staring at me.

One of them said, "Who? Shoot who?"

"Them. Both," the official said, and frowned at me. "She's an Earth agent."

"She is no such thing," Kit said. "And while as a noncitizen she doesn't have any local relatives who can charge you blood geld, I can, since she came here under my protection. And my family will charge you for me, and they will make sure you pay for all my potential lost wages. Do you know how much a cat makes, in the prime of his working years? And how many years I have left?"

"You can't..." the official said, glaring at him. "If you are a threat to Eden, I can have you killed. I do not have to pay blood geld."

"No. But what if you can't prove either my guest or myself were threats to Eden? My family will demand proof." He spoke almost kindly. "My father and my mother and...did I mention my oldest sister is Katherine Denovo? No?"

I had no idea why, but, at the name, the official visibly blenched. He backed and told the fifty, "Don't shoot," then looked at Kit. "But what can we do with the two of you, short of putting you indefinitely in containment? What if you are carrying a bug and cause all of Eden—"

"Call a doctor. My doctor. I'll even pay for it. Doctor Bartolomeu Dias," he said. "Fourth enclosure. Tell him it's for me, he'll come as quickly as he can. I'll cover the fee. He'll do a scan and he can tell you whether I or my guest are a danger to Eden."

The official didn't say anything for a while. I suspect it was because he was still hoping he could find a reason to have Kit shot. It had to gall him that Kit had stood there, flaunting all his orders and countering his authority with logic. And Kit hadn't exactly been subtle about driving his point home. But whatever the threat of the unknown Katherine might be, it clearly held terror for the official. He frowned, glared up at Kit, then at me, then frowned again. At last, and in the tone of a man making a threat, he said, "Very well." He gestured at the armed boys. "You may go out, but wait in the next room, ready to shoot anyone who leaves without my express permission." As they filed out, he glared at Kit. "Right. Don't think you can get out until you've been thoroughly examined. I shall call Doctor Bartolomeu Dias. You will not leave without his say-so."

And then he stalked out after the hushers. And closed the door behind himself, leaving me alone with Kit, who stooped to pick up his undertunic and slipped it on. He looked up at me, and the corner of his lip quirked upward. "Not that I mind the show, Patrician, but ... perhaps the tunic would be better on you?"

I blushed. I had been afraid to put the tunic on while the guns were pointed at me. With boys that nervous, any gesture, any movement can be viewed as a threat, and I did not want to get accidentally burned. I put the tunic on.

"This doctor..." I said.

"He's okay. He decanted me."

⟋⟍ FOURTEEN ⟋⟍

"SO, CHRISTOPHER, YOU BRING US EARTHWORMS NOW?" DOCTOR
Bartolomeu Dias said. He was an old man, smaller than anyone else I'd ever seen and so wrinkled that it looked as though
someone had taken double the skin needed for the man and let
the extra hang out in folds and strange excesses. He looked like
nothing so much as the old gnomes of legend, tiny and wrinkled
and wearing what looked like ancient clothes—dark brown pants
and tailored brown jacket.

He had shot Kit the barest of glances upon coming in, then
given me a slower, appreciative look and a smile. Kit greeted
him with the most natural smile I'd yet seen from him, and the
answer that, "She came into the *Cathouse*. What else was I to do?"

Doc Bartolomeu—which was what everyone seemed to call
him—gave me another, more attentive look, where something
like a smile melted into a worried frown. "I wouldn't have done
anything different, Kit," he said, his voice echoing with amusement but also reassurance, as if he meant it but also found the
situation interesting.

I did not know what was so amusing, other than the fact that
I was a woman and that Kit Klaavil clearly—judging by his various looks at me—appreciated women, and that he traveled alone.

"Lie down," Doctor Bartolomeu said, gesturing towards the desk.
Kit Klaavil did.

"So the idea," Doctor Bartolomeu said, "is that Earth put some

91

sort of bug on you." He cocked a curious eyebrow. "They say you went to Earth. Did you go to Earth?"

Kit shook his head. "No. She was fleeing through the power-trees. In a lifepod. It hit the *Cathouse*. I took her in."

"Through the powertrees in a lifepod," Doctor Bartolomeu said. He looked over at me. "And you come from Earth?" He rooted in the capacious black bag he carried as he spoke.

His manner, his oddness, made me suddenly shy. It was like when I was very little and Father and all the other Good Men gathered for a meeting, and he called me in to . . . show me off, I suppose. They looked so different from my nannies and my play friends and the world of the nursery that I was speechless. Or nearly so.

I heard my voice come out, in that stilted polite little girl tone, "I come from Syracuse Seacity. My name is Athena Hera Sinistra."

His head snapped up, for just a moment. It was the thing of an instant, and it might have meant nothing. But I noted it, even as he pulled an instrument from his bag. "I used to know someone," he said. "Alexander Milton Sinistra. I don't suppose he'd still be alive?"

As he spoke he stood over Kit holding something that looked like an oversized dimatough magnifying glass with a clear interior. He held the handle in a way that suggested he was pressing buttons, while he looked through it.

And of course he wasn't alive. At least Alexander Milton Sinistra was my ancestor who had become the first Good Man of Syracuse Seacity after the turmoils and then others, up to my grandfather. But that had been . . . My grandfather had died more than sixty years ago. "It can't be the same person," I said. "The first lived three hundred years ago. And the last about sixty or eighty or so. And even if you're that old," I said, as it occurred to me, "you can't have gone back to Earth at that time, and anyway, no, he's not alive."

"Uh. Oh?" Doctor Bartolomeu said.

"The first Good Man of my line. My ancestor. And then about every other one up to my grandfather."

He looked away from the nonmagnifying glass and at me. "Your ancestor. No. It couldn't have been the same person. Coincidence." He looked back at Kit. "I don't see any bugs, Christopher," he said. "But your stomach has been troubling you again, hasn't it?"

Kit shrugged, sitting up.

"I could—"

"No," Kit said. "No tampering with my mind. You know that."

Doctor Bartolomeu sighed. "Very well. Have it your own way. You tend to." He looked over at me. "I suppose I should have a look at the young lady. If you would lie down..."

I obeyed him, lying along the old desk, while Kit stood aside. I didn't look in his direction, as I had the odd impression that he was watching me.

Doctor Bartolomeu looked through the loop at the end of the handle at me. Seen from this end, I could see a white-light pulse in the center of it. I supposed it told him something. "Very healthy," he said. "And no spy bugs." He frowned at me, as if trying to solve a puzzle. "What possessed you to take a lifepod through the powertrees? I suppose it wasn't truly outfitted for maneuvering."

Klaavil snorted and, upon Doctor Bartolomeu looking at him, said, "Like a barge with a pole. I'd have had to use all my skill to make it through in that. She must have a hell of a lot of luck."

"Indeed," the doctor said. "But why?"

The why had bothered me all three months, and I couldn't say that I was any closer to knowing for sure than I'd been when it all started. There had been Father...Had it been Father in Circum?

Half the times I thought about it, I was sure it must have been. The other half...the other half I was just as sure it couldn't have been. A hologram. A hologram with a very well-programed voice. And I'd fallen for it, and they'd jumped me. "There was a mutiny aboard my father's space cruiser," I said. I frowned. "I think my father was killed. I escaped, and they pursued, in lifepods. I had to go where they wouldn't dare follow." I didn't mention my excursion into Circum, and Kit's coming to get me. I thought that if Kit hadn't mentioned it, there must be a reason. Besides, if all these people were so worried at the idea of my having come along with him, how would they feel about his having had actual contact with the dreaded Earthworms.

As though he'd read my mind, Doctor Bartolomeu looked up at me, "We're a small world," he said. "The remnant of a persecuted people, the vast majority of which died centuries ago. Don't think ill of us for our defenses. The hushers are volunteers. For years our young men have volunteered to keep us safe."

I understood all that. Or I tried to. But with all that, it still seemed to me like too much caution to be this scared of me. Oh, many people had been this scared of me in the past, but these people had no reason to. Kit Klaavil hadn't even let me try anything against the boys with guns. They had no reason at all to be scared of me.

Doctor Bartolomeu motioned for me to get up, as he slipped his lens back into his case. "I'll tell them you're clear and to admit you, but Christopher...What do you intend to do with her?"

Kit Klaavil stared back at him, and for a moment looked completely blank. "You know," he said, "I have no idea."

FIFTEEN

I REPEATED DOCTOR BARTOLOMEU'S QUESTION AS WE LEFT THE room, walking past fifty young men who no longer held guns pointed at us—and one or two of whom looked like they'd very much like to have the courage to talk to me. It wasn't that I hadn't thought about what would happen to me before.

Or at least, I'd thought about it in terms of *eventually, when I know how to pilot this ship, I'll take it to Earth.* I hadn't thought— or not exactly—of what to do with Kit Klaavil as part of this grand plan. It had been relegated to the something-will-occur-to-me future.

The truth was that it had started as a fantasy of hitting Kit on the head, or perhaps garrotting him, and then flying the ship to Earth. What became of him after that was truly unimportant. Oh, he'd probably saved my life when he came back for me in Circum, but he couldn't possibly have known he was saving me from anything. He must have come back because he realized that I held important information about them. He realized otherwise I could endanger all of his colony. Considering their paranoid behavior, his realizing his error and going to get me in Circum was actually fairly rational, not to say expected.

And since he'd captured me, and held my life at his whim, I felt perfectly justified in doing the same to him. Except we were now in his world and not aboard his ship. And that meant...

He gave me a sideways glance. "I have no idea," he said, as

he walked fast and purposefully down a corridor and turned, as if very sure where he was going. Because his legs were much longer than mine, this meant I must run to keep up with him, something I was quite sure he knew. "I mean, I suppose you could train for something here on Eden, right? You said you are good with machinery. There's always a need for someone good with machinery."

"But I want to go to Earth," I said.

He gave me a puzzled frown. "Don't be ridiculous," he said.

"I don't see what's ridiculous about wishing to go back," I said. "I have responsibilities. I have a position..."

He sighed. "So do I," he said. "You see..." He bit his lip. "It's a bit of a bind. I couldn't let you be killed. I simply couldn't. You think through these things and you think..." He shrugged. "But I couldn't let you be killed, and then I had to bring you here. There was nothing else I could do. And once I brought you here..." He shrugged again. "You can't go back. If you go back, they will find where we are."

"But I don't even know."

"No. But they could get it. From what you say. And I can't let that happen. There are a million and a half people in Eden, not counting the colonies. I can't risk it all for you."

"But I didn't volunteer to immigrate." Certainly not to a colony filled with Mules and their bioengineered servants. Even if familiarity with Kit had caused me to stop flinching from his odd eyes, I was sure I would meet with further horrors in Eden. And it wasn't right. It simply wasn't.

"I know," he said, "and I owe you a debt of honor, for taking away your choice in this matter." He sounded solemn. "But you must understand that I didn't have a choice, either."

I didn't understand any such thing, but neither could I discuss it right then, as we'd entered a busy, people-filled corridor, and I had to run as fast as I could to keep up with Kit. He had stepped up his pace, and I couldn't afford to lose sight of him. Let alone that the people around us were quite odd—attire ranging from uniforms like Kit's to little transparent...underwear, to a woman who appeared to be wearing an uncut roll of carpet around her middle. At the same time, Kit sped up, dodging among people, moving faster, faster. I noted that the people in matching uniforms to his gave him a non-look, allowing their gazes to slide across him.

"You don't have many friends," I said, before I could think.

He gave me a quick glance. "I told you I don't play well with others," he said, as he stepped around a group of people wearing what looked like pearlescent raincoats.

Clearly. I caught up with him as he rounded a group of people in blue and red uniforms matching his, just as he stopped short and I realized he had come face to face with a black dimatough desk and a man sitting behind it.

The man looked about Kit's age, bland and blond and bored. "Christopher Bartolomeu Klaavil," Kit said, coming up short in front of the desk. "The *Cathouse*. I brought back six ripe pods and..."

He got a pursed-lip expression. "Six pods? A thousand hydras minus the rental price."

"A thousand?" Kit said, sounding dismayed.

The conversation became a bargaining session, with the blond man insisting they currently had a surplus of pods and Kit countering that he could not possibly pay that much—around three hundred hydras, give or take, though it seemed to fluctuate through the discussion—for rental of the *Cathouse* and listing everything that was wrong with it.

They settled on twelve hundred for the pods and two hundred and fifty for rental of the *Cathouse*, with Kit insisting it be given a once-over before he took it out again.

Forms came out for the imprinting of his thumb and we were about to leave, when the blond man cleared his throat. "Before you leave, Cat Klaavil..."

Kit turned. I felt my heart sink anticipating another round of discussions I couldn't understand. I needn't have worried. Because as I turned back, at the same time Kit did, to face the man behind the desk, the man slid another form—on the sort of paper that was sensitive to the genes of those touching it—across the desk at him. "The incoming officer advised us not to let you leave without signing the agreement of responsibility for your ward."

"My...ward?" Kit asked. It was sort of like someone had just said he must be responsible for his third arm or his extra eyebrow. I confess I was no more enlightened than he was.

"The young lady from Earth," the man said, giving me the barest of glances. "Will you sign an agreement of responsibility for her as your ward?"

Kit touched the paper with just the tips of his fingers, clearly avoiding any field that might be marked with "if you put your thumb imprint here, you agree that—" He looked up from scanning it, "And if I don't agree to this?"

"Well..." the man demurred. "It will have to go before the boards what to do with her," he said. "And until then we will have to keep her confined in some way. You understand, to release her into Eden without anyone who could claim blood geld for her death, without anyone who would have an interest..."

"Yes," Kit said, but his lips snapped shut as though he'd said "No." He scanned the paper again. "She is nineteen. An adult."

"But not conscious of our customs and not integrated in our society. She doesn't know the laws here, even if inclined to obey them and—"

Kit frowned. "Fine," he said. He pressed his fingers in a deliberate way, in what had to be pre-marked places. Then glanced at me. "Come on."

I followed again. He was clearly in a worse mood—and I was not sure exactly why, since I was the one who had just been made his effective prisoner. You'd never guess it, as he stomped and marched his way through an even thicker crowd of people, down a new hallway. And here, perhaps responding to the glower on his face, people gave him a wide berth. Even those wearing matching uniforms to his dispensed with the acknowledgment nod they'd been giving him before and went straight to jumping across the corridor as far away as they could from him, a look of horror on their faces.

It made me wonder what they knew about my friend the Kitty-Cat that I didn't. Doubts and suspicions that I thought well submerged since after all he'd failed to kill me, rape me or do anything unpleasant to me—except for lecturing me about politics and history—while he had me at his mercy, now came back. What did the people in the place he'd grown up, in the very corps in which he worked, know about him that I didn't?

I followed him, watching the looks on others' faces. What had he done to upset what seemed to be an entire world—even if a small one? People looked at him with a mixture of confusion, horror and fear. Even I hadn't managed that kind of reaction, not even after I'd laid waste to some institution. Oh, people looked at me with fear often, and sometimes with the kind of horror that comes from fear. But it didn't come close to the look of horror mingled with disdain and flinching repulsion that they directed at the man walking just ahead of me.

He walked as if he were completely unaware of them. As if he were completely unaware of me too, for that matter, and of the fact that my legs were considerably shorter than his.

While I ran to keep up with him, I became aware that some people were glancing at me, too. Quick, distracted looks, as if afraid...for me. It was a novel look. I wondered if they knew what I was, if news had spread yet that I was one of those dangerous Earthworms, or if they just saw my efforts to keep up with Cat Klaavil and assumed that he...What? What was my charming companion in the habit of doing to women? From the look in people's eyes, nothing good.

We fell down two grav wells in succession, Kit Klaavil landing with the sort of soft tip-of-toes fall that would have earned him high marks in my ballet classes, and surging into striding speed without faltering.

I landed a little heavier, which resulted in my falling yet further behind him, as he walked down a busy corridor with grey ceramite walls, which gave the impression of having been poured in a hurry and never smoothed over.

Though it was full of people, the crowd behaved more informally—large groups going by, laughing and elbowing each other—as if they were not quite in public. The feel it gave me was of a utility corridor not part of the main building. Even here, though, the large groups became subdued when they saw my companion. And his expression—a mix of stone-faced pride and subdued fury—didn't change. He pushed elbow-first through a door membrane at the end, and I followed him into the cooler, cavernous recesses of...a garage. It took me only seconds to deduce this from the fact that there were vehicles parked in every spot—ovoid-shaped, though each varied slightly, and each seemed to have a different color—clearly flyers, private-size.

Klaavil walked among them, turned sharply twice, then walked up to a violent red flyer which managed to shimmer with a gold sheen. It was so reminiscent of his taste in clothes—requiring the squinting of eyes not to hurt the retina—that I was not at all surprised when he unlocked it. He held the door open and said, "If you'd go in."

And he jumped. I had no idea what prompted him to jump. Much less what prompted him to land on me before I could run away. Slammed against the not-so-clean grey ceramite floor of the garage, under his weight, I said, "What the hell?" and tried to squirm up, but he held me down and then, before I could gather up my knee to hit him on what he claimed was my idée fixe, a burner ray flew over us, burning a hole on the flyer door, and Kit jumped again.

Dazed, I looked in the direction of the jump and was only mildly surprised to find him—in far less time than should have taken him to traverse that distance—holding onto the wrist of a smaller man. Details registered one by one, as my mind adapted to the circumstances. The smaller man, dark-haired and wearing what looked like wrinkled pajamas, was holding a burner. Kit held the wrist of that hand, just as he held the other hand behind the man's back, effectively immobilizing him.

"Come on, Joseph," Kit spoke in a remarkably soft, almost apologetic voice, considering the man had just shot at him. "You don't want to kill me."

The man muttered a string of largely unintelligible syllables that sounded like insults and I took to mean that yes, he very much wanted to kill Kit.

"You do not," he said, very calmly. "How would you pay the blood geld? You'd be indentured the rest of your life." As he spoke he wrenched the burner from the man's hands, and pocketed it. "Go home, Joseph." He patted the man down, efficiently frisking him with what seemed like practiced ease. "Go home."

"I challenge you," the man said. "To a duel."

"I can't duel you," Kit said. "It is not legal for a cat to duel a non-cat." He let go of the man, turning his back and walking towards the flyer.

I'd gotten up from the floor, though I didn't remember doing it. He barked at me, "Get in." I got in, as he climbed in the other side and strapped down. I could see, through the front visor of the flyer as the man slouched—like a puppet whose strings were cut, but before I closed my door, I heard him shout, "Then how can I have justice on my sister's murderer?"

Kit didn't say anything or acknowledge the comment. Instead he slammed his door. A muscle worked on the side of his face. He started the flyer, just a few inches off the ground, but veered to avoid the man as he stepped in our path.

"Who—?" I said.

He didn't look at me. His eyelids were halfway down, as though veiling some kind of inner turmoil. "My late wife's brother."

I felt my hands clench onto the seat as if of their own accord. His late wife's brother? Was that Blondie in the pictures? And if so, had Kit Klaavil murdered her? Surely her brother believed so.

◖◎ SIXTEEN ◎◗

"LOOK OUT, LOOK OUT, LOOK OUT." MY HANDS WERE CLENCHED tight on the seat, since the seat belts crisscrossing my chest prevented me from physically ducking under the dashboard.

We'd exited from the garage through a vertical shaft and emerged into...bedlam. What we entered must have been a tunnel, since Eden was colonized inside, not on the surface. But at first glance it looked exactly like a busy city street on Earth. Buildings hemmed it in on either side and above something shone, vaguely blue, which might have been the sky.

We had no time to look up because the moment we emerged from parking, a large flyer with a semi-open back, loaded with what appeared to be crates of live chickens, headed for us at full speed.

The scream had barely finished tearing through my throat, when I realized both we and the chicken transport had veered at the last minute, managing to miss each other in the echo of my scream and the loud squawks of chickens, audible even through the hermetically closed windows of the flyer. Which got on a collision path with a large flyer in whose shadowy depths I could barely discern a large family with anxiously hopping children. And we veered onto the path of an antigrav wand just like the brooms I rode on Earth, only this broom was loaded with a man, a woman, a toddler and an infant in arms, all of them making for our windshield.

I screamed and closed my eyes. Through the dark behind my eyelids two facts slowly penetrated. The first, that we hadn't been hit. Or at least I hadn't heard the splat of a small family shattering against our windshield. The second, that Klaavil was chuckling.

I opened one eye and looked at him. He was leaning back in the driver's seat, perfectly at his ease, his fingers dancing on the keyboard.

"Don't puncture holes in my upholstery," he said, in an amused voice. "It's bio upholstery but it takes awhile to heal."

What? The seat was alive? I looked down, and it looked like suede, but I eased my grip on it somewhat. Maybe that was why it felt warm. A glance at the window showed that we were still being aimed for and flown at full force by a varying mob of flyers in all sizes and shapes. We were also missing them all, but not by much more than inches. "Have you people never heard of traffic rules?" I asked.

"No, what are they?" I'd have thought he was joking, only he turned to look at me, and his surprise and curiosity were too obviously real.

"Look at the damn traffic," I screamed, as we missed a family flyer with yet fewer inches than normal to spare.

"I am looking," he said. "What are these traffic rules? Are they programmed into flyers or something?"

I demurred. There had been a brief experiment with just that: making the flyers fully safe—incapable of obeying drivers' commands to break traffic laws. The problem was that sometimes—apparently—obeying the rules to the letter would lead to accidents. At least, I wasn't very clear on the details, but the whole plan had been scrapped some time before I'd been born. "No...no. But there are lights that control when people go and when they let traffic in the other direction go. And there are laws about which altitude various flyers can fly at and when, and there are traffic control towers, which issue orders, based on the traffic of the day and your size and all." I glanced out the windshield and shrieked, "Look out, look out!" and then, as we missed the flyer with the dimatough extruder on its back by what must have been millimeters, and as Kit Klaavil gave vent to a full-throated low laugh which in other circumstances I might have considered pleasant, I said, "It's not funny."

"It's hilarious," he said, controlling his chuckling. "I'm sorry, I shouldn't laugh at you, but I don't understand your reaction. Do you think these people are trying to hit us?"

"Well, it looks like it," I said gruffly.

He grinned, looking fully at me, while playing the keyboard and ducking under and around several other flyers. "You understand it would hurt them as much as us, if not more? Or do you think there is a vast class of suicide drivers in Eden, who get up in the morning with the express intention of going out and hurling themselves at other drivers?"

"No," I said, and waved my hands impotently. "I think that it's... I think that since you have almost no rules relating to traffic, it is inevitable that sooner or later people will hit other people. I don't understand how you can drive in this chaos."

"You drove through the powertrees in a lifepod."

"The powerpods weren't flying at me with malice and intent."

"Granted. But other flyers won't explode when touched. Unless you hit them entirely wrong." He seemed to mull this for a moment. "At any rate, the powerpods also weren't trying to actively avoid you, which other flyers are."

"But..."

"We have very few accidents," he said. "Now, this might not compare to no accidents, as you might have under a system with traffic rules and all, but... you said something about towers giving instructions?"

I seized onto this, instead of trying to explain that there were still accidents under systems with rules. "Yes. Your car sends signals of position and, you know, ID, so they know your size and all, and the tower sends back instructions."

Kit nodded. "See, that would never work in Eden. People would rip out the transmitters."

"Why?"

"Princess, we're descended from people whose relatives, friends and co-workers were hunted down one by one and killed in brutal fashion. They were hunted down because they had IDs. The government knew where they were, who they were and to what extent they were modified. And once the government knew it, the killer mob could find out. We are not so eager to let everyone know everything about us. Do you understand that?"

"Don't call me 'princess.'"

"'Patrician Athena Hera Sinistra' is a mouthful," he said, as we entered an area with sparser traffic and he sat back, visibly more relaxed. "I must call you something. You seem to object to 'Earthworm.'"

I had a strong feeling I was being teased. I didn't understand this strange place and this strange man. I would give quite a bit to be reassured the man wasn't a murderer or that I wouldn't be consigned to living the rest of my life amid a people who considered traffic rules anathema. But I remembered all too well that I'd told him to call me my full name, when I'd thought my acquaintance with this man would last no more than a few hours. Hell, even the broomers called me by my nickname. "You may call me Thena," I said. "My broomer lair calls me Mad Thena Lefty. Or most of the time, just Lefty."

He gave me a quizzical glance. "The left-handed thing?" which he'd found out very early in our practice fights.

"Yes."

"Fits. But I'd prefer just Thena, if you don't mind?"

I didn't mind. Or at least, I didn't think he was any worse a person than half the broomer scum of the Seacities who knew me by that name, and often no other. The scum, of course, being rival lairs to mine, but all the same, everyone knew me as Lefty, and often had no idea whose daughter I was. *Thena* was no worse.

We were now flying over a more sparsely traveled area and, as I relaxed, it gave way to almost completely unspoiled area— unspoiled defined as neatly fenced plots, most of them gardens or orchards, with deceptively close "horizons" of blue skies on either side, as well as above.

"The sky?" I said.

Kit spared a look up. Here, without the distraction of the traffic, I expected him to be more relaxed, but his features had clouded. He stared ahead. "Oh. Holograms. Humans don't do well with stone tunnels on either side. This is a suburban neighborhood," he said. "Relatively expensive. I couldn't live here, if my family hadn't chosen to live in a compound. As is, with three active cats and two navs in the family..." His voice trailed out. "And Mom does runs to Proxima Thule and Ultima Thule, though her eyes are no longer good enough for the powertrees, so she and Dad are retired."

"Oh. Proxima—"

"Colonies." He looked as if he had come to some internal

conclusion. "Mostly Europa, Jupiter's moon? Water. We have long outstripped the naturally available ice on Eden..." He shrugged. "Eventually people will have to emigrate, I suppose."

I supposed a little potato-shaped asteroid could only—I'm sure—support so many. But as a new arrival, I had no clue about any of this, much less what could be done to make people emigrate or to entice them to do so.

He flashed me a confused look, as if he'd just realized that he'd asked me a question I could not reasonably answer. "I'm sorry. I suppose emigration will happen when the conditions in the colonies, or even potential colonies, loom more comfortably than in Eden. It's when things usually happen."

"Or when people are told they must leave."

He shrugged. "There's no one to tell them so."

"Patricians?" I asked. "Governors?"

He grinned. "Nothing of that kind here. After... the era of the bio-lords, we... we chose not to have any rulers."

"No... rulers? Who decides where one can build? Give permits for marriage? Certify contracts? Make laws?"

He looked at me, quite blankly. "Laws are common consensus. Sort of. We don't have laws. We have traditions, which either worked or were discarded. We do have services that archive contracts, for a fee. But... permits for marriage? It's a contract..."

"But what if someone wanted to marry more than one person?"

He looked completely confused. "Well, then," he said. "He'd have to get both their consents to the terms... or however many. I don't think there are many groups larger than three. You need to find more than two people who are willing to live together in that intimate a relationship. Two people seem to be hard enough."

I choked. "It's not illegal?"

"Uh. I... we don't have laws. We have traditions. If it doesn't hurt anyone else..." He gave a distant smile that managed to make him look sadder and colder than his frown had managed. "I must tell you the idea of being married to more than one person would seem to be punishment in itself."

I didn't say anything. I was thinking of the man yelling that Kit had killed his sister.

"You said these are suburbs," I said, stabbing in the dark at something, anything to change the subject. "I suppose they're waiting to be built on?"

"What? No. They're quite...Oh." He shook his head. "We build mostly underground, you know, with the garden above."

"Of course," I said, thinking that this was how everywhere in this world seemed to be, then I said, still trying desperately to keep the conversation going. "No rainstorms." Since that was the biggest impediment I could see to building all houses underground. Oh, they existed, and the ones lined with dimatough or ceramite could be reasonably watertight. But it seemed that working against the force of gravity sooner or later became a losing game and those houses sprung leaks.

This got me a more genuine smile. "When I see holos of Earth with snow or rain it seems unlikely enough I'd think it was a lie if people like Doc Bartolomeu didn't tell me it was true. You know...all that water just falling from the sky."

"We have lots of it in oceans too," I said, piqued.

He grinned this time. "That I also have heard is true and I've seen in holos, but for the sake of my sanity I prefer to pretend that the holos are merely distorting small man-made lakes."

If he hadn't talked about his difficulties with spouses before and reminded me that he might be a wife killer, his somewhat embarrassed admission of his incredulity when it came to water would have made me laugh. Instead, I managed a pale smile.

He nodded, as if understanding my reaction and looked ahead. "Listen, I don't know who will be at home just now. It could be either of my sisters and their husbands, or both of them, or of course neither. My sister Anne is...twenty years older than I. She's a nav. Her cat is Bruno. My sister Katherine—she goes by Kath, because our family has a sense of humor—is married to a wonderful nav. No one in Eden is quite sure how or why Eber married her, but they seem to be happy. Between the two couples, they have a varying number of children. I never know which was decanted last."

"De..."

"Taken out of the womb." He gave me a curious sidewise glance. "Possibly you use a different word."

"Born." It had dawned on me with a feeling of great weariness that this place was utterly strange, if even their word for being born was different.

He frowned. "No, the bio-womb."

"The...?"

"Artificial womb, you know, so women aren't tied down . . . Ah. I guess you don't have them?"

I shook my head, trying to imagine that. I wondered what creatures it created, devoid of the stimulus of sharing life with another human being while developing. My host seemed human enough, despite his odd eyes. Well, he might be a murderer, but that was all too human, if one was to believe the oldest legends of mankind. All the same . . . I wondered what deep flaws he hid. And not wanting to think about it, I forged into, "Do all cats marry navs? Is it a . . . tradition?"

He smiled. "I suppose you could say so. It's just that we tend to train together, from primary grades on. And then, you know, during your useful years, which for cats are till about forty, when your eyes stop being quite acute enough, you spend most of the year traveling, confined in a ship with someone, it's easier if the person you are going to be confined with is your spouse." A shadow crossed his face, and he visibly forced a smile. "At least so I'm told."

"Well, brace yourself," he said. "The Denovo compound coming up."

"Denovo . . . Your name is Klaavil."

"My late wife's name. Oh. You take your father's name on Earth, don't you? I recall something from a vid. Genetically it makes more sense to take the mother's. Or at least . . ." He smiled. "So they tell me."

He veered towards one of the fenced-in plots. The fence around this one was the sort of wrought iron—or at least looked like the sort of wrought iron—popular in the ancient Victorian era. Inside the fence itself was a rioting garden of flowers that should not possibly all be blooming at the same time. To be honest, some of them shouldn't be blooming in the open air at all, such as several varieties of orchids, but then I supposed this wasn't the open air.

We skimmed a massive rose bush, plunged behind a tree loaded with camellias and came to rest on a stretch of flat grass, next to three flyers. One bright red, one a restrained brown, and one blue. "Ah," he said. "Mom and Anne and Bruno are all out. Whether to the store or on runs, I don't know. But that at least means you meet only a few people at a time. Strange, Waldron doesn't have his own flyer yet, unless he's also out, of course. Though he's very young. But he's advanced and almost a fully trained cat." He gave me a look, while I was trying to figure out who the unexpected, unintroduced character might be, and said, "I suppose you find it strange that we all choose to live in one compound."

"Uh . . . not at all. Wealthy families on Earth often do. For security."

"Oh. Here it's more . . . you see, my father doesn't travel since he and Mother retired from powertree runs. That's when they chose to have children, and he raised us while she did runs . . ." He shrugged. "Everyone staying in the compound when we got married allowed him to keep a stable home for the children while the rest of us were traveling. Fortunately they could afford cat ELFing for one child."

I almost reminded him it was for two children, at least if his sister Kath was also ELFed as a cat, which he'd said she was. But the idea that a man had stayed home to raise his children while his wife traveled all over the solar system had taken hold of my mind. How odd. The whole idea of children being gestated away from the mother, and now this. I wondered what kind of strange women were in Eden.

And met one almost as soon as we left the flyer.

⦿ SEVENTEEN ⦿

SHE WAS SUNNING NUDE, ON HER STOMACH, ON A FLAT EXPANSE of ground just past another bank of flowers I could not identify. Frankly, sunning seemed like a very strange idea, considering that I suspected this was not natural sunlight and also that she was a pale-skinned brunette, of the type that, when sunning, might turn a little less pale, or perhaps acquire a few more freckles.

"Kath!" Kit said.

The woman flipped over, revealing she was holding in her hand a gadget of some sort. From a hologram of text quickly vanishing, I assumed that she had been reading. To my relief she was wearing something—triangular silver patches over her breasts and pubic area. How they were held I had no idea. They might very well be antigrav activated.

I should explain that I don't have it in me to be embarrassed by skin as skin. At least seeing someone my own age naked would have rated no more than a shrug. But I was given to understand this woman was older than Kit and, in fact, had children of her own—not that her flawless figure hinted at this—and for some reason this made me embarrassed.

"Kath, this is my . . . uh . . . guest Patrician Athena Hera Sinistra. I trust you have—"

"Had a call from the Center? Yes." Her eyes looked like Kit's but dark, instead of green. She looked over at me, "Patrician? How should I address you? You're the first person from Earth that I've met."

"Call me Thena," I said, feeling more than ever regretful over my bad humor that had caused me to give Kit all my names. Now he would introduce me this way to everyone.

"I'm Kath," she said. "Since you already know my brother, you can guess how the family sense of humor goes." She turned to Kit. "Dad was waiting dinner for you."

"Anne on a run?"

Kath nodded. She picked up the gadget she'd been using to read and followed us into the house.

By now I shouldn't have expected the house to look like anything on Earth. We entered by climbing steps down to a landing and then down again into a sort of tunnel surrounded by walls with little holes that served as planters. Someone seemed to have picked herbs for these planters, so it was like walking amid a symphony of scent into...

A place that didn't look all that different from the outside. The carpet on the floor was either green, or there was lawn on the floor. While I'd seen people on Earth go overboard with the concept of house plants, including having flowerbeds with trees right in the house, clearly Edenites believed in a more... organic approach to house plants. There weren't flowerbeds as such, but trees, bushes and flowers seemed to grow right where they very well pleased.

The man who appeared in the middle of all this greenery was fortunately wearing more than antigrav boosted triangles—to wit, loose shirt and shorts. He had dark hair running to grey, seemed to be about sixty years old and looked, I thought, quite unlike his son. But he smiled at us and said, "Hi, Kit. Hi..." He paused.

"Thena," his daughter supplied from behind us.

"Thena," the man said and smiled pleasantly at me. He stretched a hand. "Jean Denovo." He looked like someone keeping a dozen things in his head at the same time, and trying to coordinate them all. "Dinner is ready, Kit, but I assume..."

"Bath first," Kit said and, with that personal neatness I'd come to know in the *Cathouse*, started shedding clothes as he walked, taking off for parts unknown and dropping first his jacket, then his undertunic and then his pants.

Confused, wondering what I was supposed to do, I thought that at least I could always follow the trail of clothes, find him and make him tell me what I was supposed to do next. But his father called after him, "Kit? Will your friend be bathing with you?"

And, as I felt a flood of red climb my face, Kit turned around, framed by greenery, wearing nothing but his underwear. "Uh... I'd...Um...Do you mind terribly," he said, "if she has her own bath? I'll pay for the water."

His father looked startled and that, combined with Kit's offer to pay for the water gelled it for me, not as an assumption that we were involved with each other but as a matter of water price and water saving. Which meant Kit's objection to bathing with me was not modesty—which frankly his culture seemed to be strangers to—but probably squeamishness in bathing with an Earthworm.

I barely heard his father say, "Nonsense. Water from the common fund, of course," but I had composed myself by the time he turned to me and said, "If you'd follow me, Thena?"

He led me through a corridor that looked much like the stairs we'd come down, then into a room—which like everything here seemed to lack a door and be entered through a narrower tunnel. Inside it was a pleasant-looking room and almost Earth-normal. A holo-window, revealed as such only because I knew the view from it was impossible, displayed a panorama of mountains and sky. The bed in the middle of the floor lacked even the strangeness of being round like the one in the *Cathouse*. Instead it looked like an absolutely standard dimatough bed frame with mattresses and a yellow cover.

Kit's father showed me how to open the doors to the built-in closet, though I was at a loss for what he expected me to put in it, then led me through another tunnel at the left to a tiled bathroom that echoed of Rome. He started the water flowing into an inset bathtub of generous proportions, then smiled at me, as though interpreting my expression as shock, "We can afford it because we filter and recycle much of the bath water. Don't worry that you're giving us extraordinary expense."

I wasn't even vaguely worried, but rather craving immersing myself in that much water with an almost physical need. Back home I was used to swimming every day as well as to full-immersion baths whenever the mood struck, and having to make do in the ship, for months, with a few sprinkles of water and air jets had left me feeling as though I were filthy. Yes, yes, I know, jets of air are supposed to make you just as clean, and perhaps it is all psychological, but to me it didn't add up to a bath unless I could have water.

Though I did wait till my host left, it was not more than a few seconds later that I climbed into the tub and let the water cover me. I'd just located the shampoo, next to the tub, and was lazily washing my mop of hair, when I realized there was someone staring at me.

Frankly I half expected it to be Kit—not that he'd ever shown any tendency to break in on me while I was bathing in the *Cathouse*, but because I'd got to know him and that peculiar single-mindness of his, I imagined he'd come up with something to tell me, and had come into the bathroom before remembering social niceties.

But when I looked to the side, Kath was standing there. She had put on what looked like a white silk robe and she was frowning at me, with an expression not all that different from Kit's when he considered something. As I looked up at her, she smiled, a polite social smile. "I brought you some clothes," she said. "They're on the bed. I vibroed them to what I think is your size."

"Thank you," I said, and meant it, because I'd been contemplating climbing back into the badly-vibroed dirty suit I'd been wearing.

"You're welcome," she said, but said it with the expression of someone who is thinking about something completely different. She frowned at me again, not a look of disapproval but more a look of trying to consider something. She put her hand up to her head and pulled back her hair, in one of those gestures people do while immersed in thought. "Has Kit...uh..." She paused and took a deep breath. "How...how do you get along with Kit?"

There was so much trepidation in her voice that it brought back the *I don't play well with others.* But I really didn't have any complaints, so I spoke truthfully, "He saved my life," which he had, even if he had also, arguably, kidnapped me. "And he has been a good host, though he has a tendency to lecture, but then every male does."

This earned me a real smile, with a dimple, "Don't they? And what did Kit lecture you about? Music?"

"And history and literature and, occasionally, science."

She grinned. "He must be expanding his horizons. He usually limits his obsessions to music. I'm sure he'll be taking you to the music center as soon as he can convince you to go."

I wasn't sure of anything of the kind. I wasn't sure he would want to spend any time at all with me. For that matter I was fairly sure I wouldn't spend more time with him than strictly necessary save for one thing—he was the only person I knew in this world.

Kath left, as if perfectly happy with our exchange, and I finished washing and drying. The clothes on the bed ranged all the way from Earth-retro to things I wasn't absolutely sure how one would put on.

I picked a dark red, tailored dress with a long, fluid skirt. After I discovered a brush and combed my hair back, I looked all right in the mirror in the corner. I couldn't find shoes, but then I realized that everyone else I'd seen in the house had been running around barefoot.

Stepping out of the room, I wondered where dinner would be and how to find the room. I needn't have worried. Kit was waiting for me in the hallway. He gave me one of his odd, almost frankly approving looks and condescended in smiling. "I take it Kath visited."

I nodded. He smiled. "Dinner is fairly informal, but . . . my sister vibros clothes much better than I do."

I nodded again and followed him down the hallway, then another and around a series of turns until we emerged into yet another pseudo-garden room, this one with people reclining in a group near the center. I recognized Kath, and the dark-haired man next to her looked like the man next to her in the family group photograph. Eber, I gathered. Also, Kit's father was reclining near them, as was a tall young man at that age when boys stop growing but have yet to fill in anything resembling adult muscles. He looked like Kit's father, and had cat eyes. The young man greeted us with an enthusiastic shout, "Uncle Kit!"

Kit did a theatrical double-take. "Waldron, child. Your mother hasn't killed you yet? What saintly forbearance."

The young man grinned, and must have taken this as normal affectionate family banter, because he answered with, "I am taking my cat exams this week."

"Ooh. Growing up, then. Will your mother let you drive a flyer once the Energy Board clears you?"

Waldron frowned. "I asked Jenny to marry me . . . We could get an assignment to fly next week."

Kit frowned. "So early?" He looked perturbed, then took himself in hand and visibly forced a smile. "She said yes? Poor girl." As he talked he sat down. No one introduced me to Waldron, whoever he might be—I presumed he was one of Kit's nephews, but I had no idea by which sister. A group of children younger than him were sitting some distance apart, talking and giggling.

Little robotic servers that looked like metallic turtles bearing trays came bouncing towards us over the hills, somehow maintaining their cargo safely.

They first brought us plates, then brought a variety of foods. The second wave of bots had a hollowed carapace and little pseudo arms with spoons at the end, from which they filled the plates. They understood yes, no, more and stop. I was fascinated. On Earth all this was done by humans.

No one noticed my interest as the bots served something that seemed like couscous in a curry sauce and then fish. Instead they talked. I noticed that no one asked about me, or how Kit had come by me. Surely this must be some form of politeness, or perhaps they knew everything from a call from the center.

Instead they discussed pod runs. The best ones, the worst ones, and the odd trouble with the *Cathouse* when it rolled. Here I was mentioned for the first time, and I had to be grateful that Kit didn't choose to tell them that I'd tried to kill him. I wondered what they would do. As it was, they looked at me, intently. "She repaired the nodes?" Kath asked. "Without training?"

"She says she has a natural ability with machines," he said. His look from under his half-lowered eyelids told me not to tell them anything about our mind-talk. It was just as well. I had no intention of doing so. It hadn't happened again except for the brief moment on landing, and I had no intention of letting it. The strange sensation of another in my mind, of thoughts not-mine forming in my brain made me squirm just remembering it.

"Oh, good," Kath said. "There's always jobs for mechanics. I know they are looking for some at the Center, for the refitting and checking of ships before they go back out." She smiled at me. "It's well paid too."

"I don't even know how much things cost here," I said numbly. Inside my head, I was protesting that I wasn't staying here. Not for a minute. I wanted to go back to Earth. I had responsibilities.

But the fact was that until I could find my feet and figure this place out, I couldn't do anything. I was effectively a prisoner.

"Oh, that's all right," Kath said. "I'm sure you can live here until you figure Eden out."

Her father made an encouraging sound and smiled at me, a smile of real welcome. I felt my stomach clench, but I told myself it truly was for the best. Yes, staying here made me more of a prisoner, but I must stay here until I got my bearings.

"She has to stay at least until I take the next run," Kit said. "The only way they'd let her out of the center was for me to sign for her as my ward. I'm responsible for her."

Silverware clattered. Without looking up, I knew that it was Eber who had dropped it. He'd spoken very little, but he now said, "Kit, why?"

"Well, she doesn't know the rules and is the only one in Eden, except Doc Bartolomeu, who has no kin. Not one entitled to demand for blood geld," he said. "What else could I do? Otherwise they were going to detain her or something."

I looked up then, and saw the whole family looking aghast at Kit. This must have made him feel as good as it was making me feel, because he said, in a forced tone, "Anne went out early, didn't she?"

Kath let out breath with a hiss and said something under her breath.

"Beg your pardon?" Kit said.

She repeated it. It was a foreign word with the feel of ancient Spanish and it must have been a swear word. The word after that was Klaavil.

"Kath..." Kit said. "Joseph—"

"Joseph is all over the Center, telling everyone you killed his sister," Kath said. "Oh, no one tells it to me, but they know Anne is more polite than I am, and she hears it all. Your... ancestry is brought up." She shrugged. "Anne couldn't take it. She and Bruno went out early. Eber and I were thinking of going out next week too. We just stayed till Waldron takes his exams."

"I see," Kit said. He said it with the sort of finality that one expected of a door closing. A muscle worked by his lips, pulling at them in a spasmodic tic.

"You could... pay blood geld," Eber said, looking towards the area where the children had stopped eating and were playing, in one big, noisy gaggle.

"I've tried."

This seemed to surprise his family. His father looked up in turn. "You have?"

"Yes."

"You never told us," Kath said.

"No reason to tell you. Oh, I didn't want to. It's an admission of guilt and I'm not guilty of it, not in fact, even if I am in..." He clicked his tongue and stopped, then resumed, his voice very calm again. "Even if I might be in circumstances. But I'm not so proud that I'd put my family through this or risk...talk. I offered to pay."

"And they wouldn't take it?" his father asked.

Kit shook his head. "Joseph wants a duel. He wants a chance to kill me."

"But..."

"Impossible, yes. The only way I'd not defend myself, and possibly kill him, is if I'm asleep or tied down. I've not completely defeated my will to live. It might come."

His family traded looks and then stared at me. I wasn't at all sure what they expected of me.

Kit got up, leaving his still-full plate to be picked up by the turtles, then walked out of the room. He left me lost, sitting with his family, completely dumbfounded by the significant looks they gave me. What were they trying to tell me? That Kit needed my help? How was I supposed to help him? And why? All right, so he'd saved my life, but he'd also kidnapped me. And besides, we were somewhere between friendly acquaintances and total strangers. What could I do for him, even if I wanted to? I, who was a stranger here.

On the other hand, I thought, perhaps that wasn't it at all. Perhaps it was that he was dangerous. What had he said? That he had helped kill his wife through circumstances. What circumstances? What did he mean? There was a fact that if you pushed someone out the door in a spaceship you could kill them without physically wounding them. Was that what he meant?

I remembered his backing me into a corner, looking dangerous, murderous. If the *Cathouse* hadn't rolled then, would he have pushed me against the wall too hard? Would he have killed me?

Kath was saying something to her father about, "Partly it's his temper, you know that. He gets his back up and then—"

"He can't help it," his father said. "And there's—"

He didn't say anything else, before—seemingly noticing that I wasn't eating—offering to take me to my room.

In the room, I hung up my borrowed clothes and then I undressed and got into bed. I lay awake I don't know how many hours. Despite some things I couldn't understand—such as what Kath meant by speaking of Kit's ancestry because wouldn't it be hers, too?—it was clear to me that his family's intent looks meant in fact that they were afraid he'd kill me, as he'd killed his wife.

What they didn't know is that I had no intention of allowing it. I'd get out of here as soon as possible, and keep my relationship with Kit Klaavil as casual as I could and, if possible, always see him with other people around me.

In the end I fell asleep. And in the morning, Kath Denovo took me to the Energy Board Center, where I got a job inspecting and repairing collector ships.

∙◦ EIGHTEEN ◦∙

YEAH, KIT HAD LIED WHEN HE'D SAID I'D REPAIRED THE *CATHOUSE* on my own. But then over the time of the trip, I had gotten acquainted with the tech. The manual for the ship—electronic, erasable should the ship be captured—was one of the few things aboard I could read without being quizzed on it by Kit.

And besides, machines are to me as music or ballet are to other people. It's like another sense. I can feel how machines are supposed to work. I can nudge them towards their perfect state. It's not something I think about—just like you don't think about breathing. It's just something I do, once I minimally understand the basics.

I got a job inspecting the darkships, which in most cases were working perfectly and needed no help. Also, the cargo ships to Thule, which needed very little help as well. I started realizing just how much of a wreck the *Cathouse* was, an old training ship, flying on outdated technology.

I did not encourage talk, though I swear every maintenance person in that center came to see me and talk to me. I thought it was just that they had never met anyone from Earth. After a while I realized that wasn't all. There was also morbid curiosity about Kit Klaavil and exactly what had happened between him and his late wife.

To make things worse, Kit had taken to picking me up after work. To be honest I think it was just that he took his responsibilities as my guardian seriously. What he was afraid I would do after working ten hours repairing, fixing or lubing engines, I have absolutely no idea. But I would come off of the work area when quitting time arrived, and find him standing there, wearing one of his eye-searing outfits—which I'd learned were normal for cats, because their vision made them see every color more muted—with his hands deep in the pockets of some pair of loose pants, waiting for me.

Most of the time he didn't even talk to me, just waited till I changed out of my coveralls and then took me home. Home was very quiet just now, since Kath and Eber had kept their word and gone on an early run. Leaving me with Kit and his father, who seemed to speak in monosyllables when at all. There was—I gathered—an intimation that Joseph had tried something against Kit again.

Neither told me what. But Kit's father alluded to it, and Kit shrugged and said he'd never been in any danger.

The second week he took me to a concert at the music center, a performance of Liszt. It was done with real, live instruments, and it could easily rival any of the performances on Earth. People dressed up for it too, the men in dark tunic-and-jacket-and-tailored pants, the women in dresses. I wore the red dress I'd worn the first dinner with the Denovos.

No one approached us even at intermission, and I realized the bubble of solitude that Kit moved in. I realized I was unable to refuse his other invitations. Not that they came often, and they were mostly music-related. Other than home, he seemed to live at the music center.

I discovered other things about him, such as that he played the violin, though I'd never seen him do it in the *Cathouse* and he didn't do it at home—or at least not in front of anyone. But his father said he played it and used to play with the orchestra at the music center—all of the musicians were amateurs, with other employment. He'd stopped because it made other players uncomfortable. The reason it made them uncomfortable was never mentioned, but I understood. As a rule, people don't play well, thinking they have a murderer in their midst.

It turned out his room was right next door to mine and sometimes late at night I'd hear snatches of music drifting in through the doorless entrance tunnel—curling, twisting scraps of sound like something or someone crying musically.

I didn't ask. I just wanted to work at my job, learn the strange rules of this place—which seemed to be mostly based on a complex form of codified tit for tat—and become a free woman after which . . .

My imagination failed at this point, but there were many things I could do after this. Such as, for instance, stealing one of the newer ships and making it to Earth. I didn't want to hear, and I didn't want to know anything about Kit Klaavil. But as I said, it was almost impossible to avoid the people who wanted to tell me.

One of them was Darla, a blonde girl who reminded me of a mid-twentieth century cartoon, probably because she wore her short hair in mannered curls, painted her lips into a cupid's bow and unnaturally darkened her eyelashes and the way her work suit was tailored to emphasize her breasts and her tiny waist. None of which should be taken to mean she did anything inappropriate or that she was in any way bad at her job. As far as I could tell she was very good at her job. And frankly her manner of dressing had at least the advantage of being charmingly retro. People could come to work in anything or nothing at all, and though the use of work suits was strongly encouraged for safety and identification reasons, we had at least two gentlemen and a lady who worked stark naked. Or rather, stark naked with a tool belt. No one seemed to care, and I wasn't stupid enough to mention it.

But Darla was—besides a good mechanic—the designated local gossip. I never got along with women. Probably comes from the fact that my breasts came in at eight and that I had what could be called a womanly figure long before anyone else in my age group. The other thing of course was that my mother had left when I was very young. And that there weren't many women among the children of Patricians. All of which amounted to the fact that most of the women I knew or met at boarding houses or reformatories were not predisposed to like me, and they were my social inferiors, which always caused some grit in the social machinery.

But Darla was friendly like a kitten is friendly. Friendly for her own sake, not caring on whom her bouncy interest and babbling conversation was bestowed. She started talking to me about simple things, coming by to check how my work was going, offering a hand here and locating a difficult-to-find piece there.

And then about three weeks after I'd started working there,

we were going over a Thule collector ship together and she came right out into the subject she'd skirted many times before. "So, Kit Klaavil," she said, sitting back on her heels, as she pulled the lid off the panel that controlled air purification and looked at the entrails, comparing them to a diagram. "Are you two an item?"

"What?" I said.

"Well, you know," she said, as she took tweezerlike tools to the strange bio-wires inside. "Are you friends, bundling, or going to get married eventually?"

"Uh," I said. I wanted to ask what business it was of hers, but it hit me that if I said that then it would be all over the center by the next day that Kit and I were indeed bundling, an idiom whose meaning I could guess all too well. And it wasn't even that I had a reputation or cared for it, but I could imagine half of these people waiting for me to be found dead or something. Better answer Darla's questions now, as much as possible, and maybe avoid having quite so much curious prying into my life. "We're acquaintances," I said.

"Oh, come on," she said. "You're staying at his family compound and he's taking you places. And he signed for you. As his ward."

I shrugged. "He felt responsible for me, I guess. He gave me asylum when I was escaping from some trouble in the powertree ring."

She gave me an appraising glance, as if she was dying to ask me about Earth but knew that would be pushing too far, then sighed. "His wife was very nice, you know. So sad."

I didn't say anything. I'd started taking apart the navigation system. The cat who piloted the ship had complained that it pulled right. Only by millimeters, but enough that it could cost them their lives in a tight spot.

"They say he spaced her," she said. "Just, you know, got her to go out to fix something on the outside of the ship, and then didn't let her back in. He never brought the body back. He says she committed suicide, but you know, with the training and all, everyone knows everyone, and Kit Klaavil has a foul temper. He used to get in fights all the time when he was young. More fool of Jane Klaavil to marry him, I say. But she was the first in her family to be ELFed and I guess her people didn't know any better."

I continued not saying anything and went on with my work, but in my mind was that moment I'd been out of the airlock, on the skin of the ship, and felt like Kit would not open the airlock for me. Had it been like that? Had she stepped out and screamed in his mind and he refused to let her in? I thought of him glaring ahead, when his family tried to discuss things with him. I thought of him as he pinned me to the wall of the cat chamber after I tried to garrotte him.

Oh, I was quite willing to concede this wasn't the normal Kit, the man who teased me—as he still did—over my fear of traffic in the downtown Eden, the man who could laugh at silly things and joke with Waldron. But Kit in a fury? Yeah, he could lock a woman away from air and life. He'd regret it afterwards, but it would be too late.

This was in my mind a week later, when Kit picked me up at the center and said, as I stripped my work suit to emerge in the silver jacket and pants I'd worn in the morning, "I thought we could go to the half-g gardens." He had his hands stuffed deep in his pockets and an almost sulky look.

I looked over at him and thought that his father must have been talking to him about the situation with Joseph Klaavil, or perhaps something else that Kit didn't wish to discuss and that Kit was trying to avoid going home. Part of me wanted to tell him to forget it.

First, I'd been uncomfortable around him since listening to Darla's confidences. More uncomfortable than I'd been before, which is to say very. Second, I was exhausted after a full day of work and wanted nothing more than to go home, allow myself one of my baths—I took them rarely because Kit's father insisted on not letting me pay for them—and fall into bed.

But there was something to Kit's face behind the sulk, a sort of anxious loneliness around his catlike eyes, and I thought of the disquieting music winding out of his room late at night, and I said, "Half-g?"

He smiled, though the anxiety remained around the eyes. "It's exactly what it sounds like. Though it's not gardens, or not exactly, except around the picnic grounds. It's an area that's been carved, with huge rocks forming outsized stairways and caves and . . . that sort of thing. And the whole area is a playground. Families tend to go there a lot, for picnics and to let the kids hop around. But on a weekday and after work hours, there will be fewer people there. Because it will be dark soon."

Though Eden used a combination of piped-in and simulated sunlight—depending on where Eden was on its erratic orbit—it kept to a standard Earth day and a standard Earth week, with Friday, Saturday and Sunday the days off when everyone did family things or played. On week nights the type of amusement was more likely to be of an adult sort—bars or dancing—and not what sounded like a kiddy attraction.

I wondered why Kit wanted to go there and tried to work up some alarm over the fact that he wanted to take me to a half-deserted place, just the two of us. But the thing was, while I was willing to consider and even to believe that Kit might have killed his wife in a fit of temper, even with the worst will in the world I couldn't bring myself to believe he would plan anyone's murder. Not even mine.

In fact—strangely—given my record of making people loathe me on sight and exactly how badly our acquaintance had begun, I'd started to believe Kit Klaavil liked me. Oh, nothing romantic like Darla would no doubt think, but he enjoyed my company. He had worse social habits than I. At best he was reserved, at worst sullen. But when he was showing me some place he loved—like the music center—or talking about some memory of childhood, he could be animated and almost fun. And, disquieting though it might be, we seemed to have similar senses of humor. I could look up after hearing Waldron or one of the other children say something that struck me as funny and find like amusement in his eyes.

"All right," I told him, and it seemed to me he was relieved.

He grinned. "I got dinner packed."

And so I'd let him fly me out of the confusing traffic downtown and down a tunnel we'd never taken before, then up and up another level. I remembered his threatening to dash the *Cathouse* into the half-g gardens and realized it must indeed be quite close to the surface.

We parked in an almost deserted parking garage. The parking attendant made me flinch, because she was obviously mentally deficient. I'd seen mentally deficient people on Earth before, of course, but none with six arms, one of which collected Kit's money, another of which handed him a token for retrieving his flyer and yet another of which locked a curved bar over the flyer which could only be opened with the token.

As we walked out of the garage, I was silent, filled with horror at what had been done to this poor woman. Given the ability to bioengineer your children in the bio-womb, why have a deficient one at all? And if you chose to have one, why have her so grotesquely...dehumanized?

"You're very silent," Kit said, as we emerged into what looked like a meadow with trees and picnic spots consisting of flat ground and very even grass. The gravity was normal there, the grounds being just a convenience provided for patrons of the half-g gardens.

I fully expected him to ridicule me, but I stammered out my horror at seeing the poor girl bioed to resemble an octopus and at her obvious mental deficiency. "I think it's that sort of thing," I told him, "that caused people to rebel against the bio-lords."

He stopped. We had been walking towards one of the picnic spots and a rather retro picnic basket dangled from his left hand as he turned to face me. "She's not bioed. Her family is probably one of the religious people who do not believe in bioing or ELF-ing. Otherwise they would have corrected her problem in utero. In fact, she was probably born in vivo and not in a bio-womb."

"But I thought everyone was born of bio-wombs?"

"Oh no. One of my grandmothers was staunchly against it for religious reasons. A Gaian naturist, you know, and my mother was born in vivo."

"But then...how come this girl has eight arms?"

Kit blinked. Then he laughed. "She was wearing a bioed vest, Athena. Well, probably part biological and part mechanical, like our server bots." He looked at me and smiled. "I know it's not exciting, but it allows the poor thing to earn a living."

"Oh," I felt my cheeks heat.

He touched my arm, very lightly. "It's all right," he said. "I take it you don't have anything like that on Earth and so you were justified in guessing..." He shrugged.

"I only hear about bio-wombs and no one seems to carry their children..."

"Well, those who choose to do so are a small minority," he said, and shrugged. "Though there are people who believe the bio-wombs are wrong, the vast majority of women enjoy the freedom and being relieved of the reproductive price."

I didn't intend on ever having children, but if I did, I could certainly see the advantages of letting a bio-womb carry them.

Kit said that the wombs were provided with caretakers, who simulated the sort of environment they would have had in the mother's body, and the people I'd met seemed neither better nor worse than those on Earth.

Kit and I had our picnic, and then he returned the basket to the flyer and led me into the half-g gardens proper.

"We came here a lot when I was little," he said. "It's very safe. The only time there was an accident at all was when the gravity got full-forced in a freak malfunction. My mom said she used to play here as a child."

I can't really describe the half-g gardens. As best I can try to give you an idea, they were a vast area filled with the sorts of constructions one expected in fairyland, or perhaps in children's book illustrations. Impossibly tall spiral towers rose, pale, encircled by gleaming staircases. Inside, spiral slides made of white dima-tough led one by gentle stages back to the bottom. Then there was the stepping stone area. It was exactly what it sounded like, except that there was no river—just a series of spires ending in round footholds. By jumping just right you could hop from spire to spire. And if you missed and fell—which I did quite a bit at first—the ground beneath, while looking exactly like normal ground, was actually a soft, spongy substance.

When I'd got the hang of hopping properly from spire to spire, Kit said, "My nieces and nephews and I used to play this game..." He tried to explain it and it made no sense at all, even taking in account that it had involved seven people instead of two. It sounded like a cross between checkers and tic-tac-toe in which you were a piece—or actually several pieces—and you hopped between the spires to mark your place.

"Like this," he said, and jumped.

I saw the flash in the air, but had no idea what it was. It seemed to me, for a moment, a mere glint, perhaps from the windshield of a passing flyer. Kit's scream seemed odd, but as he fell, between the spires, I thought he was joking, and hopped closer, half-annoyed, saying, "Come on, Kit, you were explaining..."

I hopped down near him, and recoiled, as I saw that his shoulder was all red. "What?"

I wheeled around and saw Joseph Klaavil. He stood on the nearest spire, and was aiming a burner at Kit.

It all happened very fast. I considered stepping in front of

Kit, but Joseph's pinched, intent expression probably meant he wouldn't care and would cut me down on the way to getting Kit. And then I put on my desperate speed, jumping up to a smaller spire, then up again, to crowd Joseph on his. I hit his arm, and he turned to look at me, with the kind of shocked, blank look that meant he'd never seen me coming—he hadn't seen me move.

I hit his arm, making the burner fall and then I kicked him hard, where Kit said I had a habit of hitting men. He fell off the spire, and I jumped down, to where Kit was, as excitement faded and I thought Kit was dead. Kit was dead and I was his ward and I didn't even want to think what they'd do with me now and—

Kit was sitting up, his hand clasping his shoulder tight. "What did you do to Joseph?"

Oh, thank you so much for your effusive gratitude, Cat Klaavil, sir. "I hit him." He gave me a level look and I added, "Yes. There. He fell. I disarmed him."

Kit sighed. He was pulling at his jacket, which had a horrible, jagged tear at the shoulder, which matched the horrible, jagged tear in his flesh beneath. "I need to go to Doc Bartolomeu," he said, his voice muddled and thickened.

"Can't we call him?" I asked. Communication devices of various kinds, usually embedded in rings or bracelets were all over Eden. "And ask him to come out?"

He shook his head. "I didn't bring...I wanted to be out of reach."

I cursed silently. I hadn't brought any sort of communicator, either. I hadn't figured out how to buy one yet, and besides, I didn't have any friends or anyone to call. And Kit dropped me off and picked me up. What could happen that he couldn't deal with?

"Right," I said. "Can you stand?"

He blinked. His inner eyelids were attempting to close horizontally across his eyes. I had seen enough real cats—of the feline variety—on Earth to know this was definitely not a good thing. But thank heavens we were in the half-g gardens. I managed to boost him up—though he was much taller than I—and hold him up, pulling his sound arm over my shoulders. I started half-leading, half-dragging him towards the garage.

And found Joseph in front of me, another burner held in his extended, trembling hands. "You killed my sister," he said.

"Don't," Kit said. "Don't. I—"

But I was furious. I had had enough of this. Let Kit not defend himself, if that was what he intended to do. Let him not react. Perhaps he couldn't react. His nictitating eyelids were now almost completely closed. But I could.

I jumped and kicked Joseph's weapon out his hand. I punched him hard, sending him back into a spire. He fell in a heap, immobile. He was a light man, only slightly taller than I and of a slim build. I grabbed the burner. I pointed it at his head.

"Don't, Thena," Kit said. "Don't."

I looked over at him. He was very pale, clutching his shoulder. He shook his head. "He's Jane's only brother. He's the only child his parents have left. Don't."

I bit my tongue. I wanted to splat the creature's brains all over the ground. The fact that he was unconscious didn't even bother me. The thought that Kit might or might not have killed his sister didn't bother me. I knew the procedure in Eden was to take blood geld or fight a duel. But this type of pursuit, and firing at Kit from cover was dishonorable, and trying to kill a wounded man struck me as evil. Trying to kill a man who wasn't—wouldn't—fight back seemed despicable. I was filled with rage.

But I was Kit's ward and I had some vague notion I could get him in horrible straits by killing Joseph Klaavil. So, instead, I pocketed the burner and returned to dragging Kit towards the garage.

By the time we got there, I had to jam his hand in the gen pad to unlock the flyer. And then I realized Kit couldn't drive the flyer. Actually, by then he was so close to full unconsciousness that I wasn't sure he could tell me where I was supposed to fly.

I thought I could just drive to the nearest populated area, land and scream for help. People would be bound to come. But then I looked at how much bigger the dark, wet area on Kit's suit was, than it had been in the half-g gardens, and I wondered if he would last long enough for someone to call specialized help.

He'd said he wanted Doc Bartolomeu.

I was crying as I dragged him into the passenger seat of the flyer and locked him in place, then examined the half-dozen routes programmed into the memory. There was home, and the music center, and a couple of stores and . . . no Doctor Bartolomeu. And nothing that could be a hospital. I wanted to punch something and scream.

Instead, I turned towards Kit, whose eyes were barely open. "Kit," I said. "How do I get to Doc Bartolomeu's?"

He opened his mouth, and then his eyes rolled into his head, and his body sagged.

◖NINETEEN◗

WONDERFUL. JUST WONDERFUL. SUPPOSING I SURVIVED THIS, without anyone accusing me of killing Kit, I'd still be left alone in Eden. How would it work? I now worked for the Energy Board, but did that mean that I would be allowed to go free after work, and live in Eden on my own? People seemed to be very leery of Kit Klaavil, but at least half of them were as leery of me.

I looked over at Kit, on the passenger seat. Right. It went beyond that. He had saved me, once. I didn't understand his forbearance with this man attacking him, but it was clear there was a lot more going on than I knew. Did I like Kit? I didn't know. I knew that over our months together, for all his occasional dark moods, he'd been the only one to ever look at me as more than a token representative of Earth, an Earthworm. And when I'd mistaken the girl for an awful bioengineered monster today he hadn't sneered about prejudice of close-minded Earthworms, or even about fear of science.

Reaching over, I shook his good shoulder, slightly. "Kit. Please tell me where Doc Bartolomeu lives."

There was no answer. Like most flyers on Earth or in Eden, his was genlock activated. Time and again I'd seen him reach to the dashboard of the flyer and press his finger into the grey membrane slot to have his genetic fingerprint recognized and start the flyer. This time it took my unsnapping him from the restraints and pushing his finger into the dashboard. He felt warm and he was breathing. I had no idea how seriously he was injured, but I knew enough from broom accidents to know people could die very quickly from bleeding out.

Damn it, damn it, damn it. I'd seen him drive often enough that taking off was no problem, nor was maneuvering outside the garage, into a tunnel surrounded by holograms making it look like peaceful countryside. And now what? I had a vague idea how to get to Downtown Eden and I supposed there must be some sort of hospital or med center there, though I'd never asked or had a chance to look for it. *Damn it, damn it, damn it.*

Thena, Kit said, his "voice" or the feeling of it so clear that I jumped and looked over to see him still slumped in the seat, kept upright only by the seat-belt restraints.

He hadn't talked. He couldn't have talked. *Wonderful. I'm hallucinating now,* I thought as I sped what must be at least a frowned-upon speed—even if they didn't have traffic regs—in these bucolic parts.

Not . . . hallucinating. He said. *Mind . . . link.* There was a pause of nothing, then urgently, *Let me use hands/eyes. Words difficult. Faster.*

What?

If you let me . . .

I felt him nudge me—push me aside, clamber close inside my mind, crowding in. It was as though my mind were a piloting chamber and he'd entered it. Whatever restraint he'd employed before was now absent. He was coming in with all he was, holding nothing back. There was a hesitation as I tried to figure out how to move over, how to let him have the controls.

And then he was . . . there. In my mind. All of him. Complex. Contradictory. Alive. Still alive. He must remain alive. A moment. Two. He was looking out through my eyes, using my hands. The flyer took off. *Your reflexes are unnervingly slow.*

That was the last time I heard his voice in my mind as a voice. Something odd was happening as his presence there didn't so much push me out of the way but tried to . . . mingle with mine. Our thoughts shuffled and clung, our memories intermingled.

I remembered being a boy child in Eden, playing games in the half-g garden with a lot of boys and girls, one of whom was clearly a younger version of Kath. I remembered a mother and father who loved me, who delighted in me. I remembered flying a ship for the first time, the joy of the controls in my hands, and the world in split-second snatches of light and sound and color, strange and yet not strange. Different eyes. The dark a symphony of singing colors. The light muted by obscuring contact lenses.

I remembered a violin in my hands, the wood old and glowing under my fingers, and a voice that sounded like Doc Bartolomeu's saying, "It was your father's," in a tone that mingled loss and hope. I remembered playing, the music flowing.

I remembered a blonde girl—first a girl, maybe fourteen? And then a woman, warm in my arms. I remembered loving her—loving her till my soul lost itself in it and it was like playing the violin.

What remained of me tried to pull back. It wasn't even possible for me to do the things I was doing in those memories, and I had never, ever, ever felt that way about a woman. Nor did I want to.

But the memories held me, carried me, like a river that submerges and pulls, and I felt cold, cold, cold. I felt my body shake, and realized it was Kit's body I was feeling, that he was going into shock as he lost too much blood. My/his fingers flew on the controls. Scenes flew by that made no sense to my eyes and that made him struggle, because everything looked different.

The memory of standing outside an airlock, calling, calling. The memory of mind-voice screaming *Jane, no!* of not being able to reach, of feeling through mind link as her body imploded, as her blood boiled, as the all-too-loved companion vanished forever into the cold of space, possessed my mind, obsessive and unrelenting like a drumbeat signaling an execution.

And then loathing came, in waves. Loathing and regret for being too cowardly to follow her out there. To put an end to it. Because it was my fault. Mine. His.

What remained of Athena in this odd mingled mind screamed *no*. And Kit pulled away. He retreated. His presence vanished from my mind.

I looked at him. He looked very pale, very still. But his chest was still moving. And we were stopped on a private plot by a little hill.

TWENTY

"DOCTOR BARTOLOMEU." THE LITTLE HILL HAD A DOOR, A THICK door that looked like oak held together with iron bands and rivets, but which was probably cleverly disguised ceramite. I pounded on it with both hands, before I realized that there was a knocker, and then I grabbed that—almost too large for my hand—and pounded that. "Doctor, please!"

What if he was out? What if he was gone? What if he didn't come back? What could I do to make Kit stop bleeding? The wound was on his shoulder. I couldn't use a tourniquet. What could I do? What if he died?

Another part of me, still shocked by the self-loathing and pain it had felt from him insisted it might be better if he died, if he rested, if he were at last healed of grief. But the other part of me, still reeling from the most intimate contact I'd ever had with another human being, refused to let him go. Forget that he would leave me alone. Forget what his family might think. Forget that I might be suspected of killing him. I didn't want to let him go. I couldn't let him die. "Doctor Bartolomeu. Please."

The door opened. The man who had come to the center to check us for bugs stood there, looking like he'd been asleep and had awakened to my pounding. "Who..." he said, then ran his hand backward through his sparse white hair. "The Earth... Sinistra. What is it?"

"It's Kit. Kit is wounded. Kit is dying."

I don't remember the next few minutes all too coherently. I know Doc Bartolomeu got his bag from the depths of the house and did something to Kit before he even tried to move him. And when he moved him, we laid him out on an antigrav platform, which he steered into the house.

The house itself was odd. I'd only seen the like in museums and holos and illustrations showing the mid-twenty-first century or older.

The room we entered was so low-ceilinged that, had Kit been on his feet, he would have been obliged to duck. It descended at steep angles, on both sides too, a strange affectation in a home carved out of living rock and lacking a traditional roof or, in fact, a roof of any kind. To the right was a dining table, just like in all those holos and reproductions, just big enough for four people, and doing a fine job of looking like innocently carved oak. Around it were four matching oak chairs, with high backs. Past it, a fireplace burned merrily and in front of the fireplace were two high, dark brown leather chairs. Past that again, a long, narrow living room, with a sofa covered in checkered material. The sofa had what looked like an honest to goodness paper book—I knew these because Father owned a library with hundreds of them—on its face, cover up. I read the title without meaning to. *Dragon's Ring.* Doc Bartolomeu removed it from the sofa and onto a low table in front it, and then I helped him lay Kit on the sofa, where the doctor proceeded to do other things to him, things that involved seaming and bandaging, and at the last threading an IV into the vein on the inside of his elbow and suspending a bag of blood nearby.

"Don't look so pale," he said. "Yes, there are other things I could have done, to make him produce more blood faster. But in a pinch the old treatments are the best, and this is what I first learned." He smiled at me, rearranging the wrinkles on his ancient face and looking gnomish.

Kit was naked from the waist up—smooth muscle with reddish-blond hair and skin disrupted by an irregular seam up his shoulder.

"It's a good thing that Joseph Klaavil is such a horrible shot. How far away was he?"

"Uh...Ten meters."

"At that distance, it should have gone through the heart," the doctor said, and shook his head as if the sheer incompetence pained him.

I heard myself say "No!" aghast, and Doc Bartolomeu gave me a curious look. "I assure you it should. However, I'm glad it didn't." And then, curiously, tilting his head to the side a little, like a bird thinking about something. "Are you worried about Christopher?"

I nodded and swallowed and then I said, "No," and then, "I don't know."

Doc Bartolomeu grinned at me as if I had done something particularly clever. "I see," he said, in an avuncular tone, which grated at some level I couldn't even identify and which prompted me to say, "It's not that. He's been...very kind to me."

He nodded. "Christopher is kind. A fool, but kind." And then with great curiosity. "Did you kill Klaavil? Joseph Klaavil?"

"No," I said. "Kit wouldn't let me."

"Christopher. Yeah. A fool." He walked to what looked like a kitchen straight out of an historical holo in the corner across from the sofa and washed his hands at the sink. Bloodstained water ran down. "He's going to be asleep awhile, and I think you are in shock."

"Uh. Me? No." I'd never been in shock before. Not even when I'd flown the broom against the wall and—

"Do you drink hot chocolate?"

"What?"

He was fumbling in what looked like a cupboard but which I realized was a cleverly disguised cooker. "Hot chocolate. Do you drink it?"

"You have chocolate?" I asked, because I hadn't even seen coffee in Eden, where the caffeinated beverage of choice was either tea or a clear, sickly sweet stuff that everyone called bug juice, and which might very well be just that. I preferred not to investigate.

"Almost everything that was once available on Earth is available in Eden. Sometimes it's expensive to synth," he said. "But I'm blessed with more money than I could ever spend." He looked at me, something like a smile flashing in the dark eyes, amid their nest of wrinkles, "And more time than anyone could wish for."

He removed two steaming mugs—that looked like handcrafted clay, thumb marks and all—from the depths of the cooker, and handed me one. "Mind you," he said, "it's hot. Hold carefully. Go on to the left chair by the fireplace, there's a girl."

I went. Normally I detested being treated with that kind of

fatherly affection, but in this case it seemed genuine and also strangely well-practiced, as though he played father to half the world and more. Or as if he were extending to me the clear affection he felt for Kit.

He came along moments later, carrying a cup and two small plates held together in one hand. He handed me a plate, which had two cookies in it. "I surmise you like chocolate," he said.

I nodded, not knowing what to say. The hot chocolate was thick and sweet and as I sipped it, I was aware of calming down.

"How did you find me?" the doctor asked. "Christopher must have been unconscious for at least half an hour, wasn't he?"

"Ab-About that. He...was in my mind."

A small clatter as the cup came to rest on the plate. "Indeed?" he said, and his eyebrows rose. "How?"

I shook my head.

He took a deep breath. "My dear," he said. "I know the limited telepathy...if you wish to call it that, that's engineered into cats and navs. I worked in the team that...Never mind. It can only be activated by another cat or another nav, and even then, it usually requires a bonded couple. Married. Though it's been known to happen between best friends raised together from childhood." He took a sip of his hot chocolate. "Would you care to explain?"

I shook my head again. "I can't," I said.

"Is it something you can do?" he asked. "Something you were born with?"

"Not that I know," I said. "It's never happened before. And Earth has no ELFing."

"No," he said. And then. "They used to, but I suppose that's been outlawed along with all the other modifications."

I didn't say anything. I thought even in Eden that was a matter of common knowledge. The fire crackled and from the sofa came the sound of Kit taking a deep breath.

"It interests me," he said. "Someday when we both have time, I'd like to examine you."

For some reason, his tone of deep interest made me think of scalpels and labs. I doubted that's what he meant. It would go oddly with the fatherly tone and the clearly kindly look in his face. On the other hand, he'd acted upset that Joseph Klaavil hadn't hit Kit's heart. I wanted to ask about Joseph; about Kit's wife; about the reason Kit loathed himself and Joseph Klaavil loathed him; about the reasons Darla had gone on about Kit's ancestry. Instead I said, "You thought you might have known one of my ancestors?"

"Alexander?" he said. "It would take a miracle for him to be your ancestor. But you do look a lot like him. Enough to make me wonder if a miracle happened. He was my friend...on Earth. Before we left. I...I tried to bring him with us, but there were... problems."

"You came from Earth?" I said.

"Yes. Oh, yes." He blinked. "More years ago than I like to think about."

"But you're not..."

He opened his mouth, closed it, then smiled, "What? Old?" He chuckled. "I am old, young lady."

"Yes...but...three hundred years..."

He shrugged. "I told you Earth had ELFing. And bioing. And Eden...we grow body parts when the old ones wear out. Three hundred years is...unusual, but not...impossible."

"Oh." I wanted to ask him about the turmoils. To ask him about what kind of people the Mules had chosen to bring with them—how grossly bioed they were, how odd. But I didn't dare. If he'd been one of them...Images of people killed, of heads on pikes, of men and women torn down on the streets swept through my mind from the old holos. And again I careened into the first sentence that crossed my mind. "Kit's middle name is Bartolomeu. After you?"

His eyebrows arched. "I decanted him."

"Is that normal? To name the child after the decanting physician?"

He looked like he was considering something, his eyes sharp and attentive. *He's trying to determine what I will believe.* "The Denovos are friends," he said. "I don't have many. And Christopher is their only son. They thought...I'd like the gesture." He frowned. "I did. Christopher is an interesting person to watch, as he matures." He looked towards the sofa, though he could not possibly see Kit from there. "Though more troubled than I'd like, and a lot of it self-inflicted."

I wondered how much self-inflicted. I remembered the pain at his wife's death, but also his certainty that he had caused it.

"The girl was a bad idea," the doctor said, as if he had read my mind. "He had to know it was a bad idea before he ever married her. He had to know . . . what he owed her." He chewed his cookie. "I wonder if he knows what he owes you, and if he'll honor it."

"He doesn't owe me anything," I said heatedly, feeling my cheeks flame and sure that this old man who looked like a gnome and lived like a relic was imagining me as the despoiled maiden prey to the handsome darkship thief. Kit hadn't touched me, except in fight practice. I suspected that other than the normal attraction of a healthy male for a healthy female about the same age, he didn't even like me much.

"Doesn't he?" the infuriating old man said. "I wonder."

There was a sound from the sofa. A moan, and then the sound of feet hitting the floor, and a grunt and what sounded like an IV line being pulled with a needle being allowed to dangle loose and hit the IV stand. Kit stumbled towards us, his fingers pressed to the IV site.

"Hello, Christopher," Doc Bartolomeu said, as if this were perfectly expected, and he stood up, even as he reached out and more or less pulled Kit into his chair. "You might not want to stand. I don't think you're quite steady yet . . ."

"I'm steady . . . I'm . . ." He shook his head. Looked at me. Then at the doctor who now stood by the chair. "What were you telling her?"

"Nothing," the doctor said. He ambled away to the kitchen and I heard plates knock together. Kit put his head back and closed his eyes, and I wanted to ask him what he was so afraid that the doctor would tell me, but I didn't want to ask, not while he still looked like death warmed over.

The doctor returned moments later, with yet another mug, bigger than ours. He touched Kit on the shoulder and, as Kit opened his eyes, handed him the mug. "Drink. You need it."

"I don't—"

"Drink or I pour it over your head. You had no need to tear out the IV."

"You were telling her . . . you . . . You were about to tell her . . ."

"Drink."

Kit drank.

"I hear you made her spare Joseph Klaavil."

Kit shrugged, winced. "He's his parents' only son."

The doctor made a sound that could normally be transcribed

as *umph*. "Why don't you put an end to it all, Christopher? Why not depose under hypnotics?"

Kit looked surprised. "It's not my secret to tell," he said. "Even if I were willing . . . even if I didn't mind . . ."

"Do you mind?" the doctor asked. "So much?"

He shrugged again and this time the wincing was more pronounced. "I don't want it to splash on the Denovos. You know what people are."

This earned him a smile. "Oh, very well. Very, very well, Christopher. I saw it up close, remember?"

"Perhaps it was a bad idea," he said. "Me. My . . . parents. Everything."

Doctor Bartolomeu raised his eyebrows. "I've always thought there was a very good chance that it was all a very bad idea from the inception of life on Earth onward, but that's not the point, is it? You particularly"—the doctor's turn to shrug—"aren't a much worse idea than any of the rest."

Kit drank his hot chocolate and I felt that not only was I in a gnome's house, but I'd fallen down the rabbit hole like that girl in the ancient story, and entered a land where everyone spoke in riddles and where words didn't necessarily mean what I thought they meant.

"You should tell her," the doctor said at last, and on the assumption I was the *her* involved, I wanted to scream that I was right there, and shouldn't exactly be talked about in the third person.

But Kit sighed. "Why? Why should I? What is the point of it all?"

"Not to repeat a stupid mistake," the doctor said. "Once was an accident. Twice is stupidity."

"Once was not an accident," Kit said. "It was cowardice."

"Then what would you call the second time?"

Kit shook his head. A smile formed on his lips—seemingly without their cooperation—as though it had ambled onto his face and shaped his lips to it. "You want me to give fair warning?"

"Call it what you will."

He drank his hot chocolate. "I will consider it." He looked at me, his eyes narrowed, not so much with a speculative look as with an indulgent one. "I am sorry I took over your mind, Thena. I know it must have been disorienting."

Disorienting. Is that what he called it? And in calling it that, and in apologizing he made it impossible for me to ask about his feelings, about his wife's death, even about his music playing. "It's all right," I said, as I finished my own hot chocolate and handed the cup back to Doctor Bartolomeu. "It needed doing."

"I suppose," Kit said. Then looked at the doctor. "Not here," he said, as if he were continuing an interrupted conversation. He started to rise, first holding onto the chair and then, experimentally letting go.

"You shouldn't," the doctor said, "try to leave so soon."

Kit shook his head. "Piloting is second nature and driving is piloting," he said. He looked over at me. "Are you ready, Thena?"

As ready as I'd ever be. I nodded. We said our goodbyes, which seemed more formal and more prolonged than I expected. The doctor gave Kit a shot of something that was supposed to increase his blood production, recommending he drink a lot of water. He said the medicine was shockingly expensive and made a joking reference to deducting his fee from Kit's account, but I wasn't sure if he meant it, or if it was some elaborate verbal sparring between them.

I followed Kit out to the flyer and this time sat on the passenger seat, which had miraculously remained clear of blood, probably because most of it had gone on Kit's now discarded shirt and jacket.

"Are you cold?" I asked, though of course there was nothing I could do if he was. Except perhaps take off my shirt, which would probably make us both far warmer than we wanted to be. Or at least me. He was wearing a white bandage across newly seamed skin, put on by the doctor to keep the area undisturbed, he said. I understood though it was never explained the bandage was actually a bio construct and would drop off of its own accord when the wound was healed.

He shook his head. "It's no time at all to home," he said.

But when we got home, he parked the car and made no move at all to get out.

"Do you need help?" I asked. "To get out?"

He shook his head. "No." And gave a small, almost feral smile. "The grass is soft here, and the bio rug inside, should I fall." He took a deep breath. "Doctor Bartolomeu thinks I should tell you..."

"Doctor Bartolomeu assumes you and I are involved," I said. And, feeling my cheeks flame, "I think. He's very old-fashioned, isn't he?"

Kit drummed his fingers on the dashboard. "Yes, but . . . not in a way you'd expect. And no, I don't think he thinks we are involved. At least not if you mean physically."

"Uh. He said . . ."

"No. If we were involved physically . . ." Kit shook his head and looked away and out his side of the dashboard at the camellias in front of the flyer, as though they were worthy of a lot of attention and close scrutiny. "He'd probably have yelled at me."

"Because I'm an Earth—"

"No. Stop," Kit said. And his voice was so authoritative that I did stop before pronouncing the second half of the pejorative which he hadn't used for me in months. "No. Because I haven't told you . . . He thinks I should tell you . . ." He took a deep breath.

I bit the tip of my tongue, but I've never been good at keeping my mouth shut. It's just not part of who I am. I suspect it would have made my life much easier overall, let alone keeping my father untroubled for much longer if I'd been able to stop words from coming out when they wished to. "You don't need to tell me anything," I said. "We are not . . . we are not . . ." But it occurred to me that we were *involved* in an odd way. I'd been in his mind. He'd been in mine. What kind of link had that formed? What did it mean?

He took a deep breath. "Sometimes, when a child is in the bio-womb, both his parents die."

I had no idea what he was talking about and made a sound of complete confusion. He ignored the sound, or at least acted as if he'd not heard it. "When that happens, it is customary to decant the embryo. Unless, of course, someone is found who wishes to adopt it. Particularly if it's viable . . ." He took a deep breath. "When I was in the bio-womb both my parents died."

"But—"

He took another deep breath, noisy in the small flyer. "My father killed my mother and then himself. Normally, with us knowing what we know about heredity, and that certain . . . tendencies, if not the actions themselves are inherited . . . Well . . . In those circumstances . . ." He stopped, and took another deep breath. He was looking out his window and determinedly not at me. His fingers were playing over the dashboard, touching everything at random, very lightly. "The advised course is definitely to decant the embryo. And I wasn't . . . viable yet. But . . ." He shook his head.

"My father was one of Doctor Bartolomeu's friends. His closest friend you could say. And the doctor..." He shrugged. "He talked to the Denovos. They adopted me in the womb. Kath...Kath was fifteen. Anne was twenty-five. And they hadn't planned on having any more children, but my father is...He likes children. They were good parents to me."

"Why...Why tell me this?"

He looked at me then. "The doctor thought I should tell you," he said. "And after thinking about it, I thought I should too, because it will help you understand the situation that I've inadvertently thrown you in the middle of. You see, my wife...I never told Jane about my biological parents. I knew, but..." He shrugged. "It all seemed like something very distant. My adoptive parents told me when I was twelve, but they are the only parents I've ever known, and as I said, they've loved me and given me as stable a home as if I were of their blood. I know...I know I have a terrible temper." He smiled ruefully. "As you probably know too. But it was not something I thought about much. And it wasn't so much that I was keeping it from Jane, as that I never thought to tell her. And then...she noticed things. During...during our year of marriage. And we had an argument, while in space and I told her, and she..." He took a breath that sounded as if he were drowning. "She didn't take it well. And her family..." He shrugged and audibly whimpered, casting an annoyed look at his shoulder. "Her family heard about it and assumed..."

"That you killed her? Because of heredity? That's ridiculous. The doctor said something about deposing under hypnosis?"

"Not hypnosis. Hypnotics. There are certain drugs that will guarantee one tells the truth, or at least that one can't self-censure. And I could have someone guide me through the memory of Jane's death and talk and make a de facto record, but..."

"But you don't want the story of your real family to splash onto your adopted family," I said. "But...Kit, I think it's known. At least, one of the girls I work with...I mean, she hinted at it."

"Who my father was? That he and my mother..." Kit asked. "Sure. But not the details. It is the details I'd prefer aren't known." He took a deep breath and I could see him attempting to force himself to relax. "And now, if you'll forgive me, I'll go to my room and lie down. I don't think I'm quite as strong as I'd like to be."

⚜ TWENTY-ONE ⚜

FOR SOMEONE WHO WAS ONLY HALF STEADY ON HIS FEET, KIT moved fast enough. By the time I got into the house, he was nowhere in sight. His father was in the living room, watching a holo of what looked like news. He gave me a curious look, as I came in.

"I didn't injure Kit," I said, defensively. "It was Joseph Klaavil."

His father smiled. "I know that. He told me." But the curious, attentive look on me continued, as if he were trying to figure out what I'd done to irritate Kit. I couldn't tell him. He said, "He'll be fine, you know? He has an iron constitution."

"Yeah," I said. I could guess that from the fact that he'd gotten up from that sofa and torn off his IV without collapsing.

I realized I was shoving my hands into my pockets in exactly the same position that Kit usually held them while he was waiting for me to get off work. But then I didn't know what to do with them, and held them awkwardly in front of me, in a vaguely Asian pose. His father didn't seem to notice anything amiss.

"I'm sorry I didn't notice Joseph before he fired his burner," I said.

This got me a curious glance. "You're not Kit's bodyguard," his father said. "He's a grown man. If we could convince him to put an end to this...Duel the man or something, then pay the blood geld since it will always be considered a murder, when a cat duels a non-cat." He sighed. "But he is reluctant to do that."

147

I found my hands shoved in my pants pockets again, and this time tightened into hard fists. "He must have loved his wife very much."

"Jane?" his father said. "I think so. It was a boy-girl thing. First time he ever fell in love, you know?"

I knew. Or at least I suspected. I'd never loved anyone myself. Oh, I suppose Simon and I...could be more than friends. And I'd had lovers before, of course. But I'd not ever been in love.

My mind was full of the images and feel of his adoration for this woman who'd killed herself because she...what? Found out Kit's father had killed his mother then himself? What did that mean? Did she think that Kit was condemned to follow the actions of his ancestors? That didn't even make any sort of sense.

"Have you eaten?" Kit's father asked. In my mind he was always Kit's dad. And he wasn't even his real father.

"I've eaten, thank you," I said. "Kit brought a picnic."

He nodded. "I saw him assemble it." He opened his mouth, closed it, cleared his throat. "I just thought the shooting might have happened before you ate."

"No, it was afterwards," I said.

He returned to watching his holo. The house was very quiet which meant, I guessed, that all the children had gone to bed. And Waldron—who had been allowed to drive his grandfather's flyer until he could buy one of his own—would be out with his fiancée. I felt an incongruous wish to have Kath nearby. I had a feeling she would talk to me. Though exactly what we'd talk about and what she could tell me, I couldn't even guess. *I'm confused by looking into your brother's mind. I'm wistful. I didn't even know people loved each other like that. And for someone to kill herself when...*

I found I'd somehow made it to my room. From Kit's room came a swelling melody. For once a recording, not violin. Of course it wouldn't be violin. How could he play with his shoulder like that?

I stomped around the room. I didn't mean to stomp. It just seemed my steps turned into stomping. I was charged, nervous, full of energy I didn't know what to do with, and strangely very, very angry.

If I were on Earth, I'd be going to my broomer lair right now. I needed a flight over Syracuse Seacity. I could imagine the night sky above, the city lights under me, the wind rushing around me. I could almost taste the mix of sea air and city smells. I could feel the leathers on my body, protecting me from the cold of the upper air currents. I could imagine climbing more and more, till I had to put on the oxygen mask. I could imagine my lair behind me, the hand signals. *Climb, climb, climb.* Simon and Max and Fuse...

My hands were clenched tight. Very tight. So tight that my relatively short nails bit into my palms. I wanted to go home. I wanted to be where I understood the rules. I wanted to be where I had some control of the situation.

I stomped from one corner of the room to the other, diagonally skirting the bed. What the hell was I going to do? I truly was like the girl who had fallen down the rabbit hole and ended up in a world where up was down, down was up and nothing meant anything.

I wanted to go home. That's all I'd ever wanted to do since I'd escaped my father's goons in the powertrees. I'd been looking for a way out. I'd been looking for a harvester who would take me in. Instead, I'd found—

It was strange because I could remember my shock on first seeing Kit, remember it as clearly as if it were happening now. Those odd eyes, the shock of calico hair. Where had it gone, the instinctive repulsion I was supposed to feel at his bio-modifications? And why didn't I feel it? Why had I grown accustomed to his face, until I could read the expressions in his odd, inhuman eyes better than I could read human expressions?

The flinching, the pain, the impenetrable reserve. And behind it all those images of lost love playing, just like he obsessively played the gems of family times in the *Cathouse.*

Oh, he was the most *infuriating* man. My hands clenched tighter, which should have been impossible. Tight enough that my knuckles hurt.

And what the hell did he mean by telling me all these things about his father, about his mother? Couldn't he just have said that something had gone wrong, that he'd had a fight with his wife and she'd committed suicide? Why would he want to tell me this? More importantly, why did Doctor Bartolomeu think that he needed to tell me that? *The first time is an accident, the second is stupidity.*

I'd like to know what the good doctor thought he'd meant by

that. I'd like to know what he thought this was the second time of. I'd stomped all the way to the front of my closet and glared at it. I hadn't even bought any new clothes with my earnings. So far I'd deposited all my money into an account. I had a gem which gave me access to it, and that was it. I hadn't spent a single hydra.

My hands, somehow, shifted from my front pockets to my back pockets. I didn't want clothes. I didn't want to stay in Eden. I wanted to go back to Earth. I had responsibilities on Earth. Let Kit stay in Eden. Kit with his strange eyes, his stranger history, with this interminable feud that he refused to put the only logical end to.

Why had Doctor Bartolomeu assumed . . . Why had he thought that Kit needed to tell me anything? Why did he think I had a need to know?

I saw their interaction. The doctor knew him very well. Kit said that he knew we weren't physically involved.

Oh, it was hopeless. These people didn't have morals, just like they didn't have laws. But they did, they did, all the same. They just didn't write them anywhere, and it was impossible to figure them out.

The music from Kit's room swelled and fell in grandiose harmonies. I imagined him lying in his bed, his eyes closed, dreaming the music—being the music. His mind emptied of everything but the music.

The music seemed to be so much a part of who he was. It wound through all his memories like a bright thread. His memories. The memories I'd gotten from his mind.

The idea that he must, surely, have gotten memories from my mind as well, as surely as I got them from his, hit me full force. I stumbled back towards the bed, and fell to sitting on it.

What did he get from my mind? Images and experiences offered themselves. Boarding schools blazing brightly; mental specialists held at bay with sharp objects or even shards broken off furniture; my father in a fury standing over me, screaming; my broomer lair on a rampage laying waste to a bar in Olympus Seacity.

Oh, dear and merciful gods. What had he gotten from my mind? What had he seen? Was there anything he could have seen that wouldn't have horrified staid, self-controlled, responsible Kit Klaavil? Kit Klaavil who would rather endure fear of death than kill the brother of his late wife? Kit Klaavil who would rather risk his life, who would rather be shunned by the whole world than hurt his adoptive parents?

I heard a sound and felt it escape my throat, and didn't know if it was a laugh or a sob. No wonder he'd said he wasn't as strong as he wanted to be. No one was. Not when dealing with Mad Thena Lefty.

The music from his room crescendoed and fell and crescendoed again. He was probably submerging himself in the sound to wash away the unpleasant images and thoughts he'd gotten from me.

I don't know how long I sat there thinking. It wasn't as though I was thinking from point A to point B, or that I was thinking with any modicum of logic or intelligence. Instead thoughts crisscrossed in my mind that wouldn't bear examination in the full light of day. Such as that cats married navigators. And that no one—no one on Eden—married Earthworms.

And it was on this that I realized the crazy path my mind had taken, and I took it firmly in hand. I didn't want anyone to marry me. If, as I thought, Father was dead, then I would have to marry someone. In the fullness of time I would have to, to leave descendance to my line. But meanwhile, I would have Syracuse Seacity to rule, and a voice in the Council of Good Men, even if only as a regent because a woman couldn't hold governance of her own accord.

But if Father was dead he deserved that I, at the very least, try to avenge him. He hadn't been the best of fathers, though it could be argued that I hadn't been the best—or anything but the worst—of daughters. Duty was duty, and I was a Patrician of Earth and had been brought up for nothing if not to do my duty.

I had intended, in the nebulous future—or not so nebulous—after Kit went on his next run, which I understood could be spaced as little as two months or as much as six months apart, to break into my place of employment and steal a ship.

The cargo ships that flew to Thule were a lot like Earth flyers and I'd been flying those since I was ten.

I knew I could fly the cargo ship to Earth. I'd seen maps enough since I was here, and calculating where Eden was on its irregular but predictable orbit was a matter of memory and spacial reasoning, both of which were my strong points.

Oh, I knew Eden's fears of betrayal. And I wouldn't betray them. No. Not because of Eden. I didn't give a hang about Eden, in the end. With their fear of Earthworms, their strange non-law laws, their certainty of being in the right, they were no better than Earth and they might be worse. But I did care about Kit, who had saved my life. And for his family who had sheltered me for a month—even his father who seemed eternally concerned over whether I'd gotten enough calories and had quite enough water to bathe in.

I wouldn't do that to them. I wouldn't betray them in exchange for their kindness. But there were many places on Earth I could land undetected and burn the ship. Most of old Europe was depopulated. And from there I could find my way to a communication device and call for rescue. Once I was on Earth...

My body ached for the sun of Earth, for wind on my face, for the sight of the ocean.

I had intended to wait, but this wouldn't do. For all I knew, from what the doctor had said, that only married couples could communicate telepathically with each other, Kit would now feel obligated to marry me. As though I were some Victorian maiden and he'd compromised my honor. It sounded exactly like the stupid sort of thing the infuriating man would decide he must do. Like...keep alive an idiot who was trying to murder him.

And he must not be allowed to marry me. No. There was misery. And then there was the sheer torture Kit Klaavil and I could inflict on each other. And no one deserved that. Not even Kit Klaavil, not even my—admittedly troublesome—self. Marrying me would be the shortest route he could take to his natural parents' end.

I threw the closet open again and picked out a black tunic and a black, fitted pair of pants. The gem that gave me access to my entire account, such as it was, went into my right-hand pocket. The burner I had taken from Joseph Klaavil—and that no one had thought to ask me for—went into my left-hand pocket.

A change of underwear or spare clothes seemed unnecessary. Any ship I could take would have a vibro unit. And I would be alone, so why bother changing clothes beyond vibroing?

There was a side entrance to the house by Kit's room. I took it, as I went silently out into the night to steal a collector ship.

◖◖ TWENTY-TWO ◗◗

I COULDN'T TAKE ONE OF THE FAMILY FLYERS. NOT THAT IT WAS possible for me to do so without tampering with the genlock. Of course, if the genlock was like on Earth, you could bypass it completely, so I probably could do that. But it would take too long, it might set off an alarm—or two—and even if everything went as perfectly as I could hope for, it would be a really bad thing for it to be discovered before I left. Without it, they might think I'd simply gone somewhere in the house and was taking in a virtus or swimming in the pool on the lower level. The thing was that without a careful search for me, they would never know I was gone. And they had no reason to do a search for me.

But I'd learned something, in the times Kit had been unable to pick me up. You could call a cab from various points in each neighborhood and from each public building. There were these little towers that looked remarkably like miniatures of the traffic control towers on Earth. You could punch your details in them, and where you wished to go and an automated flyer would come, which would drive you to your destination without your contributing anything to the flying.

The vehicles were safe, Kit said. And he should know, because he dodged any number of them while flying across town. On the other hand, at the time I was leaving the Denovo compound even most bars, certainly most restaurants and almost all public buildings were closed or staffed by a skeleton crew. Enough that I wasn't

153

too afraid, even as the flyer came to the Center and dodged the inevitable late-night partygoers and people returning from visits.

It parked me in front of the Energy Board Center and let me out, after I swept my gem through the reader, paying for the ride. I knew at night the building was unattended. I didn't know if it would let me in. The genlocks had been programmed for me, but that was during the day.

However, as I pressed my thumb to the gen-reading membrane on the side door—which I normally used when coming to work in the morning—it popped unlocked for me. So far so good. I slid to my locker, got my work suit—a bright yellow and made of some material that eschewed stains. If someone caught me wandering around the complex and I were properly attired and carrying my tools, I could claim I had come to work early because some problem in one of ships under retrofitting bothered me. If all else failed, I could claim that I had been sleep-walking. And the tools might come in handy in space. And I happened to know that Kit had paid for them.

The ship we'd gone over this afternoon hadn't been cleared from the dock—meaning that we still had access to its genlock. On the other hand, I knew, from having crawled all over it just this afternoon, there was nothing wrong with it.

To make it better and to assuage my aching conscience, the ship was not privately owned—as most ships were—by the couple flying them. It was one of the few rental ships owned by the Energy Board itself—like the *Cathouse*. They were usually rented by couples starting out and saving to have their own ship built. I had no idea why Kit rented the *Cathouse*, though it probably had the lowest rental fees ever, but it was on the borderline of unsafe.

I considered stealing the *Cathouse* and, to be honest, if it had been where I could get it, I might have. But I also knew it was on a long contract with Kit, which meant his possessions were in it, and stealing his gems with family occasions seemed like the last of unkindest cuts.

As it was, I was sure that he would feel betrayed when he found me missing. Relieved too, I thought, but definitely betrayed. And I wished I could have left him a note. But I could not afford to have them discover it too soon.

So I would make do with this ship. It belonged to a young couple, Dawn and Sean Heigle, and it was christened *Howl At The*

Moon. They preferred to do Thule runs, normally the province of those too old to do pod runs. Who knew why? Probably because it demanded less concentration and they were honeymooners.

I climbed into it, through its extended ladder—unlike the *Cathouse*, the door was a good bit off the ground—pushed my thumb into the lock. Then closed the door. Above me was one of the ejection locks—it was there because someone was supposed to take *Howl At The Moon* out in the morning to test it, since we hadn't found any of the issues the couple flying it had complained about.

From the testing and the manuals, I knew the procedure for getting out. First you turned on the systems, which needed to warm up for about half an hour. I was in the cat cabin, because the navigator cabin, though it had screens, had no controls. Just the ability to dictate controls to the cats.

I turned the engines on, then started doing system checks, while I adjusted the screen to be able to see in it. It could be adjusted because repair people, obviously, weren't cats. And mechanics had to be able to see.

While the engines warmed and the systems ran self-checks, I started mentally calculating my path out of here, via that opening right above me. Oh, lifting straight up sounded easy. But how fast would I be going? It had to be calculated to give the membrane time to open, but not so slow that you scraped your way out.

"*Howl At The Moon*, what is happening? Who is in there?"

The voice, deep and masculine, startled me.

Voice only, of course they couldn't see that I was wearing my official work suit and had my tools at my feet and everything, so that wasn't going to act as my shield of righteousness, was it?

In this type of situation, there were two things you could do. One of them was to tell the truth. The other was to tell a lie. And then the third which was my way. "I'm Athena Hera Sinistra," I said.

"The Earther?" the masculine voice said. "The mechanic? What are you doing in the *Howl At The Moon*?"

"Testing it."

"In the middle of the night?" the voice said, and then, after a pause. "You are not cleared to test it."

"I thought I'd solve some issues with it." I was checking the warming-up status of the ship. Damn it. I wasn't going to be able to take off in under half an hour. "Nav Heigle said she had some unexplained issues with the air system."

It wasn't that the engines could not lift me off well before that, mind you, it was that none of the life support systems would be ready to go. And even I was a little leery of lifting off world without air, water or lights. Particularly since lifting off before they were ready could damage them.

"Truly, I'm just checking some things. I'll be out in a moment," I said. Which was true. I intended to be out of the world as soon as humanly possible. Of course, I sort of hoped he wouldn't take it that way.

The problem with this was that pumping up the air and water systems meant literally filling reserve tanks. Sucking things from pipes attached to the ship. Which meant they would show in the dials of whoever was monitoring this. I wondered who it was. It sounded like the same lovely man who had welcomed Kit and me to Eden.

"Why are you filling the life support systems?" he asked. "It is not safe for them to be filled while parked." And he threw the override switch.

Fortunately, while I am, often, many kinds of fool, I am not exactly trusting. I'd thought he might do this, so I had already taken the front panel off the relevant part of the *Howl At The Moon*, and was happily tweaking it, so that the override would have no effect.

"Stop," the functionary said. "Stop immediately. You are in contravention of the orders and regulations of the Energy Board."

Um. Soft soap and *I'm just testing* had probably lost its usefulness. Yeah, I'd only cursorily considered it, anyway. I knew sooner or later, they'd realize they were being robbed. I had twenty-five minutes left.

I leapt across the control room to the controls and slammed my palm hard against the button that shut and sealed the door. This done, only the Heigles would be able to get in, and I doubted they could get them out of bed and here in time. Still, because I am not a trusting woman, I slammed an additional lock across the back of the door, manually. It made the genlock ineffective. Why it was there, I couldn't figure. Except that I was starting to think Edenites were more paranoid than I. They probably expected to be boarded while in one of the Thules, and they wanted to be able to lock from the inside in case someone defeated the genlock. Right. My being from Earth, the idea sounded lunatic to me. On the other hand, having seen how Kit first received me, I doubted it was as lunatic as it sounded. Kit didn't strike me as particularly paranoid—not about Earth, not after knowing me. If he had believed that his ship might be boarded in the energy trees, then doubtless all of them did. At any rate I was grateful for the locks, as I turned to survey the progress of the system warm-up.

"You locked the ship!" the voice squawked over the communicator.

I hadn't known they had a way to tell. And I didn't bother to answer. I didn't know what I could tell them that would calm them down in any way. Instead, I looked at the levers and studied the levels of various things. But staring at the gauges wouldn't make them go any further, so I went down the hallway to the nav cabin, to see what could help me find my way to Earth.

The maps were programmed to be erased at the push of a button, at least on Earth runs. Were they programmed here too? Maps to Earth? Or just to the Thules? Well, I had seen maps while traveling here with Kit, the orbit of the asteroid that had been co-opted to create Eden was available in school programs which I'd been free to peruse for the last month. And the nav cabin contained some of the best calculators ever invented by mankind. In the *Cathouse*, they were consolidated into the cat cabin and I'd seen Kit use them.

But I had no time to worry about any of this and Kit was, for now, irrelevant to my plans, except that I must get away from Eden as soon as possible before I made his life worse. I was trying out the calculators to confirm that they were as simple to operate as I'd thought from watching Kit. Well, simple for anyone with an understanding of space mathematics.

Of course, it had never been part of my curriculum, but I'd studied it, nonetheless, when I'd gotten bored with everything else.

The speaker crackled and I sighed. More from the man in the control tower.

I started towards the cat cabin, determined to turn off the com, so they couldn't talk to me anymore. What was the point of talking. I was going to take off and that was that.

"Thena!"

It wasn't the man in the control tower, the anonymous stranger I'd been bucking. It was Kit, his voice strange. It sounded like he'd hiccupped at the end of the word.

I didn't answer. Not obstinate. I couldn't speak. I couldn't find words or voice. What could I tell Kit? I'd hoped he didn't find out till it was too late. I hoped he wouldn't care.

"Thena!" More imperious, with a touch of fear, as if he thought I was dead—as though he thought I'd locked myself in someone's long distance ship to kill myself. A grand and ridiculous gesture, worthy of Earth's baroque period. Kit liked music. Did he like opera?

"I'm here," I said, speaking in a soft, trembling voice, towards the nowhere in particular that picked up sounds.

A heavy exhalation that I shouldn't be able to hear, and then something that ended with "Blazing Light," which was his way of swearing. And then, "What are you doing? They say you're stealing the ship. What did you do to make them think that?"

Before I could stop it, laughter gurgled up and out of me. "I am stealing the ship," I said. "As soon as I can make it take off."

A long silence extended after that, punctured, oddly, by sounds of heavy breathing, as if he were running. Was he hurting? Had he hurt himself again? I thought I knew what was happening. The traffic controller had patched through to Kit's home, had got him on the home com. I was linked through two coms. But why was he breathing as if he'd been running, unless he were in pain?

"You shouldn't have left the doctor so soon," I said.

"What?" He sounded as if I were speaking a foreign language, and didn't follow the conversation. "You can't take off, Thena. Please unlock the door. Put the stairs down."

"No."

"You have to. What are you going to do?"

"Go to Earth," I said. My reasoning, not clear but intense, in my room before I decided to come here, erupted out of me in semicoherent words, "I'll never have a place in Eden," I said. "I'm not... I'm not a cat, or a nav."

"You're a mechanic!" he said. "What do you mean you have no place?"

"I don't..." I almost said I didn't belong to anyone, but what kind of reasoning was that? I didn't belong to anyone on Earth, either, except to Father and I'd rather not belong to him. "I'll never be at home here."

"Rubbish!" he said. More of the labored breathing and something that sounded like a gasp. Also a hiss, steady, intermittent. It sounded, I thought, like the torch I used in welding ceramite, while working. But it was not going steady. It was hiss, stop, hiss, stop, hiss. "You are home."

"No. I could . . . If I lived here my whole life, I'd still not be home."

Something like cursing, low, under his breath. A mutter, mutter, mutter that could not be fully understood. And then a sound like something hitting the door hard.

"I don't want to betray Eden," I said in a rush. "I don't want to betray you. I'll go back and land in a deserted place. I'll destroy the ship. I'll—"

"Nonsense," the word barely audible through labored breathing. "Athena Hera Sinistra, unlock this damn door."

I didn't know why. I didn't know how, but I knew—knew with absolute certainty that he was outside that door, that he'd done something to bypass the genlock, that only the additional lock was keeping him out.

I couldn't let him in. I had no idea how he could have gotten up to the door. With the stairs retracted—which they were by virtue of the ship being closed—the only way up was by rolling a cumbersome ladder up. Had Kit done that? The thought of Kit, as I'd last seen him, still recovering from that wound, climbing a ladder was not something I wanted to contemplate.

What would possess him to do that? The foolish man must truly feel he had some duty to me.

I rushed across the cabin to the board and glared at the indexes for readiness. It was almost—almost ready to go. Almost. I closed my eyes and made an executive decision. Simon always says sometimes you need to close your eyes and say *what the hell*. Of course normally he means this just before jumping off some sort of peak, headed for almost sure death. But this—but in the details—was the same.

It was as if I'd been run off my feet and peacekeepers were on my tail, and ready to book me. I had to get out of Eden forever or allow Kit to condemn us both to sheer hell.

"I will never betray you," I said, hoping he was still listening to the com, and I shoved both fingers on the starting buttons. Below me the engines hiccupped and choked, then hummed their starting song. Now, now, now, any second now, they'd kick to full life and take off.

"Damned idiot." The words were clear, very clear. They were also roared. And followed by a hiss like a thousand torches cutting at the door.

And then the door... well, it looked like it caved inward, followed by Kit tumbling into the control chamber. He was pale as death, so pale that it looked impossible for him to be standing. He wore the pants he'd been wearing before, and a rumpled tunic that looked like he'd rescued it unvibroed from his laundry pile. Which was probably exactly what he'd done.

His hair was wild and uncombed, his teeth clenched tight together, visible through lips parted in a rictus that wasn't a smile. He had a five-o'clock calico shadow. He held a burner in his hand. It was cocked at full power.

⠶ TWENTY-THREE ⠶

A BURNER. COCKED TO FULL BURN. THE WORDS FORMED AS I was sailing through the air, in best ballet form, my foot arched gracefully towards his burner hand.

And my foot was caught in his hand and I was on my back on the floor. Again.

Only this time, unlike our sparring in the *Cathouse*, he didn't stop to make pithy remarks. Instead, he had gone past me—cat-speed, I thought, *the reason cats can't duel non-cats*—and he was at the controls, pushing the cancel buttons. Beneath me, the engines spluttered and died down.

I dove at his ankles, pulled. He fell with a sickening thud. He crashed as if he'd not had time to prepare—which was wrong. *Cats always fall on their feet.* No, wait. That was Earth cats. Kit was all homo sapiens.

I looked at his face. He'd fallen on his back, and he was still, his eyes wide. *I've killed him.* But I had a suspicion that, just like vampires, Kit couldn't be killed by anything short of separating his head from his body and burying the two on different sides of a river. Hell, for him, different *ends* of a river.

As if to prove me right, his chest rose once, deeply, then fell, he turned to look at me, his eyes wide open. *Thena.*

He was in my mind. I pushed back, pushed him away from controlling my body, dragged myself to my knees, forced myself up to the controls, reached for the buttons.

Thena, no. Damn you to all the hells of the ancients. What kind of man thought that at you in a soft, sweet way, as if he were gentling down a child.

Whatever kind of man he was, he was on me. More or less literally, pinning me between himself and the controls and doing something, fast, fast to the keyboard. His fingers danced the entrechat on the keys, something beeped with a final sound.

I turned on Kit, without pausing to think. I flailed against him, all teeth and nails. He'd turned off the ship, and now I was here forever. I was trapped in Eden for eternity. A stranger. Lost. I'd never see the ocean again, I'd never see the sky of Earth. I'd never glide, silent and sure above sleeping Syracuse Seacity. I'd never—

Hush, hush, hush. His hands held my wrists. He held me clamped down just off the control panel on the surface that, in the *Cathouse,* he used to balance a reader or—sometimes—to put his feet on, while he shepherded the progression of the ship through its slow path to the powertrees and back again. I saw him there, as I'd seen him so many times onboard the *Cathouse.* In a month—or less—he'd be gone on his route. I'd never see him in the *Cathouse* again. Eventually the whole problem with the Klaavils would die down, and he would be married again. And I...I might get to detail their ship.

Thena, this is not the time. I had no idea what he'd got from my mind, but he was holding me tight against the panel, his hands almost cutting circulation to my wrists, his body holding me immobile. Incongruously, his mental voice was full of tenderness and laughter. And I tried to twist out of his grasp and—

The side of my work suit was soaked. Looking down, I realized there was a blood stain on me and Kit's dark tunic—though it barely showed it, being a silver-grey—was dark down the side.

Kit, your wound, you—

Not the time. His mental voice now sounded clipped, short.

We must—

"Cat Klaavil? Mistress Sinistra?"

We sprang apart as if we'd been doing something indecent, which I suppose we had—mind-linked and pressed together—and turned to look at the man who'd come in. He was not the bureaucrat who had received us. This was a younger and more composed model, the vigorous and purposeful category, with dark hair and a nicely fitting uniform. From the steely spark in his eyes, he was the sort of man one expected to see in history holos framed over some caption like *the general on the eve of the battle.*

Instead he was a second-class bureaucrat, manning a control tower at night. The chasm between his abilities and his actual post clearly galled him. He strode towards us with the look that—were we an enemy army—would have made us lay down our arms, and possibly weep for redemption.

We weren't an enemy army. Kit let go of me and stood straight, squaring his shoulders. His cat eyes, now easily readable to me, reflected utter disdain for this intruder. "Yes?"

"You are charged with crimes against the Energy Board— vandalism of property and attempted theft. We can get a judge on the case, or we can total a bill for the damages and send you the accounting. Do you have some doubt about your legal responsibility?"

If Kit managed to look any more disdainful, the sheer force of his haughtiness would turn the functionary into a puddle on the floor. "None whatsoever," he said. "I will give you my account."

The functionary's eyes sparked back. I knew that look. A wolf smelling a tasty sheep. "It is likely to come to around a million hydras."

Kit's shoulders went yet more square. The side of his tunic was now dark, from the shoulder down. I wondered if the functionary didn't realize Kit was bleeding. I did. I could smell the sickening-sweet scent of blood. "If I do not have enough, you can indenture me for the remaining."

"I will."

"This is nonsense," I snapped. "I'm the one who should be indentured for the remaining," I said. "I am the one who tried to steal a ship. Not him."

Now the functionary turned to me, and his features managed to reflect even more disdain than Kit had bent on him. Kit, meanwhile, was not even looking at me, but straight ahead, his features steely.

"Did Cat Klaavil not sign a contract of responsibility for you, as his legal ward?"

"Yes," I said, but then because this made no sense. "But it doesn't matter. I am of age, I have a job. If there is a bill to pay, I should be the one paying it." I made fifty hydras a month. Kit made a thousand or so per trip. His trips took...three to six months? Everyone tried for the times when the Earth was closer, but if you wanted to keep bringing in pods, you had to work year-around. How many could he take a year? I know they had downtime between the trips. I tried to calculate it. As I was in the middle of trying to figure out how many zeros to carry on my way to realizing I'd just signed Kit's life earnings away, I heard Kit say, "It's irrelevant. She is my ward. I will pay. You may call me at home. If I am not there, you may leave a message either directly or with my father."

"Kit."

This is not the time, Thena.

But you can't. You didn't do anything. This will take your entire life earnings.

Not. The. Time.

I stared at him, but he just looked ahead. "Feel free to call me with the total," he said. "I shall discuss the means of settling it, then." And with that haughty, looking-above-it-all expression he strode out of the ship. *Come, Thena.*

I wouldn't have obeyed. After all, what I really felt like doing was testing my theory of the vulnerable points of the human male on the bureaucratic twit who was facing Kit. But if I killed him—and I might very well, if I got going—then I would stick Kit with the price for the blood geld. So I ran after Kit as he marched from the ship and down the steps the twit bureaucrat had, at least, had the decency to provide.

I caught up with him by his flyer, which was parked just steps from the ship, which meant that he had somehow managed to fly into an area that was technically closed to traffic. I wondered if he'd flown through the building. I was sure that this was impossible, that some of the doors were too small.

However, I was about to get a lesson in how wrong I could be, when he got in, sat down and barked at me: "Buckle."

For the next two minutes we flew—sometimes upside down or sideways through the doors and across the halls of the Energy Board Center, until we exited the main door. We flew over flyers being repaired and sideways between the desks of the processing office, while I held my breath. Instead of heading to the garage, the way we had when we arrived, he took the way up as I did when I met him in front of the building.

As soon as we were through the front door, Kit landed in a

parking space, pulled on the communicator pin he was wearing on his sleeve, and said, "Doctor Bartolomeu."

By the time the doctor answered, his voice sounding tinny through the pin, "Christopher?" Kit had opened the door and was throwing up, noisily, onto the pavement. I wanted to hold his head, or smack him for being an idiot, but I couldn't do either. Instead, I spoke into the pin.

"We're outside the Energy Board Center," I said. "I think Kit tore open the seam on his wound."

✺ TWENTY-FOUR ✺

"DRINK," THE DOCTOR SAID. HE HELD A CUP TO KIT'S MOUTH. For a moment—considering the way Kit had behaved for the last hour—I expected Kit to press his lips together, or turn his head away. Instead, he took the cup in his left hand and drank, while the doctor worked on his right side.

We were in the doctor's flyer, a large one—probably originally designed as a carrier van. In contrast with his house, the place—he called it his surgery, like doctors in the ancient British Commonwealth, referring to their offices—was modern and immaculate. All glimmering surfaces and smooth dimatough.

Kit was hooked up to at least three machines and the doctor was doing something to his shoulder that involved glasses and something that looked like tweezers but wasn't. It looked like he was gluing the two halves of the wound together, but he'd snapped at me when I'd asked. "No. I'm seaming them properly together with new-healed growth. Deep seaming this time, unlike last, when I thought I could trust Christopher not to tear his shoulder apart again."

Kit had tried to protest, "But she was going to get herself killed. She was—"

"Shut up," the doctor had ordered. "You don't have the strength to talk and I'd like to keep you alive, heaven knows why."

Kit had lost consciousness before the doctor arrived and despite the fact that he'd been given an injector that was supposed to help him produce more blood, despite the fact that he was hooked up to an intravenous drip that was replenishing his blood, and despite his having another three machines doing who knew what to him, he still looked half dead. The eyelids he shared with the rest of the human race were half lowered. From beneath it, his nictitating eyelids kept trying to close and protect his eyes. He looked... miserable, like a child caught playing in the rain and scolded.

The doctor worked steadily, mending his shoulder. "I didn't do this before," he said, "because it takes a very long time. And Christopher doesn't like to stay still or in a position of weakness for very long. Do you?"

"I—"

"No, don't talk. I told you you haven't the strength." The doctor glanced up at me before returning to work on Kit, and said, "As for you—"

I braced, afraid of what he might ask me to do. I was very much afraid he would order me to dance while standing still. It seemed to be the sort of thing he was doing to Kit.

Instead he said, "I don't understand how, but you must be related to Alexander."

This didn't seem to be anything I could answer. I caught a desperate glimmer from Kit's eyes that read like a warning, but I had no idea what the warning could be. What the doctor said seemed just disappointed scolding, as he added, "What did you think you were doing?"

I clenched my hands. I stood near Kit, watching him sip whatever the concoction was in the cup, and there were things I was not about to tell the doctor, particularly not in front of Kit. Like the fact that I'd realized I needed to run away from Kit because I was afraid he would tie us together forever out of some misguided sense of obligation.

Instead I said, "I needed to go to Earth. I have reason to believe my father is dead. I owe my domains on Earth a duty that—"

Kit glared at me and looked like he would open his mouth to speak, and I decided to stop him before he could. "I was not going to betray Eden. I beg you to believe that I have more sense than that. Most people here never did anything to deserve being betrayed." Was that a shadow crossing Kit's veiled gaze? "And I don't want a world's destruction on my conscience, anyway. I was going to fly to Earth and ditch in one of the areas of Old Europe that are depopulated. Then I was going to find the nearest station and call for help. After I destroyed the ship."

Doc Bartolomeu was quiet for a while. When he spoke, it was to make a deep, vibrating noise that sounded somewhere between *um* and a groan. "Have you no sense?"

"She's nineteen!" Kit put in, in the tone of defending me.

"And you're three years older," the doctor said. "What is that supposed to mean?"

"That her life hasn't been like ours," Kit said, his voice acerbic.

"You're talking. I told you not to speak. You have no strength to speak."

Kit used whatever strength he did have to say a very nasty word in ancient German before sipping his medicine again. The doctor countered by pretending not to hear.

"I don't see where I'm failing in sense," I said. "It is my duty to go back to Earth. I understand it is not in the best interests of the people here on Eden, but it is still my duty, and I thought this way I could fulfill it with minimal damage. I can't see how this was so irresponsible."

"Christopher would have been indentured beyond his productive life. Just the repairs on the ship, as is—"

"I don't see why he should be punished for my actions!" I said, mostly to avoid the deep, abiding feeling that I would, in fact, have been paying back Kit's kindness with a horrible injury. I hadn't asked him to save me. Twice. I told myself that, but it didn't seem to help.

"My dear girl, have you no respect for contracts, obligations and one's word of honor?"

I didn't. I'd never given anyone my word of honor and never entered a contract, so I had no idea why I should respect what other people did on my behalf. Kit was not my father, nor my guardian in fact. The notion seemed nonsensical.

"He brought you to Eden and he freely assumed responsibility over you."

It was on my tongue to say I didn't ask him to, but I met Kit's gaze at that moment, serious, concerned, as he stared at me. "That's not why I went after her," he said. His voice sounded distant, dreamy. I wondered what was in the beverage the doctor had him sip. "I went after you," he said, looking at me now, "because otherwise they would have shot you out of the sky. You see, I should have told you, should have explained long ago that if you try to leave Eden without being cleared, you will get killed, and the ship destroyed with you."

I opened my mouth. He'd saved my life yet again. And I still hadn't asked him to. I felt vaguely angry at his interference and mad at myself for being angry. "I didn't ask—"

"No," he said, very softly. "I didn't want you dead. That's all. Screw the payment. It's just hydras. I can always make more. But I didn't want you dead."

"Oh." If I had a way out of here without stealing his flyer—which right now seemed a way of adding insult to injury—I would have taken it. I didn't want to think about the fact that he didn't want me dead—or that he was the first person ever to express that opinion. "My father would be disappointed in you."

I meant it as a joke, but he didn't laugh. Instead, he turned to the doctor, "Is this going to take much longer?"

"Yes. Be quiet. The more you talk the longer it will take. Considering how little you like talking, I wonder at the sudden garrulousness. What possessed you," he said, and did something with his tool that caused Kit to yelp, before he caught himself, "to go climbing while your shoulder had only the thinnest seam of skin over a healing wound? And you had taken only one dose of blood replenisher?"

"I don't know. I was bored. There was nothing good on the sensi. *Why* do you think I went climbing with an ill-healed wound?" It was the first time I'd heard Kit snap at the doctor.

"Uh. See, you're not well enough to speak. This irritability is one of the symptoms of near shock. As is nausea." He looked at one of the machines. "And you're still tachycardic."

For a moment, as Kit pulled the cup away from his lips, I thought he was going to throw it across the flyer, probably breaking something expensive and irreplaceable. He gave every impression of counting backward from a hundred, then forward to a hundred again. "You," he said at last, "could make a dead man tachycardic through sheer annoyance."

To my surprise, as I expected them to escalate the fight, the doctor laughed. Or rather he cackled, a delighted cackle that went with his gnomic appearance. "You are so like your father."

"So I'm told," Kit said. And then, before the tone of his voice—flat, unemotional—could draw comment, he said, "I climbed the side of the ship because Thena wasn't opening the door and lowering the stairs." He took a sip from his cup, then added, "I melted shallow depressions with my burner and climbed."

"And it didn't occur to you this might kill you?" the doctor asked.

Kit tried to shrug and got an almost-growl from the doctor, which caused him to say, "All right, all right. Yes, it occurred to me, but damn it, if I didn't do it, she was going to die."

"Your mouth out of order?" the doctor asked. "You couldn't tell her they would shoot her out of the sky?"

"I wouldn't have believed him," I said, thinking I had to defend Kit. If he really was too ill to speak, and heaven knows he looked it, I didn't want to cause him to die. Besides, it was true. "I would have thought he was lying to me to get me to open the door."

The doctor looked up at me, snorted. "You make a fine pair."

He returned to work on Kit's shoulder. "And what are you going to do now, Christopher?"

Kit made a sound at the back of his throat. "I was thinking of taking up stripping for additional money."

This was probably the effect of whatever the mixture he'd been drinking was, because the doctor looked at him as if he were stupid. Kit sighed. "The official who met us on arrival wanted me to strip."

The doctor snorted again, this time impatiently. He looked at me. "Miss Sinistra... Would you try to do this again, if Christopher went on one of his runs and left you behind?"

I shook my head. I wouldn't. I wouldn't because I hated the idea of being indebted to anyone. And I hated the idea of getting Kit into yet more debt than he was.

"And why should we trust you?" the doctor asked. "If you have no respect for contracts?"

I didn't know. In fact, all of my history argued for not trusting me. I looked at him and was silent.

TWENTY-FIVE

"YOU CAN TRUST ME, KIT, TRULY," I SAID, AND I WAS ALMOST sure I meant it. We were back at the music center, and I was wearing the red dress because, for reasons unknown to me, it seemed to be Kit's favorite. Which was odd, as it was a lot more staid than most things people wore in Eden. Kit was wearing what was for him a frankly subdued suit tailored much like his uniform—meaning it looked like what a renaissance doublet and hose would look like after death if they had been a particularly good suit of clothes and deserving of heaven. It outlined his shoulders, highlighted his waist and did things to his leg muscles that would make a sculptor cry in despair at not being able to capture that sort of beauty.

All of it was enough to make me forget that the cloth shone in clashing flashes of silver and gold whenever he moved, and that he was very silent, even for Kit.

We'd sat through the entire program in silence, of course. Even I wasn't rude enough to talk while others were playing well-rehearsed pieces. Music as a rule doesn't do much for me. Oh, it takes my head to a blank space, if that makes sense. I can appreciate the music on a sensory level and I'd sat through enough holo lectures on music and the history of music that I could have talked for hours about this technique and that innovation.

Wasn't about to. Not unless someone made me. It wasn't true, any of it, as far as I was concerned. It was just like all the other stuff you learned so you could make polite conversation, but which meant nothing much. I didn't want to do that to Kit and besides, Kit understood music. Music was somehow wired into his mind in a way that it was like a language. Even while he sat, listening to the program, I could see his hand moving, his eyes narrowing. I didn't know and wasn't about to ask if it was just that he'd detected some minor error in the performance or if it was something else—like it had just occurred to him why that movement worked. I'd had enough of Kit's lectures on music in the *Cathouse* and it all worked out to one thing—I didn't understand it and he did. Having him go on about it wouldn't make me any more enlightened on the matter than having an expert explain to me the syntax of a language I didn't speak. Ancient Norse, perhaps.

Instead, I'd waited for intermission and started trying to talk to him then. Little things, you know. *Should we go get something to drink?* And *Isn't it a lovely night?* If we'd been on Earth I'd have been talking about the weather, only of course, the weather, like law and order, was not something that had ever visited Eden.

Kit smiled a little at a couple of my questions, but didn't answer. He took me to a table on the side of the broad terrace that sprawled in front of the music building, punched in codes and got me a fizzy blue drink with a little umbrella, just like in old-time holos. It didn't taste alcoholic, but nothing in Eden tasted alcoholic. I sipped it. He got himself something clear, which could be water or bug juice or perhaps some high-octane alcoholic concoction. He sipped it in silence. I tried to ask polite questions, but he just smiled. His eyes were as unreadable to me as when I'd first met him and his expression was bland and good-humored, but it didn't seem *right*.

I got tired of the sound of my own voice and shut up. We went back inside and listened to the rest of the program. And then we came out again. Kit started down the steps to the flyer he'd left parked on the street, but I grabbed his hand. "No."

It was the first time I touched him without his expecting it—at least outside my attempting to kill him—the first time I touched him at all outside our practice fights.

I half expected him to somehow grab my foot and leave me sprawling on the dimatough that someone had striated to look like pink-veined white marble. Alternately, I expected him to pull his hand away and continue down the steps to his flyer.

I would have followed, of course. What else could I do? I had no other way home. Oh, perhaps a cab, but I didn't want that sort of anger between us the day before he left to go out in the *Cathouse* again. Which he was doing and which, of course, was what this was all about.

But he didn't even pull his hand away from mine. Instead, he looked down at our hands. His hand felt warm. I had grabbed hold of his thumb and index finger, awkwardly. "No?" he said.

"No. We must talk," I said. "I don't want you to leave like this."

He frowned and smiled at the same time, his forehead wrinkling, his eyebrows arching, his mouth tilting upwards a little. "Have to, Thena. Have a debt to pay."

I wanted to stomp my foot and scream at him that I knew damn well. But I would not, because he was leaving tomorrow and I didn't want that between us. "A million hydras," I said.

"Nah." His smile got more mischievous. "The idiot was grossly exaggerating. Barely five hundred thousand. If I were doing a normal collection, I could pay it off in five years, no problem."

"Normal...?"

"With a navigator," he said. "And not the *Cathouse*, but a proper ship."

"Why the *Cathouse*?"

"They won't rent me one of the better ships," he said. "Flying alone is a high risk, and they just won't do it. And then..." He shrugged. "I can't collect as much because I have no nav. I can sort of do the turn of a nav, but it takes very long, and I can only collect while the powertrees are on the dark side. Otherwise the harvesters from Circum will be out. And they'll see me."

"Oh." I'd never asked, though all of it were things I could have realized, of course, if I'd thought about it. "You could stay two nights?"

"Would have to get away so far during the day and use so much fuel to go back it would make the rest of the collection less profitable till it enters diminishing returns. But mostly...it's high risk. They teach us never to go back, not two nights in a row. If someone has spotted us, it makes the chances of our getting caught that much higher. They could be keeping an eye on us..."

I wanted to tell him that Eden was paranoid, that as a collective society they were more paranoid than even I managed. But again, I didn't want to upset him on the eve of his going off to space. This being-nice-and-polite thing was probably going to kill me. All the anger and casual irritation I was used to giving vent to, would just grow up inside me and suffocate me.

Instead of speaking, I pulled him politely to one of the fake marble tables, where we'd sat before. I noted—though I'd stopped *noticing*—that, as every time I was with Kit, we moved within a space of solitude. It wasn't anything so blatant as people scampering to get away from us, with horror stamped on their features. It was more like they contrived not to be in the space around us, or the place where we were supposed to go.

The effect of it was that we moved in our own private bubble. It sometimes made me wonder what would happen if we should both undress and dance on top of tables. But I had a strong suspicion no one would really see us. Kit didn't seem to notice the space of solitude, nor the way people's glances slid off him. I wondered if this was true. I had learned the concoction Doctor Bartolomeu made him drink the night I tried to steal the ship was something that helped his stomach. Which appeared to be what hurt when Kit was very busy not showing either anger or pain.

Though as I pulled him to the table and sat down on one of the chairs, more or less forcing him to sit down across from me, he looked neither angry nor upset, just vaguely amused as if I were a kitten or a child who had just done something particularly clever.

"You're going out tomorrow, and I wanted you to know..." I took a deep breath. "I wanted you to know I meant it."

The vaguely pleased expression vanished under a wave of utter bewilderment. "You meant..."

"That I will not do anything to get you in trouble. That I will not cause you problems by the time you come back. That I will not—"

He laughed. A short laughter, like a hastily bit-off chuckle. "I know that."

"You do?" How in living hell could he know that, when I wasn't even sure? I was just determined to make a lot of effort.

"Yeah," he said. "I'm more worried about what you'll do to yourself. I'd take you with me in the *Cathouse*, only..." His voice died down.

Only he wasn't sure he could trust me not to garrotte him and steal the ship to take down to Earth. The problem here was that I couldn't tell him I wouldn't. I was fairly sure I wouldn't, but I had nothing to go on, no past actions to use to bolster my belief. I could tell him I wouldn't till I was blue in the face. It was convincing me that was the tricky part.

"Well," he said, speaking like someone who has gathered his thoughts for very long and is now ready to speak. Suddenly I felt as if his entire silence, this evening, had been designed to gather his mind to tell me something. I had no idea what. "I said I'm more worried about your doing something stupid to hurt you than me, and I am. I want you to try very hard not to get in arguments, not to get in duels, and not to get married to the first idiot who asks you."

I snorted. "There aren't idiots big enough. On Earth or on Eden."

He gave me a crooked smile. "You'd think that, but people are very dumb about whom they marry. Don't. You don't know enough of Eden. Ask my father before you fight any duels or enter any contracts, please. And do try not to kill anyone."

"I wouldn't," I said gravely. "I said I wouldn't cause you more expense, remember. And I gather if I killed someone I'd leave you stuck for the blood geld."

"Almost certainly," Kit said. "Unless it's a lawful duel and of course you don't know how to set that up. So, ask my father."

"Uh . . . am I to continue living . . . uh . . . to stay in your house while you're gone?"

He looked startled. "Do you wish to go elsewhere? Did we . . . have we offended you?"

Offended me? I used their water, I got their son in trouble, I took up space and they offended me? "I don't pay rent," I said. "Your father won't let me. And people . . . people will assume . . ."

I couldn't tell him people would assume we were a couple. If he didn't know it, I was fairly sure I could not explain.

"People will be people, as Doc Bartolomeu says." He frowned. "If you do get into some trouble you can't tell my father about, would you go talk to him? I have no idea why—he says most people are only tolerable well boiled and with a lot of salt—but he likes you, and he should be able to help you if you're in real trouble."

Weirdly, I didn't doubt that the doctor liked me. Yes, he snapped at me and glowered every chance he got, but I could tell he liked Kit, and he treated him much the same way. I got the impression that for the gnome-man it was the lack of rude conversation that would mean you were held at a distance.

Kit reached across the table. For just a second I thought he was going to cup my face in his hand, but what he did, instead, was pull my hair back. "You have this tendency to make an explosion out of a tap on a powerpod, because you're too proud to ask people how to operate the collector."

I raised my eyebrows at him. "There hasn't been anyone to ask..."

"Yeah. I know that," he said. And the tone in which he said it made me wonder what, exactly, he'd got from my mind when we'd been linked. "But there is now, and you must learn to ask."

And with that he got up. This time he held my hand and pulled me, all the way back to his flyer, where he handed me into the passenger seat, as if he were afraid I would, otherwise, not know exactly where to go. He waited till I buckled myself in, too, before he closed the door and went around to take the pilot's seat.

"You can drive my flyer while I'm gone," he said. "If you wish."

I had about as much wish to drive his flyer as I had to grow a pair of fins. But it occurred to me that without Kit there I might have to. I couldn't exactly ask his father to pick me up at the Center every day. Yes, I still had my job. I'd checked.

The funny thing was that with Kit being my legal guardian, everything I did wrong went against him, not me. I'd tried to explain I didn't deserve my job, the day before, and got handed my tools and sent to bay fifteen to inspect a ship. And I got told not to talk nonsense. My bosses said that Klaavil should have told me what the problem was. Klaavil's fault, not mine. And I got looked at oddly, as if I were suspected of harboring feelings for this particular Klaavil.

I'd read that in the Middle Ages princes and those considered too holy to be touched were given whipping boys who were beat every time they made a mistake. When I'd read it, I'd thought it was the most stupid thing I'd ever heard. Now I was not so sure. I suspected it could be a very effective punishment.

And if I still had my job, then I must get to it somehow. Of course, I'd never asked Kit to pick me up and drop me off either, but he'd done it without being asked.

"You can drive in very early in the morning and back home before traffic picks up," he said, as though reading my mind.

I nodded. I would have said I'd buy my own flyer, but Kit was paying all this money for my mistake and I was damned if

I would let him do it alone. I'd been collecting all my pay, and I was going to hand as much as I could over to him to help pay the stupid debt down. My contribution might be so small as to be ridiculous and it probably really wouldn't pay it down any faster, but at least it would allow me to sleep at night.

We drove back home mostly in silence, except as he helped me down from the flyer—yes, helped me down, as though I were small and frail—and he said this little set piece about a lovely evening that could have come straight from two-dimensional twentieth century movies.

I followed him into the house and to my room, but that night, when I heard the violin music wind out of his room, I got up—in my repaired silk slip—and went to his quarters.

He'd been playing with his eyes closed, but he opened them as soon as I entered, though I swear I didn't make any noise, being barefoot, in the grasslike carpet.

The violin came down gently and the hand holding the bow came down too, slowly. "Thena. Is anything wrong?"

I shook my head. The violin glowed mellow-gold. "I just... How long will you be gone?"

Like someone waking from a sleep, he put the violin away in its case, then the case away in his closet. He turned to his bed, where there was a small case open. He'd told me that normally you didn't pack for a voyage. Not as such. The reason his wife's spacesuit was in the *Cathouse*, even though they'd flown an entirely different ship, was that it was the cleaning and fitting staff's job to clean everything the couple had in the ship—and move it to another if they were changing ships. I didn't ask what had happened to Kit's wife's clothes. I suspected anything might have—from her having spaced them before herself, to their having been carefully packed at Kit's orders and given to her family. The suit was not with the normal clothing, so it would have stayed.

But Kit's clothes in the *Cathouse* would be vibroed and put away. And all his other effects. The only things cats and navs packed were little travel cases, no bigger than would last a weekend if they had everything in it. Reading gems. Music gems. Virtus gems—I saw Kit drop a string of the amber-colored ones into the case and wondered what was in them. Granted, as small as recording equipment was, one couldn't really be sure when virtus collection was happening. Particularly since he'd be collecting it through his own senses, so the collector might be under his clothes. But I didn't remember us having any parties with butterflies and kittens. Waldron's wedding probably, though I was at a loss how it could take up so many gems. However, Kit was addicted to family occasions as virtus recreations, so that had to be it.

"Probably about three months according to their calculations," he said. "But Anne and Kath should be back soon enough, and they will keep you company till I return." He looked up and seemed amused at my expression, which I was fairly sure reflected all the uncertainty in the world. "Oh, don't worry. You have your job and my family aren't ogres. It won't be that terrible."

He was, of course, completely wrong.

❦ TWENTY-SIX ❧

THE TROUBLE STARTED TWO WEEKS AFTER HE LEFT, THOUGH AT first I didn't know it was trouble—or that it was trouble for me, at least.

At first all I noticed was that people were giving me a wide berth and that I moved around in a bubble of solitude and silence almost as impenetrable as Kit's had been. All my workmates said nothing at all to me, unless it was strictly required by the job. Even Darla wouldn't come by with her gossip, her news and her mostly well-intentioned babble. Which was why, of course, I missed all the news, and failed to understand what was on people's minds.

I assumed that they must be equating me with Kit because he was paying for my debt and hadn't renounced his responsibility over me despite my rather cataclysmic faux pas. Then I gritted my teeth and told myself that all was well and fine. I'd be a model citizen just to spite them all. Besides, I'd promised Kit to behave.

At work I performed my duties. I even volunteered for extra hours. At Kit's house, I mostly ate as little as I could—since they wouldn't let me pay—and then went to bed.

Which is why I heard nothing about the disappeared ships until I got in late one night—so late no one should have been up—and found Kit's father in the common room they used as dining and living room, in front of the holo, staring at the news with an expression so dismal I couldn't just walk past him.

I was so tired that I could barely think straight—I'd worked two shifts, doing my best to make sure that the money I had to give Kit counted, and also making sure I didn't think. Or not too much. When you're too tired to stay awake more than a minute after hitting the mattress, you're in no state to wonder what you're going to do the rest of your life as a stranger in a strange world.

But Kit's father looked worried and, for all he looked nothing like Kit—something that made perfect sense if they actually had no genetic background in common—he had the same gestures. In this case, he'd shoved both hands down into the pockets of his pants managing to convey the same little-boy sullenness that Kit conveyed with the gesture. Though in both cases I was sure that was not what it meant. In Kit it was a sign of worry and defensiveness.

"What happened?" I asked.

He turned to look at me, as if surprised I was there. No. As if surprised I existed. Which was perhaps not unreasonable considering I'd done my best to stay out of his sight for two weeks now.

"Ah..." he said. "It's the ships that have been disappearing. Anne has been missing for...for weeks. She should have been back weeks ago. A week is normal, but..."

"Missing?" I said. I didn't think of Anne at all. I thought of Kit, out there alone. The cat who travels alone, Doc Bartolomeu had called him.

"Everyone seems to be delayed, pretty much," he said. He sounded miserable. "But every day people return, and there are stories." He looked at me, frowning. "At this point I don't know what stories are true, and which are...Well...people under stress..." He frowned just like Kit too. "But the ships can't all be having serious failures and delays, one after the other."

I looked at the holo. It had a list of ships under Ships Returned: Ru and Rob Knox flying the *Voshells Mill*; Tom and Kate Golding's the *Hairball*. John and Syl Wagner had brought their ship, the *Drool*, back home safely and Christine and Jody Runnalls had brought back their ship, the *Quilly Bomber*, all unscathed, including their toddler, Tripp. Beneath it was a list of ships self-destroyed to avoid capture, presumed dead: Sabrina and Jonathan Iffland flying the *Jena*, Kevin and Dona Molinaro in the *Catseye*, Brent and Mary Roeder, in *Fowl Reciprocity*, Kateri and William Travis in the *Indiscretion*. And beneath that, again, a list of ships still missing and now more than two weeks late. I skimmed it.

Chris French, flying the *Beaver*—I wondered if like Kit he flew alone and why—Mark and Julia Verre, flying the *Revoir*, Sean and Hugh Kinsell flying the *Madonna* and there, at the very bottom, Bruno and Anne Denovo, flying the *Fireball*.

I tried not to think of the name of their ship as a bad omen and instead said, "Ships self-destroyed?"

"The ships that return..." Kit's father said. "You see, the ones that return say that they've seen other ships..." He took a deep breath. It was as if this idea was so outside his experience and perhaps his imagination that he didn't know how to express it. "My...when my great-great-grandparents came here," he said, "they lived in fear the Earth would capture our cats and navs when we sent them back for the energy." He gave a little mirthless laughter. "We didn't have a choice, you see, it's not like...We had the technology for the powertrees. Sort of. I mean, at least the one Mule that stayed behind with us was their architect and he knew how to create them. But we didn't have the manpower and more importantly, we didn't have the natural resources." He shrugged. "We presumed as we expanded outside this world, we'd find..." He shrugged again. "Most people were never interested in expanding, though. They wanted to settle and raise families. They're...we're...just people."

"Yes, but ships self-destructing?"

He sighed. "We had to go back to Earth orbit to harvest the pods, because our whole machinery was designed for it. Besides, there really weren't many other ways to find that much energy. And we needed the energy to make Eden livable. So we took the risk. But we expected them to lie in wait for us. Wherever they were, they had to know we needed to come back. We expected them to lie in wait to capture us. The ships were—and still are—built with all sorts of safety features, starting with the fact that they're darkships, able to hide in the dark of the powertree night. Then there's evaders and of course the cat's ELFing plays into fast evasion. But each ship is also equipped with a final self-destruct button that will make the inside of it a burnt-out, hollowed hull. If you are captured and can't escape in any other way, then you must self-destruct." He took his hands from his pockets and looked at them as if they were alien artifacts and he was not quite sure where they'd come from. "For three hundred years no cat and no nav needed this feature. We...all trained in it. But the legions of Earthwo—Earthers hunting us never materialized. We realized, from what you told us, that we'd become a legend of sorts."

He took a deep, wavering breath. "Until now."

"They—" My legs had gone very weak and I sat down heavily on the soft grass. "They are hunting for darkship thieves." It wasn't quite a question, though I wanted it to be a question, and one that caused Kit's father to laugh. But he didn't. He nodded, once.

"They're using . . . well, probably some form of detection mechanism. Our engines make not imperceptible noise, of course, and they give out a power signature, but . . . They never looked before, but now they are, and they're lying in waiting and they're . . ."

"Firing on ships?" I asked, hoping against hope that was true, because if that were true, then it wouldn't be so bad. It would just mean they'd lost patience with the energy thefts and they'd decided to put a stop to them. Though of course firing on anything in the powertrees was dangerous and they had said that the ships were self-destructing.

Kit's father was chewing on the corner of his lower lip, something Kit also did. "No. They're pulling them with tractor rays. Trying to get them to Circum Terra." He made a little gesture with his hand, as if he were trying to dispel bad thoughts. "So far all those observed being captured have behaved with great sense of duty and have self-destructed. But it's disrupting the power runs. People are going back again. Some of the ones that returned went back three times and came back with half cargo. And the others . . . managed to evade the ray but sustained damage and had to repair it. I'm hoping that's all that happened to Anne."

"Me too," I said. But I was thinking of Kit getting damaged in a way that blinded him and without a nav who could go out and do repairs. I wanted to cry or scream or die. By preference die, because then I wouldn't have to think of it again. I looked at Kit's father. "It's all my fault, you know. They're looking for me."

He seemed startled. "For you?" His eyebrows went up. "Well, maybe finding out that you disappeared from the powertrees, lifesaving pod and all, gave them the idea we exist. But I don't think they're looking for you specifically."

I was hugging my knees. "Kit went right into the bay," I said. "In Circum Terra. To rescue me." I realized that over time I'd become convinced that's just what he'd been doing. Made perfect sense. After our mind link, I realized that when I had realized I was ambushed I'd probably screamed out mentally. And Kit had picked it up. Which also had to mean he was hovering far closer than the hour away he'd said he was. "I don't know the exact circumstances, because I was unconscious," I said, and told him the whole story.

He listened, his eyes rounding. "He can hear you? Mind-talk?" He shook his head. "He is trained. He probably felt your distress from the moment you knew there were armed men around you." He frowned. "But you realize you can't be right."

"Beg your pardon?"

He shook his head. "It couldn't have been the same people who were chasing you and then waiting for you in the bay," he said.

"They were," I protested. "My father's goons. I know them."

"But . . ." Kit's father said. "How would they know you were going into that bay in particular?"

I opened my mouth. "They saw me come in?" I asked.

"But that means they must have had the whole of Circum waiting for you. They must have mobilized observers. That would take a great deal of manpower. It can't be just the men who were after you."

"But—" In my mind the conspiracy expanded to include everyone at Circum. Perhaps everyone on Earth. Well, at least all the Good Men. Perhaps this was a plot to get rid of the Sinistra line. "But that would indicate it is me they're looking for." I looked at him. "If you send me back, there's a good chance they'll leave you alone."

"But we can't do that," he said. "They would have you then and know everything about us. And we don't know they would stop. Once they've found us, they might decide to exterminate us."

I almost told him that they would probably just kill me and forget all about the darkship thieves. But I was afraid he would actually consider it, if he thought only I was at risk. And when it came right down to it, I felt that I, like Kit, couldn't quite muster the will to die. Even if, in my case, part of it was because I'd promised him not to do anything stupid.

Of all the idiot promises to make, when I'd, in fact, spent most of my life doing something stupid every minute I was awake.

I waited up with Kit's father, as long as I could keep my eyes open, but Anne did not arrive. No other ships arrived. No news. Finally I crawled into my bed, exhausted, my eyes burning.

And found I couldn't sleep. Behind my closed eyes passed scenes of Kit alone in the *Cathouse*, a tractor ray having destroyed all his nodes, without a navigator who could go out and repair them. In these images he was blinded, though I had no idea why he should be, unless the tractor rays were luminous also.

I knew rationally he wasn't even at the powertrees yet. I knew he couldn't be. But I didn't want him to go there, either. Screw the debt I'd got him into. Screw it all. I wanted to know Kit was safe.

In my mind I screamed for him to come back, screamed that there was danger ahead. Of course, there was no reply and no sense that he had got it. The ridiculous ability appeared to have a range, which was stupid. What was the point of telepathy if you couldn't just communicate instantly across the universe?

Probably something designed by the Mules like the stupid, stupid powertrees, the stupid, stupid bio-improvements of ELFed people, and possibly the stupid, stupid bio-wombs. Without bio-wombs, Kit would have died when his mother died, I would have died in the powertrees months ago. In the frame of mind I was in, this seemed by far the preferable consummation to the whole matter.

My eyes burning as though I'd stared too long at the sun, I lay in bed, and wished Kit back, willed him safe.

It wasn't that I didn't care for his sisters—I must, at least to the extent that Kit's father would be made very unhappy by their disappearance. And I liked Kath, anyway. I'd seen her for a very little time, but she seemed to be the sort of woman who kept Kit safe despite his own idiotic self-sabotage.

But if I had to choose one of them to be alive and well, as much as I would regret it, I'd pick Kit. I made the baffling discovery that I couldn't imagine a world without the annoying creature—that I would in fact miss his tendency to lecture me, his obsession with music, even his sullen silences and his tendency to grab my ankle and make me fall on my ass whenever I tried to attack him.

I don't remember getting out of my bed, much less going to Kit's room. But I woke up in his room. And though I also didn't remember getting his violin case from the closet or opening it, it was open next to me, and my hand rested on the glowing wood.

Very carefully, I closed it and put it back.

I had a feeling things were going to get worse and I was right.

❧ TWENTY-SEVEN ❧

OVER THE NEXT FEW DAYS, THE LIST OF SHIPS NOW DELAYED GREW. Donna and Jim Bova in the *Speedball*. Sanford and Lillie Begley in *Finnian's Rake*. Everitt and Dottie Mickey in the *Troglodyte*. Alan and Margaret Alexander in the *Pounce*.

Also over the next few days, I noticed Kit's dad paying more attention to energy expenditure than before. Turning the lights down when fewer people were in the room. Putting two of the serving robots out of commission. Cutting down on trips to the store. "The Energy Board has raised prices," he said. "If that doesn't work to preserve enough energy for urgent tasks, they might have to institute brownouts."

Good news was much rarer. The next two ships arrived almost together, a week later, while I was at work. Work had got insane overnight, as well, because practically every ship that came in needed major repairs. I worked on bashed nodes, destroyed steering systems.

I understood the bubble of silence now—or at least I thought I did. Of course my co-workers would assume this sudden vicious-ness of the Earthers was because I had arrived. After all, this had never happened before. Now I was here and it was happening.

That they thought I was a conscious spy or a traitor, raining destruction on them and that they were wrong didn't matter. What mattered was that they were right in the essentials. This was my fault. If Kit hadn't saved my life and brought me here, all those people who had self-destructed in their ships would still be alive. It was a sobering thought and a terrible one, not made any better because I hadn't intended any of this or because all the laws of every world, even presumably the non-laws of Eden, gave one the right to save one's own life.

The death roll haunted me, but not as much as the idea that Kit might be added to it. Most nights I couldn't sleep unless I were in his room, touching the violin. This was insane, because it wasn't as though the violin preserved his scent or a feel of him—which might have calmed my anxieties. But somehow, it made me feel closer to him and therefore I did it, half afraid his father would find out. But his father didn't seem to care. At least not now.

So I was half asleep and my eyes burned with tiredness as I went through a checklist on the latest ship, trying to figure out whether I'd got every one of the life support systems working as they should. The fact that the nav had made some interesting improvisations didn't make it easier to fix, though I was glad it had limped home, of course.

And then I heard cheering. It was less than a month since Kit had left, but I wasn't exactly sane—not then. I was flying on tiredness and half a dream and I thought maybe my thoughts had reached him, maybe he'd turned back.

I dropped my tools and stumbled through the corridors, towards the arrival bay. It wasn't hard to find the specific one, because there was a throng going in that direction. This will tell you how strange things had become, because normally mechanics couldn't care less when the ships arrived, except when we had to repair or rearrange something the crew had messed up.

But now a ship arriving at all was a cause for celebration. A ship arriving with actual pods in its hold was an event. There was—though nothing had happened yet—talk of rationing power-pods, talk of prioritizing functions that got power first. How they were supposed to do it without any ruling body, I didn't know.

I stumbled along, hoping, hoping, hoping that it was Kit who had turned back. But before we even got to the arrival bay, I heard the name of the ship. It was the *An Suaimhneas*, flown by Ginger and Mary Alice McCaughtan. The crowd seemed particularly happy that the couple's little boy was also safe and the ship undamaged.

It wasn't till I got to the bay that I heard the name of the other ship—and it was definitely not the *Cathouse*. It was the *Freedom*, flown by Hugh and Amanda Green. Amanda Green, the nav, a tall, imposing woman with strawberry curls, was talking loudly to the receiving officer, as I got back. I could hear the echo of her words, on the emphatic parts. *Explosion, salvageable, arrival, light beam* and then a name that chilled me to the core, *Anne Denovo*.

Not Kit's sister. I thought of what this would do to his father. I thought of what it would do to Kit. I knew from his mind how much he loved his family, how attached he was to them.

I couldn't hear anything else, above the crowd noise. But before I could push my way to the front or ask someone what she had said, someone near me repeated it to a friend. "The Earthworms are using a light ray, trying to blind the cat and confuse the nav before they can self-destruct. The Greens saw Anne Denovo's *Fireball* get hit with it, but it got them with a powerpod on the grabber, and the powerpod blew."

"They're dead?" the friend asked, as I felt as if someone had dipped me, headfirst into ice.

"No, no," the first speaker, who sounded like Darla, said. And before I could take a full breath of relief. "Fortunately the nav wasn't in his cabin, which was hit pretty hard. They're both fine, but they have asked for special landing, because the ship will have to be radiation scrubbed. About half of it is unusable."

I rushed away from the crowd, and thumbed my ring to connect to the Denovo compound. I got Kit's dad, and started to tell him, "Anne is—"

"I know," he almost shouted. "Isn't it wonderful?"

And it was, of course, and I was the last person to tell him I wanted his son home. Instead, I assumed—rightly—that the household would be celebrating. I also assumed I wouldn't be welcome to the celebrations, though perhaps I would. You really couldn't tell with this family. They'd been more forbearing and kinder to me than anyone could imagine. The fact that through the long nightly vigils with Kit's dad, waiting to hear on arrivals, he'd never once said this was all my fault, probably meant they were a very forgiving clan. But all the same, I couldn't go back. Not to a celebratory dinner, which Kit's father was now talking about.

I couldn't go and celebrate anything, while I knew there was a very good chance I might never see Kit again. I excused myself and explained I'd be working a double shift, then went and signed up for it. It would mean leaving the building late at night, but I figured if no one had killed me yet—something I was sure I owed to the prestige of the Denovos and to whatever terror Kath seemed to strike in the minds of her colleagues. The terror was true, I'd seen it. And I figured that it was the only thing standing between me and a quick death.

When I left the compound, late at night, exhausted, for a moment it was as though I were back on the day of my arrival with Kit. Particularly because I was using his flyer.

The compound wasn't empty. Or at least the garage wasn't, as several people had worked double shifts. We were trudging into the garage, where the light was burning at half-power, when I heard a sound.

I can't tell you what made me pick the sound over the scraping of feet, the opening of flyer doors, the slamming of other doors, the woosh of warming engines, but I did. It was the slip-slide of a burner safety being pulled off.

Because in mind I was back to my arrival here with Kit, I dropped to the floor, before even thinking. And as if it were a bad recreation of that day, a burner ray flew over me, burning a hole into the pilot door, exactly where it had been before.

I couldn't think. At least not clearly. But I could move. Before I could stop, I had leapt in the direction the sound and the ray had come from, and I landed on Joseph Klaavil.

Not being rational or under my own control, I was wild, insane, a state I normally only reached at the end of a furious fight.

Each of my actions registered only as I completed it, and I became aware I'd done it. I'd torn the burner from Klaavil's hands and thrown it, not caring that with the safety off it might fire when it hit. And I'd hit him hard in the place that Kit said I liked hitting men—and then both knees before he could fall.

And because I wasn't rational, I found myself standing over a man curled in a fetal position, while I rained punches on him with my bare hands and screamed an incoherent babble about his being a murderer, about his having tried to kill Kit, about my killing him, killing him now.

I stopped to catch my breath, my face covered in tears, my breath coming in ragged sobs. Through the sobs, I heard voices from the crowd that had assembled to watch this.

"She attacked him for no reason," one said, clearly having missed the first shot.

"She's going to kill him."

"Cursed Earthworm, protecting that murderer, Christopher Klaavil."

And I realized, with a sudden shock that I was doing exactly what I'd told Kit I wouldn't do. I'd promised him not to get in trouble. I'd promised him not to kill anyone, and not to make him pay blood geld.

All of me, all my impulses, all my thoughts, wanted to kill, to destroy, to maim. But I couldn't. Not and have yet another debt accrued to Kit. Kit who had put up with all of this, Kit who didn't want this creature killed. Kit who had best come back and soon. Kit who was a cat and therefore couldn't challenge a normal person to a duel.

I stepped back. My voice shook, but I yelled as loudly as I could, "Joseph Klaavil, I'm challenging you to a duel because you have several times and without cause tried to kill me and Cat Christopher Klaavil."

He sat up at my words. His lips moved. His "I accept" was spoken in a low voice, but it echoed through the garage. The crowd cheered, and I was fairly sure it was for him.

And I...I was in more trouble than I knew how to deal with. I climbed into the flyer and closed the belt around me.

I'd best go see Doctor Bartolomeu. This asking for aid thing was odd and I'd never done it before in my life. It wasn't fear for myself that forced me to it, it was fear of injuring Kit further.

ꙮ TWENTY-EIGHT ꙮ

"WHAT HAVE YOU BEEN DOING TO YOURSELF?" DOC BARTOLOMEU asked, as he opened his door. He had much the look of someone continuing an interrupted conversation and acted as though I should have my response ready.

I don't remember what I mumbled, at the door. He took me in and sat me in one of the tall, padded chairs, and put a cup of hot chocolate in my hands, and somehow—I still wasn't discounting the idea that he was some form of supernatural being—I found myself telling him what had been going on in my mind. I would never tell it to anyone else, but it just came pouring out of me. Of course, he didn't play fair, and perhaps he had put something in my hot chocolate. He was a doctor after all.

At the end of long and often contradictory outpourings, I found myself staring at him, while he stared back at me, frowning slightly, not as if he were mad at me, but as though trying to solve a problem. "So you came to me over the duel?" he asked.

"I ... well ..." I thought I had. "The duel made me realize I should come to you. Kit told me to come to you if there was something I didn't want to discuss with his father, and today of all days ..."

"Would be a very bad day to discuss duels with Jean Denovo?" He nodded. "Probably, though you realize that there are only about two hundred ELFed families—or at least ELFed for energy collection—and therefore everyone knows everyone else. He will hear of your duel challenge."

I thought he would be quite likely to throw me out, then. Father would have, had I got myself in that sort of position. They'd put up with me so long... "And of course, once I'm out of Denovo protection," I said, "I will be...Everyone can call me a spy or challenge me to duels."

He gave me a very curious look, his dark eyes sparkling under bushy eyebrows. "Eh. Don't jump to conclusions." He paused and looked at his fireplace, which was burning brightly, though it didn't seem to make the room really warm. And I supposed it wasn't a true fireplace—not log burning—because where would Eden find that many logs? If cows were expensive, wouldn't logs be also? "You didn't come to see me because you thought Jean would cast you out, did you?"

I shook my head a little, then shrugged. "I hadn't even thought of that," I confessed. "I haven't been sleeping really well. I worry about where Kit might be...what...how he'll survive this mess. No. I was worried because I wanted to make sure that Kit wasn't going to pay for...that he wasn't going to go further in debt because I kill Joseph Klaavil. And then, you know...Kit has kept the man alive all this time, heaven knows why. He could have killed him and paid blood geld, but he keeps saying that Joseph is his parents' only remaining child, and he clearly means that he shouldn't be killed. And now I've challenged him to a duel." I put my face in my hands and moaned as I realized the complete mess I'd made of things. Why did I keep getting myself in these situations that spun out of control?

I thought I heard a chuckle, but he might have been clearing his throat. A hand rested gently on my head. It should have been creepy, but it wasn't. It should have felt sexual, but it didn't. More a touch of encouragement or benediction.

"Thena," he said. "Listen to me. Not all duels lead to death. You can pick the form of the duel and restrict it to first down. I understand what you mean about Christopher wanting the creature kept alive, though I can't say I understand it. What I can't quite make out is why you think that they would make Kit pay blood geld. Surely you understand that if a death occurs in a fair duel there is no blood geld due?"

I groaned again, deep in my throat, and I looked up at him, above my fingers. "That is the problem," I said. "Fair duel."

"Uh?" His bushy eyebrows climbed his wrinkled forehead. "I don't understand. Are you *planning* to cheat?"

I removed my hands completely. "No. It's one of those things...
like, like the mind talk. When I'm pushed, or scared, or angry, I
go... faster than normal humans. I don't know how else to explain it."

"Hysterical speed?" He asked. "It happens, like hysterical
strength, you know, and it doesn't mean you're that much faster
than normal, just that your senses give you the impression that
other people have slowed down."

"No. Not that. I can *almost* match Kit. Not quite, but close
enough. Sometimes, you know, I almost catch him... though he
usually ends up catching my ankle and I usually end up with my
ass on the floor, but..."

The doctor grinned as though all of this made a lot of sense,
and said, under his breath, "If I were a hundred again..." Then
cleared his throat. "Uh... Are you sure it's not your perception?
Or that Christopher isn't pulling punches?"

I told him about trying to garrotte Kit, about our fights in the
Cathouse, when we'd first met, and then about our training fights.
I expected him to be horrified, but he looked hugely amused,
an almost manic grin pasted on his face. "I see," he said, at last.
"Yes, if it's that obvious, you could end up having to pay blood
geld. It would be assumed you had been ELFed to an unfair
advantage over him." He collected my cup, refilled it and came
back, this time with a deep, rounded glass of something amber,
for himself. "Well... you are going to have to meet him, you
know? Now that you've challenged him, you simply have to. And
if you don't fight to the death, but only to first down, you have...
Well... They might still accuse you of assault, though everyone
knows he's been pursuing Christopher and trying to kill him, so
you'd think..." He looked at me. "No, that won't do, will it?" He
sipped his drink. "They'll find a way to blame it on you and, by
extension, on Christopher."

"They said I attacked him," I said sullenly. "Out of the blue.
I'm sleep-deprived, but I don't think I am that sleep-deprived. I
would remember."

"Likely." The doctor sipped again, then brought the drink down,
sparkling like a golden jewel between his gnarled hands. The red-
dish flames or pseudo flames brought out deep tones in the amber
liquid. He sighed. "The problem with all this is Christopher's...
ancestry. He told you?"

I blinked up at him. "That his biological father killed his mother, then himself? Yeah, he told me," I allowed derision into my voice. "I know Edenites like to think that Earthers are barbarians, but even we aren't stupid enough to think genetic predisposition is destiny."

He stayed quiet a long time, and pressed his lips together in a way that made me wonder if he was offended at me for saying that about Eden. But I'd be damned if I was going to apologize. Edenites had made Kit's life a living hell all over a stupid thing that he could not have helped.

At length Doc Bartolomeu said, "Ah." He sighed hugely, as if he'd been keeping from breathing the whole time he was silent, and had now to set the balance. "Is that what he told you?"

"He . . ." I took a deep breath. "Are you implying he lied?" I had been in Kit's mind. I had the feel of him, if not all the details, and I was sure, if I was sure of anything, that Kit was not casually untruthful.

"Oh, he's not lying. His biological father—for a given value of father—did kill his mother—for a given value of mother—and then himself. But that's not the worst—or the least of the rumors that people spread about Christopher. And none of it is as bad as the reality."

I have no excuse, except that I hadn't slept in almost a week, or not more than an hour or so a night. I found I'd got up and set the cup on the chair—of all places—somehow managing not to spill any of the rich liquid within.

I stood beside the chair, my hand on the arm, swaying slightly, because I was that tired. "I thank you," I said, politely, in my best Patrician manner. "I thank you for the hot chocolate, I know it's expensive, and I want to thank you for the explanation you meant to give me, I know you mean well, but I truly don't think you can help me, and I don't see what can be served by my sitting here and listening to . . . calumnies."

He didn't move. For a moment, he just looked at me, his face as close to blank as he could get it, but then the wrinkles rearranged into an ironical smile, and the dark eyes sparkled. "Indeed," he said. "If I were standing would you be trying to kick me in the testicles?"

I clenched my hands together, tightly, till the nails bit into the palm. I bit my lip but I couldn't bite it hard enough to keep the words in. "You are old," I said, carefully. "I don't fight with elderly people."

"Oh, honey, don't let that disturb you," he said, and cackled, a short, immensely amused cackle. "I will probably outlive you by a hundred years." But then his face went grave and he wrinkled his eyebrow and looked attentively up at my face. "Or perhaps not. You do look an awful lot like my old friend. Though if they managed that..." He lapsed into silence.

He was old. He was wandering in his mind. I would not throw a fit because an elderly man was confused. But I was also not in the mood to sit here and listen to him tell me that Kit was... what? Something terrible, he'd implied. "I'll be going to the Denovo compound," I said. "I'm sure I'll figure out a way...I'll just have a non-killing duel with—"

"Sit down!"

No one spoke to me like that. No one. I started towards the door.

Behind me I heard an annoyed huff, like the not-quite sneeze a cat does when tempted beyond endurance out of the depths of its dignity. I ignored it. He was old. I was not going to fight with him. I was not.

I reached for the doorknob. And he was there. Somehow, he was there, in front of the door. "You put something in the hot chocolate!" I said, because that was the only way he could have got there before me. "Only Kit—"

"I put milk, chocolate and a touch of cinnamon in your hot chocolate," he said, grinning. "When you leave I'd like to give you sleeping tablets to take, because you're running on nerves and spit. But I don't give patients anything without their consent. Not unless they're total idiots, and you don't strike me as such."

"Please, let me out," I said. So I was so tired, he'd gotten to the door ahead of me. But that only meant nothing could be gained by continuing this conversation with him.

He cleared his throat and tried to look dignified, which some-how only made him look like an impish gnome. "Patrician Athena Hera Sinistra, would you do me the great honor of returning to your seat, removing the cup of hot chocolate from it, sitting down, and letting me speak to you? I will attempt not to offend your sensibilities—though I can't promise I won't since I'm not sure I fully understand your upbringing." He lowered his eyes, and I was sure it was just to prevent me from seeing the amusement in them, though I had to admit he was trying. "Some of what I have to tell you—and I do believe I have to, since Christopher balked at it and you have been dragged into the midst of this unholy mess—will probably shock you and offend you. However, I beg you to believe that I don't mean any form of disparagement to Christopher, whom I consider as an adopted son of sorts. He is, in many ways, admirable, even if he tends to go weak-kneed around women."

I didn't like the tone of that last sentence, but even my sleeping brain had to admit that Doctor Bartolomeu seemed to love Kit. That much was obvious, as was the fact that the doctor was deeply concerned for Kit, and had been concerned for our relationship before I had any idea we might, eventually, have a relationship. "I'll come back," I said, stiffly. "But you let me leave the moment I wish to."

He lowered his head, this time in a deliberate movement, half bow, half nod. "If you wish to leave after you hear me, I will let you." He looked up and his eyes sparkled with that impish look. "I won't even make you take a packet of sleeping pills."

I came back to the chair, of course, not fully sure I could trust him. But if he blocked my path again, I would forget he was more than a centenarian.

I picked up the hot chocolate and sat down looking at him. He took his time sitting down, and took a sip of his drink and a deep breath, before saying something I didn't expect at all, "What do you know about the Mules?"

For a moment I was speechless. The last thing I expected was a history test.

"They were bioengineered," I said, dredging up the paragraph from my history lesson pertaining to it. "Sometime in the mid-twenty-first century. The ... governments of Earth had run their course one way or another before then. Monarchies and democracies and all that, and none of it worked. So people, as a whole, decided that government was too important to be left to benighted multitudes or even to inbred aristocrats." I smiled a little, as it occurred to me that inbred aristocrats might damn well apply to the Good Men too. Which was probably why Kit had accused me of being an Earthworm and inbred when we first met. "So they created people who were far smarter, far more healthy and ... well ... better at everything than normal people. And they delivered the government to them."

He didn't say anything, and I thought I was supposed to go on, so I said, "They were rational, of course, and very smart, but they didn't seem to understand ... well ... they didn't get humans. Quite. Or perhaps they simply didn't work by human values. Which might make sense, since they weren't, quite, human. So they did things ... They viewed people kind of like humans view livestock. But I don't think they ate them."

A flicker of something in the eyes, and a look up, "Not most of them, no."

I didn't even want to pause and think of that. "And they moved entire populations around, and they experimented with bacteria that were supposed to improve the soil, and which killed vast portions of Europe, leaving it depopulated. And they started massive wars. And when they were done ... Well ... people revolted. There were riots and massacres. They revolted against the Mules and against the bioengineered people that were the Mules' servants. And they killed them all. There is a legend that some of the Mules and some of their servants escaped in a spaceship that they'd been building. There are many versions of the story. I suspect it grew through the centuries. There are those who say it was FTL, built by the same Mule who seeded the powertrees—though most of our historians think it was a team effort, not a single Mule, but ... I guess legends are like that—and some say that they have a new world outside the Solar System, where they're growing their bioed armies to attack Earth some time ..." He was still silent, looking at me attentively. "I suppose that I thought it was all a dream or a legend, until I met Kit, because they say the Mules and their servants come back in darkships to steal powerpods. But of course, it's just Edenites."

He stirred. "Eden was founded by bioed refugees of Earth," he said. "What you would call the servants of the Mules, I suppose."

"Yes, Kit's history books said that."

He looked at me a while longer, and then took a deep swig of his drink, finishing it. He set the empty glass on the floor beside his chair, and stretched out his legs, so that they were almost at the fireplace. He stared at the flames, as if trying to read the future in them. "History is a funny thing," he said. "Live through enough of it and you start wondering what these people are writing about." He looked up at me, and his eyes looked clear and, for a moment, startlingly young. "You see ... It wasn't like that. It wasn't the Mules that depopulated Europe. For a soil-improving microbe to attack people would take a massive kind of screw-up which would forever put paid to the notion that the Mules had any kind of superior intelligence."

He frowned at the fire. "It wasn't like that at all. By the mid-twenty-first century it was obvious that Europe was dying. There were other problems too. The last gasps of a religion that refused to integrate into modernity had caused a war..." He shrugged. "All very involved and you either read the outlines of it in your history lessons, or it's not worth going into. Suffice it to say that, semantically, in many ways, it was a psychotic period."

"Kit says it was a psychotic period in every way."

"Oh, probably. But the fish rots from the head, they used to say when I was little. And the head, the way we order our thoughts, is language. Somehow they'd got themselves twisted around till they confused culture with race and religion with both. The war with this backward religion brought with it a wave of racist thinking. Particularly in dying Europe, which was very... worried... about losing its supremacy in the world."

"But they'd lost it hundreds of years before."

"Ah, but nations are like somnambulists. They wake in their own time. And continents..." He shrugged. "Anyway, it started first, in silence, almost in secret, in the frozen steppes of the area that was then called Russia. The idea was to create enough Caucasian babies. Only, you know, like everyone else, they thought they were men of their time. But none of us are. Humans... the legends of humanity fester in each of us, like a wound that can't be acknowledged or lanced. The men out of dragon's teeth, and other creations of not-exactly nature haunted the designers of the Mules. They wanted children, lots of them, armies of laborers and inventors. Millions of people who would fill their echoing streets, work for the state and pay their taxes..." He made a face. "So they decided to make these people so they couldn't mingle with normal humans—so they couldn't change the tenor of humanity, or, as they put it at the time, change the precious inheritance of humanity.

"They made the Mules all male. They said they also made them sterile, but that seems like taking too much of a precaution, for with whom were they going to reproduce? They locked it so that this time there would be no taking any Eve from Adam's rib." He grinned at my expression. "But I am speaking in riddles, aren't

I? They hobbled the genetic code of their creations, so that no female could be made by slightly altering a cloned Mule. So that Mules would not have another generation. And at the same time, of course, they started encouraging their precious, natural, Caucasian population to reproduce." He frowned. "Mind you, not just Caucasian. Every race was trying to get its citizens to reproduce, as though there were a prize at the end of the competition. Which, of course, there was. It was never the meek who inherited the Earth, unless the meek were also very fertile.

"But I digress. Of course in making the Mules, they had come to understand how to improve all humans. So the parents who could afford it started picking the characteristics of their children and improving them. Beauty and brains. It could be said that the end of the twenty-first century saw the finest specimens of humanity ever to run the Earth. Just not many. People who could spent their entire life savings to make one perfect child. Not for them the brood of natural brats."

"And the Mules governed..." I said.

"No, no." He shook his head. "Heavens no, child. Think about it. If you could create someone to do your work for you, would you hand them direction of your life?"

I shook my head.

"No. Neither did your...ancestors. They weren't stupid. Or at least they weren't stupid that way. Besides, you're not seeing the full picture. How many Mules do you think there were?"

I blinked. No one had ever asked me this, and I had no idea what it could matter. "Uh...fifty or so? The rulers of countries and...and the divisions of United Europe? And...and maybe some of the seacities?"

He laughed. He got up, and picked up his glass, then looked at the cup in my hands. "Here, let me warm that up for you." He came back with his glass filled and handed me a cup of hot chocolate, and sat down again. "There were millions, child. Millions. All the animals big enough were drafted to carry babies. You see, there was an aging generation that must be taken care of..."

I blinked. "Animals?" I'm sure the horror showed in my voice.

"Oh, yes, no one had bio-wombs yet. That was much later. Invention of the Mules in fact..." He took a sip. "They just poured little Mules into the world and educated them in creches, by the massed multitude."

"But..." I swallowed. "The environment in the womb...the... enzymes...it would be different. It wouldn't be...right."

"No." He shifted in the chair. "They didn't care. The first generation of Mules were, I suspect, near retarded, probably intentionally, but possibly due to the means of raising them. They filled the factories, they tended the farms. They were not actually more anything than most humans."

"And they only lived about as long as other humans. But... of course...they were not good at innovation. And Mules... well, think about it. All males, barely socialized...They required supervision like slaves—which in many ways they were." He narrowed his eyes at the fire, as though the fire had offended him. "I think that's when a lot of the ideas about the Mules formed. When I was a child, we could still see old newsvids—I suppose a lot of them got destroyed in the turmoils? Must have. Either that or no one looks at those—of breakouts of Mules from factories and farms, of entire towns where the men were killed and the women raped. I mean...They couldn't reproduce, but they still had all the urges of normal men. Normal men who had never learned the niceties of civilization.

"So people thought, why not make supervisors for the Mules. Other Mules who would be...supervisors. Who would hold the whip over their own kind."

He looked at me, his eyes very intent. "And then they made us."

꩜ TWENTY-NINE ꩜

I THOUGHT I'D FALLEN ASLEEP AND DREAMED THAT LAST SENTENCE. The words *beg your pardon?* formed in my mind and almost came out of my lips. But then I realized he was looking at me with an extraordinarily intent look.

I couldn't breathe. I couldn't speak. I'd heard about the Mules. I'd learned to fear the Mules. They were the enemies of Earth. They were going to come back...

But this was Doctor Bartolomeu, who reminded me of nothing so much as what I'd like Father to be. I took a deep breath. "And?" I asked. My voice shook, but it seemed to reassure him. He smiled.

"Who created you?" I asked. "And what happened?"

"In my case? My own group was created by the governing body of United Europe. The European Congress voted on it and some minister without portfolio got the assignment to see the project through."

"Isn't that a fairly high level for slave supervisors?" I asked.

He grinned. "Give the lady a cigar," he said, completely confusing me. "Yes, indeed. But myself and my...companions...my brothers, were created for other purposes, connected to those who supervised the slaves, or at least that, but up a chain of command several levels high. We were to report on the Mules to the human government. To do the jobs they could not do. We, as well, were supposed to be the innovators, the creators. To find a way out of the genetic mess humanity had created for itself and to render our own kind obsolete eventually."

"Scientists?"

He shrugged. "Some of them. Do you know the term *renaissance men?*"

I nodded. "People who are good at everything."

"Kind of like that," he said. "We were truly designed as everything you've heard about the Mules. Created to be smarter, faster, healthier, live longer... The latter because we were expensive. I don't know how many years of work it took to assemble a viable embryo for one of us. The later experiments... Well, even cloning one of us turned out to be very hard, so I imagine designing from scratch was more so, and generated any number of culls.

"At my level there were about two hundred of us, maybe five years apart. In Europe. We were, you see, treated a little better than our sad brethren in the fields and factories." He was quiet a long time. "Young women were paid or conscripted into carrying us. That was one big difference. And though we were still raised in creches like the others, we were raised in a creche where... A lot was demanded of us, intellectually. They gave us teachers and demanded we learn. We were culled for intelligence and ability to learn as well as everything else."

He shrugged and smiled at me, a smile that managed to look infinitely sad. "I'm not going to say we were any better adjusted than the rest of the Mules. No. We were smarter, designed to be so. And we were learned. But... Well, I suppose it was no grimmer than the average Victorian orphanage of a couple of centuries earlier. But... you see, I can't blame them. By then they had twenty-five years of Mule riots and Mule crimes. They didn't trust us. They might have suspected it was the way we were gestated, the way we were educated, but most of them thought there was something wrong with us. At a very fundamental level. Dragon's teeth and all that. Their religions told them we were unnatural. Their instincts did too.

"We weren't so much socialized as broken to rules and bound to behavior, till we didn't know who we were, but we knew which set of silverware to use for which meal.

"At first," he said, "we did what we were supposed to. We took our jobs between the upper echelons of the Mules and the lower ranks of government. And we did it well, and we developed other

interests. Music, art…" He shrugged. "You have to understand…
we were smart. Designed so. Trained to learn. It didn't stop when
they stopped whipping us to make us memorize things. We filled
every niche, from secret courier to researcher. Sometimes one person filled several of those. We had no personal lives, after all. The
time other people filled with children and parents and…" For a
moment I'd swear there were tears in his eyes. "All that didn't exist
for us. We were humans but not humans—creatures not related to
the past of humanity and with no room in the future."

"But… but you could make friends!" I protested, mostly to stop
the flow of the narrative because in my mind I was seeing a line of
little boys dressed in grey studying the proper fork and spoon to use.

He threw his head back and laughed though tears still shone
in his eyes. "Oh, yes, I had friends. There were three of us who
were very close, in fact. One of them was the man I have called
your ancestor, though he can't be—more on that later—Alexander
Sinistra. The other was…" He took a deep breath, the sort of breath
people take when alcohol is applied to a wound. "Jarl Ingemar." He
pronounced it like people from the Norse region of Europe did, the
J as I, the Ingemar like he was trying to talk through a mouthful
of sticky oatmeal, and looked at me as if he expected me to know
the name, to react to it.

I didn't. I'd never heard it. He sighed and shook his head. "The
things that people choose to erase…" He got up and opened
what looked like a compartment in the wall, and fumbled in it.
When he came back, he handed me a small translucent cube. I
knew what it was, because I'd seen them in museums. They were
the early forms of holos. Activated by the warmth of someone's
hand, they projected a little 3-D image above the cube.

The image that formed, slowly, hesitantly, like a ghost from
beyond, looked like a man of twenty, maybe a little older. He
looked very familiar, and yet not like anyone I knew—then again
the image was small and somewhat faded, as such images get
with the centuries.

He was a green-eyed redhead with the sort of gracile build
young men have—though he had broad shoulders and a squarish
construction to the face. Handsome, I supposed, in a very Norse
way. Put a beard and a few years on him, and he could have
been a Viking pirate—though the women of the targeted villages
might have made sure to trip as he approached.

"Once upon a time," Doc Bartolomeu said. "Jarl's face was as well known to everyone on Earth as...as Einstein's a century and a half earlier. And for the same reason. You have to understand, we didn't long stay servants, or even...in the quaint idiom of an earlier age, middle managers. We knew we were brighter, smarter, more efficient and definitely more creative than the bureaucrats we served. There was no revolution, or not as such. First we did someone's work for him and then...when he died, we took over. Jarl was not...ambitious as such. He took over the small Sea-city of Olympus. What he cared about and lived for were three things—I should explain we all had obsessive hobbies. They made up, I think, for all we lacked. Or at least we hoped they would. Jarl's were biological research, space travel and music."

"Music?" I said and looked at the faded hologram and bit my lip and hoped I was wrong. There was no telling. The hologram was too small, too faded, too...unrecognizable.

"As we were ruling the world—and I will agree with you we might have been unfeeling and uncaring, and perhaps inhuman—Jarl was designing things. The bio-womb, for one. And...and seeding the energy trees. We called them Jarl's folly. Until they worked..." He took the little hologram from me, gently—as though the person who'd been captured in it might still have feelings—and carefully returned it to the enclosure in the wall.

"It couldn't last," he said, as he returned to his chair. "We weren't bad rulers, but we weren't good either. It might be impossible to exert power at that level, that concentrated, and not be inhuman. And we had a head start on it, as you might say. Fifty years and Jarl said we should build a spaceship for escape from Earth because the time would arrive they would come for us with torches and pitchforks. The idea caught. We started building. The revolt broke out just a little before we anticipated—it spun out of control faster than we expected. And some of us...enjoyed it. Reveled in it. There are no external marks of being a Mule. And most of us were never that sane.

"We got as many as we could to the spaceship—Jarl christened it *Je Reviens*—and we...took off. Only...at the last minute, in the riots..." He shook his head, and looked at me, miserably.

"I've seen holos," I said. "I know they're classified but I..." I shrugged. "I'm good at defeating safeguards on machinery. I've seen holos of the riots. Kit says that here they make children feel being one of the victims during the turmoils. He said that...he said that they made virtus..."

"Yes," Doctor Bartolomeu said. His voice had gone unaccountably hoarse. "Yes, they do. I'm not sure it serves anything but instilling hatred of non-bioed Earthers. But...Then it's always easier to instill hatred than caution, isn't it?"

"Jarl died in the turmoils?" I asked, thinking I knew how this story went.

He started. "No. No, no, no. But before we were in the ship and the ship sealed, we'd realized two things. First, a lot of the people who'd been bioed and who'd worked closely with us—as functionaries, as scientists, as artists even—were at as much risk as us. And the other was that a lot of us simply couldn't be taken to space—not if we wanted to establish a colony somewhere and not have it be hell on Earth. They would bring the hell with them, you see?" He took a deep breath. "That was Jarl and I, between us. We accepted the responsibility for it, for...misdirecting some of our brothers, for...knowing they would end up dead and knowing themselves betrayed. We were in charge of coordinating getting everyone to the ship. Jarl...Jarl was somewhat of a legend by then, and we...we had lists, we went over them." He looked at the fire. "One of the people to whom we gave the wrong directions, the wrong time, was our childhood friend, Alexander Sinistra." He finished his drink. "We argued over it, and worried over it, but Alexander...he enjoyed his craft. What he did for the rulers. It wasn't...nice. He thought humans were...livestock. I didn't think we could trust him with the bioed humans aboard, or...with the other Mules, even.

"Jarl and I were blamed by the others. Everyone had dear friends, beloved brothers left behind. In the ship...it was... uncomfortable. And it was difficult to coordinate the two very different populations. We hadn't counted on the bioed humans. They'd reproduce, of course. And though the ship was FTL, it would take us very long to find a livable planet. We had anti-aging meds and we were sure we could...survive a long time, find a world, perhaps finally, in the time we'd have, find a way to defeat our curse and reproduce. But if that were to happen, no Mule wanted to share the world with normal humans. It would be just Earth all over again. So the decision was made to have the humans settle in Eden. By then the situation with...with Jarl and me and the rest of our brethren had become untenable and Jarl and I chose to stay behind with the non-Mules."

"Jarl stayed openly as a Mule—a renegade Mule, you might say—but he told me not to tell them what I was. They didn't know, you see, in the confusion. We had a few thousand humans aboard. The Mules all knew each other, the humans not so much. But everyone knew Jarl. He couldn't hide.

"His story was that he was staying behind to... shepherd them. To get them to a point where he'd find the way to seed other powerpods—where we'd have enough resources to do that." He shrugged.

"He didn't have a choice, but he also wasn't trusted... I was welcomed among them, set up bio-wombs, decanted children. I made friends. And if people noticed I was aging a little slower, it wasn't that different. With transplants and care, people live a good hundred and twenty years, here. I am now only... three hundred and fifty. Only three hundred in this world." He shrugged. "They think me a freak of nature, I believe, but not a Mule. Oh, some people might suspect, but I make it a big point of being eccentric in a very human way." He gestured around his home. "And people really can't believe two Mules would stay behind. Jarl maybe, but..."

"So you and Jarl remained friends," I said, "for the next three centuries."

He nodded. "Yes. And we had other friends, and their descendants inherited us, in a way. Some even knew what I was."

"The Denovos," I said.

"Ah, yes. I don't know if they were ever told, but I think they know. And yes. But Jarl... Jarl was never right, after we left Earth. I did say none of us was exactly stable? His instability was not of the kind to endanger others. There was never any reason to leave him behind. But he was not..." Another deep breath. "He blamed himself for the people left behind, Alexander in particular. And he... he..." Shrug. "Well... He didn't live well with himself. A few decades ago he got very depressed, and you must understand, he was the only friend I had left, from my childhood, the only one of our kind. I convinced him of this plan, to... to create a clone of himself. I thought watching himself grow up would give him something to live for. In his case, I think it was more important than that, an almost religious idea of absolution. He would be born anew and pure.

"It's not like that, of course. It's just genes. Which ones express, even, is different. And he knew that. But this wasn't about reason.

"We're difficult to clone. It took us over ten years. And then we found him a *wife*, the daughter of one of those families who knew about us. You see, we wanted to set it up so no one knew the child was a Mule. No use saddling the child with that. The idea was that his wife had a child designed to look and be almost like him but human. That was the story we'd give out. It . . . Some people had done it, before the turmoils. I suspect Alexander had, and that you're descended from that child—thus you look like him, but not quite, and some of the traits came through in the blood. That's what . . . That's how we wanted to set it up for Jarl's clone."

I couldn't breathe. There was a knot at my throat. The music. And that face, so strange and yet familiar. With different hair and eyes . . . "Is that how . . . is that how . . ." I wanted him to under-stand. I wanted him to say no, to laugh at me.

But he looked at me, his eyes unreadable, and lowered his head, in that odd little nod-bow. "That was how we created Christopher."

⤳ THIRTY ⤵

I WAS ON MY FEET. I WAS MAKING FOR THE DOOR. THERE WAS A lump in my throat the size of an egg and I felt like I could only get breath in around it with an effort.

He was at the door ahead of me.

I clenched my fists. "Let me go. You said you would."

"When I was done," he said. "I'm not done."

My breath was fast, my heartbeat pounded at my chest making me feel like my ribs would crack. The hissing of blood in my veins seemed to be rushing through my ears, making a sound like twin rapids. "Oh, you are done."

"No," he said. He spoke very calmly. "No. I'm not. You came to me to find out why Christopher was doing what he does. You will be told."

My nails were probably drawing blood from my palms, and I didn't care. I stomped my foot on the floor and even as I was doing it, realized how childish, how futile my fury was.

"You haven't slept properly in a week," he said soothingly. "And I wouldn't choose to tell you this now. Christopher was supposed to tell you all this the night he was first wounded, but I guess his courage failed, and after what he's been through I can't say I blame him, or not too much. But now you will hear."

"You are lying," I said, hoping it would stop it. "You're lying, saying Kit is a Mule. An unstable Mule."

It was his frown that undid me, that pierced through the denial

211

I was trying to build. He frowned as if he were considering what I'd said. As if he was seriously pondering whether Kit might be an unstable Mule. "A Mule, I suppose," he said at last, frowning a little, as if the term had no pejorative associations, which I supposed it didn't, for him. "A Mule, yes, but not unstable or... not as such. I think he was a perfectly normal little boy. Atrociously stubborn and capable of the most Machiavellian plans, but a happy child. The Denovos were a good family for him. I...I often wished Jarl had gotten to see him."

I swallowed, trying to get the air-blocking egg down.

"You see, the woman who was legally Chirstopher's mother had sole... ownership of the embryo. Jarl was trying to keep it...untainted. I don't know what...what happened. He didn't tell me. Neither of them did. But something convinced her that we were doing the wrong thing. Perhaps she was aware that Jarl's depression was hereditary—such things tend to be—and decided it wasn't right to bring a human being into the world to suffer through this. She decided to have Christopher... prematurely decanted. Aborted, I guess you'd say.

"Or perhaps she didn't even decide it, but merely considered it. Wanted to discuss it. But she hadn't known Jarl for hundreds of years. And if she guessed the guilt eating at him, she didn't know how bad or how strong it was. She didn't know that in his mind, this clone, this child was supposed to be his redemption..."

"He killed her," I said.

"And then himself." He looked at the little compartment where he'd stowed the hologram. "Which was probably for the best. I don't think he could live with the guilt of another death. He made me his heir..." He inclined his head. "And he was hers. This means I had responsibility for Christopher. Her family might have disputed it, but they didn't. The Denovos offered to adopt Kit. We had already arranged to have him ELFed to obscure any too-close resemblance. Not that he...well...cat-speed is the same thing we have and forms of telepathy are limited. The idea was that he'd been designed to resemble his mother's husband but not so closely he looked like the pictures in the history holos, which was fortunate when the Denovos adopted him. Kit didn't know he was adopted until he was twelve, and I don't think he gave it much thought after. He attended the school for the energy collectors. He served in the Energy Center Hushers, as a volunteer. He fell in love and proposed."

"And got married," I said. "And she killed herself."

He gave me a curious look. "You know I never knew for sure? Oh, I'm sure Christopher wouldn't kill her unless he had a very good reason, but like Jarl he has a horrible temper, and given a good reason and fury in a closed space alone with her..."

I shook my head. "She killed herself. I got it from his mind." He was leading me by the arm, back to the chair; he made me sit down; he offered me a glass of water that he had seemingly conjured from thin air. "Drink," he said. "Drink."

I drank. It could be poison, but I had to drink, because I had to be able to breathe and the damn egg wouldn't go down. I drank, then drank again, then I hiccupped, then I drank once more. The egg remained, but now allowed some air through.

Doc Bartolomeu knelt by the chair, his hands on the arm, looking up at me, as if I held some kind of magical power. "Are you sure? Are you sure you got it from his mind? That he didn't kill her?"

I nodded. "You're only thinking he did because his father killed his wife," I said, hearing disdain in my own voice. "Kit loved this woman...his wife. Loved her madly. I got that from his mind, too. I...shared his mind and she was in his mind as she died. She was in mind link with him as she died. He was begging her to come inside, trying to suit up to go get her."

"Cruel," the Doc said.

"He didn't know I was getting it. He was mostly unconscious when I got that."

"Not Christopher," he said impatiently. "Jane Klaavil. She wanted him to remember forever."

I hadn't thought about it that way, and suddenly I felt a wave of anger at the dead woman so strong it made me nauseous. Doc Bartolomeu seemed to read it in my eyes. "Yes," he said. "And no, it's not a surprise. I thought at first...you see, Christopher is not quite a son to me, but well, he's the...genetic twin of a very dear friend. I thought that I was only behaving as though no woman were good enough for him. But the more I've had time to think about, I think a more disastrous match couldn't have been arranged if it had been done on purpose. I think that's what attracted Christopher to her.

"He knew himself to be brighter than his classmates. Not...not Jarl's level of brilliance, but then he hadn't been forced. I think the potential is there and that it's the same. He felt odd and out of place. And in his family, he knew he was adopted. Jane was... uncomplicated. She was the first one in her family to be ELFed. Her family are working class—manufacturing workers. They're... It seemed... these things do, like an uncomplicated choice, a way to be something other than himself?"

I nodded. In a way I felt that way often enough, looking at the families of Father's employees, at couples on the street and dreaming that I was them, that I could become that simple, that uncaring. Not that I thought they truly had simple lives. I was sure that had I known them better I would have seen all sorts of complications. But the dream could be a very powerful attractor.

I'd never thought I could abdicate my life as a Patrician, but if I could, I would have.

"I told Christopher he was a Mule when he got engaged. I advised him to tell his wife. After all, navs and cats communicate, mentally, and in a marriage it's sometimes hard to control what the others get. But...he couldn't do it. I suppose because he was afraid she would talk..." He shrugged. "He told me he let her know after a year, when she wanted to find out why they weren't conceiving a child. She very much wanted children. The next year...He hasn't told me, but I can guess well enough what it was like. She was the type of woman who sulks and cries, none of which Christopher takes well to."

"He sulks too," I said.

He smiled. "Ah, yes, but it's a different type of sulk, isn't it?"

I shrugged. "He gets over it if I mock-fight him in the exercise room."

"Oh, definitely things would have gone much better if Jane Klaavil had just aimed a kick at his gonads and gotten over it..." He seemed to mean it. "But she didn't seem to be the type, so she would cry and act wounded. And Christopher is stubborn. I don't know what precipitated the crisis, but I suspect it had spun all out of control.

"And after she died he refused to depose under hypnotics and her family accused him of killing her, and rumors started leaking out, each more outrageous than the other... And he became a pariah."

"But... why didn't he depose?" I asked.

"Well..." the doctor said. "I thought he might be guilty. I didn't push him. But I think it was the Mule thing. Not just for himself, but because people would look funny at the Denovos for adopting him and . . . well, when I broke it to him he was a Mule, I told him I was one also. I told him the whole story, as I told you, just now."

"But would that have to do with his wife's death?"

"I suspect the final argument was about what he was, and that Christopher is afraid . . . you know, that it will come out. These depositions are public. Open."

"Oh. So he can't, but the only reason people can imagine for it . . . is that he killed her?"

Doctor Bartolomeu nodded. "Exactly. You see where that leaves him."

I did. It left him in hell. The only way to get out would cast him into a bigger hell. Maybe it was because I was so tired, but I really didn't seem to give a damn that he was Mule-born. Trickling through my mind was the thought of what Kit had endured, to protect those he loved. What was there more human than that?

"Are you sure . . ." I asked, confused, unfocused. "I can't kill Klaavil?" But even as I said it, I realized I would just be adding to the guilt Kit carried. I sighed. "Well, at least I can beat him up."

The doctor looked at me and smiled. "That's the spirit."

"Why did you think . . . Oh, you wanted me to understand what is happening with Kit . . ." He must have put something in the water, because my thoughts were calming and getting more coherent.

Doc Bartolomeu nodded. "In a way. I also wanted you to understand . . . I wanted you to know. He should have told you, but I didn't think he had the courage, so . . ."

I nodded. "And you're not afraid I'll talk?"

"Curiously?" he said. "No. The other reason I told you is so that you understand the depths and confusion of the rumors about Kit."

"And to that," I said, "is added bringing an Earthworm who starts the destruction of Eden power collectors."

Doc Bartolomeu shrugged. "I'm getting very tired of people blaming themselves for what they can't help. After three hundred years, it's grown rather old."

I understood that, but still, I wished he would understand I messed up whatever I touched. It was a gift, of sorts. One I could do without. If only there was something I could do to compensate Kit.

Doc Bartolomeu rose. "I'll give you some of those tablets now, and a data gem about duels. You have a reader?"

"Kit gave me one."

"Good. I want you to sleep, though, before you send any message to Joseph Klaavil. And I want you to think whether you really want to return to work at the center. You can help me, you know? I always have...work. And I can pay you, if that's your worry."

"No. I like mach—" The idea formed in my sleepy brain all in one piece, without my remembering assembling the thoughts to get there. "Doc? Since I mind-linked to Kit, could I depose under hypnotics? To clear Kit?"

Doctor Bartolomeu turned, holding a little glass jar full of pills. "They could only ask you what you got from his mind," he said slowly.

"Which means they couldn't ask me what the conversation before was or what caused the argument, because I wasn't there. I know nothing about that. Not of my own experience."

The thought drove the duel and any worry about it from my mind. It was now merely a distraction on the way to this grand scheme to clear Kit's name. If I could, I must do it. Even if I suspected Kit would hate me for it.

❧ THIRTY-ONE ❧

NOTHING IN EDEN WAS AS STRAIGHTFORWARD AS IT SOUNDED. The duel took a month and a half to arrange.

In that time, the brownouts started, reducing all of Eden to semidarkness for hours a day. It was more difficult to institute things like power-pack rationing when one didn't have government. The Energy Board did what it could by raising prices to exorbitant levels. I didn't notice that much economy at the Denovos', but less insulated families had to be hurting.

With the list of presumed-missing ships growing by the day, only a handful came back: Steve and Laurie Shay in the *October Fury*, Francis and Miho Turner in the *Gramondou*, Steve and Patti Ludwig in the *Darolme*. All of them with less than half a cargo of powerpods in their hold. And all greeted like heroes, which I supposed they were.

The willingness to go back out had grown into such a rare thing that Ru and Rob Knox's decision to go back out in their ship a month after arriving had entitled them to various interviews in nightly broadcasts. Rob Knox had, famously, declared that the ships from Earth were like rats guarding the cheese of energy and they wouldn't keep Edenites cowed. No one laughed. Perhaps he was a little insane, facing going back into peril.

And when Tom and Kate Golding chose to take the *Hairball* back out, we were treated to a holo of a green-haired—I hoped artificial—cat-eyed gentleman and his wife climbing the stairs to their ship under massive acclaim from what sounded like hundreds of gathered friends, shouting "Hurray for Captain Silkfur McFluffy." Anne had giggled on seeing it, so maybe it was an in-joke for cats and navs, but I wondered what the rest of the world made of it.

Meanwhile, my own matter crept forward. For a world that had no laws, they had a lot of traditions, cultural assumptions and hoops to jump through. Even though the duel was not technically to the death, it was a serious event that had to be prepared for and witnessed.

By the time it was all ready, Kath Denovo was ready to be my witness, having arrived back when we'd all but despaired of seeing her again. She brought me no news of her brother, but also she and her husband hadn't been disturbed by the tractor ray and had arrived with a full load of powerpods. They said they'd seen the Earth ships move through powertrees, searching, but they hadn't been found. And Kath had assured me that Kit was an even better pilot than she was and that she was sure he was all right.

I knew there was a reason I liked the woman. She was also the only one who found out I was sleeping in Kit's room, on the floor, with my hand on the violin.

I don't know what tipped her off to this—her room was down the hall and perhaps she chanced to see me enter Kit's room—or perhaps she was coming to Kit's room for some reason of her own.

All I know is that I woke up, on the day of the duel, with Kath calling me, "Thena?"

I'd opened my eyes to find her standing at the door, staring at me. "That can't be comfortable," she said.

I'd blinked at her. I'd only been able to sleep like that for over a month, so at that point I wasn't thinking of comfort so much as that this was what worked. Even with Doc's tablets, if I weren't right there, touching the violin, my subconscious refused to turn off and let me sleep.

She'd hesitated at my look, then said, "You've been doing this since he's been gone?"

It was a question, but I felt I wasn't giving her any news when I nodded. "You could sleep on his bed, really," she said. "I don't think he'd mind."

"But what if I push the violin down from the bed?" I'd asked. "In my sleep. He'd mind that."

She hadn't argued, but that night, after the confusion and legalities of the duel, I'd found a sleeping bag on the floor, next to Kit's bed. And she told me to leave the violin case out of the closet, instead of bringing it in and out. Whether she told the rest of the family, I don't know. I never asked.

I'm not going to describe the duel itself, mostly because there is nothing to describe. Joseph Klaavil not only wasn't at the self-defense level of the various young men who ran the military schools I'd terrorized, he wasn't even at the level of the various very neurotic psychiatrists who had ineffectively tried to convince me that I did not want to hurt them.

Partly he was that neurotic, though he seemed to like burners—even if he was very bad with them—he had no idea what to do with his fists. I'd walked in, amid a circle of spectators, walked up to him and floored him with a single punch—which shouldn't have been possible since he was taller than I.

I'd walked out, amid the silent crowd—since the duel had taken place at the center—and back to the flyer in which Kath and I had flown home.

"It won't put things to rest, you know?" Kath said. "He will still try to fire on you."

"I know," I said.

"It's because of Kit," she said.

"I know," I said, all the while wondering how much she knew and how much I could tell her. So I told her the one thing I could tell her, "Doc Bartolomeu is arranging for me to testify under hypnotics."

We were flying over the suburbs at that time, which is a good thing, because she swerved all over the peaceful little road, almost hitting the false ceiling. "Testify?" she asked. "About what?"

"About Kit," I said. "And his wife."

She was looking at me as if I'd taken leave of my senses. "But you weren't there!"

And then I realized she had departed by the time Kit had been hurt and I'd had to drive him to Doc's. I told her about it. The hit—which made her foam and again almost hit the holographic ceiling while she gave me her considered opinion of Joseph Klaavil—I think "that weasel" was the nicest thing she called him—the mind merge and the drive to the doctor. I didn't tell her that Kit had ripped out his IV to interrupt the doctor before he could talk to me, but clearly she'd learned the aftermath of the incident, because she said, "Oh, so that's why he was bleeding after stopping you from stealing the ship." She grinned at me. "I told John Wagner it was nonsense to think you'd shot him."

I was suddenly very glad I'd never told her that I'd tried to kill him within minutes of entering the *Cathouse*. Though frankly, knowing Kath, she was very likely to tell me that he'd brought it on himself by tying me up. She both loved her brother, her husband and her sons, and had an absolute certainty that there was something very odd about the male brain and that sometimes this required drastic measures.

But she did look at me, frowning a little. I expected her to say that she was relieved Kit hadn't killed his wife, but frankly she didn't even ask if he had. Just went on to, "I'm glad you can do that. Kit will be glad to be out from under that mess." And then she'd patted me on the arm, in a reassuring way—swerving to almost hit a fence, then correcting at the last minute. "And it's so good that you can communicate just like a nav. And are good with mechanics. You can pretty much do everything a nav does. Very useful to him, aboard ship. If only you had the visual memory to remember the powertree maps and development."

I didn't know whether to laugh or cry at her serene assumption that Kit and I were going to be a flying—and life—team. I found myself blurting out, "I can. I mean . . . I can do the maps."

She'd flashed me a huge smile, and patted me again. "I knew how it would be from the moment you two came in. I know my brother. He'll do better with you."

I don't want to give the impression that Kath was a bad pilot. She did drive through the traffic in downtown Eden as ably as Kit did, and she managed not to hit anything even while gesturing wildly. It was just that as far as Katherine Denovo was concerned, there were far more important things in life than staying on the correct path at every minute. Things like jumping to conclusions about one's brother's love life, for instance.

Not that she was alone in that. Kit's mother, Tania Denovo, had come flying in, two weeks after Kath. She started dropping her clothes off at the door, just like Kit did—making me realize where Kit got it—and smiled vaguely at her husband as he picked them up and tried to introduce me.

"I heard at the Center. Isn't that just like Kit? He always was eccentric. Only an Earther would do for him."

Though this serene assumption that I was engaged to Kit in all but announced fact disturbed me a little, I did find myself liking all three women in the family. Anne was the quiet one, her silences, like Kit's, filled with observation, sometimes interrupted with the one word that either changed the tenor of the conversation or caused everyone to erupt into laughter. Exuberant, talkative Kath was always ready to jump into the conversation and say what she thought of anything and everything—even when she manifestly knew nothing about it. And then there was Tania—who was like a combination of her daughters. Her conversational gambits could take you completely by surprise, until your realized she had jumped two or three points ahead in the conversation, having disposed of all other points in her mind.

All three of them seemed determined to find me clothes. Daring clothes, interesting clothes and demure clothes. If I let Kath have her way, I'd dress like a cat, and my protests met with an assurance that "Kit will like it."

At any rate, their absolute certainty that Kit would come home—that he was even now speeding home to us—did me good and sustained me when he was a day late. Two days and I started feeling frantic. Three days and the only thing that kept me what could pass for sane—under a dim light and if one squinted—was that I had the deposition at the end of the week.

By the day of the deposition, I was frantic. I concentrated on fear of the process rather than on counting the minutes, the hours, the days that Kit was late.

The deposition was to take place at the judicial center. You will ask what the judicial center was doing in a place that had no laws. At least that's what I asked. Kath had looked at me as if I were completely insane. "Well... we don't have written laws, but we do have customary laws. Laws don't need to be written or come from a central body to apply." And when I admitted that I supposed it was true, she'd shrugged. "The center is where they have jury trials. And where depositions like this take place."

"Jury?" I said.

"Well, you can have twelve people weigh in on your question, when you can't prove it one way or the other. They ask you questions and then they state their opinions and their reasons. This is published, and usually is enough to squelch bad opinion." She frowned. "If the judgement is favorable to you, that is. We tried to convince Kit to do a jury trial a year ago, but he said they'd hang him, which is weird, because they really couldn't. Well, not without paying a serious blood geld fine. He said he'd rather be tried by twelve than carried by six, but that he still had no intention of being hanged." She'd looked at me, her blue cat eyes wide and puzzled. "I think my brother reads too much."

We were at breakfast and she was drinking quantities of clear, sickeningly sweet bug juice, the main caffeine vehicle around these parts. I was drinking tea because Doc Bartolomeu had been sending over packets of the finest oolong. I was fairly sure it was synthed, not grown, but I couldn't care less. The idea of drinking a liquid that came from the poop of bioed bugs made me shudder, and I didn't care how hygienic they told me it was.

I understood Kit's joke—at least vaguely—as a reference to twentieth century laws against gun ownership, and had to agree with Kath that the man read too much. "I suppose," I said, "that over the last few years Kit hasn't had the opportunity for a rousing social life."

"Oh, he never had a real social life," Anne said, sitting down. "He's a lot like me. He prefers a few friends, but trustworthy."

And Tania had jumped in, as she sat down and poured herself bug juice, "Oh, not to say that this whole thing hasn't been a nuisance. More than a nuisance, if what Jean tells me about Kit being wounded is true, but don't go imagining that Kit has been some sort of a victim. I'm sure that the general silence around him has annoyed him, but very little more. We used to say the whole world could implode or disappear and Kit would be perfectly happy provided the music center and his violin were left untouched. He'd never even notice we were missing."

I thought of the gems with children's birthday parties, and of the thoughts of them in his mind, when I'd shared it. I didn't say anything. I was willing to share part of his memories only because it could lift a threat from his head. But it was none of my business to tell his adoptive family how loved and cherished they were. At any rate, I was sure for all their protests, they already knew.

The judicial center looked like a Greek temple from the outside, with massive columns just outside an outsized door. Over the door was something in Greek, a language I didn't read. Beside the door, Doc Bartolomeu was waiting, dressed all in black, carrying his black case and looking very solemn.

"There won't be a jury for this," he said, "because the facts are incontrovertible. You got it directly from his mind and—if the hypnotics can prevent you from lying, there is no way the evidence can be vitiated. Everyone knows that you can't lie in mind link, which is why one normally only does it with one's spouse."

He seemed to know where we were going, and I let him lead me along huge, echoing hallways. At the end of the final hallway there was a double door, which led to a massive amphitheater. Every seat was taken, and most of them seemed to be taken by people wearing cat or nav uniforms. I also recognized quite a few members of my own profession.

As Doc took me to the platform at the end of the amphitheater, he said, "It took this long to set up because we needed to advertise it. Though the recording will be available, it is more effective if as many people as possible witness this."

On the platform was a chair—much like an Earth armchair. I sat in it, feeling demure and little-girlish, not least because the thing had been designed for a large person and, at a little over five feet, I must look like a child in it. I was wearing a white silk dress that covered my knees, and for reasons known only to her, Kath had insisted I tie my hair back and wear pearl earrings.

The Doc stood facing the people and explained he was going to inject me and with which drugs, inviting them to research the effects. And then that he was going to ask about the facts that I'd gotten from Cat Christopher Klaavil's mind.

And then he touched an injector to my neck.

❦ THIRTY-TWO ❧

OF THE VARIOUS DRUGS I'VE TRIED—THOSE GIVEN TO ME BY doctors and psychiatrists, those administered by peacekeepers trying to keep me quiet, and those I've sought out for myself, Eden hypnotics are the worst—just above Morpheus on the list, and only because Morpheus makes me sleep for hours and I don't like being unconscious and at people's mercy.

What Doctor Bartolomeu called judicial-grade hypnotics didn't make me sleep. After the first moment of blankness, my mind tiptoed in, hesitantly, like a child entering a suspicious house. I could hear and—once my vision did a sort of flip-flop thing, where fog covered the room and my eyes seemed to be trying to blink nictitating eyelids which I didn't have—see. I could feel my hands, clasped on the arms of the chair, my legs, demurely crossed, the silk of the dress against my legs. What I couldn't do was control what came out of my mouth.

I didn't realize how complete my lack of control was till after the doctor had introduced me, by explaining that I was an Earth native, rescued by Cat Christopher Klaavil in the energy trees. I guessed he was afraid of having to ask me the question of how I'd ended up aboard the *Cathouse*, because I'd blurt out that Kit had gone all the way to Circum to rescue me. And that would probably get most of Eden furious at him for endangering them. And perhaps rightly.

You see, I wasn't fully aware of how these hearings were held.

225

I knew the Doc would ask me questions. What I didn't know was that the audience got so much participation.

After the introduction and stating that he thought I might have some facts that would weigh on the death of Navigator Jane Klaavil, the doctor turned to me, but before he could ask any questions, someone in the audience—a sharp, shrill voice—asked how I could know that, since I wasn't even there at the time, was I?

The doctor phrased it more coherently as, "Please, state for the citizens of Eden how you came to know the circumstances of Jane Klaavil's death."

I had the time of a hesitation, but it was only a moment, and then I heard words pour out of my mouth. I heard myself telling of the attack on Kit in the half-g gardens, of my violent response to it, of more or less dragging the fast-bleeding Kit to the flyer, of needing mind contact to be able to get him help.

Oh, there were gasps. Plenty of them. Just as I said that I would have liked to kill Joseph but Kit told me not to, I realized that in the part of the amphitheater facing me, on the second row of seats at my eye level, sat Joseph Klaavil, between a man and a woman who, by their look, were his mother and father. The woman looked like an aged version of the little blonde in the holos. But my voice ground on, with neither compunction nor pain, even as my brain registered recognition.

I explained the mind communication, or at least said I had it with Kit, and what it felt like, and then stopped. That was the question they'd asked. How I'd come to have knowledge of the circumstances of her death, and not what those circumstances had been.

"Yeah, but—" a voice said, from the audience.

"Please, Nav, not now," Doc Bartolomeu's voice said, smoothly. "You may ask questions later. For now, will Patrician Sinistra please describe Jane Klaavil's death as experienced through Cat Christopher Kaavil's mind?"

I did. I started with her going out for what she said was a routine repair. Once outside, she'd removed her helmet, and then very quickly stripped off her suit.

She was mind-linked with Kit the whole time and as soon as he realized what she was doing, he had searched frantically for his suit. My mind and my voice felt all this as if it had happened to me, as though I had seen a much beloved spouse commit suicide, as if I'd felt her death in my mind.

Her suit had clung to the ship, due to the nonmagnetic attraction to the ceramite. Her body—grotesque, desiccated, unrecognizable, had floated away in the vastness of space. She'd hidden Kit's suit. Kit had not found it till much later, and then he'd brought hers inside—the only thing left after her self-destruction.

When I finished speaking, I was wracked with sobs and my face was soaked with the echo of the tears he'd cried then. I heard something much like a gasp from my right, and would have turned to look in that direction, only my body wasn't so much out of my control as such an unimportant thing that it was beyond me to figure out how to move it. Still, I was aware of someone moving in my far-right periphery vision and even at that distance, that blurrily, I noted calico hair and unruly calico beard.

Someone from the audience asked about the reason for the quarrel. Before Doc could either ask me the question or say I didn't know, Kit's voice cut in, clear, familiar, at once immensely welcome—because if he was talking it meant he was here, and if he was here, he hadn't died in the powertrees—and terrifying, because I wasn't sure what he'd think of my meddling in his private life. I wasn't sure what he'd think of this at all. All I knew for certain was his voice, politely crispy, "Please," he said. "You've already heard more than I would have liked to share. May I have some privacy, please?"

More than he would have liked already. I felt my fingers clench tight on the leather upholstery of the armchair and I missed whatever the person in the audience said.

Kit made one of those sounds he made—half snort, half sigh—when someone exasperated him. "The general reason for it, I think, was the fact that our marriage had proven sterile and of a form of sterility not likely to be solved in a laboratory. Jane...." He paused and drew a deep breath, like people will do when a sore spot is touched. "My wife wanted children." A pause. "Does that satisfy your curiosity or do you wish to give me hypnotics too?"

I listened and was glad my expression couldn't change, because my heart clenched in my chest at the thought that the stupid idiot in the audience would take Kit up on that offer. And then they would find out what Kit was. But the grumbled mutter from the nosy spectator clearly meant that no more explanation was needed.

And then the questioner who'd spoken first, asking me how I'd come to have mind contact with Cat Klaavil, asked, "Yeah, but how come she ended up in the powertrees? And how come people started disappearing afterwards? And the Earthworms started hunting us?"

"I hardly think this is any—" Kit said.

"It is a pertinent, if confused question," the doctor said. Turning to me he asked, "How did you come to find yourself in the powertrees and at the mercy of Cat Klaavil?"

I wasn't sure what would come out of my mouth till it came, and then was relieved to hear the succinct answer: "There was a revolt aboard my father's space cruiser. His guards or former guards were chasing me. They told lies about me to Circum, so I couldn't go there. So I fled to the powertrees, where I crashed into Cat Klaavil's ship."

"And he offered you asylum?" Doctor Bartolomeu asked.

"No. He tied me up," I said. I heard laughter from the audience. "And told me to stay out of his way till he was done collecting." The laughter redoubled. Kit had come all the way down and into my field of vision, on the right. He stood in front of the front row of the amphitheater, his arms crossed, his expression unreadable. He'd let his beard grow and it hid the lower half of his face. Above it, his eyes were half lidded.

"And in response?" the Doctor asked.

"I tried to garrotte him and scare him so he would take me to Earth."

This time the laughter was so loud and lasted so long that even though Kit turned to Doctor Bartolomeu and asked something, I only caught the tail end of it, "—unwarranted invasion of privacy."

Doctor Bartolomeu shrugged. "So? Challenge me to a duel when this is over?" And after Kit's noise of derision, he turned back to me. "To your knowledge, did you somehow bring persecution on Eden's power collectors?"

"No."

"Is there some way in which you might have?"

"Not that I can imagine, and I've tried to figure out the logistics of how this would happen."

This time there was no laughter, but just a continuous murmur of discussion in the background. The Klaavils, I noted, got up and left, wending quietly between amphitheater rows.

"So," Doctor Bartolomeu said, "you are not in communication with anyone on Earth?"

"No," I said. "I am not."

"And you have no intention of being?"

This one was confusing and my drug-befuddled mind had trouble unwinding it. "Not unless I somehow find myself back on Earth and have a need to talk to someone. It would be very strange to not communicate with anyone in the world if I were there."

The laughter returned, and I thought even Kit's shoulders shook, though his arms remained crossed at his chest.

But the doctor said, "Somehow find yourself on Earth—does that mean you have no intention of returning now? Do you prefer Eden?"

"I do not prefer Eden, but I also have no intention of returning to Earth."

"Why not, if you do not prefer Eden?"

I moaned because I knew what was going to happen the moment I figured out what he was going to ask. Kit was there, staring at me with those half-lidded, unreadable eyes and I couldn't see his mouth through the wild calico beard.

To my horror, I heard the words coming out through my lips and could neither stop them nor call them back. "If I returned to Earth, I would endanger Eden. To achieve it, I would probably have to endanger Kit. And then I would never see Kit again and that," I heard my voice say, uncaring of the fact that I wanted to make a hole on the ground and hide, "would be unbearable."

Kit's expression didn't alter but a strong, dark red blush climbed from beneath his beard and up to his forehead.

This brought absolute silence, the sort of horrified silence that falls on a party or a social occasion when someone says one of those things that never should be said in public. I swear there were shuffles from the upper rows as people left.

Kit turned to glare at Doctor Bartolomeu. But the doctor, after centuries of life, was perhaps tired of it and had a death wish. As he entered my field of vision carrying a delicate, pink injector, he gave Kit a big smile. "Would you help me help Patrician Sinistra to the recovery room, Cat Klaavil?"

I'm fairly sure that Kit said yes, but perhaps it was the effect of the injector touching my wrist, because I would also swear that yes meant *just wait till we're alone.* Even as my body became more controllable—not normal, but closer to me, like it had been a balloon unsteadily tethered a long way off and had now come closer and therefore easier to push and pull—I wondered just how furious Kit was going to be. One thing I knew about Kit was that he despised having his affairs aired publicly—or at all.

Even with his family, who doubtless knew most of what there was to know, he spoke in half sentences and veiled references. I wasn't sure if the reason he hadn't told me what he was had been not so much fear of my reaction as a genuine, gut-felt reaction to having to tell anyone something he considered private. Kit Klaavil hoarded secrets like a miser hoarded coin. And I'd just aired his secrets for all the world to hear. More the pity, I'd also aired mine.

I felt his arm come around me, just under my arms, warm and strong, lifting me. "Up you come," he said. I fully expected him to say *and down you go,* and fling me from the stage. But even as Doc Bartolomeu approached to help me on the other side, Kit's other arm came down under my knees and lifted me up. My face came to rest on his chest just short of his shoulder, against the red stuff of the uniform, just beside the emblem with the apple and the serpent and the words *Je reviens.* Still half in a dream, afraid of how furious he was going to be, savoring his warmth and strength, I said, "*Je reviens.* I'm glad you did come back."

Something that might have been laughter rumbled through his chest. "So am I," he said. "It's ever so much better than the alternative." As he spoke he was carrying me to the one side of the stage not surrounded by seats, and through a small door there.

On the other side was a narrow corridor, and Kit carried me after the doctor, down the hallway and through a door to the left, into a very small room empty save for a single white bed, a white armchair, and an array of medical equipment.

I expected Kit to drop me, or at least to set me on my feet, but he didn't. He carried me all the way to the bed and laid me down upon it. He patted my shoulder—half absently, as if I were a child in need of reassurance—and then crossed his arms on his chest and turned to the doctor. "Of all the despicable—"

"Can it."

"You had no business—"

"No. But something I have learned, Christopher. When the people who do have business don't take care of it, it falls to those who *don't* to resolve it." The doctor's back was turned, as he poured something from a bottle, but the way Kit was glaring at the spot between the

Doc's shoulders, I fully expected the doctor's shabby dark suit to start smoldering and smoking.

However, when he turned around he looked completely unconcerned, and Kit's next foray was "I could not do this. Not without giving away secrets that aren't—"

"So we took care of it," he said, as he approached me and brought a cup of clear liquid to my lips. "Drink now, Thena."

"But you had no right!" Kit said, looking very much like he would have liked to say much stronger words.

"You're very welcome, Christopher."

Kit turned towards the wall nearest him, and punched it—hard. The sound echoed through the room. The doctor looked at him, a smile forming on his wrinkled face. "Oh, come," he said. "You know if you break your fingers I'll charge you top money to fix them. And you'll want me to fix them, so they're in shape for piloting."

Kit turned around, his other hand holding the one that he'd punched with. "You're the most infuriating, the most meddling, the most exasperating old man I've ever had the misfortune to run into."

The doctor smiled. He took the glass away from my nerveless fingers. "I said you were very welcome."

Kit let out a long, exasperated breath. "Thena," he said, "let's go home."

✦ THIRTY-THREE ✦

IT WASN'T THAT EASY OR THAT QUICK. MY LEGS FELT EXACTLY AS if they were balloons full of water and my eyes kept insisting on crossing. It was the worst—or the best—drunk I'd had since Simon and Fuse and I had highjacked that liquor transport in Olympus Seacity.

However, Kit observed a dignified silence the rest of the time we were in the room, as though by pretending he was no longer there, he could act as though he were on his way home, and therefore didn't really have to acknowledge the presence of Doc Bartolomeu. The doctor either respected this or decided to go along with it, because he too was silent, though a smile kept touching his lips now and then.

He gave me another glass of white stuff that tasted like sugared water, then a glass of green stuff that tasted both hot and vile, like the distilled sins of humanity, and finally a glass of violet-colored stuff that tasted like burnt sugar.

By this time my eyes had uncrossed enough that I could see clearly and was starting to believe I might be able to stand up without falling. Even then, as I started to stand up, Kit put his arm around me to prevent my falling. He led me out of the room and through a long maze of corridors.

Though we were not at the center, the corridors were full of people I knew from the center—cats and navs and mechanics. Most of their glances still slid away from Kit, after looking at him, but it was a different sort of slide. It was an I'm-sorry-to-intrude glance away or an oh-I-didn't-need-to-know-that look or—twice—the sort of half-amused smile that denoted they remembered what I'd said about my feelings more than what I'd said about the death of Kit's wife.

Kit didn't slow down for the glances or the smiles. And I was too dizzy to even reply to Darla's rather guilty, "Hello, Thena."

In the garage, Kit helped me into the passenger seat of his flyer, and buckled me down, before he jumped into the pilot seat and buckled himself down. He tore out of the space with every impression of wanting to get out of there as fast as humanly possible, and paying very little attention to any other flyers that might get in his way. Of course, he didn't hit anything. He just twirled and ducked and made my stomach feel like it would come out through my mouth.

"I suppose," he said, after a while, "that I should thank you."

Oh, please, don't overwhelm me with gratitude, I thought, and almost said, but the drugs had worn out of my system, and besides I could fully understand how embarrassed the poor bastard had to be, having heard the Earthworm that had forced herself on him more or less declare love in front of all his associates. I mean, what was he supposed to do now? Any way he behaved he would seem ungentlemanly.

I found my hands pleating the silk skirt of my dress, while I said in a voice that seemed entirely too small and feminine, "I'm sorry. I had no idea it would be such a detailed description, or so personal."

Kit muttered a string of unintelligible words, as the flyer spit out of the garage and into full midday artificial sunlight. The only part I caught was, "*He* knew better."

I cleared my throat. I thought, from my reading—particularly of Kit's old-fashioned Earth books—that this was the type of situation in which one girded one's loins, and if there had been the glimmer of a gird around, I would have done just that before I said what I had to say: "You know, I think he only did it because he was worried about you." A sideways glance showed me that he was frowning intently as he wound through the traffic around the judicial building at a much higher speed than could possibly be necessary. "I think he thought he was doing it for your own good because . . . I think he loves you as a son, you know."

"I know," he said. He said it as if it were a curse. "I am per-fectly aware the low-down, amoral bastard loves me. Would have shot him otherwise."

I nodded as though this made perfect sense, cleared my throat again and tried to reach for something soothing to say.

I realize that I was the daughter of a Good Man and that in theory I had been trained in saying the right thing in diplomatic situations. I'd been taught, from birth, just the right word to smooth over a quarrel that might become a trade war; to quiet animosity among guests at a party; to make the servants do my will with a smile on their lips.

This is why in all disciplines there is a class in theory and one in practice. I knew the theory very well. What I had was abso-lutely no practice in social chitchat or peace-making. I did best at Daddy Dearest's parties by keeping my mouth shut and looking pretty and then tearing out of there, putting on my leathers and speeding to my broomer lair.

Soothing and polite simply wasn't in my repertoire. So I did the next best thing and changed the subject completely, "You didn't have any problems in the powertrees?"

He shrugged and jabbed something hard at the controls, which caused us to drop in what seemed like freefall, before stabilizing and diving under a cargo flyer, then above a family one.

"Eber told me that you and my mother and my sisters were at the judicial building, and I thought I might as well come and see what they'd gotten into." He gave me a sideways look, frowned. "Sorry I didn't shave or bathe...I was afraid..."

What on Eden could he have been afraid of that was worse than what he'd actually heard? And then I realized it. "You were afraid I'd killed someone?"

"Well..." he said, as he jammed the lever up. "At the center, you know, I didn't exactly ask and no one exactly talked to me but I heard something about you and Joseph Klaavil and a duel."

"I didn't use weapons," I said, aware even as I said it that my voice sounded sulky. "I just punched him out."

"Ah, yes," he said. "But, you see, part of no one talking to you is that you can't ask logical questions. You just hear whispered words and you assume—"

We tore off down the side road headed home, and I glared at him, "You assumed the worst."

He didn't say anything for a long while. Instead he looked out at the road, even though he couldn't possibly need all his attention to fly here, where there was almost no traffic. Finally he sighed, then gave a dry chuckle. "Well, Princess..." he said and smiled a little, an infuriatingly sweet smile.

"Don't call me princess," I said.

"*Princess*, you know, considering our acquaintance... what else could I assume?"

I bunched my hands into fists. "Land," I said. "Land now."

"What? I know you're still dizzy but we're nowhere near home."

"Land, damn it. Let me out. I'll walk home."

"What? While still recovering from the effects of the hypnotic?"

I fumbled with my seat belt, unbuckled, then reached for the door unlocking button. He reached for the door lock a second too late. I'd already unlocked it and was holding the button down. I pushed at the door and would have opened it too, if it hadn't been for the air pressure. By that time I was shaking and there were tears rolling down my cheeks. I knew half of it was shock and confusion and tiredness, but the other half was that he'd heard me declare my love for him and he was lording it over me.

As though out of nowhere came a memory of my mother talking to me. I couldn't have been much more than five, but she was speaking very earnestly, as though I'd been a peer and capable of understanding. *Never give a man your heart. He'll just twist and wrench it out.*

"Land and let me down, damn you," I said. "Or I'll jump off as soon as you slow down and you know you can't land without slowing."

Kit gave me a half-frightened look, then said. "I'm landing. Don't jump."

He slowed and I could see he was dropping, dropping, dropping, slowly, until we came to rest by the side of the road, outside a row of fences. He landed and turned off the engine, and turned to look at me. "Look, Thena."

"Don't want to hear it," I said, pushing at the door, shoving it all the way out. Mom was right. Give a man power over your life and you would have it go seriously wrong. Just look at what Father did to me, and the only power he had over me was judicial. With a man I loved it would be much, much worse.

I slid through the open door onto the road. Like most suburban roads, it was soft grass that looked a lot like the living room carpet at home—No. Not home. Not my home. It was the compound of Kit's family, and I would have to figure out how to move out and soon.

Kath was constitutionally incapable of not telling Kit about my foolishness, sleeping on the floor of his room with his violin. Which meant now the only way I would be able to call my soul my own would be to find a way to get back to Earth. And then I would never see him again, a prospect so desolate it made me even more miserable than the prospect of living under Kit's thumb.

I stomped along the road towards the Denovo compound, making a remarkable speed and only stumbling now and then, because my legs must still be getting rid of the effects of the hypnotics.

I'd gone through all that trouble to get him free of suspicion, and look where that got me. Nowhere at all. I should have known the other stuff would come out, but did it need to come out in front of everyone I knew or could possibly know on Eden? Now for the rest of my life here everyone would look at me with a half-pitying look. And when Kit married, which was now inevitable, sooner or later—since he'd been upgraded from murderer to rather romantic widower—everyone would give me a pitying eye.

Well, see if I care. There were several good-looking mechanics at the center. And now that they knew it wasn't my fault that ships were disappearing, I was sure I could get them to take me out. Two could play this game. I would be so busy making the acquaintance of every handsome male in Eden that—

"Thena!" Kit said, just behind me. His steps made no sound on the stupid grass road, and he must just have caught up with me, because he was panting.

"I bet you didn't exercise nearly enough without me in the *Cathouse*," I said, and wiped with the back of my hand the tears that were forming in my eyes, doubtless because it was so bright out here and I was still suffering a reaction to the drugs.

"Not nearly," he said, meekly. "I spent most of my time in the virtus."

I sniffled. That figured. In the virtus, dreaming of his time with his precious Jane. Damn it, Thena, you are such hot stuff you can't even compete with a dead woman.

"Look," he said, practically running to catch up with me, which should show him once and for all to stop taking advantage of his longer legs to set a faster pace than I was comfortable with. Because it wasn't all in the length of the legs, and he might as well get used to *that.*

"Look, Thena," he said. "I'm an idiot."

Did he expect me to defend him? What was I now? The official clearer of Kit Klaavil's name?

"I've probably always been an idiot. Would you please stop and turn so I can talk to you?" he asked. "Or at least slow down?" He reached for my arm, wrapped his fingers around it.

I stopped and turned. Some things are automatic. The only thing I can say is that I didn't kick him as hard as I could have. He keened and went down on his knees, clutching himself.

"Oh no," I said. "You shouldn't have touched me, you idiot!"

He was three shades paler than normal, as he looked up at me, and his eyes were full of the kind of tears brought on by sudden and sharp pain, but he was smiling, even as he sucked in a lungful of air in a way that sounded like it hurt. "I know," he said, and smiled wide. "I told you I was stupid."

"Granted," I said. "You win on that. Are you all right?"

He took another deep breath. "I will be," he said, and got up, in a testing sort of way. He shook his head. "You didn't kick as hard as you could have."

I crossed my arms on my chest, refusing to admit to anything. "You wanted me to stop so I could talk to you. Now talk."

"Give me time. You know how the prospect of hanging concentrates the mind wonderfully? A kick to the groin doesn't."

"Does this mean you don't remember what you wanted to tell me?" I asked. "Right. I'm walking. We can talk at home—at your—at the Denovo compound."

And the stupid idiot reached for my arm again, though this time he managed to stop himself just before he grabbed it, his hand hovering so near that I could feel the warmth of it. "Thena, no. I know what I want to say. I'm just not sure how to say it. And I don't want to make you ang—angrier."

"That," I told him, "would be pretty damn hard."

"Wouldn't it?" he asked conversationally. "But not after being kicked." He looked expectant, but I refused to acknowledge his low joke. He hissed breath out. "Listen, Thena, I need a nav."

"I'm sure there will be dozens of them ready to travel with you now that they know you're not a murderer!" I said.

"Probably. The Denovos are a good family," he said. "We have prestige. We have Kath's brilliance and quick temper, besides Kath being the most devious avenger who ever lived. Anne is a legendary nav. Everyone loves Mom and Dad. I'm fairly sure there are dozens of the younger navs and a few of the loners my age willing to pair with me."

"See?" I said. "Problem solved. As Doctor Bartolomeu said, you're welcome."

"So . . ." he said. "You've been on Eden now for a while. What kind of nav do you think I should pick?"

Oh, was that how he was going to punish me? How he was going to show his power over me? Very well. I'd play his game. "You need someone quiet," I said. "Someone who doesn't get angry easily."

"Really?" he asked. He looked surprised. Clearly he hadn't expected me to pick up on his gambit.

"Very much so," I said. "Because, you see, you have such a sudden temper. If you were to . . . partner or marry a nav with the same temper, you would end up killing her." I realized what I had said, and amended, "I don't mean literally but . . ."

He inclined his head, looking infuriatingly unaffected. "I see," he said. "So I need a meek and mild woman," he said. "'Her voice was ever soft, gentle, and low, an excellent thing in woman.'"

"Shakespeare," I snapped. "*King Lear*." Did he think I was totally uneducated?

He grinned and bowed slightly. "What else?"

"Well, she should be blonde, because you clearly like blondes. And well read. And she should be a musician."

"Oh, yes, that would be great," he said, and beamed. "Then we could play while on the trips. It would be very nice."

"Yes," I said. "Wouldn't it?" I considered kicking him again. If I kicked hard enough, I could get a good way down the road before he recovered. Of course, if I kicked hard enough I might cause permanent damage, and though that shouldn't matter, it seemed to.

"There are . . ." He thought about it. "Last I paid any attention to any of them . . . Well, I think there are about five of the single navs who fit that profile."

"Good," I said. "Then you should fly to the center and ask one of them out, right about now."

He frowned at me, "I should, shouldn't I?"

"Yes," I said. "Now if you'll excuse me—"

The bastard used cat-speed. Before I knew what he was doing, he was on me, clasping my wrists together in one hand behind my back and, before I could stop him, bringing his lips to mine.

I moved around, trying to get the right angle to knee him in the gonads. And found he had his other hand in front of them. I squirmed. If I raised my knee just right, and shoved to the side, I could push his hand away and—

Thena!

His voice in my mind jarred, and his lips moved gently against mine—firm and yet soft, soft and yet seeming insatiable, asking for and getting my attention. For a moment, my mind went blank and diffuse, like cotton candy spread thinly against a light, and his tongue slipped between my lips to meet my tongue. It felt demanding and insistent. It tasted of bug juice, which mingled oddly with the taste of burnt sugar left by the last drug, but he didn't seem to care.

I cared, but I couldn't think very clearly because there were weird things happening to my body—probably as a result of the drug residuals. My knees had gone rubbery, and there was this great heat spreading from somewhere in my lower stomach, as he pulled me closer to him, my body squeezed tight against his muscular chest, his calico beard tickling my face and those damned feline eyes all half-lidded and tender.

Princess, will you marry me?

I couldn't talk, but I could think at him, and I thought at him the impression of a swat, the whole of my aggrieved pride behind it. *Stop making fun of me you . . . bastard!*

There was a low rumble of laughter deep in his chest, though he never broke our kiss. And now I was going lightheaded. Oxygen deprivation.

Never said I wasn't a bastard, but what does that have to do with my wanting you to marry me and be my nav? Too good for me?

No! Yes! I pushed back from him and managed a ragged sentence, as I tore my lips from his, "Damn you."

His expression didn't alter—or not much. His eyes were still soft, tender. "Please?" he said. "Please marry me. Or at least be my nav. You know I can't be trusted in space alone. I live in the virtus. And I need someone to do repairs and . . . please? I promise to let you kick me twice a week and four times on Sunday."

It had to be the most absurd proposal ever made by any man to any woman. And it was insane. What the hell did he want with me, exactly? "You like being kicked?"

"No. But if it will get you to say yes..."

"Are you insane?"

"Possibly. But look, I really need a nav and—"

"And next thing you know, you'll tell me you need a woman to cook your meals and bear your children." As I said it I remembered what Doc Bartolomeu had said. No children for Kit, ever, not unless he contrived to clone himself, and it wouldn't be the same. I looked away.

"Oh," Kit said. "I wondered if he had told you." He let go of me. We were suddenly very serious and I didn't feel at all angry at him, at least not enough to kick him.

I cleared my throat, searched madly for words.

"I'm sorry I bothered you," Kit said. "I thought... if you didn't know, you might..." He seemed to realize what he was saying. "I don't want you to... I mean, I knew you wouldn't do what... what Jane did... when you found out, and I thought when you found out, by that time, you'd have reasons to love me, and understand that... that I really am just a man, like other men. But now... I completely understand you could never knowingly marry a Mule."

His words were so formal, his tone so perfectly contained, that I had to clench my hands tight. I should have kicked him then, but I couldn't trust myself not to make it too strong. "You are stupid," I said. "Rude too. Assuming you know what my answer is and why."

"Uh... You were afraid... when we first met... you were afraid I was a Mule."

I put my hands on my hips and glared up at him, "Oh, yes, but that was when I thought Mules were all-powerful evil beings. It was before I got to share a ship with one and understood his was a more pedestrian form of evil, consisting of not picking up his damned dirty clothes, as though vibroing were an arcane mystery; and of being a hothead who is too proud for his own damn good; and of not being a gentleman."

He looked confused. "Not being a gentleman?"

"No gentleman would propose to a woman by mind talk while making her completely irrational with the best kiss she ever experienced."

His eyes widened. A little chuckle mingled with a shocked gasp, and then he used cat-speed again. The man really was a very good kisser. I wondered if he'd learned it from the late, unlamented Jane, in which case, he might be forgiven for having married her.

With his arms—both—wrapped tight around me, his body molded to mine, his mouth attacking mine with intent and malice, I felt like I was surrounded by Kit. I smelled the long-distance ship smell, but also the smell I'd come to associate with Kit—clean male with a hint of soap, but very male, warm and vaguely musky. I think I moaned, though I refuse to admit it. It might have been him for all I know. After all, our mouths were joined. Who knew who made what sound?

Marry me, Thena, please.

I tried to sigh and would have managed it, had he left me enough air space. If he intended on kissing me like this a lot, I was going to need a nose mask and oxygen tanks in the future. *Yes,* I said, reluctantly. *I think I must.*

It was perfectly clear to me that the poor man had become disturbed in his reason, and in those conditions it would be cruel and unfair to send him to space alone, much less when space had become so dangerous. I must marry him, just to make sure he stayed safe. It was the least I could do, since I was fairly sure I'd started him on this road by trying to garrotte him and reducing his supply of oxygen to the brain.

Yes, yes, you must, he said. *It gets very boring in the* Cathouse, *without anyone to kick me.*

Poor man. Madder than a broomer hopped up on oblivium.

ᓚᑯ THIRTY-FOUR ᒧᑌ

WE WALKED BACK TO THE FLYER, HAND IN HAND. IT SEEMED TO take a long time, possibly because Kit felt the need to kiss me now and then. He said he had to check on my breath rate, because of the drugs to emerge from the hypnotics, but how you checked on someone's breath by stopping it was beyond me. Not that I was complaining. His kissing seemed to stop my brain for long periods of time, too. Which is the only reason I can give for why it took me so long to wonder if it was such a good idea to marry him.

Oh, don't get me wrong. It was a good idea for me to marry Kit. In this world, where I seemed likely to be confined for a long time if not forever, Kit was someone. He had a profession that paid very well. His family was warm and welcomed me. And... well, I wanted him.

The problem is that I did love Kit. At least, I thought I loved Kit. It was very hard to say for sure, because I had never even imagined I loved anyone before. Simon was a friend. The other half-dozen acquaintances and friendly strangers who had been my sometime lovers—including a very nice harvester in Circum, who had to be twice my age but who had been very sweet and kind—were just that: friends, acquaintances, gentle strangers. I'd never thought myself in love, not love like the poets talked about.

I'd come to the conclusion that all the poets either lied or got hold of something a lot more potent than oblivium, and that all this nonsense they went on about was just that. Nonsense. Stuff out of their minds. I was fully with Shakespeare, in what I assumed was one of his more candid moments, when he'd said that men had died and the worms had eaten them, but not for love.

Then there was Kit, and I found myself doing stupid things, like wanting to touch his violin while I slept. Thinking of him all the time. Feeling a bit lost and out of sorts when he wasn't with me. And if that wasn't love, I didn't know what else it was—and I hoped it was bacteria, so they could cure it.

But the worst symptom of it was that I wanted Kit to be happy more than I wanted me to be happy. Which is why it hadn't mattered so much that I had declared my feelings in front of all of Eden. I was upset that Kit had heard it, because he would feel obliged. And now, after walking silently for a while, I started wondering if that was why he was doing this. Because he wanted to spare me embarrassment.

I think I blurted it out, but I don't know if it was mind or voice. The result was a shout of laughter and my finding myself, again, suddenly captive in his arms and thoroughly kissed.

"No, but is that why?" I asked, as I came up for air.

"Thena!" He chuckled. "I'm not a philanthropist. I'm not a bad person, but I don't tend to put myself out. Ask my parents. I wouldn't endure a day's discomfort—much less a mismatched marriage—to save you embarrassment if I didn't love you."

"Oh, but...but marrying me... Look, I'm no bargain. I have hell's own temper. And I don't get music, not the way you get music. And I have a weird sense of humor. And—"

"And I don't vibro my clothes," he said, with a quirk to his lips. "What is your point? Were you under the impression that only angels could marry?"

"No..." We walked a bit more, and then I thought of something else. I didn't know if it was important here. It was damned important on Earth and at my level in society, though I'd never thought about it much, because...well...anyone marrying me, wouldn't be marrying me. He'd be marrying Daddy's inheritance and my own little flaw wouldn't disturb him much. But I'd never thought I'd marry a man I loved. I took a deep breath. "You should know," I said, "that there have been...others. Not many. I mean, I don't have to take my shoes off to count them, but—"

He actually stopped and looked at me with such an odd expression that I wondered if I'd been speaking Glaish or if my brain was so scrambled I'd been making senseless sounds. He frowned. "Woman, are you trying to tell me you're not a virgin?"

I swallowed. "Ye- Yes."

"Oh, well, then," he said. "Of course you can't be my wife, then. We *might* be able to squeeze you in as second concubine, at half pay, if you promise to behave the rest of your life and wear a chastity belt while away from me."

If it weren't for the quirk of his lips and the unholy spark in his eyes, I think I would have run away. As was, though, I slapped him. Or I tried to slap him. An open-hand slap across the face was all I intended. Practically a caress. But of course it never landed. His hand caught my wrist halfway and he pulled me to him and kissed me again. "You are such a strange creature," he said when he was done scrambling my brain some more. "It will shock you to know I am not a virgin, either."

"You were *married*," I said with considerable annoyance.

"Ah, so. Well, I wasn't a virgin when I married, either, and she was not my only lover. Are we really going to swap lists of everyone we've ever been with? I'd rather presume it's all in the past and we love each other now?"

"Yes," I said. I took a deep breath. "Please. It wasn't . . . I've never loved anyone before."

I half expected him to laugh at that, but he smiled. "Even that," he said, "is more than I require and far more than I ever expected."

We'd somehow reached the outside of the flyer, and he was handing me in. He climbed in on his side. But he didn't lean forward to put his finger in the genlock. Instead, he frowned intently at the dashboard.

"Uh . . . what . . . what are your plans for your wedding? I mean . . . how did you ever imagine it being?"

I blinked. This seemed like the oddest of times to plan the wedding. Oh, sure, I supposed we had become officially engaged. But did we need to do a bridesmaid count right now? "Big, formal, uncomfortable," I said. "I always assumed too that Daddy Dearest would need to have me either doped, tied up or under some sort of blackmail, to get me to agree to marry whoever the bright boy was he had found."

He looked at me and, unaccountably, looked terribly relieved. "So . . . so you don't have dreams about a specific dress, or . . . or . . . specific music or . . . roses or all that."

"Roses would be nice..." I said. "But I don't have any specific dreams about my wedding, no. Or my marriage. You see, I never thought I would marry—not really. I thought eventually Daddy Dearest would sell me to the highest bidder, but that's not the same."

He nodded.

"I suppose we can do whatever you and your family want," I said. "I don't care. It is the after the wedding I'm interested in."

He nodded again, then took a deep, loud breath. "I had a big wedding once, with a Gaian priestess and fertility rites and... a banquet and dances and things..." He frowned at me. "Would you mind terribly if we don't echo it?"

I shook my head. As long as I still got him, we could just shout it from the rooftops and be done with it. It was all the same to me.

"You're not just saying it to..."

"No," I said. "We'll do what you want."

And he smiled, and his eyes sparkled and he said, "You were absolutely right, Patrician Sinistra. I will definitely do better with a compliant wife."

At which point I'd have kicked him, but he was starting the flyer and it would have been difficult.

We flew back to the center, stopped by a florist and bought me a half-dozen white roses. And then we'd flitted back to the judicial building.

Weddings were performed at a machine, mostly because marriage was a fairly standard contract, and the computer simply the means of performing it. Kit touched the sensa screen without asking me my preferences, though I was sure he knew I'd stop him if I disagreed with anything.

He picked Mutual Obligation—as opposed to one obeying the other, Common Property, Indefinite Duration and Official Mediation Required Before Divorce Granted. All of which were good because when he woke up tomorrow morning and he realized what he had done, I wanted it to be difficult for him to run screaming into the night without thinking it over. And then we'd pressed our thumbs to the gen-sensor in the computer, and we were done.

We took a very brief moment, after that, for him to send notifications of name change to the Center and to all his creditors, as well as to insert a notice of our contract into the midday and evening news.

I was ambivalent about the name. "You don't have to change it," I said.

But he'd given me a serious glance and said, "I want to. Partly because everyone expects it and it takes too much effort to correct people over and over again. And partly because... I want to change it."

I didn't ask anymore.

And then the exasperating man insisted on taking me to eat at a very small restaurant where the tables seemed to have been booked months in advance but where a mention of "Doctor Bartolomeu's table" got us—after a quick call to the doctor—seated in a quiet corner and assiduously attended to.

By the time we got home, his family had seen the news and moved my belongings to Kit's room.

There was also a small, gold-wrapped box, which Kit's mother said had been delivered by a messenger from Doc Bartolomeu.

We opened it, not without trepidation. I think Kit half expected a challenge to a duel. Instead, inside there were two gold rings, matching, broad and flat, engraved with bas-relief roses. It looked like medieval work, though of course it couldn't be. Inside, each was engraved with *Je Reviens* and a note saying that Doc Bartolomeu had had them made for us and that he hoped my ring fit, as he had it made from his sight estimation of my size. He didn't say when he had them made and I had a feeling I didn't want to ask.

On Earth, wedding rings had long since been abandoned, though women often had a ring tattooed on their finger. But in Eden they were customary, even if, like everything else, they weren't enforced.

They fit us perfectly.

⸎ THIRTY-FIVE ⸎

WE DIDN'T LINGER ON IN EDEN. KIT HAD AN INVITATION TO PLAY
at the music center, but even that couldn't hold him. He told them
he'd play when we came back. He also bought what he called a
good, serviceable violin to play in the *Cathouse*. His father's violin
had been built by his father and aged being played by him, and
it was not something that Kit would risk to space travel.

Part of the reason for leaving was the ever-increasing roll of
casualties. The Earthers—how quickly one got used to thinking
of them that way!—must be getting more efficient at darkship
hunting. I told myself it had nothing to do with me, they'd just
decided to get serious about catching the thieves.

There was the chance, perhaps, that they'd become this interested because my father's goons had seen Kit in that bay. I didn't
know what Kit had done to them. His most complete explanation
had been, "Held them at bay with a burner. Grabbed you. Got
back to the *Cathouse*."

But even if they'd seen, it was more likely in the rush of the
moment, in the darkened bay, they'd think that they'd imagined the
cat eyes and the fast movements. It wasn't likely they'd understand it
was one of the darkship thieves. Father, maybe, if he was alive, but
more likely Good Man Navre, my friend Gil's father, had decided
he needed to be seen doing something about the darkship thieves.

I told Kit that many times, when I woke up in the night catching stray bits of guilt from his mind. But other than that and

his grave expression when the lists of casualties came in, marriage suited us. I'm not going to recommend it to everyone as a universal panacea, and in fact I'd had doubts that someone with my own, negotiated sanity, could live that closely with another human being in peace, much less happily.

But we were happy. I liked waking up next to him, or often on him, as he didn't seem to mind—given my mass—if I curled up half on top of him, with my head on his chest. The rest were almost the same things we'd done before, only now we did them together. If I was tinkering with some piece of machinery, trying to figure out how it worked, he was reading or practicing violin nearby. If we went to the music center, we held each other's hands.

I suspect marriage made us less sociable, rather than more. We'd no need of others while we had each other.

I'd quit my job at the Center and Kit and Kath had more or less bullied the people at the Energy Board into giving me provisional nav certification. They kept saying that I couldn't be a nav, but Kit insisted he was taking me aboard his rented spaceship and I would work as his nav, so they might as well certify me.

The examination was easy enough, testing all the areas in which I already knew I excelled—mechanical ability, navigation and my mind link to Kit. That one was a little strange, as it seemed to stretch farther than any other cat/nav link. I could hear him when he was at home and I in the center, miles away. I suspected it was farther than that. They might have too, but they didn't test it. After all, better than needed was not a problem.

And then a week after that, a month and a half after our marriage, we bid our farewells to friends and family and got ready to leave in the *Cathouse.* Due to my provisional status, we were still not allowed to rent a better ship—not the least because they'd lost so many ships and so many were in need of repair, that finding another ship would have been a problem.

Kit's family had gone back with us to the center, to say goodbye. The women hadn't yet decided to go back to space and everyone was a little tearful and a little worried. The hugs lasted a little longer, and I—who didn't remember being hugged by anyone but Kit, since my mother's death—was bewildered at finding myself passed down a line of hugging relatives, not only the Denovos by birth, but Denovos by marriage. I felt my eyes unaccountably moist as I stepped back to hold Kit's hand.

And Doc Bartolomeu came up, pushing through the family group. He pulled Kit into what would be a bear hug if Doc Bartolomeu were of normal height, and not a small, stooped little man. At best it was a racoon hug. Or, given the fierceness of it, perhaps a wolverine's.

He let go of Kit very quickly, then hugged me with the same fierce fervor. Stepping back, he said, "You know you shouldn't go to the powertrees. Not just now."

"We'll be fine," Kit said. "I was fine before and I was alone."

But the doctor sighed and recommended that I not do anything stupid and Kit not be a hero. We assured him that we had no intention of doing either of those. All we wanted was a quick and successful trip. At the price powerpods were now, it would put a considerable dent in our debt, and besides we wanted to be allowed to rent one of the bigger and newer ships.

As I've said before, we always get what we don't want.

The trip out was uneventful. Kit had brought his violin and treated me, late into the night, to renditions of the Passacaglia from the Rosary Sonata, or to Bach's Violin Concerto number one. I liked it. I might not understand the music as music, but when Kit played, his feelings invaded my consciousness. It was a lot like being in mind contact with him, if less clear. And if Kit spent any time at all in the virtus, I wasn't aware of it and that was doubtful, as we were more or less always together barring the fresher, and that only because it was too small to fit both of us—in fact, I was still not sure how it fit him.

Our approach to the powertrees was equally uneventful. At first we were both very tense, having timed it perfectly to go in while the powertrees were on the night side of the Earth. One of the great mysteries was why the powertrees were pegged to orbit the Earth at a latitude and speed that meant they were in darkness for two six-hour periods for each of Earth's days. It seemed like a strange idea to have solar collectors in the dark for half the day. But it was assumed there had been a good, sound reason. Some theories said it was to allow the trunks to grow, so they could support new powerpods. The others said that it kept the growth of powerpods more even. And many others forwarded other reasons.

The pet explanation, in Eden, was that it was done to allow the darkships to move among them undetected. I'd thought this was crazy when I'd first heard it, but after hearing Jarl's story, I thought perhaps not. Oh, he wouldn't know of Eden, as it would exist, but he might very well have anticipated a time when his kind would need to steal powerpods.

We'd waited, tempering our approach to make it at night—found a cluster of powerpods where I expected it to be based on the maps given by a returning navigator, from which I'd extrapolated three months' growth.

I was in the nav's cabin, looking at my screens—which were considerably better for my eyes than Kit's screens were—calculating the changes in the computers there which worked only with raw numbers and therefore couldn't give anything away, and trying to figure out where the next cluster was because this cluster had only five pods, and our ship could take ten. Eden, in power-saving brownouts as it was, could use as many as we could bring.

At the same time, by sight and voice, I was directing Kit—giving him a second pair of eyes on his collecting work.

To the left a smidgen, Kitty Cat.

Princess, his amused voice came over the mind link. *Have I mentioned what impresses me most about you is the depth and breadth of your precise scientific vocabulary?* Smidgen?

You know, a touch.

Touch? *What is a* touch?

I sent him a mental image. There was a momentary silence. The collector carefully encircled the powerpod and started closing—a fiddly operation, if you didn't want to detonate the pod.

You have a very dirty mind, woman. How did I marry such a low minded wench?

Well, you got the right length, did you not?

Indeed, he said, as he started to pull the powerpod—our third of the run—home to our storage bay. *I should hope I have the width too. Or are you complaining?*

Which is when I saw the flash out of the corner of my eyes. I had time to mind-send, *I think there's something, starboard, three clicks, but—*

And then light erupted, a flash of unbearable brightness, bright enough to blind me.

Shit, Kit said in my mind.

And then a wave of heat, like the uncovered mouth of a hellish furnace hit me. And I lost consciousness.

I don't know how long I was out, but I came to with Kit in

my mind. Not talking to me, exactly, just swearing up a blue storm. It started with *Shit*, ran up the scale of all the standard swear words, and then to an eerie silence.

I heard him moving around...wherever I was. It didn't seem to be the nav cabin. Or if it was, something had happened to me, because I was horizontal, on my back.

I assumed the person moving around was Kit. The presence felt like Kit's. There was a rustle of cloth and the sound of breathing, and then again, the low swearing, this time mind and voice, "Shit, shit, shit."

I tried to open my eyes. They wouldn't open. Or at least, the light didn't change. I tried to speak, but my mouth hurt. And then I became aware that everything hurt—my whole body. It hurt at such a high level, so uniformly, that my brain had refused to recognize it as pain, and my *self* had gone somewhere, away, far away.

Kit, Kit, it hurts. And it's dark.

For a moment he didn't say anything. Then came a deep breath. "Hold up, Princess, hold up."

Gentle, gentle hands touched my neck and then something pointy and cold made me shiver. It felt like the tip of an injector. "Painkiller," he said. "It should start feeling better soon." He made a sound like a hiccup. Maybe a sob.

I felt the bed shift with his sitting on it. Bed. We were on the bed, then. I hadn't been on the bed when... *What happened? What was that?*

"Tractor ray. Slammed into our collector claws, and then smashed pod into side of ship." He took a noisy breath, that might have been another sob. "It...burst. Right under your...right under the navigator cabin. I was looking the other way. Otherwise...blinded."

The pod. The heat and light. Radiation. I'd been radiation-burned. If the ship was undamaged—and it might be, the dima-tough and ceramite Eden used was much tougher than anything on Earth—it would still be radiation-hot. All of it. And I... *How bad is it? How bad did I get hit?*

"Bad." I heard him rummage through something. There was a sound like containers being slammed together, papers rustling. Something beeped, then again, urgently. Kit gasped.

The pain was going away—not being removed, exactly, but receding to some place far away. It left my brain able to work. That type of blast. That strong... *Tell me, damn you! How bad?*

He made a sound that I couldn't interpret. It might have been annoyance or a sob or something. And then he said, "Hold up. Hold up, okay. Wait. I'm trying to get a read on the med-examiner. Something is wrong."

Of course something was wrong. He was trying to get a read on severe radiation burn and poisoning with an instrument that was designed to diagnose and prescribe treatment for minor aches and sprains and perhaps the common cold. If I could have lifted my arms without screaming in pain, I would have smacked the side of his head. *Christopher Bartolomeu Sinistra! You know better than that! I'm radiation-burned. From the feel of it, badly burned. There is nothing in our medkit that will help.*

"It's not irreparable. A couple of weeks of regen and..."

Which shows how my beloved was functioning. A couple of weeks of regen might solve the problem—it depended on how many of my internal organs I'd managed to cook—but a couple of weeks of regen was months away in Eden. And if I was so burned I couldn't see and everything hurt, I wasn't going to make it to Eden alive. *It feels like my entire skin area is burned,* I said. He didn't answer. *And my eyes are gone. Kit, do you have your radiation suit on? I must be emitting radiation too!* As I spoke, I tried to reach for his mind, to commandeer his eyes. He pushed me back.

Can you see, Kit? Are you blinded?

No. I'm fine. Closed my eyes in time.

Let me see.

"No. Yes. I'm wearing the radiation suit." He took a deep, shaky breath. "There must be something we can do. I refuse to...I refuse to...You can't die like this."

I pushed again, past his resistence and his bewildered pain, past his defenses and his panic. I pushed and pushed, and he gave in, and I got to look...out of his eyes.

Everything looked different. I'd known that. The virulent colors looked muted pastel to him. Tasteful really.

But no amount of different vision could make me look other than what I was. If I'd been a roast, I might have looked attractive. As it was, my skin was a burnt, brownish mess, cracked in places, and mingled with the melted remnants of the dress I'd been wearing. My hair was a dark mass, best not investigated. My eyes were indeed gone.

I pulled back from Kit's eyes.

I took a deep breath that brought twinges of pain despite the painkiller. *Kit, you know what to do. You have a burner. There is nothing else you can do for me.*

"No," he said, then like an incantation. "No. There must be something. I must be able to do something. I must. You can't die, Thena! You can't."

Words from Shakespeare ran through my head on the subject of all of us being born to die. But I couldn't have told him that, not if I tried. The truth of the matter is, when it comes to matters of any importance poets are bloody useless.

Listen, lover, listen. I knew I was calm by virtue of the painkiller. I knew if the painkiller started wearing off it would only get worse, much worse. If he didn't have the courage to do what must be done, I would die slowly. You can't live long with your skin that burned. *It was good. It was better than I could have imagined. I never expected love, you see, and I got to have it. Maybe I didn't even deserve it. But we took a gamble, and we lost, and there's nothing we can do now. Nothing. You must get the burner. You must put me down.*

And then I thought if he was here, the *Cathouse* was adrift in the powertrees. Adrift on automatic pilot. Any minute now, he'd hit another powerpod and it would all be over for both of us. *Put me down and get out of here, Kit. Get out of here fast, before you crash or they board you.*

He didn't answer. Not with words. But from his mind came a storm of emotions. Fear for me, and almost unbearable grief, and then, rising, growing, a steady drumbeat of *Not again, not again, not again. I'll do as she says, and then I'll kill myself, I'll do as she says and then I'll put myself out of my misery. Not again, not again, not again.*

Kit, no. You must go back to Eden. You must go back and... Take my body? In storage. Have me cremated. Put my ashes in the rose garden atop the compound. By the white roses...Like...

But he wasn't listening. He was running. I wasn't quite in his mind, but I wasn't quite out.

I could feel him panting, running. I could feel him in the cat cabin, rummaging, finding the burner. I could feel the handle of the burner, made of smooth dimatough, cool and heavy in his hand.

He was walking. He was walking back, slower, in measured

steps. But the rhythms in his mind remained the same, the frenzied certainty that he must kill me then himself.

I felt him near the bed. I felt the tip of his fingers touch my hand. *Oh damn,* he said in my mind. *Perhaps there is . . . destiny?*

No destiny. Don't be an idiot, Kit. I must die. I'm already dead. But I want to know you will go on. I want to know you'll live.

A choked sob answered me. *Why? What's the point? It's not like I'm going to have children to live after me. It's not like there's any point to me. Just another Mule—a dead end, going nowhere. I can die now, or I can live alone hundreds of years. What difference does it make?*

It makes a difference to me. I tried to push the idea at him, the feel of how much I loved him. *It makes a difference to anyone who hears you play the violin. And Kit, there's more than one way to reproduce. You can have children, just not of your body. You can make them, mold them, see them grow. Find . . . find someone to raise them with. Name a daughter after me.* I wasn't sure what I was saying anymore. I just wanted to convince him life had value. I was sure if he just got past the grief, he'd see it too. *Your parents love you. Doc Bartolomeu loves you.* I felt the tip of the burner, cool against my temple. The thought in his mind was that he would fire like that because he must make sure that he killed me with the first shot. I heard him swallowing. I could feel him steeling himself for the shot.

Goodbye lover, I said. *Thank you. I'm so glad I didn't garrotte you.*

The burner dropped. A ragged sob answered me, then his voice, "I can't, can't, can't. Can't."

You have to!

But he wasn't listening. He was straightening himself up. I heard him walk out, calmly. I didn't think he was abandoning me. He had made a decision, but what decision? Damn fool man. Didn't he know he was in shock and couldn't be trusted to decide anything?

A part of my mind followed him. I couldn't quite see through his eyes, but I could follow. He was going around the ramp to the cat cabin. I felt him pushing the switch that erased all maps, and then the switch of the intercom, cool against his fingers, felt him flick it on.

It was ridiculous. Even if another Eden ship were nearby to be hailed, it wasn't likely to have a regen tank in its hold, any more than we did.

But he flicked that switch on and spoke into the com in his best, decisive voice. "Christopher Bartolomeu Sinistra, piloting the *Cathouse* on behalf of the Eden Board of Energy. I have an emergency aboard and I demand aid."

Of whom do you demand aid, you fool? I asked. *There is no one!*

But as he repeated the message again, there was a loud crackle and then, "Circum Terra. What is an Eden Board of Energy?"

And Kit, clearly, calmly, though his mind was one large, confused sob, said, "I believe you call us darkship thieves." There was even a hint of amusement to his tone.

For a moment only silence answered, and then a voice said. "Did you say *Sinistra?*"

"Yes. I must request rescue for my wife, Patrician Athena Hera Sinistra."

"Ath—" a series of crackles followed, and then a different voice came on.

"Mister . . . ah . . . Sinistra. Did you say you have Athena Hera Sinistra aboard, and that she needs rescue?" Daddy Dearest's voice sounded healthy and possibly even happy.

"Yes. My wife, Athena Hera Sinistra, was burned by an exploding powerpod and she needs immediate first aid and extensive regen."

A deep breath from the other side was audible through the com. "Well, well, well. So . . . What are your conditions?"

Tell him he has to let you go after you deliver me. Arrange some means he doesn't set foot in the Cathouse. *They'll kill you, Kit, if they see you. You must—*

I might as well have been talking to a wall. My husband, wonderful, ridiculous, loving, stupid man that he was, answered bravely and foolishly, "None, so long as you save Thena."

◖⟢ THIRTY-SIX ⟣◗

I WOKE UP. THE FIRST SENTENCE IN MY MIND WAS *DAMN IT, KIT.* *Doc Bartolomeu* told *you not be a hero. I'm telling.*

There was no answer from his mind, and the feeling that he was nearby had disappeared.

My call of *Kit!* went unanswered, even as I became aware of my surroundings. I was lying on something soft, but it didn't feel like the yielding and accommodating bio-bed Kit and I shared in Eden or the other bio-bed we shared in the *Cathouse*. In fact, it felt very much like a mattress on Earth—soft, but not at body temperature and not molding to me in the way only a bioed thing could.

I had binds on my wrists, binds across my middle. Something— a tube?—was down my throat, taped to the sides of my mouth. Something else obscured my eyes, or at least when I opened them I saw nothing but darkness.

Memory rushed upon me. The coup in my father's space cruiser, Eden, Kit, the *Cathouse*. A moment of brief panic whispered that it had all been a dream. I'd just had one of my many accidents with the brooms. I was in a hospital, recovering. Everything else was hallucination.

The cloying, disinfectant smell of the hospital seemed to confirm this. A dream. A delusion. Not true. My mind refused to accept it. It couldn't be a dream. It just couldn't. I could have dreamed the darkships; I could even have dreamed Kit as I'd first met him.

I could never have dreamed Kit as I'd come to know him—as a person who would love me unconditionally, who would accept the fractured confused person I knew myself to be. That, I could never have dreamed.

So Kit existed, and the whole episode had been true. Where did that leave me?

It left me here, in a hospital bed, strapped down as a mentally unstable patient, with a tube—presumably with nutrients—shoved down my throat and with no ability to defend myself. And no idea where my husband was.

The silly idiot. The gallant fool. What did he think he'd earn giving himself up to Earth? What except death? Did he think he would be on hand to defend me from whatever threatened me?

I knew that was exactly what he thought and dreaded his misguided belief. But one thing I dreaded more.

If I had been brought into this hospital to recover from severe burns, and if I was now struggling towards full consciousness, it must have been two weeks, perhaps a month, since Kit had surrendered himself and the *Cathouse*—not only endangering himself but betraying Eden's trust in its pilots—in an attempt to save me.

The chances that Kit was still alive were very low. There were laws on Earth, after all, that dictated the death of anyone bioed away from human genome standard.

They wouldn't be able to see most of his modifications. He could hide the fact that he was a Mule. But his hair and his eyes could not be hidden, and would be obvious. And besides, my father had been there. And I failed to see how my father would not want Kit dead, if nothing else, to hide the fact that I'd married what he'd consider a monstrosity.

For a moment I felt as though I'd sink into the mattress, as though my loss and grief would overwhelm all. At the same time boiling rage bubbled up, smoldering, from depths I didn't even know I had possessed.

I had been angry before. In fact, many people, including those who had tried in vain to mold me into the perfect Patrician's daughter, would claim that anger was my abiding problem. But I'd never been this angry at so many people.

I smoldered with rage at my father—who was almost certainly still alive and whose role in all this I couldn't even begin to understand. I burned with fury at myself for not having prevented Kit from coming back to danger; I felt strong annoyance at my husband's stupid chivalry—but most of all I longed to punish Earth. All of it. Land-states and dead zones, protectorates and Seacities. Them and their stupid laws. Ever since the turmoils, they'd banned an entire type of people, an entire class of bio-improvements, and for what? Were we any better than we'd been? So the Mules had been inconsiderate, perhaps violent. They'd not taken into account the will of the people they governed.

The Good Men weren't any better, and like the Mules, they had no more than a tenuous connection to the people they governed. They were just a few families, lording it over the mass of mankind for whom they didn't care any more than the Mules ever had.

My fury at Earth could have consumed the planet in a giant conflagration.

Correction, *would* consume the planet in a giant conflagration.

I made sure not to move in any way that could be interpreted as my being awake, as I listened for any noises indicating people in the room. I heard a heavy step to my left, almost certainly a male foot. From the right came softer sounds—as if produced by someone smaller—and a tinkle of glass or ceramite, as though the somebody were manipulating a tray full of objects, medicines or perhaps surgical implements.

"I still don't understand," the voice from my left said, speaking in a low rumble that confirmed my suspicions of its gender. "Why they have us here, guarding her, with weapons. She's just a little girl."

The person on the right didn't say anything for a while, and when she spoke, it was in a sort of soft, concerned tone. "I don't understand it, either, but they tell me she is very dangerous. And besides, I don't think they'd order us to guard the daughter of a Good Man if that weren't true." She sounded dubious even as she said it.

Oh, good. I liked it when I took my guards by surprise. Gently, carefully, so deliberately that I didn't seem to be doing it and could stop at any moment, I started testing both the firmness of the bind around my wrist and the tightness of it.

The bad news was that it was indeed tight. The good news, that it was made of tensile, non-rigid material, like most of the binds put on you in hospitals, where they were, after all, afraid you might damage yourself with an unconscious movement. This meant if I worked slowly, if I worked carefully, I could free that hand. Which, of course, would make it much easier for me to free myself of all the other binds.

If there was one thing I couldn't stand, it was to be tied down and blindfolded. Someone was going to die a horribly messy death for this.

I thought of Kit tying me in the *Cathouse* and tenderness fueled my rage. *Kit, wherever you are, I'm going to avenge you.*

I was pulling, slowly, steadily at my hand, loosening the bind, when I heard a response. *Thena? Thena!*

For a moment I wasn't sure I had heard it. It was that faint. But I seized onto it and mind-shouted in the direction of his perceived thought. *Kit?*

This time the response was a little stronger. *Light. Bright. Pain. Nausea. Thena? Alive?*

Oh, I am very much alive. And I'm coming for you.

Yes. The one word. So unlike Kit, and yet bearing in it Kit's personality and a curious sense of despair. And then there was something that sounded like a mental scream, like the mind-voice equivalent of a spasm of pain.

Kit!

There was no answer, and I thought they had killed him. But if they had killed him, that meant that they had kept him alive all this time just to communicate with me. Preposterous. No. Kit was alive. That scream was the result of whatever they were doing to him.

Why would they be doing anything to him?

Because he was a darkship thief. They had technologies Earth could only dream of. And besides, Kit knew where they were located, where they could be plundered or exterminated.

Oh, I'd grown up with the full myth of the benevolent government of the Good Men, who cared for their people and sought only their happiness.

Unfortunately for the mythmakers, I'd also grown up with my father. It was impossible to see my father at close quarters for most of my life and not to know—know with absolute, gut-born certainty—there were only two things Father and most of the Good Men cared about: power and their personal well-being.

Of course they would torture Kit to find out what he knew, and where the people were who knew more. And of course they would pay. It was me against the Good Men of Earth, their armies, their faithful retainers, the massed legions of those they governed.

Poor bastards, they didn't stand a chance. I had them surrounded by my sheer anger and determination. And they wouldn't believe it until it was too late.

I worked steadily, pulling my hand fractionally out, then a little more, and then yet a little more. I knew as well as anyone can that in the situation I'd found myself in, escape was impossible. Of course, this had never stopped me before, and before this I didn't even have Kit to fight for.

If Kit was alive—and I was sure from his voice in my head that he was—then it was my duty to find him, rescue him, and get his shiny white-knight behind back home to Eden. It wasn't some high flung duty, really. Mothers do it for their ducklings and dogs for their masters all the time. It was rather that most basic of all instincts: help those who have helped you. That I loved him only added icing to the cake.

I don't know how long I took working my hand in and out. Really, I wished I wasn't blindfolded because it didn't allow me to know if there were people in the room, and if there were, were they looking at me? So I kept a sharp ear out and stopped as soon as someone rustled near the bed.

Twice, someone touched me, without seeming to realize that I was working to free myself. Once there was the touch of a measuring instrument of some kind against my earlobe. I'd frozen in fear that it was an injector and that I was about to be given a sedative. But it was just a brief touch followed by a beep, that told me they were reading blood pressure, blood sugar, or perhaps degree of doneness for all I knew.

The second time was more helpful as someone flung a coverlet over my naked body. I hadn't been cold before, but the coverlet provided additional cover for my activities. I could pull on my hand more vigorously and bunch my fingers into that almost-dislocating position that made my hand into a thin, sharp wedge—then pull again.

I'd like to say my hand came free in no time at all, but I actually had no idea how long it took me. It seemed like a very long time, because I was measuring minutes in degrees of freedom. Pull, pull, pull. When my hand was finally held only by the middle of my fingers, I forced harder, and expected alarms to shout. They didn't. I moved my hand, slowly, under the coverlet, to be at my side.

To my left, the heavy man stepped, stepped, stepped, away from me, paused at that far end, then stepped back. There was no noise from the right, and either the lady who had been there had left, or she'd sat down and taken up a reader or a game player or one of those things nurses always seem to have on hand for when they're watching an unconscious patient. My ears are good but not that good. Catching the slight touch on a play pad was quite beyond me.

So . . . there was only one thing to do, and it had to be done agonizingly slowly, so as not to raise the alarm. I moved my hand, fractional inch by fractional inch, under the coverlet, towards my face, and then felt my face very slowly. The tube going down my throat felt like a standard flexible feeding tube. One advantage of having half-killed yourself in broom accidents before is that you know these things.

The thing over my eyes, on the other hand, didn't feel like the standard blindfold, but more like swim goggles—only clearly opaque. I wondered why there were there, but I had no doubt that I had to remove them enough to see—but not so much that anyone glancing at me would see what I'd done.

It is the tragedy of my life that, having been born to do things suddenly and in a big heated rush, I am forever consigned to doing them slowly, carefully and by almost imperceptible degrees.

There was no choice though. I slowly, slowly, slowly slid the mask upwards. Slowly, slowly, slowly, until a sliver of light showed through the bottom of it.

Bright, stabbing light. My body stiffened. I stopped a spasm through an effort of will. Fortunately the tube in my mouth prevented the gasp from escaping. Light. Bright, bright light.

Light. Burning light. It was Kit's mind, touching mine, the sort of mind touch we had had in the last few minutes in the *Cathouse.* *Blinding light.* His eyes hurt as if someone had put a hot poker through them, and his stomach clenched. He too was tied down, somehow, and I knew without knowing how that there were two guards in dimatough, with burners, pointing lasers at him. I heard his speaking voice as he would hear it, from within his aching head. He spoke in that matter-of-fact way he did when he was not giving an inch and would see whoever it was in hell before admitting they could hurt him. "If you don't turn the lights down soon, I will be blind and useless," he said. "And I won't be able to do whatever it is you want me to do, even if you convince me."

The voice that answered him was Father's and it dewed my body with cold sweat. I remembered him in the ambush in the collector bay. He had been in on this from the beginning. "Agree to look at Jarl's plans and tell us what we're missing, or we will burn your eyes. And regen them. And burn them again. Until you realize you are not in control. You are not home. Here, you do what we want, or you hope we kill you."

Kit. He didn't answer. I didn't think he could. Gradually the touch of his mind—pain and confusion and overarching wounded pride and worry for me—receded.

I fought against my own rage, which urged me to hurry up. Instead, I forced the rage into the channels normally taken up by strength, forced it to tame and go slow. I needed rage to do the part of strength, because strength I had not. I'd realized that when I tried to move my hand, when I tried to lift the blindfold. The force behind my actions was maybe a quarter of what I would have expected. As for the bright light, shining under my blindfold, I refused to believe they had me under high beams or—as it felt like—the light of a thousand suns.

It must be, I thought, that my eyes were made extra sensitive to light by being covered for however long it had been. I closed my eyes, opened them, closed them, opened them again. Each time the light seemed less stabbingly bright.

Of course, I remembered my eyes had been burned out. What if they hadn't been regenned properly? Fortunately the panic lasted less than a heartbeat, because I opened my eyes, and I could see.

What I could see were just bulky figures that could have been humans or objects. One out against a greater source of light, one quite near me. No, two quite near me, on either side of the bed. Guards? And then one a little further away, lower than the rest but bulkier.

I blinked again and slowly my vision cleared and the bulks resolved themselves into clearly visible objects and people, even if each was surrounded by a faint halo of light, as appears on things when you've squeezed your eyes really tight, then opened them.

I was in a large room, brightly lit by the light from two windows. It wasn't a standard hospital room in that no effort had been made to have it feel homey or comfortable, or even soothing. It was just a stark white room, with lots of white space, one of the walls taken up with blinking monitors and buttons, a bed—for all I knew a floating platform—on which I lay.

The things to my side were not guards—which was good. I'd not have had much leeway with guards that close—but large, polished medical machines. From one of them extruded the tube that went down my throat. It made a not-quite-humming noise, of the kind that can only be picked up by human ears when the human is thinking about it.

On the other side was a machine that looked much the same, but which extended myriad wires like tentacles towards my body. I'd not paid any attention to those smaller feelings before, having concentrated on the fact that I was naked and strapped down, but now, as I followed those wires to the small shapes under the coverlet, I realized there were sensors on me. Probably, judging from the monitors on the machine, they were heart rate and breathing sensors.

That was a problem, because almost anything I'd have to do to free myself would alter those readings. In fact, those would have altered already, if I hadn't taken it so painstakingly slowly and been so maddeningly patient.

I would have liked to take it slowly and patiently now, but the thing was that glimpse from Kit disquieted me. I didn't know what Father knew about Jarl or why he would be trying to get Kit to interpret any writings left by Jarl.

All right. So Jarl was the genius—even for a Mule—who had gifted us with the powertrees, a puzzle no one since then had managed to solve. Perhaps that was what Father wanted, or perhaps the secret of the legendary FTL stellar ship that Jarl had also invented. Granted, Kit was Jarl's clone, so perhaps he could solve it—though this took a twentieth century view of cloning, the naive belief that a clone was the same as the original and not merely a younger twin sibling. Still, I could see where they thought that Kit might have the natural talent to interpret Jarl's writings. The question is—even if Father had access to images and writings about history that I did not, how had he recognized Kit for what he was?

The people of Eden clearly hadn't. Oh, granted, they'd last known Jarl as an old man, probably looking much like Doc Bartolomeu.

And granted, they thought that Kit had been bioed to resemble his mother's husband.

But, Heaven and Earth! All my father had were old holos, probably grainy and out of synch as the twenty-first-century images tended to be. So, how could he tell that Kit resembled Jarl enough to be his clone, and not merely someone from the same stock? Wouldn't the eyes and the hair have thrown him off?

It didn't matter, of course. Father had found out that Kit was a clone. Something that was as forbidden on Earth as all other experimentation. Even without the additional crimes of being an ELF and a Mule, my beloved was proscribed.

I probably should be grateful that Father had realized who Kit was. I had no doubt that trying to get the key to Jarl's secrets was all that was keeping Kit alive right now. Of course, it wouldn't keep him alive *and* comfortable. And so I should get him as soon as possible. And then I was going to rip Father's head off his shoulders. And I was going to make him *eat* it.

First to get out of here. If slow and painstaking wouldn't work—or not without driving me nuts—I needed the quick and easy solution. The two other bulks in the room—one near the window—and one further away from me, to my right—were human. Or at least the one by the window was a large man in full dimatough armor. The other one was a middle-aged woman in a reclining chair.

The woman looked asleep and the man had his back to me, looking out the window. Right. That meant that Father Dearest didn't expect me to wake up yet.

It was obvious. Had he thought I was near the time when I would regain consciousness, he'd have been very careful to have two or three of his goons on guard, and at least one nurse or medtech who'd had to tangle with me before.

Granted, those people were hard to find—in the sense that once having seen me in full-blown berserker mode, most sane people refused to come near me again, much less guard me. But then, sane people did quite astonishingly crazy things for enough money, and Father had a lot of money.

And there was no way that he would have left me in the charge of two people, one of whom could decide to sleep and the other one—judging from the armor, definitely trained at guarding or peacekeeping, because dimatough doesn't come cheap—could decide to turn his back on me.

Good heavens. I almost felt guilty for the lesson in paranoia I was about to drum into these innocents' heads.

Almost but not quite. Sometimes people simply have to learn lessons. It's for their own good. And if they survive, they're better people.

I chewed at the corner of my lip. Right. These beds usually had a release somewhere, that, if pressed, made the binds retract. It was usually a single button, which made it easier for nurses having to clean the patient or turn him or whatever.

It was usually at the edge of the bed, on the underside—just. It could be at the head or at the foot of the bed. If it was at the foot, I was shit out of luck. But mostly it wasn't at the foot. It was usually near the head because if a nurse were alone, it was easier for her to control a semiconscious patient by holding his shoulders down, than by holding onto his ankles, when he could still have rolled over and fallen, or at least hit his head.

So . . . just under the top. I quested with my hand. Nothing on the right side. I pushed my fingers up and behind my head so I could feel underneath that edge. Nothing. Then bending my elbow at a painful angle, I searched as far as I could along the left side of the top of the bed. And felt a small bump. I pushed it with a will.

For a second nothing happened. Then the binds started retracting. With a whirr. The guard spun around.

Shit. Shit. Shit. The electrodes attached to various points of my body and the tube down my throat kept me as still as the shackles had done.

I reached up with my newly freed hands and tore at the tape around my mouth keeping the tube in. In the process, I sat up. Alarms sounded.

The nurse stood up. The guard walked towards me. I reached up and tore the tube from my mouth. It was down my throat. As it tore up, it seemed to bring most of my throat with it. I tasted blood. The nurse screamed, "No, no, no."

I swept my hand down my body, throwing electrodes all around.

The tube glugged a greenish mess to the floor. I realized I was in my hyper-fast mode because everything else seemed slow motion, and the guard wasn't walking, he was running. But not fast enough for me. And he was a newbie. His burner remained holstered.

Little girl like that. Ah!

I rushed him, pushed him back, grabbed the burner from its holster. Thanks heavens it was a Cinders10. I'd used those so often before—having stolen them from guards, peacekeepers and proctors—that I flicked the safety off by instinct as I backed up. I tried to speak. What I wanted to say was, "Stay still, go to the corner. Let me out and nobody gets hurt."

Unfortunately the damage to my throat was not illusory. It felt like my whole throat was raw, and my voice came out in incoherent grunts and rasps. The nurse slammed her hand against something and sirens sounded, loud. In the past I'd have burned her where she stood but . . . well, to begin with the alarm had already been sounded. And what if she had a family to go home to? What if they'd worry about her? What if her death would destroy them? They'd never done anything to me.

I'd never thought these things before, and I realized they were a weakness now. I also suspected that things were about to get far more interesting than could be solved by burning the two innocents in my room.

The nurse approached, "Calm down, Patrician Sinistra. You're just confused. Nothing is wrong. We're here to care for you."

Like hell nothing was wrong. If nothing were wrong, my father wouldn't have taken my husband away from me. If he cared, even the modicum he was supposed to have cared for me, the little bit of duty and obligation that he'd pretended—he'd have Kit hidden somewhere until I woke, and then would send him on a ship back to Eden.

Separate us? Sure he would. After all, I was the hope and descendant of his line, and for him to have a successor I must marry someone from a Good Man's family. But hurt Kit? Kill Kit? If he cared for me, he wouldn't even have contemplated it. Hell, if he were sane he wouldn't have contemplated it. Unlike the innocents here, he knew what I was.

I burned the floor ahead of the nurse, to stop her getting nearer. She stopped and wailed, "But you're naked." Which indeed I was. I guessed I'd caught some of the Eden attitude that being dressed or naked was my business alone, because I flat-out didn't care.

The guard was reaching for me—slightly hampered by the bed being in the way—and from down the hallway came the sound of footsteps in unison. I'd guess more guards, only it was probably Daddy's goons.

Father wasn't stupid. He was what he was, but stupid wasn't it. And though he might have been fairly confident—must have taken one hell of a doctor to make him fairly confident—that I wouldn't wake so soon and might have relaxed his guard, he'd always been the sort of belt-and-suspenders type of man who would keep backups just behind the next door. And the backups—only to be called in case of need—would be the best he could command.

At the same time, the innocent in the dimatough armor was trying to get at me. I grabbed the nearest thing that looked like a non-lethal weapon. The tube that had been down my throat and which was merrily spewing green liquid onto the floor. I grabbed the end, spared a glance at the machine and punched hard at the button that I thought would increase the flow. It worked beyond my wildest dreams, spewing green goo in a wide arc in front of me. This made the innocent slip and allowed me to drop it and turn, burner in hand, to meet the ten or so armored goons, who came in at double-time march. And with drawn burners. Hello. This was new. Normally they had orders not to fire on me, no matter what I did.

"Patrician Sinistra," the lead goon said, and though I didn't recognize his voice, I recognized his tone. It was that not-really-believing-you'll-listen-to-me tone those in Daddy's employ who'd had to deal with me before were wont to use. "Put down your burner. Put it down. We have orders to burn you if you do not obey."

I did some very fast calculations in my head. Like this: They might have orders to burn me, but I doubted they had orders to burn me lethally, which would kind of wreck all of Daddy Dearest's efforts to get me functional again.

Oh, I could well believe that having evaded capture in the powertrees and come back not only married to someone Earth would consider grossly bioed but also severely radiation-burned had earned me new rules. And not pleasant ones. But there was no way that Father was going to dispose of the future of all Sinistras by taking me down.

At his age, it was highly unlikely he would sire any other Sinistras. In fact, it was unlikely, period. Mother had been the fifth of his wives and the only one to give him a child. If I didn't look so much like the old bastard and if Mother—from my memories—hadn't been such a sweet, compliant woman, I'd flatter myself that she had improved the line.

But she hadn't and therefore Daddy wasn't going to risk his little daughter. Not to the point of killing. Which didn't mean that he hadn't ordered the goons to burn off a hand or a foot.

I had no intention of risking that, particularly since I had to get out of here and get my husband as soon as possible. Getting myself into intensive care would only leave Kit at Daddy's tender mercies for another week or two. No. Wasn't going to happen.

My whole calculation cannot have taken more than ten seconds, but the goons were growing impatient. "Well, Patrician," the one in the center—was that Narran?—said. "What is it going to be? Are you going to put that burner down nice and slow like a good little girl, or am I going to burn your burner-holding hand off?"

He aimed. At that point, even if Kit hadn't existed, the goon would have been on my list to kill or maim. No one can speak to me in that patronizing tone of voice and live, unharmed, to tell the tale. All right, perhaps Kit. But he'd better make it up to me really fast, after that.

I could, of course, just aim at the idiot and burn him before he could burn me. But then there were all his acolytes and one was sure to get me before I shot him. Right. Still had the bed nearby. Yeah, yeah, yeah, standard hospital bed, of sculpted ceramite and for all of ceramite's various, helpful qualities, it can't burn worth shit. But it had a mattress and a blanket and you know what? I'd come across this type of institutional mattress and cover before. Oh, they might be fire retardant, but turn a burner on them, and, baby, do they burn.

So I jumped behind the bed at the same time that I aimed my burner full power at the mattress. The fire resistance lasted all of a second, maybe a second and a half, and up it all went in a sheet of flame, hot enough to make me feel like my eyelashes and eyebrows were singeing. None of which mattered, because since I was close enough for that, I was also close enough to notice that the bed was on little floaters to allow it to be moved.

I aimed a kick at the ceramite frame, making contact for as short a space of time as I could because the material would be getting hot and I was, after all, barefoot.

The kick worked beyond my wildest dreams, sending the bed— now filled with an inferno of flaming bedding—sailing across the room at the goons, who broke ranks and ran their several ways. Allowing me to pick Narran off, then three more of them.

There is an art to hitting men wearing dimatough armor. You absolutely have to hit them at the line between the neck and the head part of the armor. Even then, you're unlikely to kill them, because the hinge is protected. But if you hold it long enough, you heat up the entire face and head plate, and the subject tends to collapse unconscious.

Of the two innocents, the nurse was huddled behind her chair and from the sound of crying and hastily muttered words, she was either praying or exorcising me. I doubted either would work. Neither had worked before. The gods wanted nothing to do with me, and if there were demons around I was it. I didn't think it was possible to exorcize an actual demon. The guard remained lying down in the pool of green goo.

Was it possible the fall had killed him or knocked him unconscious? Sure it was. It's also possible to survive a hundred-foot fall unharmed. It's just not likely. Those suits aren't only near-unbreakable, they're also padded inside to minimize trauma from falls. The innocent was staying down because the innocent had some brains and preferred to live to become, someday, less innocent.

On the other hand Daddy's goons were reassembling, and one actually took a potshot at me, right through the haze of flames, risking hitting a vital spot and Daddy's full displeasure.

And then my luck kicked in. This is where I have to explain that I used to believe when it came to luck I had none. I had revised this somewhat since meeting Kit. Even if I must run into a darkship, there were so many others my lifepod might have hit. It had to be luck.

Well, this was luck too, or rather that form of luck that I should have anticipated, but didn't even think about, until a deafening shriek sounded. I was not sure what the shriek was, but I did note that Daddy's goons started and jumped, which gave me a chance to move, super fast, past them, running on my bare feet, holding the burner.

Okay—super fast was not so fast, because I almost fell in the pool of green goo, myself, but that was fine, because before I got to the goons, stuff started falling from the ceiling—thick, foamy, shocking pink stuff.

Fire retardant! I thought, even as—blinded by the stuff that clung to my skin—I ran past equally blinded goons and—thanks to a great spatial memory—out the door into the hallway, where pink goo was also falling. Behind me I could hear the hesitant, but approaching sound of footsteps from Daddy's goons. Which meant that they were living up to their outrageously high price tag and trying to keep up with me.

I was in an institutional hallway completely devoid of all attempts at decoration. What I could see through the gently falling flakes of pink foam was greyish, polished dimatough. Doors each way, lined up so that each of them faced the blank space between doors on the other side. Then at each end, windows.

Right. If you're ever in a hallway like that, there are two possibilities. At the doors at the end, there will be a stairway leading up and a stairway leading down. All right, there are also two other possibilities. That the stairway will lead only up or only down. But in this case, that was unlikely. My father knew me—clearly not as well as I knew myself, but pretty close. And knowing me, he had to be aware that keeping me at ground level was a mug's game. If one of those windows at the end of the hallway—let alone the windows in my bedroom—were at a level from which I could jump to the ground, I would. And never mind if the windows were unbreakable and unopenable. There simply was no clear dimatough in the world. And any other type of clear material, including ceramite, could be melted by a burner, not to mention a hundred other incendiary contraptions.

Putting me at the top floor was almost as much of a mug's game because—though it looked rather unlikely, just now—Father couldn't discount the possibility that I could get hold of a communicator, call my lair and have them sweep me off from that perfect landing pad—the roof. I had, after all, done it before.

So I was probably on a middle floor and the floors above and below were filled with guards. If Daddy knew what he was doing, which he usually did, that meant going either way was stupid. And now the steps behind me had fallen into stride. So...that left me...

Ducking into some corner—not possible, as the hallway was as straight as the road to hell—and letting the goons go past me. Truly, that only worked in twenty-first-century comedies, even if I could have pushed into one of the doors around here.

Turning around and picking them off one by one—yeah, because

I would have time to do that while running backwards. And
Daddy's handpicked guards *would* just let me pick them off and
not call someone on the com to ambush me from the other side.

Right.

What were the chances that the other rooms on this floor
were filled?

Low, unless they were filled with guards—and I didn't think
even Daddy was that paranoid since he'd only given me ten
guards, not a hundred. Daddy wouldn't want me to have ready-
made hostages. I had used those to get what I wanted, before.

I aimed for one of the doors on my left and ahead of me
and held the burner there. It erupted into flames almost immediately. Good old wood. Sometimes you had to love retro trends.
Wasn't it great someone or other had done studies proving real
wood actually killed germs and was therefore better for hospitals? Very nice.

Still not breaking stride, I ran through the burning door, holding my breath and hoping that it wasn't something like a linen
closet and that I wasn't just managing to burn myself to death.

Luck held. It wasn't a linen closet, but a room exactly like
mine, only empty. And the flames didn't do anything to me. I
didn't expect them to, since I was covered in a nice coating of
soothing pink, fire-extinguishing foam.

So I hardly broke my stride as I reached for the bed and peeled
off both sheets, grabbed what looked like an old fashioned IV
stand and threw it at the window.

The window broke, which just goes to show you. I would have
expected it to be unbreakable, but long experience taught me to
always try the simpler solution first. And besides it only took a
second.

I set fire to the mattress with the burner, which gave me a
chance to take a look out the window.

I was only on the third floor, which should have been good
news, but I'm no more stupid than Daddy Dearest is. I could
climb down to the green lawn and the peaceful-seeming parking lot below. But by the time I finished climbing, there would
be two dimatough-clad guards down there, ready to hold me
fast. In fact, even as I tied the knot on the sheet, to make the
two sheets into one, I was fairly sure one of Daddy's goons was
already calling backup.

It is a good thing that I've never been one for an obvious or trite frame of mind. And it was even better that with the two sheets tied together, and secured to the foot of the still-burning bed, well below the flames—ceramite was a mite hot, but not enough to burn the sheets—I could swing like that ape-man guy in the twenty-second-century jungle series and get atop the wall that ran six feet away and at about the same height as this window. I was fairly sure there were no such congenial arrangements near my room. Which, again, is an advantage of my not having a conventional frame of mind.

The other advantage of this is that I'd already thought on the need for some distractions. My burner was still at almost full power and I put it on the long-distance, high-power mode with a flick of the thumb.

I hit the two nearest flyers, for the smoke, then two as far off as I could, to cause confusion, and then a couple, random, in the middle. I was in fast mode, and the laser on very high power, so none of this took more than a few seconds. It takes much longer to explain than to do. All the flyers went up almost immediately. Because I know how to fix flyers. And that means I also know where to hit them to make them go boom. Two exploded, two started to smoke heavily and the other two—further off—broke out in smoldering fire. It's hard to aim that well at that distance, so it would have to do.

Fortunately the pieces of the exploding flyers fell on other flyers, started other fires and added to the general chaos and mayhem.

I had no holster for the burner and like hell was I about to leave it behind. So I put the butt between my teeth, grabbed the end of the sheet and jumped through the window in wassname-of-the-apes style. I did not, however, do the trademarked cry, partly because people were starting to appear down there, as the affected flyers started to scream in alarm. And there was just enough smoke for them to be sure where I'd gone.

I swung to the wall, grabbed onto the rough-poured ceramite top, and shoved the sheet back, so it would seem to have gone straight down and hopefully convince my pursuers that I'd gone somewhere into the parking lot. I wish I had. Stealing a flyer seemed like heaven right about now.

Particularly since the wall didn't lead to freedom—not that I really expected it to—but to a sort of enclosed yard, surrounded by yet higher and, judging from the sheen of circuitry on the top of the ceramite, more-than-likely-alarmed walls.

Right. I let myself drop down into the enclosed space, while thinking that if it could be said that I had traded a roofed prison for an open-air one, at least this one was remarkably goon-free. Oh, it wouldn't be for long, but sometimes you take what you can get.

I got hold of the burner, and held it in the two-hand mode as I did a circuit of the little enclosed yard. Why have an enclosed yard like this surrounded by alarmed walls, on the side of an otherwise enclosed, guarded facility? Well, when the facility was a hospital there could be only one reason: to comply with regulations.

I found the effluvium pipe for hazardous bio-waste right where I expected it—where the yard widened a bit to allow a biohazard robot ship to land. It was a black pipe, thicker around than I was wide and capped off with one of those nipple ends that was only supposed to be opened by the matching end of the biohazard ship.

And right on target—though this was not surprising because I knew these ships made collections on a fairly close schedule, to prevent any great accumulation of what could, should it overflow, be a danger to all—I saw a ship with the biohazard symbol painted on its side do that daft dance that robot ships do as they land, sensing their homing unit.

I looked back at the pipe and wished—wished with all my might—for my nice, impermeable spacesuit back in the closet of the *Cathouse*, with its lovely, lovely helmet and oxygen tanks. Then I looked up at the ship.

Fine. I'd done worse. And besides, it wasn't like I had a lot of choice, and I'd rather travel as bio-waste than be bio-waste. And I'd much, much rather travel as bio-waste than have Kit be bio-waste.

I turned the burner onto the nipple end of the pipe, causing fluid and things better not investigated to flow from it. There probably was an alarm somewhere, but I'd bet you there was a delay on showing the leak, and the ship was going to be coupled with this outlet in seconds, thereby probably neutralizing the alarm.

I took a deep breath and climbed, backwards, inside the pipe.

There was time for just another breath, before the ship coupled with the outlet and started vacuuming. I tumbled head over heels, in mostly liquid mess to float in yet more liquid mess, my lungs bursting for a breath, my heart trying to speed up into panic.

I forced myself to think. First, so far so good. Though very few of the biohazard ships had this, it was all too possible this one might have been equipped with blades or a thresher. So I'd been lucky once already. Now to be lucky twice. Which way was up?

I'd once read a book that advised, should you ever be caught in an avalanche, you should pee yourself to track which way the pee flowed and thereby discover which way was up.

Charming though the idea was, I didn't think it would work so well in liquid.

Instead, I concentrated on where the hum of the motors was coming from. The left and beneath me. So there was a good chance—or at least a decent one—that the upper part of this container was upward, in the direction of my head.

I swam that way praying with all my might that the container wouldn't be filled to the top, and just about crying when I felt my head poke through into the air. I knew it was only logical. They didn't overfill these because they were afraid they would overflow. But when you're in the soup—and in this case greyish green soup that smelled gaggingly of chemicals—you really don't take anything for granted.

. I rubbed my slimy hand across my slimy eyes, which shouldn't work to clear them, but did, and opened them, while taking big lungfuls of very caustic-smelling air.

There was a good chance that floating for very long in whatever the hell this was would cause me to be as thoroughly burned as I'd been in the *Cathouse*. Which was why I had no intention of doing so. Instead, I waited while the robot ship did its idiotic take-off dance, then waited as it gained speed. I wanted it well away from these facilities, because what I had to do next would doubtlessly make me visible.

First I located the vent hole. It was where I expected it, in the center of the hollow sphere that formed the shell. Yes, all of these had a vent hole. Think on it. Otherwise, depending on what they were carrying, they might very well build up pressure and blow up. Which actually had happened once or twice—according to the news—when the vent hole had become closed.

The vent hole had a prime-quality filter, but that didn't matter, because I had a burner and burners—praise be to whoever was responsible, at this rate, probably Kit's biological dad—were a solid-state, hermetically-sealed piece of gadgetry.

So as soon as I estimated I was safe, I swam to right underneath the vent, aimed the burner at it, and blazed. I actually held my breath, fearing that whatever was in here was explosive. Which was probably silly, since bio anything usually doesn't blow up. Well, sometimes, but not too often.

This time it didn't blow up, the filter just caught fire and then its housing melted. They fell into the biohazard with a plop. I'd worry about coming in contact with whatever the filter was made of, but if I hadn't come into contact with anything lethal by now, there was a very good chance I might be living a charmed life. So instead of worrying about that, I stretched to reach the edge of the hole and to pull myself up.

Fortunately these robot ships never went very high or very fast. In fact, they tended to travel as much as possible over uninhabited zones and fly low and slow, where they couldn't come in contact with piloted craft, or otherwise interfere with the traffic lanes. This was because, of course, the experimentation with robot-driven flyers hadn't been a rousing success, even if they always followed the rules.

Fortunately—as I expected—I'd been held in Daddy's territory: Syracuse Seacity, an artificial island off the coast of the North American protectorate.

Founded as tax havens in the mid-twenty-first century—as soon as tech became available to grow artificial islands out of what looked and felt very much like lava, but was actually a man made and biological compound closer to coral, only exponentially faster growing—they had soon become independent republics, and then after that principalities, of sorts. Inhabited initially by a disproportionally skilled and educated population, they'd also become immensely wealthy. It was where Glaish had developed, first as a patois, then as a language.

Now, each seacity was surrounded by miles and miles of underwater farms, where algae and fish were grown for food and medicine and industry. It wouldn't be out of the question to say that each of the seacities was worth the equivalent of as much as the biggest metropolises of the twentieth century had been.

But what mattered to me right then is that we were indeed in or, rather, flying towards the edge of Syracuse Seacity, by the time I poked my grimy, slimy head above the ship.

Why did this please me so much? Because in a seacity created, designed and built from the beginning as an urban environment, every area was densely populated, though some areas—such as the low-rent district we were now flying over, composed of warehouses, narrow streets and robot factories—were less vital than others. What this meant was that to comply with safety regulations, the biohazard ships got around the seacity by going around the seacity. Literally.

My hopes were answered when I spotted the glimmer of the ocean ahead.

Of course I had a plan B if this hadn't happened. I always had a plan B. And more often than not a C, and you'd be amazed how many times I'd had to resort to a plan F. Plan B was to jump the next time the ship started its idiotic landing dance and hope that it wasn't over a biohazard site.

However, I much preferred plan A, as it was shaping up, leading me out over the ocean and about ten feet above it. Because, if you're going to have to jump from a ship, you want to jump into water.

I waited until we were over water. I couldn't really recognize this area of beach, but the shores off the seacities are not like the shores off real islands. They are never rocky, unless the Good Man was crazy enough to have rocks planted. To my knowledge, Daddy Dearest wasn't that crazy yet, though heaven only knew how he'd be once he learned I was gone.

As soon as I was sure of not falling on land, I pulled myself up and all the way off the ship through the roof, and fell into the blessedly cool and clean water below.

I went down, down, down, then up again, broke water, took a deep breath...

Shore was about twenty feet away, and though I knew I was really going on strength I didn't have, I must reach it. And then I must find out how to get to Kit and rescue him. All before Daddy figured out where I was.

◦⊚ THIRTY-SEVEN ⊚◦

I REACHED THE SHORE—FINE BLACK SANDS, CREATED FROM THE
initial grinding down of the pseudo coral that build the island.
Even though it wasn't particularly hot out—I tried to calculate
what the season would be and failed, since Eden kept its own
calendar—the sands were very warm. I found a place hidden by
the contours of the tiered cliffs that led to the interior. From the
smell of the area, this was not exactly a beach. Well, at least not
a recreational beach. Unless my memory failed me, this was an
area of flyer factories and warehouses.

The chemical smell seemed to emphasize that it was indeed industrial. But of course, that could have been my own residual smell.

By the time I reached the shore the strength I'd borrowed from
myself had failed me. The hysterical sense of do-or-die fading, I
knew I was going to collapse and possibly stay collapsed on the sand.

So, I buried my burner—not so far down that I could lose it,
in fact no further down than a hand's width—then lay down on
top of it. Listen, you sleep with a burner next to you on a beach
that's not exactly the safest in the world—hell, in any beach—the
best that could happen in those circumstances is that someone
would steal your burner. The worst ... could be much, much worse.

I don't know how long I slept, but I woke up with a questing
mind touching mine. I knew that touch and that mind-voice
before I was fully awake and responded to it, *Kit.*

Thena! You're alive. They said ...

281

I felt for the burner under my body before I woke, and dug for it with my fingers, holding it before I even opened my eyes. Yeah, I could fully imagine what Daddy Dearest had said, probably as a way of asking Kit where I was likely to go. Although what made him think that Kit would know anything of Earth was beyond my reckoning. It was what he did. First assume what pleases you, then force other people to agree with it.

I tried to probe Kit's mind for what they might be doing to him and what might be going on, but he blocked it with his mind. *No. Thena, get to Circum. Get out. I don't know what, but they mean to do something to you. It's not good. Steal a ship. Go back home.*

I opened my eyes, looked around the beach. It was sunset. I didn't know of what day. Clearly, Kit had been told I'd escaped and that I was likely to die if I hadn't already. And my idiot beloved thought I could save myself by leaving without him. I didn't know whether to laugh or cry. Not only couldn't I imagine going anywhere without Kit, but did he really think that my returning without my husband—my only claim to be one of them—would earn me welcome parades? *No. We both go or we die trying.*

Whether they were on my tail or not—and granted they were, because, since when did my father give up that easily—they weren't here. The beach was as deserted as when I'd fallen asleep and though the dry black sand could never allow footprints to be identified, there weren't even any of the holes in the sand left by foot pressure. None but my tracks from the sea, that was. Good. The sea was a lot closer too. Full tide.

Thena! Despite the vague feeling of urgency and fear and an all-too-real sense that he was blocking physical pain from me, Kit's voice filled with a hint of amusement. *There are things even you can't do. I gather I'm in a secret prison. I—*

Shut up, I said. *Either we both leave or we die trying.* The sounds from the area upcliff from me were those one would expect in early evening. Not much in the whirring of machinery and the clanks of industrial production as there had been during the day.

Of course, these areas at night were known for broomer lairs. I didn't know of any of them, but then I wouldn't. I mean, it's all well and good to say that my lair were broomers and we were, and as illegal as they came—since no exceptions were made to the laws for children of Patricians and professionals. But we were the children of the high class. Our rebellion was perhaps easier—I thought for the first time with a pang. It had occurred to me that if I'd tried to steal a ship on Earth no one would demand I pay for the damage. Not even Daddy Dearest. But there were a lot more rebels than us.

The rule of the Good Men might bring peace and prosperity to Earth. I didn't know. I only had Eden to compare it to, and while I granted it seemed far more prosperous, it wasn't necessarily peaceful—I remembered the traffic at center—but it created its share of malcontents too.

You're not going to let me convince you, are you?

Uh? It wasn't a question I could take seriously. He knew better. I wondered if there were really broomer lairs nearby or if I was assuming there were because I wanted them to be. *No.*

He didn't say anything else, but there was a sense of bright light shining in his eyes, and I tasted blood in my mouth—which had to be an echo of his mind. Damn it. I knew how sensitive cat eyes were. I added a few more cherished fantasies about precisely how I was going to kill Daddy Dearest to my favorite daydreams.

And then I got up. I didn't know how long I'd been asleep, but I felt rested—also starving. I needed to get on with the business of finding Kit. Because we both had to get out of here as fast and as intact as possible, before Daddy got extraordinarily creative. If he hadn't yet.

If Kit was in some secret prison, I had to find out where that might be. The logical place to find that information was—curse the luck—my father's computer. Oh, not the mem he carried with him. That of course would be wherever Daddy was, and I'd rather keep out of his sight until I knew with what I was dealing. But Daddy was old-fashioned. One of those ancients who do not trust the mems alone, are afraid of losing something or that someone will break into something.

So he kept a machine in his office which no one else knew of. Well, almost no one else. I was the sole exception because I had found it, quite by accident, while hiding in the office. I would bet the location of any prisons that weren't public would be stored in that—or in the gems he kept in the safe on the wall.

I had to break into Daddy's house. There was nothing for it. And then afterwards I had to hook up with my broomer lair. Because even I couldn't exactly break into a secret prison alone.

Well, I probably could. After all, few people kept you from getting into prison. It was getting out again that would be tricky.

Clearly, I couldn't get from here to Daddy's house—which couldn't even be seen from here—by walking. And it would be a little hard to waltz in, naked, through the main entrance. Dad might hire scum. He did not, as a rule, hire stupid scum. Or not that stupid. Just stupid enough not to realize they didn't want to mess with me. So the very first order of business was for me to get a broom. I would just have to hope that this area did have some broomers.

The cliffs of Syracuse Seacity were tiered—purposely so to allow people to climb them. You could climb the cliffs from platform to platform, all around the isle except for the part just outside Daddy Dearest's palace, where the cliff was sheer and ended straight in the ocean. For security reasons, natch. Though I couldn't remember any instance of an armed takeover between Good Men, they supposedly had happened often enough in the days after the turmoils.

But here, I could go from platform to platform of black cliff, with just a normal step in between. You see, when the seacities were organized it was with the idea that they would attract the intellectual elite of the time—the scientists and the creators of technology, the storers and purveyors of data. Not the manual laborers. That had come later, as the world changed and the seacities became separate entities in their own right.

In the beginning they'd been a way to escape the restrictive rules and regulations of the natural land masses. A way for those who were doing well enough not to see all their money vanish in taxes to support the addled, the incapable, or—a lot more often—the simply lazy.

So originally this means of accessing the beach had been all important. Old holos showed these beaches full of fashionable people. Not now. As I reached the top of the cliff it was like looking into an old history holo.

I was looking down the street as it had existed when the seacity was first built. The houses—ranging from pseudo-Mediterranean villas in poured dimatough to pink, mushroom-shaped houses of glistening ceramite—had once been the height of luxury and, this close to the beach, probably expensive enough.

The thing is that as the seacity population—and industry—grew, it couldn't grow horizontally. Or maybe it could, but there were all these algae and fish farms and things on the bottom and I doubt whoever my ancestor was then wanted to pave over valuable real estate. And that's if they'd kept the technology for the islands for any time. I knew it was now gone. Whether it had been lost with the Mules or in the riots afterwards, no one knew.

So the island had grown upwards, in terraces of dimatough, supported on columns. As a rule the lower the street, the cheaper and rougher the neighborhood. This one was the lowest one. It didn't exist in the better parts of the isle, not as such, because there no one had built upwards and the old homes had been carefully and lovingly preserved, and were like a historical holo too, of a different kind.

This one had clearly become a sort of industrial hell. At least some of the houses had become factories—some were only closing now—and if I had to guess, they dealt in the most dangerous and hazardous trades. Narc creation, for sure, because more than one structure, close up, looked like it had blown up from the inside and then burned to all but the outermost dimatough or ceramite shell. Probably making oblivium. It was known to blow up if you cooked it too long, or if you cooked it too short a time and then shook it, or if you kept it at the wrong temperature or if you looked at it cross-eyed. It was street-sold in little dimatough packs, so if it blew up within, all you were out was a truly spectacular mind-scrambling high. Not three fingers and a nose.

These bottom areas had little sunlight, of course, since having a big terrace above kind of blocked all light. They had artificial lights, but how many and where depended on the location. This area was very poorly lit, which was good. By clinging to the shadows between the houses and the dilapidated sidewalks, I could almost hide the fact that I was naked. At least well enough that I could pass if no one gave me too close a look.

The burner in my hand presented more of a difficulty. Father is touchy about burners. To own one you have to be one of a few security professionals or, alternately, to not give a damn about Daddy's regulations. Though this area looked rundown it didn't mean it was lawless. Or at least, it probably meant it was only lawless when it was convenient to them. They would protect their own. Which I was not.

I carefully set the safety on my burner, then reached upward, to hide it in my hair. And had the shock of my lifetime. Where I was used to meeting with curls—and after the last few hours, probably very tangled curls—there was nothing but short, scratchy stubble.

At first I swayed in shock, but then thought set in. I'd been burned. My scalp had probably been part of it, and I very much doubted that radiation was meant to do a girl's hair good, for that matter. So, I was without hair, for the time being. Gee, I hoped Kit wasn't too attached to my curls. Or that he'd be willing to wait till they grew back.

I hid the burner. Nobody's business where. Probably not nearly as thrilling as most people will think, but at any rate, it is a trade secret of sorts, and besides, I might need to hide it there again. With it safely hidden, I continued walking between sidewalk and facade, past two probably active narc factories of some sort from the smell. Then down around the corner, past a couple of warehouses that were probably not full of stolen goods, that being just my imagination.

That was when I saw the broom come flying in, under the upper terrace and between the columns. I followed in the same direction. And found myself on a side street full of what looked like private houses, except that private houses normally don't have guards at the door. And very few of them have neon signs in the windows, advertising all kinds of brews. Bars, I thought. Bordellos. And perhaps the occasional lair—those being the ones whose guards wore full broomer leathers. You see, up there, on a broom, it gets pretty damn cold with the wind whipping around you, and for all the materials available to us, nothing *quite* keeps the cold out like leather.

Also, there were girls on the street, some in about what I was wearing, which meant that other than my hair—and that could be a weird fashion statement, for all anyone knew—I could pass. I started walking along the sidewalk, putting a little roll in my walk, so that customers would know that I was up for business. And I hoped someone would bite soon. After all, I didn't want anyone to think I was trying to set up as an independent. Not in a place where there were so many houses devoted to the business.

But I also had to snag the right customer, see? So I cooled it when a couple of men who looked like local semilegal laborers looked at me, and waited till the right prey came along. Fortunately he did just as my neck was starting to prickle.

He being a tall blond man, beefy. He was wearing brown full-broomer leathers—the jumpsuit slightly open at the chest to reveal blond hair. The patch near his left shoulder read NARC, SACK OR POWERPACK. NOBODY RIDES FOR FREE. I smiled at him and licked my lips and undulated my hips thinking that he was about to get the full meaning of that last saying.

It brought him to a complete halt in front of me. I don't think he'd been shopping, till what was in the shop window caught his eye. Most broomers—of whatever class—don't pay for sex. They have their own women, usually lair followers, although many of the broomer lairs do not allow a woman to ride her own broom. But then again, there were all-women lairs—normally referred to as Amazons—where the males were treated as arm candy, if they were noticed at all. One of the funniest air battles I'd ever seen had been between the Wicked Witches, an Amazon lair, and the Lavender Buzzers, a male lair who were not particularly interested in women. They had both ambushed a drug transport truck at the same time, then proceeded to battle each other while it got away. The Brooms of Doom—my own lair—had just stood aside and watched, while trying not to get wrenched muscles from uncontrolled laughter. We were more of the fight-in-a-bar than the stealing type.

At any rate, this broomer had just decided that whatever he had waiting back at the lair for him, he wanted what I was selling. As I stopped and gave him the minimal inclination of the head that meant I knew he was looking and I wasn't averse, he grinned. "So . . . what are you going for?"

I wasn't sure what he meant, but I smiled back and said, "Buy me a meal and we can cuddle." This wasn't intentional or fully thought through, except that the smell of greasy spoon cooking from the places we were passing was making my stomach twist with hunger. So I thought I'd better take care of that too.

He raised an eyebrow, quizzically. "Amateur?"

Prepared to run if it turned out he was an enforcer for one of the houses, I wiggled. "One time only. I'm just hungry."

His grin got wider. "Got any eating place in mind?"

"Anywhere will do." Frankly, I would have felt bad if he'd

taken me to a relatively nice place for this area. If he'd paid for something like a steak, I might have had to run away and leave him unmolested. But fortunately, he was trying to get as much bang as possible for as little buck as could be, so he took me to a soup place.

Either the soup—mostly algae of various kinds—was exceptionally good or I was starving, because I had two bowls before I slowed down.

And then he led me out of there and to where he *parked his broom*. I had done my calculations. If he'd left his broom at his lair, I would have to go home with him—or convince him to go home, my being too shy to bundle in a lair—because I didn't think I was in a condition to battle a whole lair.

Fortunately, I was in luck. He took me to his place, which was a micro-apartment sliced out of one of the bigger houses. And where the first thing I noticed on coming in was his broom, propped up near the door, next to a ratty bed and rattier chair.

While he was closing the door, I got the burner out, so that when he turned, he found himself facing it, pointed squarely at his forehead.

His eyes went wide. "Whoa there, sweet thing. Where did you get that from?"

"My armpit," I said. "Strip."

This brought a unique look of confusion to his face. "But... you don't need to point a burner at me..."

I shifted the place I was pointing the burner at. Less lethal but far more personal. "Ah ah funny. Strip. And don't even think of trying anything."

I don't know if it was the look in my eyes, or the sheer unlikelihood of the situation that subdued him. One feint towards me caused me to step aside very quickly, then run a burner ray so close to his—by then naked—arm that he must have felt his arm hair curl. "The next one makes you sing soprano the rest of your life. Now bundle your clothes and your broom, open the door and set them outside."

He obeyed. From the look on his face, he might still have been thinking that it was some sort of fun and games. I waved him aside with the burner. "Sit. On your bed."

He did. Which is when I used my special speed to run all the way out the door, ducking to pick up the clothes and broom and boots and then around a labyrinth of streets, taking random turns, until I stopped in the narrow space between two burned-out buildings.

There I pulled on the leathers. They were large on me, as were the boots. To wear the boots I had to wad up a bunch of pamphlets someone had abandoned near a pole. They seemed to be a discourse on the evils of drugs.

The leathers smelled funky, but were practically sterile by comparison to the biohazard ship. I could live with them. Besides, all my shots for STDs were up to date.

Minutes later, I was on the broom—a crappy model, but serviceable—and airborne over the ocean, headed for Daddy Dearest's house.

It was around the island and I had to fly so as not to get caught in the traffic control sensor—that is, keeping either too low or too high to trigger their attempts at identifying the unidentified blip. This wasn't difficult, though, as I was used to doing it anyway, and the habit came back without effort.

It meant over the city I flew high enough to be in the range where the scanners didn't pay too much attention because if any flyers chose to go that high they were on their own and the sea-city traffic control had no responsibility for their safety.

A lot of intercontinental transport flew at that level, anyway, because it was almost the only traffic up there, and if you were careful you didn't hit each other, and it got you there faster, for which most long flyers got a bonus.

It required pulling the hood up on the jacket, slapping the oxygen mask on and breathing from the tank attached to the broom. And let me tell you, if I thought that the leathers smelled funky, the mask managed to smell even funkier. I was truly glad my STD shots were up to date. On the other hand, the mask and hood made me anonymous. Or perhaps not entirely, since at least two other broomers flashed me greeting signs. I flashed them back "hello" moving my right hand quickly in relatively innocuous universal broomer language. I wondered if this all-brown leather getup, with the bright patch on the shoulder, was the attire of some specific lair, and prayed that whichever lair it was, there were no lair wars going on involving it. Which was sort of hoping that water wouldn't be wet.

On the good side, I found my burner, stashed into the belt of the leathers, a great comfort. Forget diamonds or dogs—a girl or boy's best friend is always a high-powered weapon.

But I found no reason to use it until I flew near Daddy's side of the island. Here I had to be very, very careful.

I'd never specifically asked, but I was fairly sure that Daddy Dearest had trigger alarms for flyers approaching the house. I would have. It stood to reason if one were so afraid of invasion by sea as to make one's approach a forbidding cliff, then one would also be afraid of invasion by air, which could come at you in just as many numbers, and make defense just as impossible.

If I could think of the need for defense from the air, so could he.

The way the mansion was located left only one other option. It sat at the highest levels of the isle, sprawling and classically comfortable. On the one side, it faced a sheer, forbidding cliff that ended in rather deep sea. The cliff was coated in dimatough, so it was as smooth as a mirror and much harder to cut. Though it could—as I remembered Kit doing when he climbed the ship I was trying to steal—be melted by a concentrated burner jet close up.

On the other side, it had a ramp that climbed slowly from the restored lowest-level neighborhoods nearby and onto the front door.

Going by that ramp was the only option. It was also suicidal. I hadn't yet reached the point where I was so tired of life that I wished to forfeit it by giving Daddy a bead on me for a very long time, as I climbed that slope. There was no way—no matter that I was wearing borrowed leathers, and even if I kept my mask on, that someone in Daddy's never-ending retinue would not recognize my gait or the way I stood. Besides, approaching the mansion in full illegal broomer's attire could be compared to slathering oneself in bacon before sauntering into a tiger's den.

That, however, was the only way to get in. Unless I did it my way. The highly improbable, possibly insane route.

Right. I knew which one to choose.

◖◗ THIRTY-EIGHT ◖◗

I APPROACHED THE SINISTRA MANSION FROM THE SEA AND, AS I got closer, I flew lower and lower, so that by the time I got near the mansion I was flying so low my feet in the too-big boots were grazing salt water.

As long as the broom worked, it was all right if I froze halfway to death in wet leathers—or went naked. It beat the alternative, which was Kit dying in whatever hellhole Daddy Dearest had stashed him.

So I flew yet lower, till the broom was barely above water—and that only because I wasn't absolutely sure this model would survive a good dunking. Brooms weren't made openly except in the rogue—and mobile—seacity of Shangri-la. Every other system in the world forbid them strictly. Which meant that they were smuggled in and cost a small fortune, particularly the good models, which were as solid-state and watertight as my handy-dandy burner.

The cheaper source of brooms, though, and one often resorted to by less pecunious broomers, was the brooms put in flyers to be used as emergency exit devices if something went seriously wrong while you were airborne. Those thus adapted—depending on the flyer they were taken from, which was usually in some flyer graveyard—were often barely air resistant much less water resistant.

Flying at near-sea level, I assessed the wall. It was sheer and impregnable. Like a spaceship. I remembered what Kit had done

291

to climb the near-mirrorlike side of the collector ship on dock, and I saw absolutely no reason not to replicate the technique here.

I started by turning off the oxygen and removing the mask. It's not that oxygen and burners don't mix, it's that when they do mix the resulting explosion tends to catch the attention of everyone in the next mile or so.

Once that was done, I clipped the broom to my belt—while still straddling it—so that as I got off it, I didn't have to worry about its falling into the depths of the sea.

Then I burned four holes—two at foot level or close enough, and then two further up about where I estimated my hands would go. Well, holes might be a form of expression, since they were actually more like four shallow, concave depressions in the wall—but never mind. Deep enough to allow me to rest my hands and feet in them.

I gave them a few seconds to cool off—no use cooking my hands—then flew up to where my left foot was level with the foothold. Stuck my left foot in, my left hand above, reached down with my right and turned off the broom, then dismounted and stuck my foot on the right foothold.

The handholds weren't at exactly the right height, but it was no problem, as I found I needed intermediary holds, about halfway up my body, for my feet to go into, and then further up for my hands. My first assumption that the handholds would become footholds presupposed that I could leap up by my whole body length each time and hold onto nothing.

I'm not going to say it was easy—it wasn't. Once or twice I put my hand into a still-hot hole and lost skin. Another couple of times my foot slipped and I was left dangling from my ragged fingernails. The only reason I had the nerve to do it at all, particularly as I got halfway up the wall and above, was that if I fell I could always use the broom to avoid crashing headlong into the sea below. Of course, I knew very well that if I used the broom, the motor would likely be enough to set off Daddy's alarms. At least that was my bet. It was quite possible this broom's low energy consumption and low vibration would be below the threshold Daddy had set, but I couldn't know that for sure, and I wouldn't bet on it. With as many illegal broomers as there were on Syracuse, he wouldn't discount brooms as means of attack.

However I will confess that a little past halfway through, as much as my arms hurt, as much as my fingernails bled, and as much as my whole body screamed that I couldn't go on with it, it took my whole will power to keep myself from just turning on the broom and flying up. But I remembered Kit, and held on.

I tried to reach out to him twice, but got nothing but diffuse impressions and the certainty that he was keeping the more unpleasant facts of his situation out of my mind and that right then there were only unpleasant facts.

It seemed endless and hopeless, even when I reached the top. The top—because cliff and wall merged—was the top of the wall of our garden. And because I was very much afraid the top of the wall itself was alarmed—unlikely but possible—I had aimed my course veering slightly right a little at a time to where the branch of a tree—I thought the apple tree near the library—protruded just over the wall.

By the time I got there, and the branch was within reach, I extended my hand to it . . . and my hand slipped. So, instinctively, I slapped my right hand down on the wall.

The noise and light were instant and deafening. *Intruder in east quadrant of garden,* screamed at the top of someone's lungs and then recorded and magnified.

My hand reached for the broom to turn it on. And then my teeth ground together. No. If I left now, and they knew I was trying to get in, I could never come back.

They've done experiments with very young children. When scared, most of them run away. A few others freeze and cry in place. And then there are those like me—they run, headlong towards that which scared them.

In my considerable experience, it was the best strategy. Some writer of the twentieth century said that it was better to be a live lamb than a dead lion, but that it was always better and often easier to be a live lion.

I grabbed onto the top of the wall, ignoring the deafening noise, and climbed on top. From there it was easy to step onto the branch of the apple tree and hold onto other branches.

The branches ended close enough to the library window—an oversight for which someone's head would undoubtedly roll, but that was Daddy's lookout—that I could balance on the last portion where I could stand, and then launch myself towards the window. The window of the library was part of the oldest building of the house and not only glass, but glass that had gone all wavy and irregular with age. Since glass is a supercooled liquid—in fact silicon ice—it runs over the centuries. It just runs very slowly. So after a few centuries the middle and above of any glass window will be the thinnest part.

The leathers should protect me from the worst of the glass, but I held my arms, crossed in front of my face, as I launched myself into the window feetfirst, in a leap that would have won me all sorts of medals had I been in a ballet competition.

My left foot hit first, shattering the glass, then I kicked with my right, as it hit, to enlarge the opening, because that would make cuts to my body and head less likely.

I fell on a heap onto a dusty oak floor, on top of a lot of shards of glass. I thought most of it had gone onto my borrowed boots, but I didn't have time to examine them. Instead, I took off running.

While the library—an old-fashioned affair of the sort that was built in the twenty-first century and never again used since gems replaced books as the main means of storing data—had been my favorite hiding place as a child, I didn't think it would work as an adult. Part of my safety as a child relied on the fact that no one knew I was there—or would think of it. So clambering to one of the top shelves and lying flat was a good way to hide.

But now everyone knew—or would know in seconds—where I'd come in. So I needed to take advantage of those seconds.

I took off running full tilt out of the library and managed to push aside a maid and a footman who, to be honest, seemed to just be going about their business and probably didn't even know what hit them. They fell butt-first onto the polished marble floor, and I ran on.

Daddy Dearest's home was set by zones. In my happy-happy days here, I'd had my own zone, where I lived and kept my clothes and hid my broom, and where my valets and maids were housed.

Then there was Daddy's personal zone. And then there was this—his private business zone. The public business zone was located up front, and consisted of reception rooms and meeting rooms and other stuff to conduct the business of Syracuse. Uninteresting. And while there were some dresses in my personal clothing I'd kill to have Kit see me in, the all-too-high likelihood that I would *have* to kill to have Kit see me in them took the fun out of it. As did the all-too-high likelihood that I would die trying to get at the fripperies.

No, having been discovered, the best thing to do was get about my business and be gone. And, of course, the best way to avoid capture was to go where they didn't expect me. Which, fortunately, was exactly where I wanted to go—Daddy Dearest's sanctum sanctorum. His business office.

So I took a sharp right in the marbled hallway and ran down a blood-red hallway accented with gilded columns. After my time in Eden, the decor of my home looked even stranger to me. I'd long ago come to the conclusion that it was proof of hereditary madness. Because it wasn't as though Daddy Dearest had remodeled and refurnished the entire house, and yet the oldest parts harmonized with the ones he'd expanded or decorated. They all had unified taste. Bad taste.

They were decorated, in fact, as if someone with the color sense of a cat had acquired a vague veneer of classical architecture—the bordello kind—and decided to implement both tastes to the hilt. The Sinistra mansion looked like a very majestic bordello over whose walls and ceilings someone had bled massive quantities of arterial blood.

But I concentrated enough on running to ignore the walls and the columns, the statues of nude and improbably endowed marble fauns and even, as I gained Daddy's office and stuck my hand against the palm lock of his office, the improbable fresco of dancing nude maidens and even more improbable nude youths frolicking about the walls, just above the gem storage units.

Instead I concentrated on Daddy Dearest's secretary and assistants, who had been doing whatever it is such people do, and who looked at me with horrified expressions, and grew visibly paler.

I gestured with my burner. "Out. Out now."

They edged towards the door. The male first—a middle-aged man who had been Daddy's secretary forever. I wondered if I'd ever known his name—which might have proven he had some sort of intelligence. The women edged behind him. Stringy and Bouncy were my names for them and I was fairly sure I'd never known their names. If you went with what Daddy Dearest called them, they were Pea Brain and Bloody Incompetent.

It's a good thing I know the signs of someone about to do something incredibly stupid. I saw it in Bouncy's eyes before she lunged for me, and I burned the floor just in front of her. A warning shot. Not that marble or the ceramite equivalent burns, exactly, but it stores heat and crackles and is altogether spectacular.

She jumped and squealed and the male secretary grabbed her arm and sort of pulled her behind him, as he continued backing towards the door and out of it. I realized they were going as slow as possible, hoping for reinforcements, and I burned the ground in front of their feet to hurry them up. "Move it, go. I'm not worth your lives. Trust me."

They went. Fast. I kicked the door shut in their wake. Then pulled one of the massive walnut desks in front of it. And then, for double security, burned the door opening mechanism from the inside. Very thoroughly. Which meant I would have to leave by one of the broad windows after I was done. And Daddy Dearest would have been a total fool if he'd not left orders that there would be a broom squadron waiting for me when I came out.

I didn't think Daddy knew that my handprint could open his doors. If he knew he would have changed the lock. I was also fairly sure he'd never allowed my genprint to open doors as such—why would he, when they led to all his most private places? So it must be a glitch, one that he couldn't possibly know about, or he'd have blocked it. However, I was sure some of his more trusted bodyguards and best goons were authorized to open the door, and I really didn't want to be surprised in there.

Not that I was where I wanted to be yet. To most of the household this was Daddy's office, where they saw him, sitting behind the burled walnut desk with the seal of Syracuse on it. But once—I must have been three or four—when I was hiding behind one of the cabinets in his office, under the principle that there was no better place to hide than the last place they'd look, I'd seen Father saunter in, shoo his secretaries out, lock the door, and proceed to do a lot of odd things. The sort of odd things you see someone do in old spy holos. Push the frame of a mirror. Open and close the third drawer of a particular cabinet four times. Twirl the knob on a sculpted faun. And on command a door opened in the wall—a door so well disguised by the fresco, and closing with such a narrow fissure, you couldn't find it until it swung open.

As it did right now, after I completed the actions.

I entered Daddy's innermost sanctum, and closed that door, also, behind me.

This secret room must have gone back to all my ancestors, because it was like a packrat's refuge in there, with mementos, decorations and data gems dating all the way back to the twenty-first century or perhaps before. I'd spent many happy hours in there, when I knew Daddy was safely away on his diplomatic trips. I'd gone through most of what must be termed junk on the shelves, reading ancient documents, prodding at old holos. The family—and I supposed I was proof of it—all ran to pretty much the same look. Short, dark-haired, with unruly hair. People always marveled at how much I looked like Daddy and at first I'd been offended, until I found a holo of him as a young man. Not quite pretty enough to be a girl, but close enough that the features, softened, made me—a not-masculine-looking woman.

Well, all our ancestors had looked much the same when young, and there were holos of them with various dignitaries around the world. I hadn't activated them all, of course. It got boring after a while. Just enough to think that yeah, all Good Men Sinistras were sawed-off bastards, hewn from the same olive-colored block.

The thing was, in all my exploring of this office before, I'd been very careful not to do anything that might leave a mark. After all it was important that Daddy not know anything here had been touched. So I'd edged around the junk—I'd planned to throw it all away when I inherited, until I remembered that I'd never be shown this office, my husband would—and played with it, but I'd never touched the desk in the center, where Daddy Dearest's backup cube sat. That desk had all locked drawers. Old-fashioned locks. Really old-fashioned. With keys.

Of course I could pick the locks, or, by preference and considering how in a hurry I was, smash them. But it would be hard to do so and not leave traces.

Right now I didn't care about leaving traces though. I started by turning on his cube. It came on—the holographic display glowing above the desk and the letters *input password* glowing midair. I glared at it as I tried to think. If I were Daddy, and thank all the gods in the various heavens I was not, what would I have used for a password?

Evil seemed an unlikely choice, as did *Rattlesnake*, for meaner than—no matter how much they fit Daddy's profile. Like me he was left-handed, and I remembered once hearing one of his friends from when he was young calling him what I got called by my broomer lair: *Lefty*. I tried *Lefty* but all I got was a red glare and *Incorrect*.

Right. I squinted at the glare and on impulse tried my mother's name, *Elena*. The glare came again *Incorrect*. I ground my teeth. It figured he wouldn't even use her for a password. What had I been thinking?

I chewed on the corner of my lip, and tried to remember the name of Daddy's last doxy. But there were so many of them—actresses and porn stars, singers and painters—and they came on the scene so fast and vanished never to be heard from again so fast that it seemed scarcely likely he would use the name of one of them. Though it might give meaning to the idea you should change your password often.

Well, I seemed to be interesting to him, and perhaps even loved, insofar as something like Daddy could love an external object—which of course as far as he was concerned was part of the problem. He wanted me to be an object that could be molded and bent to his will—something that was impossible. And so he often preferred to crush me or attempt to, but the vehemence with which he went about it seemed to imply he at least gave a damn.

So I tried *Athena* but all I got back was the same damned red glowing denial, and, after a moment, another screen warning me that one more wrong password would trigger intrusion-prevention mechanisms and cause the whole system to erase.

Damn it. I didn't have time for this. But I didn't know what else to do, so I turned my attention to the locked drawers. Here, somewhere, in the junk—or perhaps documents or gems—that Daddy considered too important to let an unlikely visitor to this sanctum see, might be a clue to the password.

There were two ways to go about opening these drawers. The intrusive way and the even more intrusive way. There was no way I could get in and retain intact both the locks and the fine old oak desk. Daddy Dearest would know I'd broken in, and there was no point trying to hide that.

Which meant, of course, that any information I obtained relating to where Kit might be held would have to be used as fast as possible. As soon as Daddy saw his violated desk, he would know that I knew where my husband was. And he would move to stop me.

But I didn't have the time to break into the desk in a way

that would leave no traces and, as good as I was at mechanics, it would take me a while to figure out how many tracers, trackers and access alarms Father's computer had. He would have many, that I knew, even in this most secret of his data storage machines.

So I decided to throw caution to the winds and cast about for a likely implement to open the drawer with. I found a letter opener—or at least I thought that's what they were called in old holos—from the twenty-first, its silver handle stained and lackluster, engraved with the initials AMS. Which probably stood for Alexander Milton Sinistra, the two names having made a back-and-forth in the males of the line for centuries.

Above the handle, the knifelike top was thick and looked like some form of steel. It would do. If it failed, I'd use the burner, but there was a good chance of setting fire to the whole setup with the burner, and the dagger—though slower—at least wouldn't burn the contents of the desk.

I started with the top left-hand drawer. All right. This is perhaps just my understanding of things, but it had been my experience that the top drawers tended to contain most personal artifacts, and also that the one that accumulated most personal stuff that might be close to a putative heart—in Daddy's case, I wasn't willing to stipulate that he *had* one—was the one of the dominant hand. Which for Father was the left one.

So I went after it with a vengeance—or rather, with a letter opener. Fortunately the blade proved as sturdy as I hoped. I dug around the lock—it was guaranteed to have the sort of key that couldn't be faked by wiggling something in it—throwing chunks of oak to the floor with mad abandon. It seemed to take forever, but I don't think it did, as I was digging as fast as I could. And as soon as the wood was weakened enough, I hit hard at the lock with the heel of my palm.

It took two hits, but the remaining wood splintered and the lock caved inward.

The drawer was almost empty. It contained two small boxes and a holo-picture storer probably of twenty-first-century vintage. I frowned at that, because . . . my father is not sentimental. At least he's not sentimental in the way other people are sentimental. I suspect if you started talking about injustices he suffered and how the world done him wrong, you might be able to induce a shine of tears in his eyes. But anything else, including describing the unjust death of a million babies or butterflies or anything else would be met with a stony glare and perhaps an enquiry as to why you were wasting his time.

The twenty-first-century holo couldn't possibly be his. It had to be his ancestor. So why keep it, much less keep it in a secret drawer and not with the piles of junk all around? I mean, it was marvelous enough he never threw away his ancestors' mementos, but maybe that was pride in his ancestry. The idea that he would cherish a holo of an ancestor this much, though, struck me as odd.

Curiosity overcoming everything else, I propped the holo on the desk and flipped its turn-on level, fully expecting it not to work. Replacing batteries in these was insanely expensive and difficult, as they used power technology different from ours. However, the holo came up promptly, if faded, and I stared at the image, uncomprehending.

It showed . . . three young men. One of them I would say was Father as a young man—but then as I said, it could be any of my male ancestors as young men. Females just didn't seem to leave an imprint on the line at all. The other two people . . . The center one was the same figure as in Doctor Bartolomeu's treasured holo. Jarl Ingemar. The third one . . . I squinted at the holo, thinking he looked awfully familiar, until the eyes, staring at me out of the narrow, olive-colored face, beneath unruly dark hair fell in place. I'd last seen them staring at me from among a nest of wrinkles. Doctor Bartolomeu Dias.

They looked very young—like young men on vacation, against a blue-sky and green mountains background. My fath—No, my ancestor leaned on Jarl on one side and Doctor Bartolomeu leaned on him on the other, using him as a sort of prop by virtue of his great height. They wore loose white shirts and tight black pants and looked very much like they'd been caught in the midst of a relaxed moment.

My mind hissed, fizzed and popped, refusing to figure out what this could mean. If Doc Bartolomeu and Jarl had been Mules . . . If they had known my ancestor . . . But my ancestor couldn't be a Mule because he'd had kids. But . . . My head hurt.

I stared at the holo, then at the holo floating above Daddy's computer demanding a password.

No.

But . . . I had one more chance. Right. I gritted my teeth and dug into the desk for the other two boxes. One of them contained three data gems. The other . . . The other contained a single, broad gold ring, unremarkable in all but the fact that it was obviously made of gold and therefore expensive. The inside was engraved with *Je reviens* in flowery script.

I couldn't breathe. It was as though I'd been kicked in the stomach by a kangaroo. I realized my own ring, which had had a matching inscription, was missing, but why did it have a matching inscription? It was the same as in the collector ships' insignia, the same as the name of the ship that had taken the Mules out of the system—stopping in Eden on the way. *Je reviens*. I return.

But who returned and where?

Right. In situations like this, thinking till I got sick seemed a waste of my time. Thinking wasn't what usually got me out of trouble. Force was.

I looked at the other drawers. It would take long to break into all of them. And the thing here was that I had no idea where Daddy was or when he'd come back. I sighed, as I started, with desperation, hacking at the space around the lock on the bottom left drawer—almost certainly a drawer designed to contain papers and documents.

Then I looked up at the screen. It was unlikely, not to say impossible, that I would find a gem or a paper marked with Milton Sinistra's passwords. So whatever I found, I would have to guess at.

I bit my lower lip. Well. You know, the one thing out of place that I'd already found was that very odd picture. Oh, don't get me wrong, Daddy was as proud of his ancestors as they came, but he had never, to my knowledge, kept sentimental pictures of his long-dead forefathers in a locked desk. So it must be a clue.

The question, I thought, was first or last names, and in what order?

Well, sooner or later I was going to have to try it, and if it destroyed the files that was entirely too bad. If I couldn't get in, it would be just as useless to me. And sooner or later, I was going to have to take a chance.

Right. Sometimes you just have to say *what the hell?* So I typed into the keyboard—AlexanderJarlBartolomeu. The order the young men were in from left to right.

For a second, nothing happened, and then there was a sound

like a subdued *paff* and a red light flashed. "Destroying all secret files to protect from intrusion."

Fuck. Knowing Daddy as I did, I got up from the desk, and backed away as far as possible. Which was good, because I heard a sound from under the desk and a dart lodged in the chair. It didn't look like it would have killed me—of course. If I knew Daddy, he was trying to make the intruder sleep, so that he could later interrogate him or her at length. After all, one's inner sanctum should not be violated.

Two seconds later the hiss started. And I knew that hiss. It was gas being pumped into the chamber. Also, though at this point it couldn't possibly have an effect on me yet, I could smell the traces in the air. It was a gaseous variety of Morpheus.

In hell he'd get me this way. I was already on my feet, and shoving among the various things, trying to find something, anything, that would help me out of here.

I was fairly sure going back out through the office would be suicide. Or through the rest of the house. They would be looking for me.

None of them would be so stupid as to think I'd got into the office—which I was sure they'd managed to get into by now—and vanished. So they would be trying to figure out where I'd gone, and my sudden reappearance would be treated with joy. Uh... short-lived joy for me. Though possibly not literally. It's not like Daddy had ever tried to kill me. But he would make me wish to die.

With the sickening stench of Morpheus growing thicker in the air, I tried to think of a way out. This room had no windows. And I had to get out.

Of course, I knew, from my ability to reason spatially, that this room was located at the corner of the house, with the corridor on the other side. And that corridor had a series of windows, looking out over the sea.

The question was...how solid was the interior wall?

Most people make the mistake of thinking that walls are impenetrable barriers. Unless they are external walls, built of stone and brick, very few are.

Since from what I could remember in my mental picture of the place, this was not a load-bearing wall, there was a good chance it was made of—at best—wood.

A quick tapping confirmed this. Not hollow, but built of wood. Right. Which meant I needed something to tear through it, and quickly.

Madly, I tore around the room, tossing aside ostrich eggs, sheet music, old theater programs and other irrelevant souvenirs. Surely in their negotiations with native peoples, potentates and mad dictators, some of my ancestors had been given war maces or axes, no matter how ceremonial.

I tossed things aside, rapidly, opening and closing closet doors. Inside one such door, I found a broomer suit—top-of-the-line insulated leather—and a broom, too, a branded broom, Egalitaire, which had been a popular brand fifty or sixty years ago. Top of the line in its time, and in fact so well built that its value had gone up as a collectible.

I didn't have time to change, but I'd be damned if I was going to pass that up. Supposing I got out of here, both of these would be useful. The compartment contained a backpack with the initials MAS—who knew Daddy had been a broomer once upon a time? But the time frame and the initials were right. I shoved the suit and broom in the backpack, then the two boxes and the holo from the desk drawer.

I'd just found, in a corner, what looked surprisingly like a bayonet, when I heard a crackle as of radio engaging, and a voice sounded, above me.

"Athena."

It sounded like Zeus Pater in a fury. It was at least Pater. Mine. In a bad mood.

I turned, bayonet in hand, and looked at an oversized image of Daddy Dearest, floating above the desk. Bastard. Utter bastard. The thought that he probably had cameras around here came to mind. And that he probably had other weapons that he could use against me, too. Targeted ones, unlike the gas.

Right. I was planning to use the bayonet to open the rest of the drawers before the gas got to the point I had to use it to hack my way out. But the thing is, if I started hacking at the wall, Daddy would have his servants on the other side before I could get out.

Right. There was only one thing to do. I smiled sweetly at Father and said, "Hello, Daddy. Having fun torturing my husband?" And then I told him what I was going to do to him when I caught him. He interrupted me after the second time I mentioned castration.

"I only have one set, Athena."

"I'll make you regrow a pair so I can cut it off again," I said.

He shook his head. "Dear girl," he said softly. "You don't under-stand. If you want to keep your monstrous paramour alive, you'll do what I say. You will, right now, sit in that chair, let the gas take its effect, and wait till I come home."

"Oh, Daddy Dearest, you're the one who doesn't understand. If you touch a single hair on Kit's head...I'll...I'll commit suicide."

I didn't know where the threat came from, but as I said it, I saw the expression of panic on Father's face, and I grinned. "Right. I have, on me, enough poison to kill myself and to ensure the process can't be reversed. And that you can't harvest any eggs."

"You're bluffing," he said, but his eyes looked like quiet, unimagi-nable panic. Oh, how sweet. Now I knew what to do. I'd hold all little Sinistras hostage. No Athena, no future for Daddy's line. Look how scared he was.

"Wanna try it?" I asked. "I suggest you stop the Morpheus now."

Like that, the hiss stopped, as if it had been turned off by a switch, which it probably had. That thing about Father not being a fool probably meant he had manual overrides for everything here.

I quickly calculated strategy, which at that point was like doing quadratic equations in my head, but not nearly as much fun. I could tell Daddy to let me come out through his office and pull all his servants away. Oh, I could. Except if I were Daddy I would make sure there was someone out there, ready to hit me with a tranquilizer dart. Had to really, or he risked losing control over me, which was at least almost as bad as having me commit suicide.

If I were Daddy I'd figure out a way to do it. So, he would too.

My only other choice was...

I smiled at Daddy, grabbed the chair from the desk. It was solid with a dimatough frame. Oh, good. As hard as I could, making use of all the strange strength I could command at these times, I flung it at a blank space of wall, above a low cabinet.

The wall cracked and splintered, opening fissures. Nothing large enough for me to pass, but that wasn't needed, not really.

I climbed on a small table nearby, then leapt at the wall, feet-first. It was weakened enough to splinter in all directions, under the impact. I went through and landed on my feet atop debris. From behind me, Daddy Dearest howled, "Athena!"

I confess that while assessing the situation—a vacant corridor, with a window on either end, one of the ends no more than ten feet away from me—I looked over my shoulder and told Daddy what I wanted him to suck. The fact that I didn't have one didn't make the slightest difference.

Now alarms started sounding here too, and I could hear approaching feet. No way I could make it out of here through the mansion. No way in hell. It just wasn't possible.

So that left the window. I opened it and looked out. It gave over a cliff, and then the sea far below. The problem was that the cliff wasn't exactly as sheer as it should be. Less than two floors down, there was a protruding ledge.

Brooms tend to stall if you start them while falling. Even the best ones, which the one I was wearing at my belt sure as hell wasn't. And two floors is a low space to start, in freefall, even without a stall.

On the other hand...Sometimes you just have to say what the hell.

So I unhooked the broom from my belt. I wasn't going to use the one in the backpack till I tested it. I put it between my legs.

And then I said, "What the hell!" and I jumped.

❦ THIRTY-NINE ❧

I TWISTED AS I FELL, AND I FELL LIKE A STONE, WHICH I EXPECTED. My finger pushing at the button of the broom didn't even get me a courtesy sputter.

Which is why I'd jumped with my back to the sea. As I approached the ledge, I kicked out with my left leg. The goal was to barely touch the cliff, then pull back, before any drag broke my leg.

I hit out and my leg hurt like hell, and I wondered if it would make any difference, even as I fell past the platform which was—literally—an inch in front of my face.

Now my only worry was the water below. Of course, at the speed I was falling, the water below was as good as a concrete surface. I pushed the broom button frantically, then again.

Nothing happened, nothing.

The air rushing past me seemed very cold. I couldn't breathe. I sent Kit—forcefully—an *I love you* thought, even as my lips twisted in a wry smile, figuring that I would royally piss off Daddy by committing suicide.

And the broom coughed, spluttered, and barely gave me time to press the reverse slide before it took me full tilt against the wall.

I backed up just enough to turn it around, and, holding on with one hand, pulled my hood up with the other, because my naked scalp was starting to freeze. From the walls of Daddy's mansion, a boiling of brooms was pouring out.

My face formed a smile that must have approached manic

rictus. I whispered, "Playing tag. How sweet." Because here I was in my familiar territory.

I'd escaped peacekeepers and rival broomer gangs for years. Daddy's goons couldn't possibly have that much experience. Not on brooms.

If you ever find yourself being chased on a broom, there are several steps you can take. The first and best would be to outrun the others. I looked over my shoulder. Okay, so my pursuers were growing larger at an alarming pace. That meant...I couldn't outrun them. Right.

The next best thing—at least if you are an experienced broomer— is to hit the most populated area you can as fast as you can.

It had limitations in this particular case. Ah, yes, I know, theoretically all brooms were illegal and if caught within the seacity on a broom everyone should be treated alike.

Theories are a beautiful thing, but they have this odd tendency to not translate into practice all that often. Particularly when the theories involved so-called public servants who knew which side of their bread was buttered.

I was sure that Father's goons had transmitters which gave them some form of code for the traffic control towers, and which would stop them being detained or worse. And I didn't. In fact, if Daddy's goons didn't have a way to broadcast that I was a dangerous element, they were total and complete fools.

Right. So...there were areas of town where that wouldn't do them any good at all. The main one being the area where my broomer lair was located. Which meant flying as fast as I could around the isle, past the area where I'd stolen this broom—which was good—and down to the deepest low level.

Deep Under, as it was known, was on a part of town that had to have been slightly less expensive than the rest to begin with. Facing the sea was a structure like a huge dead metal spider, with all its legs up and half-bent. It had been, once upon a time at least, a dock-unloading robot. And this area had been the dock through which every product that Syracuse Seacity needed came, in the days before flying everything in was practical or economical.

Flying past the spider was the very first test that any broomer had to face in Deep Under. First, because there were far more arms than natural spiders. Once, in an idle moment, while standing near the base, waiting for Simon, I'd counted five hundred arms, and I wasn't near halfway.

The other obstacle was that the robot had been decommissioned at least two hundred years ago. Since then it had stood, metal parts and ceramite parts and dimatough parts forming the lifted arms, and pleading with the gods for a mercy that wouldn't come. Some of the metal parts rusted and fell apart—and did so at unpredictable times, so that flying through it, you could set off a storm of falling ceramite and dimatough as the vibrations of your passing disintegrated the metal that linked them. Even when they didn't fall apart they had a tendency to move with the vibrations of anything near.

Was there a way to get through it? Well, yes. Myself and others who'd done it—on a dare or in a desperate situation—would tell you that it was done very, very carefully.

For this my horrible borrowed broom might be an advantage. It was so low-powered that it didn't set off much vibration at all. The group following me, though, was at a distinct disadvantage.

With them still far enough behind me that their vibrations were just starting to hit the spider and make all its arms twitch and wave, like the branches of a tree in a light breeze, I started flying between them. There were two theories about the safest way to do this. One was going high. By going high, amid the rotted claws and picks and bits of things up there that had once been used to unload ships, you escaped the risk of having heavy objects fall on you from a height. On the other hand, the slightest vibration could cause a still-halfway-sound arm to pivot and a claw to grab you or a pick to pin you.

The other—and my normally preferred method—was to go as low as possible. Yes, you risked having something very heavy fall on you. My friend Fuse had never recovered from it. On the other hand, if you were alone and were very careful, the chances of setting off any movement or any disintegration were low.

I wasn't alone, so I flew as near the top as possible, concentrating both on going fast as I could, and as carefully as though I were wending my way through the powertrees.

This took all my attention plus some. I forgot about the people behind me—about everything but wending now under a claw, now above a scythe, now past a low-hanging basketlike thing.

The only thing to say for it is that it was easier than traffic in Downtown Eden, though not by much, and that I wished very much that I could borrow Kit's mind to do it, even if he found my eyes and reflexes horribly inadequate.

As the movement around me sped up, I realized that my pursuers must have caught up with me at the other end of it. A few screams and one short, sharp crunch told me at least one of my pursuers had died a horrible death.

But I didn't dare turn or see how many of them remained until I exited on the other side and was a good ways down the street. And then I turned. Two.

I reached to my belt for my burner and shot.

Deep Under is dark, but not that dark. I could see well enough to shoot. And I could tell when I hit the first broom—the one closer to me—because it exploded in a lovely fireworks of light and parts.

But when I turned to shoot the second he had disappeared. Damn. I swore under my breath, because I didn't like that. I didn't like that at all.

However, there are always things you can't do anything about. The best thing for it is to know which those things are and to isolate them from those things you can, in fact, do something about.

Right now what I could do something about was changing out of this ridiculous outfit—which was starting to get me odd looks from various broomers flying past me, since I was sure the colors weren't right for this zone—and then find my lair. Which I very much hoped was still the same place it had been for the last six years, since I'd started flying with them.

I evaded curiosity—as much as possible—by flying down and landing.

Now I know I said this was a broomer-friendly area of town, and this was true, because it had the spider on one end, and on the other end a desalination plant blocked it aft. To enter into Deep Under, you could either fly through the spider, or come in on either side of the desalination plant, where there was about a one-person-width opening between it and the columns that supported the biggest park in town—the Hanging Gardens—above us.

There were other entrances, mind you—sort of—in the alleys between the buildings at the end of each block. But those alleys were really narrow and often blocked by loading docks. Remember, this had started as a working part of town, composed of warehouses.

What this left were eight blocks of large buildings and one main street, most of it in complete darkness or as near it as could be, until someone turned on a lamp—and all inaccessible to large flyers and to most conventional peacekeeping forces.

So, of course there were illegal broomers there. And illegal coiners. And illegal just about everything else including—it was rumored—illegal bioengineers. There were generations of people born and raised in those warehouses. There was always a cloud of kids on the street, most of them wearing headbands with lights on the forehead. Everything that could possibly be done and that Daddy could possibly disapprove of took place here. There were even rumors that there was a group of fanatical Usaians plotting revolution in here. Probably wrong, although it was true that after their country fell apart, people who clung to their founding document as a religion, and who lived their lives according to it, seemed to have spread to every country in the world. Few of them were—mind you—actually descended from Usaians. Or at least, the geneticists said they weren't. But that didn't stop them being as fanatic about their individual rights as those who'd been born to it.

Because most of them were skilled—particularly in technology—most countries and city-states tolerated them, provided they kept to themselves and didn't try to proselytize. They had at least one open-air enclave uplevel, but there were a few scattered about here too. I didn't think they were plotting active revolution, but one never knew.

Daddy had been overheard to say that the whole area should be sealed and a poisonous gas grenade dropped. And there were stories that this had been done by at least one of my ancestors, but things had gone seriously wrong and this whole side of town had been contaminated.

There were stories that the people in Deep Under had drilled secret holes and tunnels, both to escape and to make sure they took others with them if push came to shove.

Which I suspected was all that stayed Daddy's hand.

But the point is that there were people on the street for me to mingle with, and as long as I took care to stay away from the conspicuously guarded broomer lairs I'd be all right. The lairs here were more hard-core than the ones above, and I had no intention of tangling with them.

I wended my way past lairs and little shops—of course there

were little shops down here—food shops, clothing shops, electronic shops. I suspected some of the goods, displayed under spotlights, had been stolen from transports, but others were obviously simply the bottom of what people could purchase and might have been culled or thrown away up above—bruised apples, half-rotted oranges and diminutive bananas.

Where two sellers' stands stood in front of an alley, I took a look between. At the other end, someone had built a house out of slabs of ceramite that were still so imperfectly joined it was obvious they'd once been part of a pavement. For the area it was a big house, and more importantly, it wasn't part of one of the warehouses and therefore probably belonged to one of the local rich men—a merchant or some other boss.

I walked between the stands, with the look of someone who knows what she's doing.

Once in the alley, I got close to the wall and started undressing. See, there is a way in which Deep Under is so much like Eden that it made me want to cry with sudden homesickness, and then wonder what was wrong with me that I was homesick for Eden. In Deep Under, unless you were clearly threatening someone, no one cared what you did, and that included undressing.

The broomer colors I was wearing were a risk because they might make some broomer lair feel threatened. Naked wasn't threatening to anyone, though it might make a few males curious.

I didn't intend to stay naked for very long. I dropped the suit, then reached in my backpack.

Daddy and I are exactly the same size. He has a broader chest, but I have bigger breasts, so it all comes to the same. This was very useful because I would bet his suit fit.

Of course the first thing I did was look it over for bugs. I wished I had Doc Bartolomeu's bug-sweeper to tell me if there was something hidden in the fibers. Since I didn't, though, I must make do with what I did have. I looked as closely as I could and didn't even detect an imperfection in the leather or a misweave in the inner lining. Good. I put the suit and boots on with a sense of relief. Wearing boots five sizes too large, with a bunch of paper squinched into the front and sides, is not exactly comfortable and with all the running and kicking I'd done, I was starting to get blisters.

I sealed the boots to the suit under my knees, strapped the

burner to the belt, and then the two brooms, side by side. I'd be damned if I was going to take off on the Egalitaire until I'd had a chance to give it a very thorough going-over. Even if it had a powerpack still in it, powerpacks got flaky after about ten years or so. Sixty years or so...wasn't worth risking.

I transferred the contents of the backpack to my pockets—relieved this suit had pockets. In fact, this suit was perfect unrelieved black, which I knew wasn't anyone's colors, at least not in my zone. But it was close enough to the Brooms of Doom, which were black with red piping.

There was one thing I must do, I thought, before going to my lair, and that was to get trading money. An anonymous gem, at least, with enough narcs in it to allow me to buy food and such if needed, because I didn't know what the lair had on hand.

Most of us were the children of Good Men or of trained professionals in the Good Men's service. Not goons, but secretaries and lawyers, accountants and managers. The children of those who ran the machinery of state. This meant that while we called the working-class broomers play broomers because they had other occupations and other duties, we were very rarely full-time broomers. We couldn't be. We had state occasions and places where we had to show up with parents or attend on our own. And the only person in the lair who ever remembered the practical side of things was Simon, who was the nominal leader. Failing Simon, no one wanted to do anything but bum around on brooms, get stoned and jump in and out of others' beds. Not exactly in that order.

So the lair would have food if this were one of the periods when Simon was more or less in residence. Otherwise it would be a wasteland of wasted broomers. And not a bite to eat.

So, I took the box with the gold ring—if Daddy could take my ring, I could take his—and I looked for one of the places where I had sold jewelry before. Usually my own jewelry. It was a small hole-in-the-wall shop, and the owner might be one of those quasi-mythical Usaians, or at least he had a tattered bit of cloth showing stars and a few stripes hung on the wall behind the desk at which he sat, and I'd always heard that this was the representation of their male deity, just like the woman with the torch was their female goddess, who was said to change into an eagle in her incarnation as war divinity.

I didn't care. I wasn't here to ask him about his questionable beliefs. He must have recognized me because, as he looked up at me from behind his holographic screen—unreadable from this side, but writhing and moving across his face like electronic stigmata—he smiled.

Nodding, in greeting more than anything else, I set the gold ring on his dark dimatough desk. His eyebrows went up as he picked it up and weighed it in his hand. He brought out a scanner, attached to his computer, and pushed the ring against it. Figures scrolled on his screen and he looked at me. "Hot?"

I almost said no. Before going to Eden, I would have said no. You see, I could get a lot more money for the ring if he thought he could sell it intact and as it was. On the other hand, if Daddy was looking for the ring—and I had a very strong feeling he would be—anyone caught with it would die a horrible death. It wasn't only that by following the links Daddy might get to me—in fact, it wasn't that at all because I had to be out of here long before that—it was that looking at this man, with his sharp blue eyes, his wrinkled, tanned face, his receding hair, I couldn't imagine causing his death by lying to him. I sighed. "Yeah. At least...it wasn't exactly stolen, but someone will be looking for it. Better as gold value only."

There was something, some internal shift behind his eyes, and I guessed that I'd passed some test. I didn't know what would have happened if I hadn't, but I know that when he paid me, he paid me far more than I had expected—a full sixty-five narcs, in the coin of Syracuse.

He gave me the money coded into an anonymous gem and I tested it, then headed out the door, towards my lair, which was down two blocks, to the right on an alley and three floors up, to a rounded, arched entryway.

Before I had flown up the full height, I knew something was wrong.

⬖ FORTY ⬗

FOR ONE, IT WAS HARD TO AVOID THE IDEA THAT SOMETHING WAS wrong, when there were dark marks—as of a fire—around the entrance, and the bowels of the lair looked charred and deserted.

Shock barely had time to register when a broomer flew into sight. He wore all black leathers with red piping, and I felt a sudden and overwhelming relief as I recognized the broad, ruddy features of my friend, Max Keeva. Max was the son of Good Man Keeva and we'd been friends before we were members of the same lair. Rumor had it that we'd clawed each other in our cradles.

He made the broomer sign for down, and pointed at the deserted warehouse. I followed.

We landed on a crunchy layer of burned debris. I wondered if I was walking on my other broomer lair associates, even as Max dismounted and turned. "Athena!" he said. "I'm glad we came here at the same time. I am so glad to meet you."

The hair I didn't have prickled right at the back of my skull. Something was wrong, very, very wrong. I didn't dismount. Instead, I set the broom on hover, near the floor, and toyed with it, acting as though I were just taking my time. I gestured around. "What happened?"

Max frowned, if at my not getting up, or at what, I don't know. "Fire," he said. "One of Fuse's booms gone wrong."

This was perfectly plausible. Fuse, aka Ajith Mason, was a firebug. Well . . . and an explosion fanatic. He'd been both our demolition

315

expert and our speed demon before his accident. After it, he'd become . . . In all the rest of his functions, he was a child of six or so—a child of six with a lame leg and the manners of a two-year-old. But he was still very good at making things go boom. He just didn't always understand when he shouldn't.

So it was plausible, but the back of my neck was still prickling and the skin of my skull would stand on end, if it could figure out how to do so. "I see," I said. "Who else died?"

He shrugged, looking impatient, and shook his head. "Not many people," he said. "We moved. We're . . . elsewhere."

"Did Nat get out all right?"

He looked up and seemed surprised for a minute. "Nat?" Then he shrugged again. "Yeah, I'm sure. Everyone got out fine. Even Fuse. We have a new lair. If you follow me, I'll take you there."

Right. Come into my lair, said the lion to the lamb. I smiled, big and idiotically, and nodded like I'd lost all my marbles. "Sure. You go ahead. I'll follow you."

He looked a little suspicious, but he got on his broom, and took off, then hovered outside the entrance, waiting for me to follow. He'd have been a lot more suspicious if he knew that as I turned to follow I had my hand on my burner and pointed at him through the leathers' pocket.

And then, as soon as I was sure he was ahead of me, leading me somewhere and not looking back, I dropped, suddenly, way down. I feinted into an alley, and I actually flew among the pedestrians, till I backtracked into another alley, where I flew down to stop at a balcony wedged between two adjacent buildings. I didn't know to whom the balcony belonged, only that the door leading to it was dimatough and shut tight. And that the balcony had waist-high, enclosed dimatough walls all around. I fell into it, and crouched in a corner, so that I was in the shadows, even if Max should fly above me.

No, not Max. That wasn't Max. I didn't know who it was, but he wasn't my friend. It was as though someone else were wearing Max's body.

I felt bitter bile come to the back of my throat.

Oh, maybe he'd hit his head and gone as potty as Fuse, but in a different way. Somehow, though, that didn't feel right. My lair mates—Fuse excepted—never called me Athena and rarely called me Thena. Or at least not unless we were in company. The rest of the time they called me Lefty.

And I couldn't imagine a place in heaven or hell where Max would be completely indifferent to Nat. Nat was the son of Max's father's accountant. He had also been, since the two of them had developed an interest in sex, Max's lover. They weren't the only monogamous broomers, but they were pretty damn rare. In fact, part of Max's interest in joining the lair had been because it gave them a place to hide in, since his father could not be allowed to discover what the two of them were up to. They had other arrangements. I'd heard that Nat had a secret passage leading to Max's room and they slept together most nights. But the lair allowed them to be together and be themselves and accepted them implicitly.

To be indifferent to Nat's survival or not sure he had survived or—seemed like—not sure who he was meant only one thing. That person . . . that thing back there was not Max.

I squeezed myself into a tight ball and had a fit of the shudders. Was it possible to erase someone's mind and superimpose another? It was one of those technologies one kept hearing rumors of, but which never seemed to exist. Maybe that was what Daddy wanted to do with me. It explained so much.

The thought of myself with a superimposed personality and memories, behaving like Daddy's Little Daughter made me want to throw up again, but I didn't have the strength to get up and do it, and besides it might not be safe. For a while I couldn't even think how to get out of here or what to do next. I could just sit and tremble.

I hadn't tried to mind-touch Kit since I'd left the mansion, partly because I'd been running and partly because I didn't want him to feel my distress, but now I did. I reached my mind towards him, and touched his.

I had the feeling of a hastily cut-off scream, and then Kit. *Thena!* And in relief, *You're alive. You must make it to the powertrees and find a ship to take you back.*

No. We are both going to go.

Thena, you damn stubborn Earthworm.

Yes, you horrible bio, my beloved husband.

I don't know . . . if it's possible to save me.

Oh, it will be. Don't get too attached to the accommodations, because you won't have time to use any of the drawers.

I got back a mental attempt at a laugh, and the sensation of his arms around me. By the time that subsided, I'd steadied myself. My mind was not going to be rewritten. I was not going to let Daddy get away with it. Because if I did, then Kit would be left alone and probably die. And that wasn't going to happen either. We were both going to get the hell off Earth and back home. Together. We were probably worrying Kath, as it was, and that was not a good thing.

I waited, in case the faux Max was in pursuit. I didn't think he would be. I had a strong feeling he wouldn't be too at home in Deep Under. I though I heard someone fly by once or twice, but there was a good chance those flights were unrelated. Meanwhile I was thinking where I could find my lair. If they hadn't all died in whatever had destroyed the lair, they would have relocated somewhere.

Right. After a while, I flew straight down from the balcony, hooked my broom on my belt and, as soon as I could, ducked into a store that sold communicators. Some of them were the classic, palm-sized computer and phone, with enough memory to keep track of several families. And a very distinct electronic signature. I didn't want that, because if the call I made went wrong, I was likely to end up having to throw it away before being tracked.

In the end I picked a ring-com. A pain to dial, really, since it all hinged on twirling three rings around, like doing a very old combination lock. But they were disposable, had a very low signature and I could discard it without tears, since it cost me only half a narc.

I walked away with it, until I found another shop—this one selling rugs. I pretended to be interested in the merchandise and walked all around, amid the people.

Since the rugs were displayed by being strung up from the ceiling beams, it created so many convenient partitions where one could hide.

I made it to the back of the store, between two rugs, and I dialed Simon. It was no big puzzle which code to dial. Not his home, since that had a good chance of being answered by some employee. You see, Simon's father...well, he hadn't exactly died, but he'd been in a horrible flyer accident when Simon was thirteen. And he'd been a vegetable ever since. No one had unplugged his life support, because only Simon could do that when he came of age and inherited in two years. Until then, his father's managers were the de facto regents, but Simon had to do all the ceremonial occasions and was often referred to as a Good Man. Which meant he had a secretary and several assistants. Not his official personal code, because something funny might have happened to that and at any rate too many people knew it.

But Simon and I had been friends-who-slept-together for several years. Oh, not like Max and Nat. We were never going to set the world on fire and neither of us was monogamous.

Simon proposed, mind you, every other month, but I had no more intention of marrying him than I had of growing a second head. And besides, Daddy, for some reason, disapproved.

Still, when you have that kind of relationship, it is useful to be able to contact each other without anyone knowing. Simon had had a com—voice only—embedded into his wrist in a shop around here, years ago. Embedded coms were illegal in most of the world, as were other mechanical enhancements, but here in Deep Under, people installed them quite gladly.

I dialed that code. For a moment no one answered, setting my heart hammering, because what could possibly be happening? If Simon was away from his wrist…

But then Simon's voice answered, husky and hurried. "Thena. Thank heavens you're alive." He sounded horribly like Kit, and the Thena part was all right, because that's what he called me in private and not in the lair.

"Shouldn't I be?"

"There's a bulletin on you. Your father said they recovered you from captivity…" He paused as if he couldn't quite believe what he was saying. "Amid the darkship thieves. And that you'd escaped…"

"While unsound of mind, yeah, I imagine. Simon, tell me, what is my favorite ice cream?"

"What?"

"What is my favorite ice cream flavor?"

"Uh … mint," he said. "But—"

"No. Who put salt in the dessert of the representative of the Northern European Territories at the banquet when we were fifteen?"

"Max."

"Why?"

"The bastard had treated Nat like a servant."

"Right."

"Thena, have you lost your memory?"

"No. What was our biggest fight when we were kids?"

"When we were playing house."

"Why?"

"I wanted to be the mommy. Thena, have you gone crazy? Why do you want me to tell you all this stuff?"

I heaved a deep sigh. "Because I just met Max."

There was a silence and then, "Oh."

"Is there an explanation?"

"Uh... several. Fuse thinks he got hit in the head by something. Jan thinks that he got hold of a bad set of oblivium and Nat..."

"Nat?"

"Thinks he's possessed. Nat has gone... uh... a little funny."

Yeah, I could imagine. I'd have been downright hilarious if this had happened to Kit. But I didn't go into that. I asked Simon about the lair. He gave me the new directions. Everyone had gotten out alive, he said. They'd used the skedaddle plans. And that, now that I thought about it, was another thing that Max didn't seem to know about.

I wasn't absolutely sure that Nat wasn't right. Perhaps it was possession.

☾ FORTY-ONE ☽

APPROACHING THE LAIR—LOCATED ALMOST UP AGAINST THE WALL of the desalination plant, where someone had carved a cave out of the material that had formed the isle—I didn't recognize the person on guard. He looked very young, too. Maybe fourteen or fifteen, that age where guys have just stopped growing but haven't put on any muscle. But he wore the right colors.

As I approached, he flourished a burner, and pointed it at me. "Evening. What business?" he asked, giving me the onceover from top to bottom.

"Lair business."

He raised his eyebrows. "No beast so fierce, but knows a touch of pity."

"But I know none, and therefore am no beast."

He gave me another onceover, this time more relaxed, and smiled, in a cheeky way a young kid his age shouldn't. I would have flattened him, but he made me think of Waldron, so I didn't. "Who are you?" I said.

"Abidan Kwasi, and you?"

"Athena Hera Sinistra."

Like *that* the burner was pointing at me. "She's dead."

"Rumors of my death are largely exaggerated." I jumped him, but remembered what Kit had to say about my obsession and kicked his hand. His burner went flying and we both ran for it.

I had just grabbed it, when a voice from the doorway said, "Abi, leave Lefty alone."

Abidan turned, and then I did. Jan Rainer was walking towards us, informally dressed as people got when they'd been in the lair for a while—i.e., he was wearing leather pants but not full riding leathers, which meant he didn't intend to go out. On top he wore one of the almost disposable white shirts that everyone seemed to wear. "Lefty," he said, and grinned at me. "Stop playing with the noob."

I still held the burner anyway, as I stood up, and slipped it into my pocket to keep the other company. Amazingly useful things, burners. One can't—really—have enough of them.

Jan knew me well enough he made no comment. Instead he turned to Abi. "I just came to tell you that she was expected. Simon called." Jan was Simon's second-in-command, when Jan wasn't in the lair. He wasn't quite so mentally coordinated as Simon, but he was good at keeping things going if Simon had given him precise instructions. "He'll be along as soon as he can get away."

Abi, who had turned a lovely shade of red, gave me a sheepish look. "I can't be blamed for not recognizing you, now, can I? You're not ten feet tall and you don't have balls the size of elephants."

I grinned at him. It was a good attempt. I was trying to remember the name Kwasi from our general circle. I seemed to remember he was the son of one of Jan's family's administrators. "It's these clothes," I said. "They disguise my height, and at any rate the balls were always largely metaphorical."

He was a cute kid, about the color of aged walnut with startling blue eyes. Pre-Eden Thena would be earmarking him as someone to get to know a lot better in three or four years. Now he just made me think of Waldron—even if he looked quite different—and feel a pang of missing the whole family. I hoped no one else had got captured...I hoped...

I followed them into the lair. It looked amazingly like our other lair, which probably shouldn't surprise anyone. Like nomadic and rootless cultures, the broomers could replace everything they owned fairly quickly. Particularly since they commanded the purse of the children of Good Men.

There were partitions, most of them made of the sort of stiffened fabric that is used to make separations in stores and offices. White, allowing the light to shine diffusely through it, it made the whole place look exotic and strange.

As per normal, there were some common areas, and then little cubes that each broomer claimed for himself and filled with his possessions—usually a mattress and any number of boxes containing more specific stuff.

Lairs were very safe inside. At least no one from outside would steal anything and if someone inside the lair stole from one of his brothers or sisters... Well, there would be hell to pay, and someone would make sure he did pay. So the little partitions weren't closed, though some people had hung rugs or towels or just pieces of fabric across the doorways, to protect their privacy.

We walked along a sort of hallway between cubes. From one of them came a sound like dice being rolled. From another came soft moans and what I would bet was the sound of copulation, and then past a cube I knew was Fuse's just from the chemical smells.

Up through to the innermost area, and Jan had his arm around my shoulders. I'd bundled with him, but it had left no mark, and I didn't think he was interested in a reprise, and besides, I was tight and coiled and had my hand on my burner, inside the pocket. One false move and he'd be a briefly glowing bonfire.

But he didn't make any false moves. He took me all the way to the back, where he called someone to get me a sandwich and a beer. There were about ten broomers in residence, counting—or not counting—Fuse, who mostly stayed in his cube and only bothered them when he wanted someone to steal explosives for him. "I think he's gone more unstable since you disappeared," Jan said.

Since I couldn't imagine a more unstable Fuse, I kept quiet and drank my beer and ate my sandwich.

It wasn't like I sat idle for very long, either. Not many minutes after I'd arrived, and I'd met the other new member besides Abi, a shy young blonde named Irma Fratelli, people started bringing me brooms, and asking me if I could take a look. It ranged all the way from "It makes a funny sound when I take off in vertical free fall"—to which I refrained from answering *if the sound is not zoom, splat, you're doing well*, though the old Thena would have said just that—to "I found this on the street and don't know if it works," ending with "My Dragonwing stopped working and you know you're the only one who can make it okay again."

By the time Simon—looking debonair in tailored leathers—made his appearance, I had six brooms in front of me, in various stages of disassembling, and someone had found me my old toolbox, carefully salvaged from the fire. I was testing the starter circuits on a Flipper that had seen better days, and eating a second sandwich with my right hand.

Simon greeted me as he always did. By hauling me up with an arm around my waist, and kissing me stupid, barely giving me time to swallow the bread in my mouth. I pulled away as soon as I could because I was almost absolutely sure that Kit wouldn't approve—though how people greeted each other in Eden ranged all over, just like everything else did.

Simon St. Cyr, son of Good Man St. Cyr—one of the reasons he often used the nom de guerre Baker—was of mostly French ancestry and looked it. His family were hereditary rulers of Liberte Seacity which had, at some point, been set up by a group of French and Swiss financiers. He looked like his ancestry too—being only slightly taller than I, slim, with an oval face and dark hair. He'd have been totally unremarkable except for two things—his nose, which was sharp and beaklike, and his caramel-colored eyes, which always seemed to know some joke they weren't sharing with the rest of his face.

"Now, now," I said, as I slipped from his arms into sitting cross-legged on the floor again. "You mustn't kiss me like that, Simon. I'm a married woman."

He raised his eyebrows, but didn't say anything. It didn't occur to me till much later that he probably thought I was joking.

Instead he looked at the brooms in front of me and at the various broomers assembled around me looking on with the anxious expressions of parents while the doctor looks at their child. He looked back at me, and this time his eyes were shining with pure mischief. "Oh Lefty, damn it. You don't have to fix their brooms. Tell them to scat, all of them. I've told them to replace the pieces of crap months ago."

I shook my head, at the same time as one of the broomers—a young dark-haired woman—protested, "But that was because we thought she was dead."

"Right. So the minute she shows up, you pile brooms on her. Do any of the rest of you work for your supper?"

I took a sip of my beer. "I like mucking with brooms," I said. "Sit down, Simon. I need to talk to you." I gave the rest of the room the beady eyeball. "The rest of you, scat. I need to talk to Simon in private. You can come back when I tell you to. I promise not to kill your brooms."

They rushed out. Like most semiliterate societies, broomers thrive on lore, but I wondered exactly what the lore about me was, that all of them were so prompt to get out. Hell, most of them knew who I was, had been my friends for years. What did they think I was going to do if they didn't run? Burn their feet off?

Now that I thought about it, I very well might. At least back in the days when I didn't have to explain to Kit why I'd done so.

I looked back down at the open broom in front of me, and Simon started pacing, which I knew meant he was about to talk, but before he could get a word out, someone ran in—or rather someone loped in, dragging one of his legs. Fuse. I stood up, because I knew what was coming. I was right too.

Fuse rushed me, screaming, "Thena, Thena, Thena." He was a good six feet tall and he'd been—before his accident—a big, beefy man and not ugly with it.

Something had happened to him after the accident, because he'd never fully recovered his weight and looked stringy and underfed. I didn't know exactly what had happened to him, after that claw fell on him, except that he'd been in regen for weeks, and this was the best they could do. His father had since had another son, to replace him as an heir.

I had grown used to him, I supposed, but after all the time away, I had to make an effort not to flinch away from his half-paralyzed face, with the permanently droopy eye and the slouching down mouth. He kissed me on the cheek, a slobbery kiss, like a small child's. I resisted an impulse to wipe my cheek. I wondered, out of the blue, if Eden, which was far more advanced than Earth, would know how to fix this, even as he said, in his usual, slightly slurred speech, "They said you were dead. Bad they." He glared at Simon, who rolled his eyes. "And no one will let me make big booms. Thena, I have to show you my new boom stuff."

"Not now," Simon said, impatiently, which was exactly the wrong way to handle Fuse. As I saw Fuse's face crumple—even more—and look like he was going to burst into tears, I said, "Fuse, sweetie, just sit there and wait, okay? I need to talk to Simon, and then I'll be right along to see your new stuff."

He looked like he'd protest, but then nodded, once, and went to sit with his back against the wall and his arms around his knees, looking expectantly at me. I looked up at Simon.

Simon looked at Fuse.

"Don't worry," I said. "Just talk."

Simon sighed. He resumed pacing. "I don't know where to start," he said. "Everything went to hell after you disappeared."

"Start with Max."

"Ah, Max," he said. And as he said those words, someone else slid into the room. Simon turned, looking like he was ready to bite the intruder's head off. You see, when Simon gave orders around the lair, they were obeyed and I would bet right now both the guard at the door and probably an additional guard set halfway up the hallway would have orders not to let anyone come in unless Simon called for him.

Fuse had slipped by because frankly, no one was ever sure how to stop Fuse. If you put your hands on the wrong place on him, it was quite possible he would detonate. And this new arrival—well, it was quite possible he would detonate too but in a completely different way.

Nat had always been tightly wrapped in a way. Max was the relaxed, happy-go-lucky one in the association, always ready to make a joke or diffuse a situation. Nat, perhaps because he was a brilliant man growing up in a system where his family had climbed as far up as it could go and yet would always be someone else's employees, perpetually gave the impression of being a carefully contained package of frustration. Except when he was with Max, when he seemed to unwind and had even been known to laugh.

Right now, it would be impossible to imagine him laughing.

He'd always been tall and thin, but now he looked spare to the point that where his flesh showed—between his gloves and his leathers, at the wrists, and on his face—it seemed to be insufficient to cover his bones, giving him the angular look of a hurriedly-drawn caricature.

His eyebrows were low above his dark eyes and his lips were slammed shut in a thin line that admitted neither expression nor protest. I'd rather argue with a hurricane than with Nat right now.

Apparently so would Simon. He looked at Nat, then wheeled around to face me again. Nat didn't greet me. He went to stand near where Fuse sat, leaning against the wall.

"Right . . . Max . . ." Simon said. "He . . . His father went on a trip to Circum shortly after your father came back. Just after you disappeared. He . . . he borrowed your dad's ship. And . . . well . . . his dad had a stroke on the trip. And Max was acting weird when he got back, but we thought, you know, being Good Man suddenly. I mean, I remember when my Dad had the accident, and I didn't exactly inherit, but I thought, you know..."

I nodded.

"But then he didn't...he didn't seem to become himself again. It could be shock..."

Still leaning against the wall, Nat said a swear word. At least I was fairly sure it was a swear word, though he said it in ancient Spanish, in which I'm not exactly fluent. "It's not shock," he said. "It's not Max."

"Oh, come, Nat," Simon said. "It is Max. I mean, we know it is Max. There is no way..."

It was my turn to intervene. I shook my head. "No, Nat is right. It's not Max."

"What do you mean?" Simon asked.

"Just...it's not Max." I told him about my encounter with the faux Max. "Even before he missed his cues," I explained. "My skull was prickling. Something was wrong. He didn't move like Max, if that makes sense."

"It doesn't," Simon said, and looked from me to Nat as though he thought we'd both gone over the exact same cliff together.

"I can tell you exactly what he moves like," Nat said. "And talks like. And acts like. Max's Dad. Good old Good Man Keeva, may he rot in all hells. I tell you, Max is possessed."

"Nat, that's insane," Simon said. "People don't get possessed. We've had centuries of science that..."

"Don't care," Nat said. "Max is possessed. And I want to send his father's soul back to the hell he should be in. He doesn't remember...he doesn't remember anything. He calls me *boy*."

My head had started to hurt. I'd forgotten what a handful the broomers were. And I was starting to wonder if I'd done the right thing in coming here. I needed to find out where Kit was kept, and if anyone was able to break into the systems where the Good Men kept their information, it would be Simon, right, since he was almost officially one of them? And if one needed shock troops to mess up a place, it should be easiest to take the broomers. But I'd forgotten why most of them were—most of them time—rebels without a clue.

"I thought," I said, tentatively, "perhaps, you know...perhaps there's a way to rewrite your brain to make you exactly what your father wants you. Perhaps they were getting ready to do that to me when I escaped." I caught a surprised look from Nat and Simon, but I'd explain later. "And perhaps Max didn't."

"There is no—" Simon started.

"No," said a suddenly forceful Fuse. Still Fuse, but forceful. "No. It's not rewrite. It's replace. They open your head. And they put their brain in your head. And then off you go—your brain—off in the trash can."

ᐦᑫ FORTY-TWO ᓬᔲ

WE ALL TURNED TO STARE AT FUSE. HE LOOKED AS HE ALWAYS did, droopy mouth and half-closed eye, but that eye and the other were full of intent thought and they reminded me of what Fuse had been like three years ago, before the bit of the spider fell on him.

"You don't know what you're saying," Simon snapped. I don't think he was so much denying the truth of what Fuse had said as wishing to make it go away as an unimaginable horror that shouldn't be visited upon the waking world. "You have no idea what you're talking about. They've tried brain transplants before. They don't work even between people with very close genetics. There's always different sites for nervous system attachments and capillaries. It's impossible. Trust me, I know something about the brain, because...because of my father."

But Fuse just looked at him, and it was a most disturbing look to see in Fuse's gaze. It was like an adult looking at a child and pitying him. "Not if you are the same..." He seemed to fish in his damaged memories for a word that evaded him. "If you are made to be exactly like your father."

"Stop," Nat said. "Clones are illegal."

"So is putting your brain in your...your...your son's head," Fuse said. Spittle dropped from the corner of his damaged mouth, but it didn't seem to matter. "My father...I heard my father talking, and I was coming here, to...tell...And then I flew through the

329

spider." He put his hand up to his head, and cupped his forehead in it. "Thena, my head hurts."

All of a sudden, the light went from his eyes, and the child was back, petulant and annoyed. I went to him, and patted his head, not absolutely sure what I was doing.

"Come and see my boom tools, Thena," he said, and pulled me by the hand towards his compartment, and I went because my head was full of thoughts that I didn't want in it. It was unthinkable. Unimaginable evil. Nasty, dark, turbulent. It was the stuff of nightmares.

And yet I thought of Daddy Dearest in that operating room. Daddy Dearest ready for a major operation. But it was impossible. It had to be impossible. "But I'm a woman," I said. It made Fuse look at me with total incomprehension, and that's when I realized that Simon had followed us in, as had Nat.

"I was waiting for you to figure that out," Simon said, sullenly.

"But I can open my father's genlocks, the ones no one else seems able to open," I said. "And..." I shook my head. Something about the Mules having labored in vain to create a female of their kind. Something about Jarl having had plans, something about his having hoped to do it. What if he'd left plans behind? What if...

I thought of Doctor Bartolomeu saying that he had known my ancestor and also that it would take a miracle for him to be my ancestor.

"You're insane," Simon said. "It's impossible. With you it's impossible... with the rest of us..."

"The rest of you all look like your fathers," Nat said sullenly. "I don't like admitting it, but all of you look like your fathers. All the way going back. And all Good Men have only one son. One son and heir. Until Fuse, and then they had a second, when he got hurt."

Fuse giggled, a tuneless giggle. "Made him give up on my body, didn't I?"

I felt a chill go up my spine, and made mechanical answers to Fuse's talk. Shaped charges. He was talking about making booms any shape he wanted, being able to cut a hole in any wall, any size and shape he wanted.

Nat and Simon accompanied me out of the compartment when I left. Fuse stayed behind, playing with his toys. We all lived in fear that he would blow us all to kingdom come one of these days. "It wasn't Fuse who blew the other lair, was it?"

Simon looked surprised. He shook his head. "No. Somehow he never does. Though the other day I had to cover up for him doing an underwater explosion off the coast, but not... Never in the lair."

"So how did it happen?"

"We were raided... shortly after... when Max... They wanted to arrest us. We escaped, then burned it to destroy what we couldn't take." He frowned. "If it's not Max... I mean, I thought it was Max who had gone over to the other side, and denounced our lair, but if not..."

"Max had a horrible memory," Nat said. "He had notes in gems. If his father found them... I mean." He seemed to realize he was talking about Max as being gone and of his father as being the current faux Max and shut up.

I remembered the gems in my pocket. What had Father kept in his secret drawer? "What else happened, Simon? You said everything went wrong. What else went wrong?"

He looked unfocused. Confused. As if his brain were continuing on a path he didn't like. "Good Lord, Thena, you disappeared, Max turned weird, our lair was blown up. What more do you need?"

"Right," I said.

"How did you get captured? What happened?"

"I wasn't captured," I said. I made my way back to the place where I'd left the half-repaired brooms. "I ran away. You see..." I told them the whole story, from waking up with a man in my room to being burned in the darkships. No. Not the whole story. I didn't think there was any reason to tell them what Doctor Bartolomeu had told me. No reason to reveal Kit's problems with his ex-wife's family, much less that Kit was a Mule. I needed help rescuing Kit, and I knew how long it had taken me to get over my fear of the Mules.

It was amazing how your upbringing could make you afraid and disgusted of people that—to your knowledge—you'd never met. But never met, the Mules remained a myth, and as a myth they had the power to frighten. I didn't want to confuse things. There was no need.

Unless we are all Mules. I shut the door on that thought. There were no female Mules. I heard Doctor Bartolomeu say it would take a miracle.

But when I finished my story, they were both very quiet. "You really meant you are married," Simon said at last, sounding deflated.

"What? Yes. I am married."

"But to a bio? Thena!"

"He's not bioed. He's ELFed. It's just his eyes." *And his ability to speak telepathically with me.* That too was a complication he didn't need. "And his reflexes."

"Yes, but—" Simon said. Then shrugged. He looked at me and seemed to read something in my eyes. "You love him, don't you?"

"Yes," I said. "I think so. I never thought I would, you know? It's not something...I mean, I don't think I ever loved anyone before." None of us had. Our parents never took any care to instill any sort of love in us. Fear of their rule, sure, but love? Why bother? Why educate children whose brains... No.

"Do you have any idea how to help me find the prison where Kit might be?" I asked. "That's all I want, to get my husband and get back to Eden."

In retrospect, perhaps Simon should have been shocked, perhaps upset. He didn't look either. Instead he looked a little wistful. He frowned at me, as though thinking. "I can look at my father's papers, but I don't think...Well...His stuff that wasn't sealed is in the hands of his secretary. His stuff that is sealed...I can break into it, but I need more than this to go on, because I'll be violating all the rules of my custodianship set by the Council of Good Men."

I nodded. The Council of Good Men of course would not want Simon near his parents' private papers. "If there is anything like prisons or...or anything..." I said. Like brains transplanted into children, for instance. "They would have been eliminated by one of the other Good Men, wouldn't they?" I seemed to remember vaguely my father and others spending a lot of time in Good Man St. Cyr's home after the accident.

Simon nodded. He still seemed to be talking out of deeper thoughts that he couldn't voice—perhaps that he couldn't bring into words even within his own head. "I think," he said, at last, "I'll stay here overnight. Perhaps we can come up with some-thing...some plan."

Some plan. Ah. Nat stayed and glowered while I worked on the brooms. He paced back and forth. After a while, he went and got his pack of cigarettes and started smoking. Smoking was somewhat of a fad among kids our class, though usually not children of Good Men. Our fathers were all uniformly opposed to it and very vigilant.

Of course they were. They wouldn't want anything to damage their future bodies.

I didn't ask Nat to stop smoking. Natural forces can take up whatever bad habits they wish, after all. You look at them the wrong way and they raze your house and piss on your cow, something that it looked like Nat was fully capable of doing.

I finished all the brooms. And set them down side by side. I was tired but I didn't think I could sleep. "Nat, do you have a gem reader here?"

"Can get you one," he said. "Where are you staying? Which compartment?"

"No idea. Did they move my things when we escaped? Did anything of mine get brought over?"

This caused him to smile. It wasn't a happy smile, but it was the best expression I'd seen out of him in a long time. "They brought your broom. I thought they were going to worship it. I think they got you a cubicle, you know, refusing to believe you were really dead."

How touching, like a mythical chieftain in a primitive culture, which I guessed we were. It turned out I did have my broom but I didn't have a compartment. Instead, Abi and a couple of the younger ones set me up a cube, very quickly, with some of the cloth and a mattress they got heavens know where. One of the younger girls whose name I didn't remember went and got me another beer and another sandwich, and Nat lent me his gem reader, before adjourning to pace back and forth in the hallway, smoking.

I wanted to ask him not to walk by Fuse's compartment, because I was fairly sure some of those fumes were explosive, but I couldn't, could I? He might think blowing himself and all of us to kingdom come was a lovely idea. Never give the suicidal people ideas was one of my mottos. Oh, all right, I'd never thought of it before, but it would be one of my mottos from now on.

Feeling like a complete and utter failure—unable to figure out what was going on—where my husband was, anything—I turned on the gem reader and popped the gem on.

I didn't know what I expected. This being Father, it could be anything. Anything at all, including porno sensies of him and one of his women friends.

It wasn't. The first thing that came up, flashing bright in the cube, were the letters "The Athena Project."

After that, the first page was notes, done by hand, in a cramped, small handwriting, very square and neat. I couldn't understand any of it. No, I mean it. I might have got some articles and the occasional conjunction, but most of it might as well have been in a foreign language.

It wasn't. Fairly standard, if old, Glaish. But for the love of sweet hell, if I understood bio mathematics I wouldn't be running with a broomer lair to relieve boredom. Hell, heaven and abyss, I would be willing to bet no one on Earth now understood these bio mathematics.

No. Well...Maybe someone. Father had kept them for a reason. Maybe he'd trained biologists in it. Maybe...I tamped down the thought, hard, and paged down, to find...dates and notations in Daddy's handwriting.

Dates and...notations on failed experiments on following Jarl's directions for breaking the lock on the Mule genome.

They'd created two before me. A hundred years ago. Sterile. They'd been married off, properly. Male clones had been created to keep Good Man Sinistra alive.

All of this was very clear from the notes, as was the fact that the females were designed so that Daddy Dearest's brain still could be transplanted into their heads. He'd left instructions she would be the first female to inherit in the era of Good Men. Daddy couldn't imagine giving up power. But he also couldn't trust anyone—even a woman, or perhaps particularly a woman—to do what he wanted her to do without his being actively in control. And of course, what she was supposed to do was be the mother of all Mules. The mother of a new race that would displace the mere humans. The mother of...

Their heads. She. No. My head. Me...

I scrambled out of the compartment, running, as fast as I could. I couldn't remember asking the guard in the hallway the way to the fresher, but I found myself there. It was a really primitive fresher, that anyone in the twenty-first century would recognize, and I found myself on my knees, losing beer and sandwiches into the toilet.

There followed a period of which I remember nothing. I came to—or became aware of myself—curled up on the mattress of my cubicle, my mouth tasting sore, my face wet, though I didn't remember crying, and feeling tired—bone-tired, as though I'd run miles and miles uphill in snow.

I gathered myself up, feeling about a hundred years old. Right. So I was a Mule. So I'd been created to give Daddy Dearest the ultimate sex change operation. Goody. Did I think that made me special? At least I was walking around, with my brain still in my head, my body still intact. It could be much worse. How much worse?

Max. And all those other Sinistra clones, born and grown to nineteen or twenty, only to die without ever knowing what hit them. Daddy had been alive...what? Three hundred years past his body's usefulness? Earth didn't have the means to rejuvenate bodies, like Eden did. And besides, catch Daddy Dearest being old and wrinkled like Doctor Bartolomeu.

Beyond all that, of course, it fit the masquerade. Couldn't just stay alive on Earth. Sooner or later, the word Mule would be used. Sooner or later.

What kind of perverse mind propagated the worst myths about his own kind? The government of the Good Men did. Oh, perhaps they didn't have much chance after the riots and the turmoils, but did they need to actively propagate it?

They'd got left behind, when the ship went to the stars. They'd got left behind...

I took a deep breath. Right. So Daddy Dearest was scum. I didn't actually feel surprised at this, so much as a little sorry. You see, in the past he'd never tried to kill me—on the contrary—so I had to abstain from killing him. Now the game had changed.

There were some deaths I must avenge. My...I guess my twin brothers, that he'd killed over the years. I could turn that gem reader on and know the exact number, but I remembered from looking at our genealogy that all children were born late—though I was unusually late. So, usually when the father was around forty. And the son would ascend at nineteen or twenty. Yes, definitely, this was Daddy's antiwrinkle solution. And in three hundred years, he had killed...let's say eight of them. And he was going to pay. For every one of them. And for what he wanted to do to me.

But first—more important than revenge—was getting Kit out of Daddy's hands. What Daddy might do to Jarl's clone...if he'd realized Kit was Jarl's clone...And he had, or he wouldn't be asking Kit to decipher Jarl's writing.

I groaned. Of course he did. He would. It wasn't just the look. He'd have known Jarl at the same age. The same gait, the same figure, the same voice. I remembered the tone in which he'd answered Kit's hailing from the *Cathouse*. To hear a voice as if from the dead would do that to someone. And maybe he'd recognized Kit even before that, in Circum Terra.

And I wasn't such a child that I didn't think Daddy would still hold a grudge for being left on Earth. I wondered why they'd left him, and I meant to find out, but not now. First, I was going to get Kit. And after my throwing up and my crying, I thought I had an idea. And damn it, I was going to implement it. Even if it required the help of someone even less stable than I was.

I ran out in the hallway and couldn't find Nat. Please, don't let him have come to his own conclusions already and have left to take his own revenge.

✎ FORTY-THREE ✎

NAT HADN'T LEFT. THE BEWILDERED GUARD POINTED ME AT HIS compartment, and I hurried to it, ignoring the guard's rather tentative motion, as if to inform me that Nat didn't beat mattresses that way. Hell, perhaps that he didn't do it any way, now that Max was gone. And if he did, I might be set to embarrass him mortally. Too bad.

His compartment was one of those which were perfectly private, an oriental rug covering the front opening so that not even light escaped from inside. If he'd left the light on.

I called, "Nat?" then louder. "Nat."

At least there were no moans coming from inside. And no cigarette smoke. Right.

I took a deep breath. Right. I poked my head to the side of the rug. "Nat?"

It was pitch dark in there, and Nat was lying on his mattress, dressed and immobile. It only needed his hands crossed on his chest to make this look like a viewing.

I reached for the lamp on a small table near the entrance and flicked it on. For a moment, I was speechless. This cubicle was furnished like no other cubicle in the lair. There were tables and a desk and a huge dark wood trunk. It looked like a real room in a real house. There was even a drawing on the wall. It was Max. I was sure of that. It was mother-naked Max done in charcoals.

337

I was staring, rather confused by the mix of artistry and nudity—not unusual but odd when it comes to one's friends—when I heard the slide of a burner being drawn, and looked into Nat's less-than-sane eyes.

"Ah," he said. "It's you." He set the burner aside, though he didn't slide the safety back on, and fumbled on his bedside table for a cigarette box, a shiny aluminum affair. He pulled a cigarette out, lit it, took a deep pull on it. "What do you need?"

I took a deep breath, despite the smoke. "I need you to come to my room. I need to show you something."

He gave me an odd, lopsided smile, that somehow signaled he was making a joke—it was as though finding that Max might truly be gone instead of having abandoned him, had led him rediscover a sense of humor. "I've seen one of those before," he said. "And I'm not that desperate."

"Not that," I said. "Documents. Gems. I got them from my father's secret office."

"Ah," he said, getting up. "The gem reader."

"Exactly," I said. "The gem reader."

I didn't know when I had decided to show the whole thing to Nat. It would imply his realizing we were Mules. It was all the more dangerous, since he was not the son of a Good Man but the son of one of the servants. A professional, well-paid servant, but still a servant. So, he wouldn't be a Mule. Wouldn't he react even more violently to the idea than the rest of them?

The only thing I knew for sure is that Nat was not in an emotional state where I could tell him a story and have him believe it. Not without showing him some proof, even if the proof was my own supposed Father's handwriting over the centuries.

He grabbed his cigarette case, and caught me looking at the portrait again. "I drew it," he said. "Years ago."

"You...really?" I was the last person in the world who would ask him about the improbable endowment. Truly. Though perhaps not all that improbable. My husband...I didn't want to think about scientists all those centuries back creating Mules with something extra. Perhaps they thought it would keep them free of envy issues?

"Yeah, I thought of going into the arts, but I'm the oldest, and Father said that Good Man Keeva—" He stopped short and took a deep, noisy drag on his cigarette.

I took him back to my compartment, and he sat down on the edge of the mattress, as he turned the gem reader on.

His first noise was annoyance, but before he could complain of not understanding anything, I told him to page forward. He did. He read Daddy's notes in silence, as his face became more and more angular. By the end of it, he looked like a woodcut. A very angry woodcut.

I don't know what I expected him to say. Perhaps *Eek, Mules!* Or the like. Instead, he looked up at me. "Athena. Born of Zeus' head. The girl without a mother. The bastard has a sense of humor." He lit another cigarette.

"Athena Hera Sinistra," I said. "Hera."

"The mother goddess. Woman, the bastard is a laugh a minute."

"Isn't he?"

He smoked in silence. "So, why did you want me to see this? Are you going to show Simon?"

"I don't know..." I said. "I suppose I should?"

"I don't know. You know him better than I do, but I think you'll at least need to go slow. Or...allow me to do it."

Oh, sure, turn to the madman for tact. "What do you mean allow you to do it?"

He shrugged. "I can tell him I saw the notes. He'll believe me. I don't need to tell him about the...you know, the little genetic difference. He's not at risk. No one is going to replace him. His father is the living dead. But if he knows—"

"He can prevent others from being—"

"Oh, no," Nat said, and smiled a sweet, angelic smile, that made him look beautiful and years younger. "No, sweetie. I intend to do that. I intend to kill each and every one of the bastards before he gets a chance to do *that*." The smile vanished, and he looked like himself again. "I've been wondering what to do with the rest of my life." Another grin, this one humorless. Oh, good. I'd created an angel of death. "I'll let you do your own bastard, though.

"But I'll still tell Simon before, you know...because...in case I get stopped," he said. "Or killed before I'm done. But I'm going to tell him that these go on, but I'm not going to tell him what he is. I don't think he could take it?"

It seemed to be a question, and I wasn't sure how to answer it. I didn't think he could take it, either, but how was I to know?

"I thought you were going to be shocked and disgusted by the Mule thing. Maybe want to kill me and . . . and the others, too."

He looked up, all shock, his eyes wide open. "You did? Why on Earth?"

"Well, we're . . . you know?"

"Mules?" He shrugged. "But if you are, then so was Max, and I loved Max. And Max was just . . . Max." A wry twist of the mouth. "Of course, I didn't have much interest in his genes."

He stomped out the rest of his cigarette and folded his hands in his lap. "So, what do you want me to do? Why did you wake me? Was it because you didn't think you could kill them all? Because I've seen you in action and you—"

"No. I mean . . . no. I probably could kill them all, given time, but this is more important. I must get my husband off Earth and quickly." I explained. Not just the fact that Daddy Dearest had to be furious at Kit, for marrying me, for taking me away in the first place, but that I thought that Daddy and Jarl had been friends, and that Jarl had left Daddy behind when he took off for the stars, and that Daddy—I thought—still held a grudge. "He will hurt Kit."

"Bastard like that?" he said. "You bet your tits. So . . . why do you think I can help you?"

"I know he's in some secret prison, or some secret facility of some sort. I have to find out where. I have to."

He said, "Yes," unblinking.

"I . . . if it's Max's dad, in Max's body . . . if . . ."

"You're thinking the bastards probably know all this stuff together? A good bet. Yeah. Lending each other ships with medical facilities and such. Sure they do. Probably the only reason they haven't put your squeeze down yet is that they figure they can make him study this Jarl's crap and decipher it for them."

I groaned.

"Yeah. So . . . you want to squeeze old Keeva's balls till he tells you where he keeps your husband?"

"I wasn't thinking . . . I mean if that's what it takes . . ."

Nat gestured, with long fingers holding a lighted cigarette. "Metaphorically speaking. And you need me, because? I mean, I know the balls in question, but I think the psychological triggers are somewhat different now."

"I thought," I said, taking a deep breath, because, heaven

help me, I truly was asking the help of someone crazier than I. "I thought you might have some secret way of getting into the house. I mean, if I remember, your family doesn't live there and if I remember..." How could I say these things without seeming to have been paying a prurient attention to him and Max. Which I hadn't been. It's just they'd been around so long, and they were—heaven help us—among the sanest broomers, or at least the smarter ones. "If I remember, you spent most nights together, so either you went to him, or..."

"Or he came to me?" He shrugged. "A bit of both. But yeah, I had a secret way into the house. It took Max about a year and a lot of bribes to get it made. And no, I don't think that old Keeva has figured it out."

"Good. So...would you...I mean?"

"Take you there?" He grinned. "My pleasure, but it's morning now. I think we want to wait till nighttime, and no offense, but you look like living shit. You take something to sleep. I'll talk to Simon."

And looking almost like his old self—was it the sense of mission? He left my room.

‹‹◦ FORTY-FOUR ◦››

WE'D FLOWN TO OLYMPUS SEACITY, THE SEAT OF THE KEEVAS, and landed on an inconspicuous little beach.

Olympus was more sprawling than Syracuse, and it had never got built up. Probably because most of its wealth came from growing patented hydroponics and underwater crops. Not exactly algae, but stuff that had never grown on Earth—or underwater—before. I understood it had some underwater habitats, too, but I'd never been very interested. Now I was getting a crash course in how the other seacity lived.

We'd gone into a natural cave on the shore, where Nat had gone through at least as complex a dance as Daddy did to get into his secret office. Only here, there was no faun whose knob to twirl. It was more this ledge and that indentation on the wall. After about ten of these, a door opened on the rock at the end, a door that was solid rock on this side and dimatough on the other side.

The corridor we entered was also rock and dimatough. Rock on the sides and above, poured dimatough underneath, polished and smooth. Nat touched the wall, and lights came on, glowing softly. He walked ahead of us, and we behind. We, because Simon had insisted on coming. I hoped he didn't hear anything that might give him an idea who I was. But he had insisted, and we couldn't, plausibly, stop him. Not without telling him, which would defeat the whole point.

He padded beside me, his hands in the pocket of his leathers, where he had a burner too.

Nat had a burner in one hand and a tranquilizer gun in the other. His idea had been to hold the gun to the Good Man's head and make him tell us what we wanted to know, and then blow the Good Man's brains out. But I'd convinced him that if Good Man Keeva was even vaguely as paranoid as my father, then he would have ways to give the alarm. Better to tranquilize him as fast as possible, and then take him away somewhere else, where we could interrogate him quietly.

And then a weird gleam had come to Nat's eyes and he'd said something about just burning him being too good for him anyway and something about being able to make it last days. I truly, truly, truly didn't want to know, and the mere mention of it had made Simon turn a shade of green.

Nat walked as if he knew the way too well to give it much thought. After a while, I realized that the rock had given way to pure dimatough. And that I could hear the waves breaking over us.

I don't know how long we walked. It was all oddly silent, and it gave a sense of unreality to the whole thing. We took two antigrav wells up. I wondered how we were going to carry an unconscious man back. We had tried to talk to Nat about carrying an unconscious man on a broom, but Nat had only shrugged and said he and Max had doubled up lots, and that it was all in how you tied the unconscious man up.

Just as we came to a door that looked like the end of the line, I wondered what if Max—well, the new Max—had changed his room? What if—

But Nat was opening the door and stepping out onto the thick carpet of the room. Nat must have been part cat, because he stepped out in utter soundlessness, and had sent a dart off from the dart gun before my eyes had adjusted. Someone—a slim blonde woman—sat up at the odd sigh that escaped the sleeping man when the dart hit him. She looked into the darkness with wide-open eyes and opened her mouth.

The tranquilizer dart hit her before she could scream. She fell, immediately, like a bag filled with sawdust.

The men worked silently. They had brought ropes and stickfast tape, and before you knew it, they had the Good Man trussed up, rolled in a blanket, and convenient handles improvised out of stickfast tape.

I won't say it was easy taking him back. Of course it wasn't. The antigrav wells were the pits. I had to help them balance the man, who, but for being warm, looked like a corpse. As we got to the cave and Nat went about matter-of-factly binding himself to our victim so they could both ride one broom, I said, "Are you sure you didn't give him the wrong dosage of tranq?"

"Oh, he should be so lucky."

Right. There definitely were things I didn't need to know.

By the time we got back to the lair, the Good Man was starting to stir, but by the time he woke up, we had him properly tied and firmly attached to a rather large and solid dimatough chair in the innermost room—the same room where I'd repaired the brooms.

Meanwhile, Nat had fretted about the possibility that the bimbo in bed with not-Max had seen something that would lead to us. "I'd have killed her, you know, but I was afraid the burner was going to cause a fire and bring people on us."

Had I been that unconcerned with the life of bystanders, before going to Eden? Perhaps. All I could think is that I didn't want to justify it to Kit. And I'd better not tell him I seemed to have called forth the living incarnation of death, either. I didn't think he would like that.

First thing the Good Man did when he came to was scream his head off. Nat ignored him, sitting across from him and smoking patiently. Simon and I let him scream. The more noise he made, the less strength he would have to oppose us.

I don't know how long he screamed. I was trying to think of the things to ask, and how to ask.

I needn't have bothered. I simply didn't get a look in. You see, Nat had apparently been thinking of *small bones in the body that you can break easily* and *curiously painful things one can do with a lighted cigarette.*

After half an hour, Simon left. I could hear him retch in the fresher next door. At forty-five minutes, the Good Man sang. Interestingly, he sang without even the promise that pain would stop. I guess Nat didn't like to lie.

As soon as I had the details about where Kit was held, I left the room, almost running. Simon, very pale, was waiting in the hallway. We'd chased everyone else from this part of the lair before we started, but we went all the way to the other extreme, near the entrance, where we could almost not hear a staccato of screams, followed by some rather curious sounds, the provenance of which I didn't want to know.

"He really . . . Nat . . ."

"Yes," I said. "He felt his skull. After you left. There are . . . scars."

"Uh . . . your . . . did he tell you the location of your husband?"

"Yes."

"So . . . are we going to rescue him?"

"Yes. The problem is how. You see, the facility is under water. Carved in dimatough."

⊸ FORTY-FIVE ⊷

WELL, AT LEAST IT EXPLAINED WHY I WAS ABLE TO CONTACT KIT, at least intermittently. You see, the facility, code-named Never-Never, because whoever went in there was never seen or heard of again, was built into the very foundations of Syracuse Seacity, either nested in a bubble left over from the pouring of the city, or melted after the fact.

It was under water though not that deeply in—I guessed because it was easier to air that way.

"We could go in through the top," I said. We'd assembled in a new war room that Simon had arranged to be partitioned at the front. Nat had vanished with the Good Man and none of us was all that eager to find out where he had gone. Or what had happened to the Good Man or whatever remained of him. I remembered all too well what Nat had said about keeping him alive for days, and damned if I was going to begrudge him his vengeance, but I also didn't need to think about it. This was clearly also Simon's idea, since he didn't even want to go to the room at the back.

We were all sitting on the floor, in a circle. All of us being about fifteen broomers, only two of them new, plus myself and Simon. Fuse had left his beloved explosives to come sit by my side, but I wasn't absolutely sure if he counted.

"We could," Simon said. "But if we do, we'll meet resistence full on, won't we?"

"Right," I said. The thing was, and Simon had pointed this out, that we had to move really fast. Oh, Nat was a fast bastard and, apparently, had cleaned up behind him, removing the sleeping dart that had lodged in the girl's neck. But we needed to get Kit out of there, and then both of us out to Circum Terra and out to Eden before someone realized that Good Man Keeva was missing, and who had done it. Any delay could mean they moved Kit. Or they destroyed the *Cathouse.*

Oh, I'm sure there were other ships we could use, but none adapted for use by a cat from Eden. And I didn't want to try to pilot the thing without Kit's special abilities. Plus, Eden might damn well blast us out of the sky as we approached. They damn well might. Collectively, they were as paranoid as I was.

"So . . . what if we go from the side?" I asked. From what Good Man Keeva had told me about the positioning of the facilities, they extended all the way to the edge, on the south side of the city, right by those cliffs that led up to Daddy Dearest's mansion. Under the water.

"Mmm. Could be done. Except we risk drowning whoever is in the lower levels, if it extends very far down."

I'd thought of how many levels there might be and I'd asked, though not for this purpose. "There are three levels," I said, "but the underwater one is the lowest one, and depending on the type of puncture we make . . ." I was thinking. "There must be some way to make a hole and cover it, so that it doesn't immediately flood the place."

At that moment I became aware of Fuse, pulling on my sleeve. "Yes, Fuse?"

"Do you remember? I told you. The sewer repair. I stole one."

Clear as mud. "You stole a sewer?" And of course I didn't remember. I had been thinking of Daddy Dearest and of whatever was going on with that. I hadn't been thinking of sewers. Or repairs.

Fuse hissed out air like a peevish child. "No, Thena. A lot of seacity sewers are access . . . access . . ." He lost the fight with his drooping mouth, but not without spraying a broad perimeter of spittle all around. "Are near the outside of the foundations, and it's easier to enter from the side. I watched them do it. To repair the sewer. You blow a shaped charge, and then you slap in a . . . a chamber, with two membranes." He looked at me, and must have seen complete, blank incomprehension. "Like an airlock. I stole it because I thought it was neat!"

We hadn't taken his word for it. Taking the word of one madman at a time was sort of my limit. I'd already filled that quota with Nat. So Simon and I had inspected the airlock chamber which Fuse had stolen. I guess you could call it that. It was about six feet long, and wide enough to let a person pass, and it reminded me of nothing so much as a buttonhole. Inside there was a chamber, small enough to let one of us through at a time. We'd have to coordinate it.

"I'll have to call reinforcements," Simon said. "And I've ... uh ..."

We were standing outside Fuse's compartment, discussing plans, but he stopped and sighed.

"You've uh?"

"I've made enquiries about your ship."

"Oh, no," I said.

"Not officially," Simon said, quickly. "Never officially. I ... have friends amid the harvesters. Well, they're my friends if I pay enough, you know how that goes."

I knew how that went.

"I went up for a visit couple of years ago," he said. "You see, I always wanted to go to space. So I went up, and looked around, and ... well, they're willing to help for a little cash."

Wasn't that the way of all the worlds? And wasn't it a wonderful thing?

"Anyway, your ship was radiation cleaned, because they were ... you know, studying it. Not taking it apart yet, but studying how it works. So I paid someone to stock it. Air, water, food. I can't promise what the food will be, but it should be enough for your trip back."

I nodded. I didn't know what to say. I hadn't even thought of that, just thought that I wanted out of here and back to Eden. Good thing someone's brain was working.

"I'll have an air-to-space ready for you to take to Circum. Do you think you can? You or ... your husband? It's a fast one. Very small. You should be able to make it up there and dock in less than three hours, if you can pilot it accurately enough."

"Kit for sure," I said. "If his eyes and mind are working." I hadn't heard from him for a while, and my attempts at mind-touching met with complete shielding on his part. I could get no more than the sense that he was alive and . . . well, not well. "And if not . . . we'll figure it out." He could always borrow my eyes and hands. Provided it wasn't a lethal wound, Eden had regeneration. And somehow, I doubted they would destroy his eyes. Not if they wanted him to do the same work Jarl had done. Or to try to understand it.

Suddenly, without warning, Simon had pulled me to him and was kissing me hard, teeth scraping teeth. I was so shocked it took me a moment to put a hand on his chest and push him back.

He smiled a little, not at all embarrassed. "I figured I was entitled to a goodbye kiss," he said. "If it weren't for that husband of yours . . ." He grinned. "Ah, well. Let's get the show on the road, shall we?"

III
Je Reviens

Ⅼⓒ FORTY-SIX ⓈⅮ

THAT WAS HOW, BEFORE DAWN HAD FULLY LIT THE SKY, WE WERE out, flying just above the water near the cliffs just beneath Daddy Dearest's mansion.

Fuse flew ahead of us and down into the water, and I hoped—hoped—that the airlock would work. I didn't want to drown Kit. Simon was very nice, but hardly a consolation prize. The problem was that I was very much afraid without Kit I'd go as crazy as Nat had gone without Max.

Fuse dove down and moments later the water splashed up. I didn't see Fuse splash up with it, but he also didn't fly back up.

I couldn't wait, so I flew down, and there was the grey membrane, on the wall of the cliff. I rode through on the membrane, with a burner in each hand.

The airlock was dry and on the other side was a hallway with only a little water on the floor, and if Fuse had come in through here, who knew where he had gone, and what had happened to him, because there was a detachment of goons facing me.

I burned in a scything motion, aiming for their necks, because their bodies might be armored and heads exploding is only interesting as a figure of speech. They all went down.

Kit, I'm here. Where are you? What level?

For a moment, there was no answer and I thought they'd moved him, I thought—

This level, he said, having got the image of where I was from

353

my mind. From his memory he sent me the image of which corridor to take, how to get to his cell, how to get him out.

Be careful, love, I'm guarded.

Oh, I wouldn't expect anything else.

But not your father. He left, in a hurry, some time ago.

I see, I said. It was, in fact, clear as mud.

໑ FORTY-SEVEN ໑

I FLEW DOWN THE HALLWAY, FOLLOWED BY JAN AND SIMON. THE other broomers were presumably either guarding access to this corridor or perhaps just causing random mayhem in other parts of the compound. While guarding the corridor would be the sane thing to do, these were broomers. If they were inclined to sanity, they'd get therapy, not shoot at things, hold up things and get people to pay them for protection. No.

I just had to hope we could make the best of what we had.

At some point Jan and Simon got ahead of me. By the time I got to the door at the end of the hallway, they'd already killed the two sentinels there.

They were about to burn the genlock with their burners on high, but I decided to play a hunch. "Clones, remember?"

Jan looked startled, but lay his hand across it. And the door spread open. I don't think he had believed any of what had spread around the lair like wildfire—the whole thing except the fact that the Good Men were Mules. I saw belief and comprehension hit him like a mallet. I though he would be out for the count.

We must have been faster with the breakin than I expected, because as we entered the room, Kit was chained to a desk. Literally chained to a desk, looking in baffled wonder at a holographic screen. I registered two things that made me feel immense relief—he seemed to be whole, and the light was turned down to the point where it was only slightly uncomfortable for him.

Probably the lowest they could take it. I'd brought sun-protection goggles for him, of course, but it didn't look like—so far—his eyes were ruined.

The other things I noticed weren't so reassuring. There were two guards in there, one who swivelled to point his burner at me, and whom Simon burned where he stood.

The other guard, though, was Good Man Rainer, Jan's quasi Father. He was punching at a com button and screaming, "Repeat, what should I do with the prisoner?"

A burner ray came over my shoulder. Jan had burned him where he stood. And then, as if nothing at all had happened, he helped me melt Kit's chains so that I could take him out of there.

Nat was going to be so disappointed. One less that he got to take care of.

◖◖ FORTY-EIGHT ◗◗

EVERYTHING WENT WELL. ALMOST TOO WELL. I'M NOT USED TO things going without glitches, and when they do, I start looking around for the trap. I've found that I'm always right.

I wasn't looking for trouble, and I can't say I was disappointed I got Kit out of Never-Never with relative ease. But my anxiety grew every time something went well or smoothly.

I tensed as we left through the membrane, tensed some more as I managed to fly back, through the water, to the outside.

Kit had panicked under the water, and for just a moment I wished I'd remembered to bring Morpheus, only I doubted I had Nat's ability for holding a tied-up man on a broom, and in fact it wasn't something I was sure I wanted to acquire.

As we flew above the water, sparkling silver in the morning sun, Kit was so quiet that I was afraid he was seriously hurt— though I hadn't seen what looked like more than scrapes and bruises—or perhaps that the glasses weren't enough to shield his eyes. But then he mind-said, *If we could take a tenth of the water we can see to Eden, we'd be so rich.* And I was reassured. My ever-practical love remained himself.

Simon had taken us to where he'd hidden the air-to-space and seen us aboard, and managed to say goodbye without kissing me, which was good because the minute Kit saw him, I swear he started ruffling feathers he didn't have and looking like were it not for a few generations of civilization, he would be pounding his chest to scare away the intruder.

The air-to-space was comfortable, and I hoped Simon got it back. We docked it where we'd been told, and got back into the *Cathouse* which was lovely and freshly scrubbed. And I'd been happy, yes, but I also felt that odd prickling at the back of my neck. Trouble was on the way, I was sure of it. And yet, was I only reacting to the stress of the last few days?

Kit had flown the *Cathouse* out of Circum without anyone even trying to follow us.

Sitting in the cat cabin, even if he had managed to lose a lot of weight and have a huge bruise on the side of his face, Kit looked like himself, and very, very happy, as his fingers played on the keyboard.

"Go get the fresher," he said.

"Are you implying I smell?" I asked.

"No. But if you go now, you can be all clean to direct me through the powertrees. I figure since we're coming back late, we might as well take some powerpods."

"You're just afraid they'll send us back if we don't."

"Kath might," he said somberly. "She'll be pretty pissy by now."

Undeniable. Though I suspected she would forgive us all the moment little brother came back alive and well.

I hit the fresher. The funny thing is even our clothes were where we'd left them. I guessed they'd just radiation scrubbed the whole ship and hadn't got around to doing anything with the contents. Suited me fine. I got a nice blue dress that Kit liked, and hoped it would compensate for the loss of hair. I tried not to look at myself in the mirror on the way to the fresher. Couldn't be helped. My head had just the littlest bit of stubble coming in. The best I could do for Kit right now would be to tie a scarf on my head.

I didn't, though, as I came out of the fresher. Just hoped Kit could get used to me like this until the hair grew back.

In the hallway just outside the cat cabin, I said, "I hope you can get used to—"

And stopped as I entered the cat cabin. Because Daddy Dearest was there. Pointing a burner at Kit's head. And Kit was moving like a robot and looking like a wax dummy.

My father turned but not so completely he'd lose sight of Kit and faced me with a wide smile. "About damn time, Athena."

"I see you wanted to see us off, Daddy Dearest," I said.

He glared at me. "Depends what you mean by off. I knew it was you when I heard Keeva had disappeared. I gave my orders. Your little friends won't get to kill my century-old friends. Not this time, *daughter*. Not ever. By now all your friends are dead. But I knew you'd be coming here. And your friend St. Cyr..." He made a gesture. "Clumsy child, nothing more. Not a tenth the man *his father* was."

He accented the familial relationship words with ironical inflection as though daring me to say something. I wasn't about to. I also wasn't about to give my friends a thought. Oh, I hoped Father wasn't speaking the truth, and if I knew the bastard, there was a good chance he wasn't. He was just trying to confuse me. But at any rate, it didn't matter. It was between us now, not the broomers.

He grinned at me, as if he knew what was going on in my head. "Well played, girly. Not even a growl back? You've grown up. Too bad that will all go to waste. I can't afford to lose you now. There aren't enough of us of the old school to restart the genetic program from scratch. So you'll come with me to Earth, where you'll be a good girl and we'll finish what we'd started in the space cruiser. And then we'll bring our kind back, in glorious splendor."

I glared at him. "Our kind?"

He lost his temper at that. Controlling himself had never been his strong suit. "The Mules. You know damn well. Don't think you can toy with me."

"Ew. You're genetically my brother," I said, pretending I didn't know what his ultimate plans for me were.

He glared, but he kept an eye on Kit and he never moved the aim from Kit's neck. "We are superior to the rest of humans. We owe it to the Earth to populate it with the best possible humans. Cheer up. Your children will inherit the Earth."

"No, thank you. I've had enough. Enough of Earth and enough of you."

"Ah...no species loyalty. Not that I expected better of you, girl. You've been a disappointment from the beginning. You were the result of centuries of research and I had high hopes. We tried to reproduce the miracle that created you, but we couldn't. The antireproduction triggers in our genes destroyed every other female embryo we created, even those cloned from you." He grinned at what must have been my ghastly look of surprise. "Oh, it was easy to get material during your medical exams, your medical crises. But none of them took, so you're all we got. And I must take over your body and make it do what it must do for the betterment of mankind."

"You're not part of mankind. And what part of replacing it is betterment?"

"Oh, we won't replace all of them. We'll need servants, after all." Casually, gently, he rested his free right hand on the back of Kit's neck. Kit gave the impression of flinching from the touch without moving, not even minimally. "Move it, Athena. Ahead of me. I have an air-to-space ready to go. You come with me now, and I'll let your play friend go back home without hurting him."

I didn't believe it for a minute. Kit mustn't have either, because he said, *Don't you dare. I'll blow my brains out the moment you leave the* Cathouse.

His words in my mind were so forceful there was no room to doubt him. *Don't worry,* I told Kit, as I made as if to go ahead of Daddy Dearest. My mouth was dry and I felt my mind dip into panic. I didn't trust the unholy son of a bitch, not further than I could throw him. And I had no intentions of throwing him. But there would be a moment, when he turned, to take me out of the room, that his burner wouldn't be on Kit.

I couldn't understand why Kit hadn't tried anything already— except that as I looked over my shoulder I realized, from the flickers on the screen, that we'd steered into the powertrees. Father had waited till we were there. Which meant I couldn't count on Kit.

Don't worry, I told Kit. *I'll handle it.*

"Move it, further," my father said. "I'm not following that close to you." And then, casually, he turned and raised his hand and brought the burner butt down on Kit's cheek, cutting a groove from which blood flowed, amid the calico beard.

Kit's eyes reflected on the screens, maddened by fear and anger.

ᗢ FORTY-NINE ᗡ

IT'S JUST THAT FATHER MISCALCULATED, BECAUSE WHEN HE TURNED to get to Kit, he turned away from me for a moment. And he didn't have his burner pointed at Kit, either.

Long enough.

I threw myself through the air and grabbed at his burner. I tore his aim away from Kit, as his finger pressed the trigger. The beam hit at the ceiling.

And then I was fighting, roaring, mad with fear, insane with protective, jealous love, caring only for keeping my father away from Kit.

My father was stronger than I'd ever thought. Stronger and better trained. His nails gouged at my skin. His feet tripped me. His hands grabbed mine, immobilized me.

Even wounded, even old, even insane, he was more than a match for me.

This close in, I couldn't use my ballet moves. I could try, but they wouldn't work—I was too close to him.

Father switched his hold to my neck, tightened his hands around my throat and pushed me up against the wall of the *Cathouse*.

"You stupid bitch," he said. "What did you think you were going to do? So glad to find a boyfriend? So glad you can't think when you're around him." My father grinned at me, his face totally inhuman. "Did I ever tell you what my specialty was, in the days before the turmoils, *daughter*?"

I couldn't breathe and the world was growing dim before my eyes.

"I was an assassin, created to enforce Mule rule over the stupid humans. An assassin, Athena. Designed to kill men and Mules. That's where you got your fighting ability, *dear*. Your speed, your strength, your sense of direction and your mechanical ability. I was designed with them so I could carry out missions in hostile territory. Alone. And you got them accidentally, through my genes. But I'm the original, you're just the copy. But you are the copy and if your bio had managed to take you with him, he'd find that you turn out just like dear old dad . . . Isn't that funny?"

Nothing was funny. Sad. Shocking. Terrible. Not funny. The world was slipping away.

My hands were tearing at my own neck, trying to pry my father's fingers away.

And my senses were running away from me, dimming, disappearing.

As from a long distance off, I heard, "And now, when you pass out, we'll kill your boyfriend and we'll go back to the flyer before we hit anything."

Flailing, feeling my life ebb away like water among rocks, I was aware of Kit's foot—as though it were my foot—slowly sliding along the floor, towards the lever that turned off the internal gravity of the *Cathouse*—a function left over from its days as a training ship, when it was needed to train recruits in null-g, *just in case*.

We weren't mind-linked. But perhaps subconsciously my mind reached for his, in fear of death. I felt the lever beneath his boot, felt it slide and then click to.

And then the null-g kicked in, and my father and I floated to the ceiling, his hands still around my neck.

⚬ FIFTY ⚬

BUT I HAD TRAINED IN NULL-G WITH KIT. WE'D MOCK-FOUGHT each other in null-g, for exercise. Kit liked the freedom of null-g and he thought I needed to practice in it.

My father struggled to regain footing. I twisted his fingers away from my neck.

I understood now why the other Mules hadn't taken him to Eden with them. He was a killer. How much was I like him? Was I destined, infallibly, to become a copy of the murderous bastard?

I surely felt like killing. Like rending him to pieces. I felt as bloodthirsty as Nat. I wanted to kill him slowly and over weeks. I wanted to hear him scream.

Both of us had lost our burners in the melee, but I'd always been more at home with fists and feet.

I kicked at him, and I twisted and wrenched at him, and I used all my ballet moves, unfettered, all the more graceful for the null-g.

Given the advantage of null-g, I soon had him cornered against the bulkhead, and I had my hands around his scrawny neck. I would kill him now, I thought.

But there were his eyes looking at me, and in them I read utter terror and complete defeat. He was bleeding from the corner of his mouth and his forehead. Blood stained the shoulder of his tunic. His eyes were dull with pain.

And I thought he was a killer. Designed to kill. Was I that

much like him that I could kill remorselessly? In cold blood? With my bare hands?

Kit kicked the gravity and we fell to the ground. I gathered myself up, painfully.

And Kit was standing by us, holding my father up. "We're in a corridor," he said. "We're safe for now. On automatic pilot."

"I can't kill him," I said, and half opened my hands. I looked at Kit and sighed. It would be more truthful to say I didn't want to kill him. I wanted to think of myself as different from him. Not made to kill.

"No one is asking you to." Kit shrugged. "He forced us onto the energy trees. You piloted through them before. He should be able to. We'll put him in the air-to-space he brought in. If he has the same capacity of movement you have, he can do it. And then, on Earth, we'll let him square it with your friend Simon. I doubt he'll have an easy match."

I agreed. Who'd have thought of Simon that way?

Kit dragged my father out to the bay. "You may get in that air-to-space and fly away," Kit said. "In two minutes we will open the outer door. If you don't fly away, you'll be spaced. Without the air-to-space."

He dropped my father into the bay and walked back and lowered the lever that slid the door closed.

My father seemed to wake up, as the door was halfway closed. He lurched at us.

"Three hundred years," he yelled. "You won't destroy it all now. Jarl betrayed me once. I won't have it again."

He grabbed at the two halves of the door and shoved hard. They still slid together, closer and closer. My father refused to give up. He kept pushing, even as the halves of the door squeezed him between them.

It all took no longer than a painfully drawn breath, but in my mind, replayed, it lasts forever—a slow agony of fear and struggle.

Kit fumbled for the lever to halt the closing, but he was just slightly slower than normal—tired and confused by being hit with the butt of the burner.

And I was exhausted. I tried to jump towards the door. Too late.

The two halves of the dimatough door clunked together.

Blood spurted everywhere—on my clothes, my face, my lips—warm and metallic.

I know I didn't pass out. Athena Hera Sinistra doesn't pass out. That's for the pampered, well-brought-up girls of Earth. Athena Sinistra was tougher than that. Athena Sinistra was a Mule.

But it must have been the earlier oxygen deprivation, and the adrenaline and all. I stared at the bloody mess caught between the doors and reality slid away from me as my vision darkened and I collapsed to the floor.

ᵍ❧ FIFTY-ONE ❧ᵍ

I WOKE UP WITH KIT CURLED AROUND ME.

Opening my eyes, I saw that we were in our room, aboard the *Cathouse*.

At first I thought he was asleep, but then I felt his hand caressing my hairless head and heard him say, over and over again, "It's all right."

"Should you be here?" I asked, with sudden alarm. "The energy trees—"

"We got out of the ring hours ago," he said. He looked sheepish. "I harvested. Only five pods. I gave you a sedative, so I could pilot us out and clean up and . . . and catch some sleep. I feel like myself again, at last." He reached for me and pulled me close. There were bruises on his shoulder, bruises down his neck, but he didn't seem to be complaining.

"Isn't it weird?" I said, half dazed.

He raised his eyebrows at me. "What?"

"That we're both Mules. I mean—"

He shrugged. "I had suspected it before. The way Doc Bartolomeu kept talking about your *ancestor*. I think he did too. It was just that . . . it was too great a miracle for him to hope for, I guess."

"Do you think . . . there will be more . . . of me?"

"I don't know," he said, then smiled mischievously. "I'll let Doc dissect you and then—"

367

I put my finger on his lips. "No, seriously. I mean, if we have children..."

"We save a bundle because we don't need to have them created in tubes," he said. "Yes, I do realize that."

"Kit, do be serious," I said. "If we have children, with whom will they have children?"

Kit shrugged. "Isn't that entirely their problem? We'll try to have daughters, all right? And then we can send them on a ship, after the long-lost Mules. We'll make sure to include a note saying they can have babies with whomever they want."

"Kit, do be serious!" I said. "There is something you're not thinking of." My mind was full of the events of the last few hours, and I felt vaguely dizzy. "What if... Father was an assassin. They built me as close as possible to him, so I could accept his brain. What if I turn..."

"Into an assassin? Unlikely. Not very lucrative in Eden. I mean, okay, some people prefer to pay someone else, but it gets all messy with the blood geld." He saw my serious eyes and sighed. "Thena... I fell in love with you as you are. Fractured, maybe. Lost, perhaps. But I'm no prize either. I'll keep an eye on you. You keep an eye on me. I don't think either of us has an affinity for wanton killing, much less for doing it for pleasure. Look how you reacted to your father's death.

"He might have been an assassin, but it took more than genetics to make him one."

◖◍ FIFTY-TWO ◍◗

THE ALARMS THAT TOLD US WE WERE APPROACHING EDEN RANG ten weeks later, while we were in bed. Eden's orbit had taken it two weeks away from us while we were on Earth.

We got up, quickly, and dressed in our uniforms so that we were perfectly official as we got to Eden.

I sat in Kit's cabin, because there was a good chance we'd be shot out of the sky and I'd be damned if I was going to go in isolation.

Kit did the last approach, brought Eden onto the screen and flicked the comlink. Still not too sure these weren't our last few minutes of life, I took a deep breath to control my fear.

He reached for my hand and squeezed it, as he said, "Cat Christopher Bartolomeu Sinistra, piloting the *Cathouse* on behalf of the Energy Board. I request permission to land."

There was a silence from the other side, long enough for my heart to almost stop. I remembered what Eden had been like before. And yet, scared as I was of our reception, I couldn't help but smile, because I had found someone I belonged to.

If Eden didn't want us, we'd find our way elsewhere.

I was not alone anymore. I belonged.

A voice that I would say was the voice of the dock controller who'd first *welcomed* me to Eden, crackled over the link, "The *Cathouse* is more than six weeks late. It has been entered in the roll of losses. Cat Christopher Sinistra and Nav Athena Sinistra are dead."

369

"Not really," I told him, while my heart hammered wildly and I had to resist an urge to shout my joy. It was just bureaucracy. We could deal with that. "Only late."

"You cannot be late. You only had fuel for a four-month trip. Three weeks later you'd be out of reserves and dead. You—"

"We were down on Earth," I said and grinned, a grin he couldn't see but might just sense from the tone of my voice.

"What?" the controller asked.

"Nav Sinistra had radiation poisoning and we stopped on Earth for regen treatment," Kit said, in a slow, wary voice.

"You *stopped* on Earth for *treatment*?"

"Well, it wasn't that simple, but yes. I'll be glad to tell you the whole story after we land."

"You'd better, Cat. And you'd better make it convincing. This is most irregular."

"Controller," I said. After all we'd been through, the Controller's bullying tones were almost funny. "We must land. Kit's family is expecting us."

Another silence. "Navigator Sinistra, if you delayed your collection run for personal reasons, you have to know that the Energy Board will fine you for the delay in supply, and all the boards will want to interview you for potential breaches of security. Also—"

"I *know*, Controller." I batted my eyes at the console, not that it helped, but hey, sexiness can be felt across links, right? "Now, could you give us a dock number, please? Before I go crazy and just give my cat instructions to dash at Eden in the area of the landing control station. We Earthworms tend to be so temperamental."

Kit chuckled aloud over the comlink.

"Dock fifty-five, but I want you to know that I shall have armed hushers ready and that you will be examined for any evidence of undue influence and that—"

I flicked the comlink off.

Nothing says welcome home like a strip search.